THE RITUAL CALLED WAR . . .

Sarah stared in helpless fascination as the two Mentors, Mrann and Revin, raised their right arms to reveal the metal bands of their office. As she watched, a line of power was suddenly visible, stretching between the Mentors, extending outward to the staffs held by their apprentices. A blink, and the line was gone.

The runestaffs still held high, the apprentices paced clockwise around the Mentors, and when they stopped, the four figures formed a square inside the boundary of the sacred circle.

Suddenly the air around the Mentors began to glow. Clouds of color that could barely be seen flowed downward from their upraised hands. Then the light the Mentors generated seemed to swell and brighten. A line of power leaped out, touching a youngling at the edge of the circle. The youngling fell back, eyestalks shriveling and body scorched almost beyond recognition.

Sarah gagged in horror, turning away, looking around in desperation for some means to halt this Terran-caused conflict which she now knew would end only when one Mentor or the other was dead. . . .

KRIS JENSEN
FREEMASTER

DAW BOOKS, INC.
DONALD A. WOLLHEIM, PUBLISHER

1633 Broadway, New York, NY 10019

First Printing, February 1990

1 2 3 4 5 6 7 8 9

PRINTED IN THE U.S.A.

For Mother, who taught me to love books, and for Dad, who taught me many other things.

ACKNOWLEDGMENTS:

My thanks to Rick Kampmann and Debbie Braun, who were there at the start; Pat Wrede, for her critique of the first draft; Warren Cartwright, Chi McIntyre, Chris Grund, and the Dragon Pit (especially Larry Andersen and Robin Brent) for their support and encouragement along the way; and Nate Bucklin and Jim Frenkel, for contributions too numerous to mention, and for their determination to see this book in print.

Trade Attache Sarah Anders scanned the news releases scrolling up the screen of her home terminal. "Damn," she muttered as a name caught her attention. Then louder, "Pause." She read the story quickly.

SEC/EX MARKET NEWS
2254:3/24, TERRAN CALENDAR

NAGASHIMI INTERSTELLAR DRIVES, INC., AND BRADDOCK-OWEN EXTRATERRESTRIAL MINING CORPORATION ANNOUNCED THEIR MERGER IN A JOINT COMPUCONFERENCE TODAY. JAMES NAGASHIMI, GRANDSON OF THE FOUNDER OF NAGASHIMI DRIVES AND CURRENT CHAIRMAN OF ITS BOARD OF DIRECTORS, STATED THAT THE NEW CORPORATION, TO BE KNOWN AS NAGASHIMI-BOEM, EXPECTS TO CONTINUE THE ESTABLISHED BRADDOCK-OWEN DIRECTIVE, SEEKING OUT AND EXPLOITING UNTAPPED MINERAL DEPOSITS BEYOND THE SOLAR SYSTEM.

ANNOUNCEMENT OF THE MERGER DREW PROTESTS FROM PAN-UNION CORP., THE SOLAR SYSTEM'S SECOND-LARGEST BUILDER OF INTERSTELLAR SHIPS. A SPOKESMAN FOR PAN-UNION STATED THAT THE COMPANY WILL FILE A FORMAL OBJECTION WITH THE TERRAN UNION SECURITIES BOARD.

"A useless gesture," Sarah said to the terminal, which did not reply. "File!" she ordered, and the computer obediently put one copy into permanent memory, and sent a second to her office at the Terran Union Interstellar Trade Commission.

9

2255:1/5, TERRAN CALENDAR
TOP SECURITY/SCRAMBLED
EYES ONLY
TO: HOWARD SANDSMARK, SECRETARY,
        INTERSTELLAR TRADE COMMISSION
FROM: ANDREW HAINSBURY,
        UNDERSECRETARY, SECTOR EIGHT

The situation in sector eight is not good. Since my last report, Nagashimi-BOEM has succeeded in edging us out of trade agreements on Hellers' World and Ichcka. Nagashimi agents dazzled the native negotiators with flashy trade goods and promises of quick riches in exchange for mining rights. The contracts contain no safety considerations or provisions for environmental protection. Strip mining is scheduled to commence on Ichcka almost immediately.

I recommend that we carry out future negotiations with extra-solar governments in secret, so as not to alert Nagashimi-BOEM and other industrial conglomerates to our activities. Planetary mineral surveys should be conducted under tightest security, and the results released only after trade agreements have been ratified. Negotiating teams should be small, with minimal support personnel to avoid attracting undesired attention.

These procedures will be implemented in sector eight beginning with negotiations on the newly-opened planet Hydra.

***************CONFIDENTIAL***************
TRANSCRIPT FROM THE OFFICE RECORDER OF
SANDSMARK, SECRETARY,
INTERSTELLAR TRADE COMMISSION.
2257:10/16, Terran Calendar
SANDSMARK: I have an assignment for you. Rich titanium deposits have been located by a mineral survey team in sector twelve, on the planet Ardel. No trade agreement has been signed with the Ardellans; I want you to get out there and lock this up before the industrial conglomerates get wind of it.
ANDERS: How large a team can I take with me? I want

Harris and Bang, and a couple of the younger people, if I can have them.

SANDSMARK: No. This will be a solo job. The first-contact report says this culture has rigid rules of protocol. Since the first ship touched down on land owned by Clan Alu, all negotiations must be conducted with the elders of that clan. They have refused to allow more than a single negotiator.

ANDERS: No backup? I'm getting too old for solo assignments. I've gotten accustomed to desk work. Why don't you send one of the youngsters?

SANDSMARK: I want your experience. *Blackhawk* will be your transport; it will stay in the area, far enough away so that it won't attract unwanted attention to Ardel. You'll be able to keep in touch with them. The first-contact report and mineral survey are queued up on your terminal, and the language tapes are waiting on your desk.

ANDERS: Anything else I should know?

SANDSMARK: You aren't allowed to take any powered weapons along. They've agreed to let you bring a single communications console and a locator beacon.

ANDERS: Damn! Do they at least have toilets?

SANDSMARK: Check the report.

Prologue

2252:5/18, Terran Calendar

The death cry swept through naArien's body, driving the spark of awareness that was his soul upward, reawakening his mind. He gasped for breath, tried to open eyes long-closed, but sticky gel still glued them shut. He sneezed, blew gel from his nostrils. Where were his mates? They had promised to be here, to help him. What was wrong?

He had a body. He was aware of that much. He could wipe the stuff from his face with a tentacle. He reached . . . and could not move. He remembered.

Strands of soft white silk wrapped his body from head to toe, holding him tight to the granite wall. The living stone pressed against his back, warm and inviting as a womb. Colin spun the silk from his six-fingered hands, winding it about naArien's plump, tentacled body. Soran, their ancient mate, watched from her platform, her gentle gaze reassuring him. As the fibers obscured his vision, naArien slipped into the deep trance of metamorphosis, knowing he would return to consciousness only when the transformation was complete.

Now Colin's death cry echoed against the stone. naArien knew the cry was his mate's, though he did not understand how he knew. He twisted away from the wall, tearing at his cocoon with the limited strength of new-grown limbs. He opened his mouth to breathe, sucked in globs of gel mixed with silk fibers, and choked. Gagging, he fought harder, pulling the cocoon away from the stone. He kicked and felt it tear, freeing his foot. There was a small hole beside his hand, and he worked at it, ripping upward until he could touch his face and clear the debris from his mouth. His other hand came free, and he wiped the sticky stuff from his eyes.

13

He blinked, and stared at his hand. Six fingers, still shining with wetness, stood out like a sunburst from the central palm. He flexed them one at a time, then touched their tips together. A joyous gurgle caught in his throat. This was a Master's hand!

Sunlight streamed in through the skylight, brightening the center of the cavernous room but leaving the walls shadowed. Bits of fiber from his cocoon danced in the sunbeams. He stepped away from the stone, letting the light play up and down his new long legs and slender torso. Shreds of silk littered the floor and hung like a disintegrating shroud about him. He saw the platform where Soran lay, her body bloated and dying. She looked at him with eyes gone black, portals opening on her soul. He went to her, the remains of the cocoon trailing from him like a soft white cloud, but even as he reached her she convulsed and lay still. A second death cry swept through the chamber, and Arien stumbled and fell. . . .

"Arien!" This sound seemed real, but Arien touched it, twisted and turned it in his mind before accepting the reality of it. "Arien, you are dreaming again!" A powerful hand gripped his arm, shaking him. Arien opened his eyes, was blinded by the bright light of the wall sconce. He shut them again, concentrating on dimming the light to a comfortable level. A cold wind swept through the open shutters, chilling his shoulders, and he burrowed deeper under the furs.

The hand was still on his arm, squeezing. He opened one eye, saw the old Healer Viela, his stiff white hair lit from behind and standing out about his head like a glowing halo, his face shadowed. Arien opened his other eye. Viela's head moved, the shadows lifting from his face, revealing the beaklike nose and narrow mouth circled by deep-etched lines of age and concern. Behind him light flickered on the bare stone walls, here and there reflecting from a quartz crystal or a patch of mica. The shutters creaked. Arien hated this room.

Twisting, Arien wrenched himself from the other's grasp and sat up.

"You must have roused half the keep tonight, Arien,"

said Viela, his voice stern but concerned. One gnarled hand crept up to touch the ceramic medallion at his chest, while the other smoothed the sleeping furs. "There is talk of banishing you from the keep if you cannot stop broadcasting your dreams."

Arien turned his back on the Healer. "Tell me how to control something I am not conscious of doing," he muttered. The shutter creaked again, then slammed shut.

"Accept the training offered by the Mentor," said Viela, sitting beside Arien. "He will help you come to terms with the loss of your mates, and teach you to live as a FreeMaster."

Arien shrugged. Without mates he would never be a whole person, never become a Mother and raise younglings. He would live a long time, alone. He faced the Healer. "I have no House, Viela. I have no past, and no future. I am outcast, except for your kindness in giving me this room."

Viela's gaze caught Arien's and held it with a power that only a Healer or Mentor possessed. "Losing your mates was a terrible experience. It is the worst thing that can happen to any of us, short of our own deaths. But you cannot change what has happened by reliving their deaths night after night. You must put this behind you."

Arien shivered. The night was cold, and this discussion was accomplishing nothing. He reached for a robe and pulled it over his head, settling its heavy folds about his slim body. Then he slipped soft tol-hide boots over the broad pads of his feet. "I am going walking," he said, rising and throwing a heavy brown cloak around his shoulders. "I will not disturb the keep any more."

The street outside the Healer's complex was empty but for shadows. Arien walked down the center of the gravel roadway, head bowed and shoulders hunched forward. His feet scattered pebbles that rolled and bounced down the hill, disturbing the foraging night-mice.

When he reached the keep's outer wall, first-moon Rea was high in the indigo sky. Its soft light illuminated the burial niches cut into the wall behind the clanhall. Arien walked there, stopping now and then to read some of the swirling runes carved beneath each niche. His womb-

Mother rested in an angular urn of blue-shot quartz, and he touched it, some part of him remembering the growing time he and his littermates had spent in her body. There were more urns, more runes, and then the last two niches, recently cut in the heavy rock wall. He stopped to caress the soft, warm marble of the matching urns, gentle fingers stroking the stone as they would have stroked his mates' bodies.

"Colin, Soran, your ashes are all that remain of our triad. Our House is dead, and there is no place in this clan for me now." Arien's hands traced the swirling design he had carved the day his mates were cremated. It was the single rune of hopeless inquiry. "Who will carve my death message?" he asked, expecting no response. The wind whistled along the desolate mourning wall, tugging at his cloak. There was nothing he could do for his mates now, and nothing they could do for him. Turning, he walked toward the gate.

The clanhall loomed dark and unsympathetic as Arien trod the narrow path that ran between it and the wall. The kitchen step was deeply shadowed. He stumbled on it, fell and caught himself, bruising his palm on a stone. He cursed under his breath, though there was no one to hear him but the dead. A few paces later the path opened onto the keep's main road, and he walked head down, his feet making scuffling sounds in the silence.

Arien stopped outside the house he would have shared with Colin and Soran. The windows were shuttered, the doorway dark. He remembered the chamber where he had been cocooned and knew that moonlight was dancing across the platform where Soran died. It would be winter before the roof-vines covered the skylight and their broad leaves blocked out the sunlight and turned the chamber below into a dank cave.

With a shrug of resignation, Arien turned back to the road. The fate of their home no longer concerned him. The House that traced its lineage from the founders of Alu Keep through one hundred and sixteen successive Mothers had died with Soran. He was alone, a Master without a past or a future. There was nothing left for him in Alu Keep.

A single cloud moved across the face of Rea, casting him into shadow for a moment. He approached the great wall of the keep in silence, and let himself out through the night gate. The door swung shut behind him and the bolt slid home of its own accord. Turning his back on the clan of his birth, he started through the fields toward the black cutout mountains. Behind him, the tiny second moon rose swiftly, chasing its elder sister across the sky.

Arien walked for many days, through vineyards and pastures and over hills. He forded streams within sight of easily-crossed bridges, and clambered over huge rocks when clear trails wound around them. He climbed slowly into the mountains, into sun-bright days and cold, clear nights and forgetfulness.

Along the way he lost his cloak, dropped in the heat of a day when he forgot how cold the night would be. Dirt matted his straw-colored hair and streaked his face, and the scarletberry juice stained his lips and hands. His robe was torn, one sleeve ripped to the shoulder and dangling to reveal the dagger sheathed on his arm. The blade had not left its sheath since Arien walked away from Alu Keep. Rodents and lizards crossed his path without fear, and birds did not flee him. He ate berries, drank from the cold mountain streams, and neglected his body while his mind traveled other planes. The skin on his hands had become translucent, revealing the pattern of veins and muscles beneath the berry stains. He survived without thinking how to survive.

One moonless dark just before dawn, he stumbled from the forest onto the shore of a small lake. The night was still; not a leaf rustled except where he had passed. The water's obsidian surface reflected the black dome of the sky, sparkling with stars. Arien stood there for a long time, arms wrapped around his chest to warm his aching tentacle nodes, toes not quite in the water, and stared at the stars and their reflections. They seemed more numerous than the urns in the mourning wall.

There was a legend that each star was a Mother's soul, returning in the darkness to watch over her children and her House. Did Soran's spirit roam the night sky, de-

spairing over the loss of her legacy? Her death, and Colin's, were minor tragedies when compared to that. It was
the loss of continuity that mattered, the dying House and
the shattered line.

A breeze ruffled the surface of the water, scattering
and multiplying the reflections. The sky brightened and
the stars faded with the coming dawn. Arien sat on the
damp shore, arms still wrapped tightly around his chest,
and began to keen. The wails tore at his constricted throat
as he rocked, eyes closed and head back. He cried for
Colin and Soran, and for the younglings who would never
exist. Finally, out of breath, belly knotted and throat raw,
he could only moan. Sleep took him as the first streaks
of rose appeared above the mountain.

It was mid-afternoon when he woke, sweating. His
throat burned, his joints and muscles ached, and his belly
was empty. He lay unmoving for a long time, staring
across the lake. Life went on around him. Waterfowl up-
ended their plump bodies and searched for tasty tidbits.
A fish jumped. Insects buzzed and flitted along the shore,
not always out of reach of lizards' tongues. Arien
stretched, enjoying the warmth of the sun on his back.
Beneath him, the matted plants were damp and cold
against the earth. He rolled over, and found that it was
not the sun that warmed him. A ball of brilliant white
shimmer-light hovered above his head.

He had made shimmer-light before, small flames to
light his way, but he had never created a ball this large.
He was suddenly afraid. Shimmer-light was common
enough, but it was always made for a purpose—to light
the darkness, to act as a marker and guide. He could not
remember setting this ball of light to glowing. Had he
dreamed a need for it, and created it in his sleep? It was
his handiwork; he recognized the subtleties of its structure. However he had built it, it was draining energy from
his body, energy he could not afford to lose.

He closed his eyes and concentrated on the shimmer-
light. He had created it. He must put an end to it, or it
would put an end to him! His eyes snapped open. He
stared at the glowing ball, basked in its warmth. It would
be an easy death, painless and peaceful. He could lie on

the cool shore until the shimmer-light consumed all his strength.

Arien realized that he no longer wanted to die.

Turning his sight inward again, he concentrated on dimming the shimmer-light. Moment by moment its warmth faded. The drain on his body lessened. The earth felt cold against his back, and he began to shiver. His robe was clammy, a cold shroud holding him down. When the last spark of shimmer-light winked out of existence, he sighed and closed his eyes. He was exhausted.

The trembling started in his hands, and soon spread up his arms and down his legs. He quaked from the cold and from the sudden fear that he would never leave this lakeshore. Water lapped against the earth near his left ear. An insect crawled across his bare right arm, and he could not brush it away. He lay there shivering until dusk's cool air reminded him of the cold night to come. Arien knew that he might not survive another night on the damp shore.

He rolled over, struggled to crawl toward the forest. His wet robe caught on sticks and thorns. He tugged it free and crawled on, until he reached a stout tree trunk. He sat there, back pressed to the rough bark, and watched first-moon come over the mountains.

Arien was aware of two things that could kill him: cold, and starvation. He was too chilled to search for food, but he could make a fire. The moonlight showed him dried leaves and twigs and small branches within arm's reach. He slowly gathered them into a pile, stopping often to rest. When it was ready, he leaned back against the tree and raised his hands, holding his circular palms toward the tinder.

A single spark of shimmer-light would ignite the dried leaves and grass. Arien closed his eyes and tried to still the trembling of his fingers, tried to concentrate on the energy he wished to control. He held his breath and visualized a tiny flame shriveling a leaf, running up a twist of grass, caressing a twig. He imagined the flame growing larger, spreading through the tinder and into the branches, until the crackle of burning leaves filled his ears, and he smelled smoke.

The fire warmed him throughout the night. He fed it carefully until he fell asleep just before dawn. It was out when he awoke, and the sun was high in the sky. He stumbled to the lakeshore and drank, but the water did not fill his belly.

He found scarletberries at the edge of the forest. Thorns on the bushes scratched his arms and chest, but he pushed headfirst into the thicket and stripped berries from the inner branches. He crammed them into his mouth; scarlet juice ran down his chin and dripped onto his arms. When he could eat no more, he made a pouch of his robe's torn sleeve and filled it with ripe berries. This he carried back to the safety of his tree.

Arien slept for most of the day, then drank, ate more berries, and gathered the night's wood. He used a branch to scrape the earth bare around the ashes of his fire. The task exhausted him. By dusk he had a small fire burning brightly in his little circle, and a neat stack of branches waiting to feed it. He spent the night dozing against his tree.

In the morning he found tongue-roots. He was walking to the shore for water when the wispy upper fronds of the plants brushed his palms. He dropped to his knees and used his dagger to dig the fleshy roots from the earth. They were small and starchy, and would taste better boiled, but he ate them raw. They made a satisfying lump in his stomach. He washed and rested, dug more tubers to roast beside his fire, gathered wood and filled his makeshift pouch with scarletberries before settling in for the night.

Just before dawn the death cry woke him. He was trembling, more from fear than cold. There was still some wood piled nearby, and he used it to build up the fire. Then he sat back against the tree, legs drawn up and arms wrapped around them, to await the day. He had thought the dreams of death were over, the memories finally under his control. Now he feared that he would never be free of them.

The morning was hot, and Arien decided to swim. While he could not wash the memories from his mind, he could scrub the grime from his body. He stripped off his robe and waded into the cold water, shivering. He bent down, grabbed the stalk of a water-fern, and stripped away a handful of the broad leaves. The crushed foliage released a sharp, clean fragrance as he briskly rubbed it over his body. Then he walked out until the water reached his tentacle nodes, enjoying the tingling in his skin as the dirt sloughed away.

A fish jumped, and fell back into the clear water with a splash. Arien looked down, saw a school of fingerlings darting between his legs. His stomach rumbled. He could almost smell the aroma of firm white flesh broiling over his little fire. He unsheathed his dagger, took a deep breath, and lowered his face into the chill water. Most of the fish he saw were too small and swift to spear. He swam farther out, turned away a poisonous eel with the point of his dagger, and was about to retreat to shore when he saw a school of flatfish hiding on the sandy bottom. He surfaced, then dove, and came up with two of the oval, one-eyed fish impaled on his dagger.

Low snarls and frightened braying greeted Arien when he broke water. He twisted and turned, trying to locate the source of the sounds, then paddled across the lake toward sunrise. His dagger grasped tightly in his hand and the fish dripping blood onto his fingers, Arien halted, staying low against the shoreline, keeping his body partly submerged. On the beach a wild tol, its silvery fur glistening in the sunlight, crouched, fangs bared and paws bloodied, before a huge braying alep. The mount stood its ground, blood streaming from deep scratches at its shoulder, its six legs straddling and protecting the body of its fallen rider. Arien could see that the Master was dead, his aura already dissipated. It was his death cry, and not a dream, that had disturbed Arien's sleep.

The tol was small. If the alep had not been guarding its Master's body, it could probably have broken the tol's back with a well-placed kick. The tol seemed to know this, and kept just out of the alep's reach. It seemed content to wait for the big animal to bleed to death.

Arien could not let the alep suffer any longer. He picked a palm-sized rock from the shore, then rose and stepped between the two animals, water streaming from his body. He flipped the flatfish from the point of his dagger, tossing them into the grass. The tol was not distracted. It crouched on its powerful rear legs and snarled at Arien.

Arien threw his rock as the tol sprang. He missed the animal's head but connected with a sleek shoulder. The snarl became a howl. The tol's slender body twisted in midair, and landed an arm's length from Arien. He stooped to grab another stone as the tol turned and leaped again, paws extended and claws unsheathed. Arien dove to the ground. His right wrist hit a rock and his hand convulsed, throwing his dagger into the weeds. He kept rolling down into the water.

The tol landed at the edge of the lake and stood there, watching Arien. He walked toward it; it bared its fangs and snarled. Behind it, the alep snorted.

Arien shivered. He felt chilled and tired. He wanted to swim back to his fire, but he would not leave the alep to die, and he would not go without his dagger. His toe touched another rock; he scooped it up and threw it. His aim was poor. The stone zipped past the tol's head and only made the animal more angry.

"I will toy with you no longer," said Arien, raising his hands and turning his palms toward the tol. "Flee now, or face the wrath of a FreeMaster." He tried to still his body's trembling as he conjured a ball of shimmer-light and sent it gliding in the tol's direction. The tol snarled again and backed away. Arien stepped forward.

"Go now, and you can leave in peace. Take the flatfish. They are my gift to you." Arien walked up onto the shore, concentrating his energies into the shimmer-light and moving it to keep the tol backing away, toward the spot where the flatfish lay in the tall grass. He spoke quietly, trying to soothe both animals with the tone of his voice. The alep was accustomed to shimmer-light, but the tol was frightened by the shimmering ball of flame. With a low growl it turned and fled through the grass. Arien could not tell whether it took the fish.

He dropped his hands, let the shimmer-light dissipate. He felt chilled to the bone, and even the sunshine did not warm him. The air was turning cold. His shoulder was scraped and bleeding, his feet were covered with mud, and his robe and boots were on the other side of the lake. He looked across the water at his campsite. It was a short swim, but he was too cold and exhausted to attempt it. He searched the weeds until he found his dagger, then went to tend the injured alep.

The big mount brayed at Arien and nudged him with its snout. He stood still and let the alep smell him. It sniffed at his hands and chest, and at the blood on his shoulder. Its breath was warm, and felt good on Arien's skin. He bent and pulled up a handful of grass, offered the seed heads to the alep. It snorted, and accepted the offering. As it chewed, Arien used the stalks to dry his body.

The alep was well-trained and well-groomed. It allowed Arien to wipe the blood from its shoulder and examine its wounds. The gashes had cut deeply into the muscle but had not reached tendon or bone. Arien had seen animals recover from worse injuries.

The Master was dead, his body already cold. He was dressed in tunic, leggings, cloak and boots, and there was no pack on his saddle. He had probably come from a nearby keep.

"I do not think your Master will mind if I borrow his cloak," said Arien to the alep. He lifted the body, which was surprisingly light, pulled off the heavy wool cloak, and settled it around his shoulders. Then he slung the body across the alep's back. He would not leave the dead Master to be torn apart by scavengers. He took the rein and led the alep around the lake.

By the time they reached Arien's clothes, the wind was sweeping across the lake in chilling blasts, and dark clouds had obscured the sun. Arien shed the warm cloak just long enough to clean the scrape on his shoulder and put on his robe and boots. Then he tore a piece of cloth from the hem of his robe, wet it, and cleaned the mount's wounds.

"Is your keep nearby? Can you lead me there?" Arien spoke soothingly as he washed the alep's shoulder. The animal stood quietly, head turned so that one eye watched Arien work. He used a pad of moss from a nearby tree to stop the bleeding, then spread the tree's healing sap over the wounds. "You should not carry much weight until your shoulder heals. Your Master's body is light. Will you carry it if I walk beside you?"

Dark clouds gathered across the lake. Arien eyed the sky suspiciously, aware that the storm season sometimes started early in the mountains. The temperature was dropping rapidly. Rain would turn to snow or sleet by nightfall, and he had best find shelter before then. He took the bridle's single rein and led the mount away from the lake.

They walked for a long time. Arien was wet and cold despite the borrowed cloak. The chill wind teased the clouds until they released their burden of rain, turning the trail into a mudslide. Arien fell, but the mount plodded right on past him, and he had to scramble to catch up. He clung to the long rein, hoping the animal knew its way home. The rain turned to sleet, and ice gathered on the branches of the trees, weighing them down like a heavy crop of summer fruit.

It was too dark to see anything more than anonymous shapes. Still the big mount plodded on, its Master draped across its back. The animal's six-legged surefootedness kept it on the muddy, icy trail, while Arien slipped along behind, struggling to keep the pace. Frozen blood stained his hands and knees. Knowing he could not continue much longer, he watched for a thicket or a stand of trees that might protect him.

A row of fruit trees coated with ice made a canopy over their heads, and Arien pulled the reluctant mount into this shelter, hoping the animal would be content to rest there and share its warmth. Arien leaned against a tree trunk. His borrowed cloak was caked with ice, his boots torn, and his dagger lost. "Perhaps," he said to the big animal beside him, "perhaps I will join my mates this night."

On the side of the highest mountain, in the midst of a vast orchard, stood the ancient guildhall of the Free-Masters. On the night of the first winter storm, Malin, newly-made leader of the guild, sat alone in his room. A ball of shimmer-light, dancing forgotten above his head, warmed him against the cold. It cast strange shadows across the sharp planes of his face, and lightened the golden hair that flowed to his shoulders. Malin stared at the intricate tapestry that insulated the outer wall, his piercing green eyes searching for patterns in the threads. The fingers of his left hand toyed with the wide band of copper and golden jewels that wrapped about his right wrist. It was a band of office, symbol of the GuildMaster, and he had not worn it yesterday.

The old GuildMaster was dead. Last night he had called Malin to his side, and given him the jeweled band. Malin had protested, and tried to refuse the gift, but the GuildMaster only laid a trembling hand on Malin's shoulder. Then he rode his favorite mount away from the guildhall, and Malin knew he would not return. Before dawn his death cry had swept through the hall, followed by the storm which had kept Malin from searching for his body. The cry still echoed in Malin's mind, mixing with the psychic disturbance of the storm. Now stray threads of fear also touched him. He shivered; his eyes caught a black strand and followed its winding path through the tapestry. It was not the storm rattling the shutters that made him tremble, and shimmer-light was no proof against this chill.

Someone nearby was broadcasting. He was familiar with the mental patterns of everyone in the guild; this mind was strange to him. Pulling his gaze away from the dark web of the tapestry, he donned his warmest cloak and boots. The door of his room opened before him, and latched itself again with a single thought as he hurried down the long second floor hallway. Torches lighted his way to the balcony and the great wooden staircase that led down to the main hall, where most of the guild was gathered beside the communal hearth. Their skills were not as sharp as his—they had not felt the fear that pounded his sensibilities.

The broadcast was weakening, and Malin knew he must hurry. He beckoned for two of the younger, stronger Masters to accompany him, and sent two others to the stable for some of their most powerful mounts. They rode

directly into the fury of the storm, ice caking on their
legs and on the thick cloths that sheltered their faces, and
stiffening the fronts of their cloaks.

Crystal-coated branches made delicate arches across
the trail, and Malin pushed them aside with quick reluctance, feeling them shatter at his touch. The urgency of
his search drove him forward, leaving no time to admire
the beauty wrought by the storm. The broadcast was only
a fine filament now, barely reaching him, but he fixed its
direction and led his party toward the source.

With a suddenness that surprised him, the contact was
broken and he was without guidance. He feared its originator had died, though he felt no death cry. Then through
the sleet a glimmer of light appeared, shimmering in the
darkness to one side of their path. As Malin approached
it resolved into a flickering ball of weak shimmer-light,
riding above the head of a young Master, who lay crumpled on the ground beside the GuildMaster's body.

Warmth seeped into Arien, slowly driving the chill
from his bones. He breathed herb-scented air that drew
the weariness from his body. When he had gathered
enough strength to open his eyes, he saw a pot of steaming tea and a plate of fruitcakes on the table beside the
sleeping platform. His attention did not wander from the
food until his hunger was sated. Only after he poured his
third cup of tea did he notice the Master who sat in the
shadows near the door.

"May the great sun smile on you," he said with formal
respect. The Master rose and came into the light.

"The sun has smiled on you today," he responded,
drawing his chair to the side of the platform. "I am
Malin. What is your keep, Master? Who shall we contact
to say that you are safe?"

Arien put down his tea and turned his face to the wall,
focusing his attention on the complex design of the tapestry that hung there. "No one," he said in tones just
loud enough for Malin to hear.

"Your House will be worried about you," insisted the
Master.

"I have no House!" The strength of his anger shocked

Arien. It was bad form to impose one's emotions on another; he had buried the aching resentment so that no
one else might see it, and had succeeded only in hiding
it from himself. This must be the source of his nightly
broadcasts. He turned back to face Malin. "I am Arien
of Alu Keep, and my House is dead."

"You broadcast well, FreeMaster Arien." The Master
extended a hand, palm outward, all six fingers spread in
a sunburst. His aura glowed soft violet. Sensing the serenity the other projected, Arien let himself be drawn
into its field. "That ability, and the shimmer-light you
produced, saved your life."

He was glad to be alive, but without a home and a
purpose, what kind of life could he have? "It might be
better if you had let me die," he said, making an obser-
vation rather than a plea. The self-pity that had been his
companion for too long was slipping away, along with
the bitterness and anger he had tried to keep hidden. Part
of him wanted to keep and nurture that bitterness, because now it was all he had.

"It is never better to die." The Master twisted his
hand, a gesture used to stabilize emotional fields. "How
did you lose your mates?"

Arien started, offended by the boldness of the question, but chose to answer it and see the other's reaction.
His emotional pain was subsiding, and he spoke with
calm detachment. "Colin was killed in a fall while I was
in metamorphosis, and Soran was so closely bound to
him that she died while I was fighting my way from the
cocoon. I could not save her."

The Master shrugged. "My mate succumbed to night-
fever shortly after our younglings were born."

The revelation surprised Arien. "Who are you?" he
cried. "What keep is this?"

"This is a guildhall, and I am Malin, leader of the
FreeMaster's Guild." He raised his wrist, the sleeve of
his robe falling so that Arien could see the precious copper band that was his badge of office. "Welcome,
FreeMaster," he said in a voice that embraced Arien,
that made him feel as if he had just come home. "Welcome, apprentice."

2257:10/6, TERRAN CALENDAR

****NAGASHIMI-BOEM INTERDEPARTMENTAL
MEMO****

TO: AUSTIN DUERST, VP/RESOURCE
        DEVELOPMENT
FROM: JAMES NAGASHIMI, CEO
   WE HAVE RECENTLY RECEIVED
INFORMATION THAT LARGE DEPOSITS OF
TITANIUM SANDS HAVE BEEN LOCATED ON
THE PLANET ARDEL IN GALACTIC SECTOR
TWELVE. DEPLOY AN INDEPENDENT SURVEY
TEAM TO ARDEL IMMEDIATELY TO CONFIRM
THIS DISCOVERY AND TO BEGIN
NEGOTIATIONS WITH THE ARDELLAN
GOVERNMENT.
   SINCE THE LOCAL CULTURE RANKS ONLY
3.5-4.0 ON THE EVANS TECH SCALE, YOUR
TEAM MUST BE DISCREET WITH WEAPONS
AND TECHNOLOGY. NO OVERT DISPLAYS OF
POWER OR VIOLATIONS OF TRADE
COMMISSION GUIDELINES BY
REPRESENTATIVES OF NAGASHIMI-BOEM CAN
BE TOLERATED. TRADE COMMISSION
REPRESENTATIVES WILL BE SHIPPING TO
ARDEL WITHIN THE NEXT TEN DAYS; WE MUST
MAKE GOOD USE OF OUR HEAD START.
   I EMPHASIZE THAT THERE MUST BE NO
REPEAT OF THE BETA BIMIDJI INCIDENT.

Austin Duerst read the message a second time, then
filed it to memory and requested a listing of available
operatives and ships. He scanned the list quickly, keep-

ing in mind the true meaning of Jim Nagashimi's memo—
use any method necessary to get the trade rights, but
keep the corporate name out of it. Nagashimi needed the
titanium. The demand for the new nearly-impervious alloy hulls was already exceeding predictions.

Duerst found the name he wanted near the bottom of
the list. Nicholas Durrow and his ship were available. He
should have sent Durrow to Beta Bimidji. The local
chieftain would still have died, but no one would have
connected the death to Nagashimi-BOEM.

Chapter 1

2257:12/3, Terran Calendar

Sarah Anders slammed the stylus down, felt it shatter
against the stone table. She cursed. The candle guttered,
threatened to go out, then flared bright again. She glared
at the perfect lines of runes marching down the writing
cloth. Would she ever master their intricacies?

She sighed. It was not the runes that frustrated her. It
was the continuous delays in completing the trade agreement. She and Clan Alu's Mentor, Mrann, had been
working on the pact since her arrival on Ardel forty-five
days ago. Each time she thought they had nearly completed their task, Mrann or a member of the clan's council found a reason to object to some portion of the
agreement.

Finally they had drafted a pact that everyone seemed
to accept. Mrann was ready to present it to the council
for approval when he was called away to a meeting in
Berrut. That had been four days ago. Sarah could do
nothing but wait until he returned.

She picked up the printout of the message that had
come through on her transceiver that afternoon. The
Union's sector authority reported activity in the Ardellan
system—its sensors had detected a ship registered to Na-

gashimi Interstellar Drives. The ship rendezvoused briefly with a shuttle, probably to restock the shuttle's supplies. That meant agents of Nagashimi-BOEM were operating on Ardel, had been for some time. Where were they? With whom were they negotiating? Did they know she was at Alu Keep?

She feared that Nagashimi-BOEM's agents would try to keep Alu's council from ratifying the trade agreement. Perhaps she should request help from *Blackhawk*. She had nothing concrete to report, and bringing the ship back to Ardel might attract attention to her presence here. Perhaps she was better off waiting for the others to show themselves. She tore the printout in half, stuffed it in the charcoal brazier at her feet and watched with satisfaction as it flared. If only it was as easy to be rid of Nagashimi-BOEM! As the flames died, she pulled off her robe, blew out the candle, and slipped between the furs on her sleeping platform.

The young Mother's death cry echoed in the stone of Alu Keep. Laril felt the psychic disturbance break through his barriers as he stood in her chamber. It tore at his heart, made him want to throw back his head and scream in pain even as it constricted his throat and drove the breath from his chest. It left him gasping, shaking, barely able to hold his weapon.

A tangle of tentacled, nonempathic younglings slept undisturbed at the dead Mother's side. Laril envied them. He had never before felt a premature death, had not been prepared for the power of the Mother's final cry. He was not of her House, not even of her clan, yet her death left him weak and trembling. What would her mate feel, when that last agonized cry reached him? He stared at the dead Mother, thought of his own mate and younglings safely asleep in Eiku Keep, and regret immobilized him for a moment.

Knowing he could kill the younglings easily, Laril turned his weapon away. The death of the Mother fulfilled his purpose. Soon the Mentor's apprentice would seek him out. Laril had planned to turn the Terran weapon against him and destroy him. Now he was not certain he had the strength to cause another death.

The alien weapon was cold in his hands, lifeless, like the Mother its tight beam had just pierced. Slipping the weapon into the sash that girded his slender waist, Laril made his way back through the silent house to the young-lings' portal and stepped outside. As he crept along the dark, deserted street behind the building, he felt the stone of Alu watching him. He closed one hand on the grip of his weapon, his six opposable fingers struggling to grasp a shape formed for four fingers and a thumb. Real or imagined, he sensed hostility emanating from the walls of the Houses and guildhalls around him. Alu was an ancient keep and the stone carried within it the essence of generations of Mothers and Masters. He was certain that it marked him as an intruder, and watched him.

Sarah woke with a start. Her room in Alu's clanhall was dark, though the shutters were thrown open; no moon had yet risen. Unfamiliar constellations glittered in the blue-black sky. She sat up, and the sleeping furs slid to the floor. The air was cold. No coals glowed in the bra-zier. Shivering, she reached for a cloak and drew it about her shoulders. The heavy fabric smelled of something like, but not quite, cinnamon. She picked up her flash-light, set it down, and lit a candle instead.

The light threw wide, diffuse shadows that Sarah found comforting. She breathed deeply to slow the rapid beat-ing of her heart, and tried to gather the remnants of the dream that had awakened her. The adrenaline rush sub-sided, but the only part of the dream she could retrieve was an oppressive awareness of death.

Footsteps echoed in the hall outside her room. Sarah ran to the door, pulled it open, saw a figure cloaked in gray moving swiftly down the shadowed corridor toward the clanhall. Gray was the color of power, worn only by the Mentor and his apprentice. Since Mrann was in Ber-rut, this must be his apprentice, Elver. Curious, Sarah fastened the front of her cloak close about her naked body and followed him, her bare feet slapping stone as she ran.

She stumbled into the great hall just behind Elver, in time to see him close his eyes and will the huge wall-mounted torches alight. The sudden wash of cool, brilliant illumination startled her, and she blinked tears from her protesting eyes.

The Masters of Clan Alu were slipping into the clanhall through the sheltered side doors. They stood in small groups, whispering and gesturing. Sarah sensed that whatever drew them had also awakened her—a silent communication that reached everyone in the keep. The perception of death had come with her to the clanhall. It was stronger here, and she wanted to flee from it, but there was nowhere to run. Even the stone walls seemed to radiate disquiet, as if they, too, were aware of something dreadfully wrong in Alu Keep.

Elver stood near one of the doors, speaking with several Masters. Sarah recognized Torma, leader of the clan's council, and the Healer Viela. When she joined them Torma and Elver cupped their hands in greeting, but the Healer refused to acknowledge her presence.

She seemed to have walked into an argument. "I can feel the intruder near the wall beside the gate," said Elver. "I must stop him before he kills again."

"You?" scoffed Viela. His tunic was open, the cord of his Healer's medallion tangled in the fasteners. With one hand he brushed back the hair from his face. "His challenge is for the Mentor."

"The Mentor is not here. Elver must go in his place," said Torma.

"He has only begun his training. He may have the power, but he does not have the experience needed to use it," protested Viela. "We might as well send this head-blind Terran against the assassin."

Elver cut him short. "Do not mock me, Healer. I have the power, and I will prevail. There is no one else to send. Would you risk the lives of any of the Masters? Like the Mentor, I am expendable because I no longer have a mate. You must play your part, and gather the Masters to the council circle. Do what you can to aid me."

Elver turned and walked away. Viela tried to follow him, but Torma laid a hand on his arm.

"Let him go. We need you in the circle." He pushed Viela toward the long table, beckoning the other Masters to join them.

Sarah did not stay to watch the circle. By the life of her grandmother, these people were such as she had never encountered before. Midnight assassinations, challenges, and personal combat did not fit with their daytime gentleness. Something was very wrong, and she feared she knew the source of the wrongness. This was just the sort of trouble she expected from Nagashimi-BOEM's agents. She slipped out the side door and followed Elver through the deserted streets. The sense of death was still with her, and her intuition warned her that it might be Elver's death she felt. She could not let him go alone.

In the last moment of darkness before the rising of Ardel's twin moons, the streets were very dark. Sarah could see nothing but the outline of rooftops and the shimmer of Elver's cloak. She had to move swiftly to keep up with his long, purposeful strides, and her bare feet suffered from the dirt and gravel of the roadway.

Of its own volition her hand went to her right hip, reaching for her stunner. It came away empty. Alien weapons were forbidden on Ardel, but years of Union training and habit died hard. She wanted a stunner not to protect herself, but to aid Elver.

First-moon was rising. Its soft light illuminated the road and the top of the keep's wall. She saw Elver in the street, facing the wall and the wide doors of its gate. Sarah crouched at the corner of a building, out of the moonlight. Her eyes scoured the shadows at the base of the wall, but she could not discern what Elver seemed to sense there.

Suddenly a dark figure divorced itself from the shadows and raised a weapon, threatening. Moonlight glinted on the bright metal of a hand laser. Sarah gasped. She could not tell whether the challenger was Ardellan or Terran, but the weapon was Terran, and deadly. It must have come from Nagashimi-BOEM's agents. Elver was no match for that laser, whatever training and powers he possessed. She cried a warning, but it was already too late.

Elver stood, cloak flowing back in the breeze, feet apart and arms outstretched in a gesture of power. Sparks crackled from his fingertips toward the intruder. The assassin braced his arm, sighted down it past the weapon to his target. A great arc of blinding white light flowed outward from Elver's hands, but the power he summoned fell short of its mark. The assassin fired.

In the great hall in the heart of Alu Keep, the Masters sat at council. They circled the massive stone table, the Healer sitting beneath the ancient tapestry that draped the high outside wall. He touched his palm to Torma's. In slow, studied motion their curled fingers interlaced to lock their hands together. Then Torma reached out with his other hand, touching palms with the Master who sat beside him. The action moved like a wave around the table as, one by one, the Masters entered the circle. Their interlocked fingers linked them in a continuous chain like the interwoven rings and six-pointed stars that danced across the tapestry. The last Master reached for Viela's free hand, and as their palms met the circle was completed, and power began to flow.

Viela sat in the Mentor's place, channeling the power. Closing his eyes, he drew a deep breath and let his mind settle through layers of consciousness into trance. He gathered energy from the minds and bodies of the Masters, weaving it into a cone of power over the table. As Healer, he was aware of the physical limitations of each member of the circle. He monitored their bodies, finding the level of power he could safely draw from each of them. When he had achieved the maximum strength in the cone, he set his mind free to search for the intruder.

Viela's mind flowed up and outward, toward the House from which the death cry had come. He was aware of many familiar presences along the way: Masters and Mothers awakened by the cry and stirring in their own Houses; curious younglings gathering at windows and doorways; the Terran crouching in the street and just be-

yond her, Elver crumpling, his gray cloak floating to the
ground with a whisper.

Elver was alive, but dreadfully wounded; Viela watched
as the life-force flowed out of him in fountains of violet
energy. The Healer's mind swooped low to touch Elver's
consciousness. He monitored the blood loss, found it
minimal. Elver's heart was strong, his breathing steady,
his mind struggling to control the pain that wracked his
body. Viela helped him stem the outward flow of energy.
His life was no longer in danger.

A thirst for vengeance rose in the Healer, transmitted
from the minds of the Masters who were linked to him.
He separated from Elver and reached out to search for
the assassin hidden in the shadows. Viela touched the
stranger, drew more energy from the Masters as he
reached into the consciousness of the assassin. They gave
to him freely, sacrificing safety in the name of revenge.

Escape. Viela touched that thought. Laril wanted to
climb up and over the wall of Alu Keep, to run home to
safety. Delving deeper, draining those linked to him even
more, Viela touched panic and a desperate need for the
security of House and hearth. He built on this fear of
Laril's, sending energy into the great wall of the keep,
wakening the spirits that rested within it.

Using Laril's memories, Viela strained to construct a
grand illusion. Pulling even more energy from the circle,
he built an image of Laril's home keep, rising from rolling fields planted with grain. Late summer sunlight cast
shadows that stretched across the plain, beckoning Laril.
A soft wind rustled the grain, moving it in gentle, rolling
waves. Draining his Masters to the point where the weakest of them lost consciousness, Viela used the energy to
project the image outward, past the still figure of Elver
to the great wall, and beyond.

Laril started forward to make certain his target was
dead, but he saw movement in the shadows behind the
body. Slipping his weapon into his sash, he turned back
toward the safety of the wall. A small flower of panic
blossomed in his chest as the stone wall of Alu Keep
loomed before him. It seemed to grow and change shape

in the moonlight just as the fear was growing in his chest, devouring his senses. He ran toward it, but it moved away from him and he was forced to run faster, harder, until his heart pounded and his chest was ready to burst. Terror spread to his belly and his mind, and his legs began to shake. He had only one goal—to reach the safety of his own hearth in Eiku Keep.

At last he flattened his body against the wall, but he could feel it fighting him, repelling his midsection with unforeseen force. He tried to climb, but had only inched his way up a few hands when he realized the reason for the stone's repulsion. Dropping to the ground, he pulled the alien weapon from his sash and tossed it into the shadows. Then he flung his body against the wall and scaled it with all the speed he could raise. The six fingers of each hand were splayed in a wide circle to give a secure grip on the stone, and the circular pads of his feet, clad in soft boots, curled over what small outcroppings they could find.

The climb was endless. Fear and panic were his constant companions, and he had no thought for anything but the top of the wall. When his left hand and then his right touched empty space above his head, he could not be certain if it was reality or illusion. He pulled himself up to look over the edge, and saw the plains of Eiku bathed in soft summer sunlight, the keep standing broad and tall only two hundred paces away. Some part of him knew this for illusion, or memory, but he was caught up in the vision as he scrambled to the top of the wall.

Laril looked out at the golden plains of his home. The beautifully sculpted stone walls of Eiku Keep welcomed him. The gates were open, beckoning, as a gentle wind carried familiar scents to his nostrils. Brushing the dirt from his tunic, he settled it in place, and stepped. . . .

Sarah Anders watched the intruder turn and run for the wall. She bent low and crept toward Elver, keeping to the dubious shelter of the shadows. Elver's pain was like a silent scream inside her head. Her breathing and her heart rate quickened as she struggled toward him.

She was reliving the pain and terror of the laser blast

that struck her down on New Kingston. The puckered
scar on her shoulder was six years old now. She refused
to have it cosmetically repaired; it was a reminder of the
ruthlessness of her fellow human beings. An independent
negotiator named Durrow had wounded her when their
tour group was attacked by a native carnivore. He claimed
it was an accident—poor aim and unfamiliarity with the
settings on the firearm he had been issued. Sarah was
able to trace him back to BOEM, but she had never been
able to prove that her injury had been deliberate.

Elver was sprawled on the gravel, eyes closed and
breathing shallow. Sarah knelt beside him and cradled
his head in her lap. Gently she examined the wound in
his side, where the laser had burned away clothing and
flesh. The moonlight was not bright enough for her to
evaluate the damage, but he lived. She could only hold
him, and wait for the Healer.

She heard rustling sounds across the street. Younglings
peered from a portal, the brave ones jostling for the best
position to view the street and the wall. Their Mother
appeared, pulled them back into the house with arms and
tentacles, and closed the door.

Rea topped the great wall, silhouetting the intruder
against its bright orb. Sarah watched, horrified, as the
assassin stepped from the top of the wall. The presence
of death was like a mat of cotton closing about her,
smothering her. She shuddered at his scream. Bending
over Elver, she sought some comfort in sheltering him.
With a gentle hand she brushed the hair away from his
face.

In the great hall, Viela allowed the exhausted Masters
to loose hands, breaking the circle. Gathering his things
to minister to Elver, he sent an apprentice to bring restorative potions for the Masters.

For the second time that night a death cry swept
through the keep. Viela was pleased as he felt it move
past him and outward, across the plain toward Eiku.

Chapter 2

The death cry touched Arien, twisting his dream. Once again he struggled with the silken fibers that bound his body, protecting it during metamorphosis. His youngling's tentacles were gone; new-grown arms and Master's hands tore at the soft cocoon. It parted, trailing behind him as he approached the platform where one of his mates rested. He was too late. She was dead. . . .

Arien awoke with a start, a new death cry mingling with the remembered cries of his dying mates. Sitting up, he shivered from more than the cool air of the late spring night. He cursed the double empathic gift that had come to him with the deaths of his two mates, so many seasons ago. The tragedy had released the latent empathic abilities that made him a powerful FreeMaster, but with the gift came the curse of sensitivity. Unguarded emotions broadcast by other Masters could trigger memories that he would rather forget; the sweeping power of the death cry brought back those fateful moments that changed the course of his life. He needed tea and a warm hearth to banish the nightmarish effects.

Arien blinked and the guest room in Eiku Keep's clanhall brightened as one of the wall sconces glowed with gentle light. The sleeping furs were strewn across the floor. He pushed them aside, and reached for a cloak draped across a nearby chair. Bending, he pulled on soft boots and settled them about the broad circular pads of his feet. His fine gray hair flowed forward to cover his face, and he swept it back, his lips pressed in a narrow line. Then he rose, tossing the cloak about his narrow shoulders.

The door of his sleeping chamber was ajar by the time he reached it, opened by the same thought that dimmed the wall sconce behind him. He paused when he saw light under the door across the hall. The room belonged to his employer. He did not like the man, but any company would be, better than sitting alone in the big kitchen. Crossing the hall, he tapped on the door. He heard the sound of muffled footsteps, and then the latch was loosed manually and the wide wooden door opened.

"What do you want?" Nick Durrow growled, planting his compact Terran body in the doorway.

"Favor, sir," said Arien politely, but without any trace of subservience. He noted that Durrow was dressed, and the sleeping platform undisturbed. "I am going to the kitchen for tea, and perhaps some fresh bread. Would you like to join me?"

Durrow ran a broad hand over his short, wiry black hair and nodded. He fiddled with the leather pouch at his hip, surreptitiously checking the knives that were hidden in his sleeves. Arien did not miss these slight movements. In the sixty days since the Terran had hired him as guide and translator, Arien had never seen the man unarmed. Durrow followed the trade rules and carried only Ardellan weapons, like the knives sheathed in his sleeves, when he could be observed. Arien had convinced him it would be worth his life to be found with energy weapons, or even a communications device that might be assumed to be a weapon. But in the Terran camp where no other Ardellans came, and on Durrow's shuttle, Arien had seen weapons that used light to destroy. Lasers, Durrow called them.

Durrow shouldered his way past the taller Ardellan, leaving him to blink out the light and latch the door. The Terran moved with the stealth of a wild tol, despite his heavy-soled boots. Arien, following, wondered if Durrow knew that the brash self-assurance of his aura announced him to the empathic Ardellans everywhere he went, as surely as if he'd thumped loudly when he walked.

The Terran's manner often confused him—it was so alien to his own upbringing in the ordered life of Clan Alu. Durrow, whose emotional aura was chaotic and disruptive, was often unpredictable and difficult to handle. Arien's GuildMaster had ordered him to work for the offworlder, and he did so without protest. He acted as chaperone and diplomat, trying to keep the trouble Durrow caused to a minimum. He would be pleased when the Terran was gone again, and he could return to the peace of the ancient guildhall, where memories from the days before he became a FreeMaster rarely troubled him.

Ignoring the narrow, winding back stairs that went directly to the kitchen, the Terran continued down the hall toward the wide stone stairway that connected the second floor living quarters with the first floor, where Clan Eiku's meeting rooms and the great hall were located. Arien followed him, wishing he could banish forever the memory of his metamorphosis from youngling to Master.

A wave of grief washed through him; for a moment Arien did not know if it was his own sorrow, or that of another. Then the wide doors opening on the hallway below swung apart with great force. Revin, the tall, white-haired Mentor, leader of Clan Eiku, burst through them. Arien's instinctive reaction was to melt into the shadows along the wall and try to slip back up the staircase. Durrow, who lacked the Ardellan's empathic sensitivity, continued arrogantly down the stairs to confront the Mentor.

"Mentor, you are back early," called the Terran as he raised his right hand, fingers curled together in a grotesque imitation of the Ardellan greeting. "Did the assembly go well?"

Revin ignored Durrow, walking past him with a swiftness and grace that denied his years. "Barnn!" He called for his apprentice only once. His name had just stopped echoing in the great stone entrance chamber when Barnn appeared at the top of the stairs. He looked confused and not quite awake. He was still fastening his robe as he passed Arien, who followed him down.

"The death cry was Laril's." Revin's anguish spoke to them all, even the Terran. Arien saw the fleeting shock that passed over Durrow's dark features. "His mate is still alive. Go quickly, Barnn, and keep her from harming herself and her younglings." The apprentice was already through the door, running down the dark street toward the dead Master's House.

Arien leaned against the cold wall of the entranceway,

drawing strength from the permanence of the ancient stone. His mind wanted to reject the words he had just heard—Laril, the young mapmaker he and Durrow had worked with, was dead. Even his empathic talent had not been enough to identify the source of the death cry. Only a Mentor's training developed that ability.

The harsh voice of Durrow demanding to know the decision of the assembly jarred Arien from his reverie. One of Revin's attendants opened the door to a small meeting room and propped it back. The other walked from sconce to sconce, willing the torches to light. Ignoring Durrow, Arien followed them into the room. He dragged a chair to the center for Revin. The Mentor pulled off his cloak and handed it to Arien before he sat. The other Masters of the clan were gathering, coming in ones and twos to the clanhall to stand talking in small groups. Durrow would not be put off. He followed Arien, confronting Revin again.

"What of the Assembly, Revin?" demanded Durrow. He was belligerent, planting his body before the Mentor's chair. Arien froze, one arm holding Revin's gray cloak out to his attendants. The Terran was being deliberately offensive, violating custom and courtesy in his impatience to have an answer. He did not understand the gravity of this night's events, and, even if he had understood them, Arien doubted it would have made a difference in his actions.

Arien felt the cloak leave his hand and drew a strengthening breath, stepping between Durrow and the angry Mentor. "Mentor," he said with great dignity, offering his hands palms upward and fingers spread in a gesture that asked pardon. "Captain Durrow begs your forgiveness for disturbing you in this time of distress, but it would aid him greatly if he could know the decision of the Assembly. Will Eiku be allowed to trade with the offworlders?" Arien felt Durrow's anger at his interference; it lanced through him but he stopped it before it reached Revin, absorbing the energy himself so that the Mentor would not feel the offense.

Revin looked up, weariness etched in the fine lines of his features. "As I expected, we will have to fight for that right. The Assembly in Berrut has accepted Eiku's claim to ownership of the great wasteland where the Terran ships land. In three days time we meet Clan Alu at the landing site to decide the dispute. If we take the wasteland from Alu, the trade rights also pass to us.''

The Terran stepped around Arien, his anger mollified. Although he had developed a good understanding of Ardellan speech in a very short time, his thick accent made it difficult to understand him. His changeable emotional aura gave the empaths a much better understanding of his true meaning. ''Mentor, I am pleased that our agreement will bear fruit to nourish both of us. When you win control of the disputed lands, you can give the people I represent the right to mine the sands. Then we can give Clan Eiku metals—all the copper and iron you can use and trade. Eiku will be lifted from a poor, powerless clan to new prosperity and influence.''

''Impatience is not a virtue, Master Durrow. Let us first see the outcome of the dispute.''

Durrow lowered his voice so that only Revin and Arien could hear him. ''I have no doubt that you will win the dispute, Mentor. You have Laril to thank for that. Tonight he went to Alu Keep to kill the Mentor's apprentice. The Mentor will have to fight alone, against you and your apprentice. You will triumph.''

Arien felt Revin's power reaching toward the Terran even before the Mentor rose from his chair. It was like an independent entity, flowing from the Mentor's body and existing only to destroy the focus of his anger. That Durrow had dared to interfere in clan matters, and had brought about the death of Laril, enraged Revin. He raised his arms in a gesture that concentrated and directed the power of his anger. The Mentor stood in the center of a blazing ruby rage that every Ardellan present could see, and they drew back from him in apprehension. Durrow never moved. Arien knew he saw only an old man standing with his arms in the air, his alien features twisted in a grotesque, unreadable expression.

''No,'' Arien cried as he threw himself against Durrow, pushing him away from the pulsing, growing power of Revin's anger.

"Do not interfere, FreeMaster, or your life will be forfeit. His life," Revin pointed to Durrow and power flowed from his fingers, touching the Terran in the center of his chest and sending him sprawling across the room, "is already lost."

Revin's attendants were standing behind him now, safely away from the potent energy of his rage. At the door of the small room the other Masters crowded around, watching the confrontation. Only Arien dared to step between the angered Mentor and his target. Arien's aura glowed amethyst, his anger with Durrow tempered by his knowledge of the Terran's flaws.

Addressing the Mentor in respectful tones, Arien tried to sense the thoughts and predict the actions of the Terran climbing to his feet behind him. He disapproved of Durrow's actions, and let that disapproval shine in his aura, knowing the Terran would not sense it. "Mentor, Master Durrow does not understand our ways. Had he told me of his plan, I would have prevented it. Laril must have agreed to take part in the scheme, and it cost him his life. It was his choice, Mentor."

The ruby glow of Revin's anger softened a bit, and Arien felt the touch of his grief. The death of an adult was a traumatic event in the life of a clan; when the mating chain was broken it could not be repaired, and the continuity of the House was ended. Laril's death condemned his mate to live out her life alone and to die infertile. The secret of creating new lines had been obscured by the passage of time and the machinations of the Healers Guild. No new Houses had been created in the keeps in many generations. Laril's House could not be replaced.

Durrow was on his feet now, moving toward the Mentor, keeping Arien's body between himself and Revin's anger. With the instinctive reaction of a cornered animal, he touched the mechanism that released the knife at his right wrist. Too late Arien sensed his intent and turned to warn him, but the knife was already in Durrow's hand. Arien felt a single thought from Revin sweep past him, then saw the blade of the knife twist beyond repair. The

Terran looked at it, dumbfounded, and dropped it as if it had burned his hand.

The twisted blade clattered to the stone floor as another death cry reached them. Its power staggered Arien, but he managed to remain on his feet. The room was silent for a long moment; then Barnn pushed his way past the Masters gathered at the door, his face twisted in defeat. "They are all dead," he cried, his hands making a gesture of warding. "She strangled the younglings before I reached her, and tore her own tentacles out. She bled to death." There were dark stains on his tunic.

Arien felt Revin's anger turn cold, saw his aura redden once more. The old Mentor stretched an arm toward Durrow, the flat of his palm facing the Terran, with all six fingers extended like a sunburst in a gesture of warding. No one in the room moved as Revin spoke. "Terran, you have done more harm than you know. Your life is forfeit here, but for the sake of this FreeMaster I will not kill you now. If ever you set foot on Eiku land again, you will be dead."

"What of the metal I can bring you?" cried Durrow, fear putting a sharp edge in his voice. "Clan Eiku will die a slow and painful death without my help."

"There is another Terran anxious to take the sands and give us metals in exchange. Mrann of Clan Alu bragged that she is at his keep. When we win control of the wasteland, she will trade with us. We have no need of you. Now go!" Dropping his arm, Revin turned to Arien. "You may stay, FreeMaster, if you wish to leave the Terran's service."

Arien bowed his head to the Mentor, and offered his hands palms upward once more. "Forgiveness, Mentor, for my part in this," he said. "I must go with Durrow. The will of my GuildMaster binds me to his service." He turned away, taking Durrow's arm and pulling him from the room before either he or Revin could say anything more. The Masters at the door stepped aside, allowing them free passage.

They were almost at the back door when Durrow stopped, tugging his arm from Arien's grasp. His dark eyes were hooded, his face a mask that Arien could not

penetrate. The FreeMaster looked him up and down, and
then addressed him sharply. "Do you want to live, Master? Revin will kill you if you provoke him once more."

Durrow nodded, looking up at Arien. "If I had my
laser pistol . . ."

"You would be just as dead," said Arien.

2257:12/4, TERRAN CALENDAR
TO: CAPTAIN SWENSON, TERRAN UNION
         INTERSTELLAR SHIP *BLACKHAWK*
FROM: SARAH ANDERS, TRADE ATTACHE/
         ARDEL
    SITUATION ON ARDEL HAS CHANGED
DRAMATICALLY. TERRAN LASER PISTOL USED
TO MURDER A RESIDENT OF CLAN ALU.
ASSUME YOU WERE NOTIFIED OF PRESENCE
OF NAGASHIMI SHIP IN-SYSTEM.
    AM IN NO IMMEDIATE PERSONAL DANGER,
BUT SUGGEST YOU REMAIN IN-SYSTEM AND
MONITOR COMMUNICATIONS CAREFULLY.

    Captain Jan Swenson threw the hard-copy down on his
desk and looked at his first officer. "If we turn back now,
how long will it take us to reach Ardel?"

    "Seventeen hours," replied Schimmel.

    "Who else can make the delivery to Bartel's Colony?"

    "Captain Wick of the *Kyte* has enough of the anti-
fungals aboard to meet the settlers' needs, but he will
need thirty-six hours more transportation time than we
will."

    Swenson uttered a curse. "That puts us in a fine pickle.
If those fools had stored their chemicals properly, we
wouldn't have to rush them a fresh supply. The Trade
Commission considers the colony's wheat crop too important to risk." He studied the status board on the wall

opposite his desk. "Anders has done well enough without us for the last forty-five days. It'll take us less than twenty hours to reach the colony, then thirty-seven back to Ardel, less if you fine-shave the jump between systems. I think she can wait that long."

Chapter 3

Sarah Anders read the last entry in her journal.

"I have no doubt that agents for Nagashimi-BOEM precipitated last night's murder of the Mother Hladi, and the attempted murder of Mrann's apprentice. I found the assassin's hand laser this morning. It is Terran-made, a smuggler's weapon.

"I must convince Mrann and the council to approve the trade agreement now, before anyone else is killed."

She underlined the last sentence with two bold strokes. Then she closed the notebook with a snap, heard the privacy seal catch. She slipped the pen into its little pocket in the binding, then shaded her eyes with one hand as she looked at the sun. It was nearly midday. Where was the Mentor?

She suppressed her impatience. Ardellans moved by their own timetables. They were less precise, more relaxed about time than Terrans. Their year was divided into six unequal seasons based on changes in the weather, they had never invented clocks, and they began and ended their days at dawn so that the length of a day was always changing. They had no deadline for completion of the trade agreement. When the matter was finished, it would be finished. Sarah had found the attitude refreshing until Nagashimi-BOEM appeared on the scene. Now she felt pressured to conclude the agreement before the conglomerate's agents could interfere further. The Ardellans' relaxed attitude had suddenly become a source of frustration. She sighed, and tucked her journal under her arm.

The boulder she sat on was just outside Alu Keep's gate. She turned her head, gazing across the fields at the scarlet conifer forest that climbed the distant mountainside. She longed to visit that forest, to see the strange animals and birds that lived there. Most of her eighteen-year career had been spent on high-tech worlds, but she preferred Ardel's agrarian society. Here no one thought it strange when she touched a tree, or sniffed a fragrant blossom. As alien as these people were, she sometimes felt more comfortable with them than she did with her own kind.

The Ardellans used such a small area of their planet. A stormy ocean separated this continent from the other major land masses, and though there were fishers among the Ardellans, there were no sailors. The fisherfolk told tales of monsters that capsized boats when they strayed too far from land. The crews were drowned or devoured by hideous sea creatures. Clan Alu's historian recounted stories of adventurous Masters and courageous Mothers leading their clans through adversity, but never tales of exploration. When Sarah asked, the historian said no one had ever crossed the desert wasteland, or climbed over the mountains to see what was on the other side. Only FreeMasters were unfettered by family and clan obligations, and they had much more important ways to spend their time. The Ardellans lived circumscribed lives on this little piece of arable land, divided among eleven clans and a half-dozen independent cities.

Sarah smiled, tossing her long dark hair over her shoulder and retying the thong that imprisoned it. There were mysteries here. She found the Ardellan culture fascinating in a personal and professional sense. Perhaps, when Alu ratified the trade agreement and the Union built a spaceport, she would apply for permanent posting. It was time to settle down. With Jeremy entrenched on Ganymede, and Merissa taking her third doctorate on Titan, she was free to do as she pleased. Permanent posting would pay less, but the children had not needed her support in years, and she wouldn't need much to live here.

And there would be no more trips back to Earth. Sarah's smile faded as she thought of the black-edged sheet of vellum covered with her mother's spidery handwriting. She kept it tucked away in her ditty-bag; she would not send her mother a reply, but she could not bear to part with the letter informing her of her father's death. It had arrived just before she boarded the ship for Ardel. The letter was written in her mother's sparse, formal style. It described the stroke, the days of life-support, the diminishing brain function until her mother finally allowed the physicians to withdraw their machines. She had given him a white man's funeral, instead of taking him home to New Mexico. Sarah sighed. That was the final wedge of many that her mother had driven between her father and his people.

The wasteland and mountains of Ardel reminded Sarah of the summers she had spent with her grandmother in New Mexico. The old woman was an artist who tried to preserve some of the ancient ways. She and her cousins kept sheep, did their own shearing and carding, spun heavy blanket-wool and dyed it in huge steaming pots. The weavings that came from her loom were prized by collectors. She had not been bitter about the daughter-in-law who had come to buy blankets for the gallery, and had taken her son back to the city instead. It was Navaho custom for a man to join his wife's family. Grandmother had often admonished Sarah to be understanding of her mother and the career that took so much of her time and energy, and to show her proper love and respect. Sarah had tried to do that, but her mother's coldness and domineering nature made it difficult. At the end, they fought about everything, until Sarah chose a career that would take her far from her mother's circle of influence.

It had meant leaving her father behind, too. She missed his warm smile, his genuine interest in her life. With his death, she had no reason to return to Earth. Her memories of him would remain as fresh on Ardel as anywhere else. Perhaps if she stayed here, she would finally find some of the peace her grandmother claimed was her birthright. She might make time to study the old woman's journals, and learn more about the way of a Navaho wisewoman.

Mike wouldn't like it, though. Marrying him had been

another sort of rebellion, an excuse to run even farther
from home. He was a xenobiologist, and she was studying anthropology. She changed the focus of her graduate
degree from American Indian cultures to alien civiliza-
tions, and followed him to Cygnus III to do her field-
work. Jeremy and Merissa were born there. By the time
they sent the children off to school, she and Mike had
drifted far apart. Their contract came up for renewal
every five years; eventually they just neglected to file the
papers. He stayed on Cygnus III, while she met Sandsmark and joined the Trade Commission. She never heard
from Mike anymore, but he'd be sure to turn up if she
decided to stay on Ardel. Not that it was any of his business. She had fulfilled the terms of their contract, and
provided him with the requisite two children. He had no
further claim on her.

Best of all, Sandsmark and the Union would have to
find someone else to take the tough assignments. Sarah
laughed, thinking of Sandsmark seated behind his huge
lucite desk, imperiously controlling the lives of his sub-
ordinates. He had lost the use of his legs on his final
mission; some said it was an accident, but others claimed
it was an error in judgment. He demanded total loyalty
and dedication from his employees. He would be livid
when he heard she was leaving the department.

She smoothed the soft copper-colored tunic, admiring
the way it fit her tall, angular frame. She had never felt
so comfortable in native dress. She wore her own boots
and her grandmother's handwoven sash. Every time she
looked in a mirror, she saw more of that old woman. The
strong sun here had darkened her skin, accenting her high
cheekbones and the gray streak in her hair. Only her blue
eyes were wrong.

Sarah looked over her shoulder at the bloodstained
rocks, and shivered. There were things she needed to
learn about Ardel and its people before she decided to
stay. Dark splotches marred the earth, and a bit of blue
fabric fluttered in the wind. Brown bones were strewn
among the rocks, bits of flesh and gore still clinging to
them. The wild tols had feasted well. The Healer had

assured her that the assassin was dead before they tore him apart.

She turned back to scan the horizon. A gust of wind lifted dust from the roadway. Younglings worked in the fields, cultivating the plants. Others repaired the irrigation system, under the watchful eye of a Master. Beyond the gardens, green shoots decorated the grain fields.

Before her, life; behind her, death. Why?

Squinting, Sarah watched an approaching dust cloud resolve into two fast-moving aleps carrying riders. They sped toward the keep, ignored by the younglings in the fields. The mounts looked a bit like horses, with large, barrel-shaped bodies and long heads, but their legs were a wonder. They ran on two pairs, The delicate forelegs and the heavily-muscled rear, with a third pair folded under their chests. For walking on rough ground, and for climbing, they extended the central pair of legs. These limbs stood out from the body at a slight angle, the feet broad and flexible on sturdy ankles, giving the aleps excellent balance and agility.

She recognized the Mentor by his traditional gray cloak; he rode ramrod straight, his soft gray hair flying in the wind. He was a powerful being, and Sarah found him attractive despite, or perhaps because of, his alienness. They had known each other only forty days, yet she thought of him as a close friend.

"Sarah, what are you doing here?" Mrann called as he brought his big alep to a stop before the gate. "I expected the Masters to greet us."

Sarah nodded. "The Masters are in council, Mentor. I asked Torma if I could meet you." She knew the request was granted reluctantly. Torma did not approve of her presence at the keep, or even of the Terran presence on Ardel.

The second mount stopped just behind the first, dropping its central limbs to stand relaxed on all six legs. Runnels of sweat made parallel tracks in the dust on its rump. The rider stared at the keep, eyes vacant, arms hanging limp at his sides. His cloak was open, his tunic covered with road dust, his hair a matted silver mass.

Jeryl was his name, and the assassinated Mother had been his mate.

Mrann dismounted, tossed his mount's rein to Sarah, and walked over to Jeryl. He eased the rein from his hand. "Dismount, Jeryl," he said firmly. The other swung his leg over the alep's neck and slid to the ground. He stumbled, and Mrann steadied him. Sarah scrambled down from the boulder and they walked into the keep, Sarah and Mrann leading the mounts.

"Hladi's death cry reached us while we were traveling from Berrut. Jeryl has been in shock since then." Mrann looked into Sarah's eyes, and the hairs on the back of her neck rose. It was not an unpleasant feeling. "Do you know how she died?" he asked. Stopping at the stable just inside the gate, Mrann handed the reins of the blocky aleps over to two younglings who worked there. The younglings trundled across the uneven ground, their ovoid bodies perched on stubby legs and bristling with tentacles; the aleps followed.

"It was the work of an assassin. What little is left of him is back there, on the rocks, and his mount is in the stable," Sarah told him, pointing to one of the far stalls. "The stablemaster examined the alep's earmark; he says it is from the Eiku herds." She lowered her voice. "I found the assassin's weapon in the street last night. It is a Terran weapon, a laser. I took it to my quarters so it would not be handled." Among Mrann's psychic gifts was the ability to receive impressions from inanimate objects. She had seen him identify the owner of a silver spoon by simply touching it. Sometimes when he gazed at her she wondered what he might learn about her through a touch, and it made her shiver. Now his eyes met hers, and she felt his wrath wash through her.

"I do not blame you," he whispered. "Bring the weapon to my rooms tonight, after I leave the council." Brushing the dust from his fine gray tunic with one hand, he took Jeryl's arm with the other and led him to the street. Sarah walked a pace behind them.

The sight of Mrann's gray-cloaked figure striding ahead sent Sarah's mind tumbling into the darkness of the previous night's events. She walked without conscious thought around the spot where Elver had been wounded, remembering the helplessness that had overwhelmed her as she knelt beside him. She was very sensitive to the pain of others, an inheritance of dubious worth from her grandmother. As an enthusiastic teenager she had entered a University program to develop her psychic talent, but within a year the constant arguments with her mother blocked whatever talent she possessed. Frustrated, she dropped out of the rigorous training program. Her case was not unusual; only one student in ten completed the training. She fled across the continent and entered an anthropology program at another school. Once she was away from her mother the sensitivity returned, but by then her ambitions had changed. She never pursued her psychic studies.

With effort she brought her thoughts back to the present. The street was quiet. It was past midday, and the road was usually crowded with noisy apprentices bouncing about their business, but today the younglings were subdued and silent. Some of the workshops were shuttered, and those that were open had few customers.

Mrann was still holding Jeryl's arm when they rounded the final curve in the road and entered the wide circle in front of the clanhall. Sarah sensed the tension in the two aliens, and saw Mrann's fingers tighten their grip. In the center of the circle, on a ceremonial bier made of Alu's own granite blocks, lay the body of Hladi, Jeryl's mate. She was draped in yellow cloth, her long, slender, new-made Mother's body still beautiful. Above her head lay the circled cross, symbol of the House she and Jeryl had shared.

Jeryl trembled as they approached the bier. His fear was a tangible presence. Dread flowed around him with a sticky seductiveness, and Sarah shrank from it. Mrann's grip on Jeryl's arm tightened as Jeryl tried to pull away.

"Let me go," the grieving Master cried, his voice quivering. "I cannot stay. Hladi's death cry signaled the end of my life. Let me go!" This time he succeeded in breaking away from Mrann, and turned back toward the gate and the great wall. Sarah stepped out of his path, trying to escape the power of his emotions.

"No!" Mrann commanded, and Jeryl stopped in his tracks. Sarah dared not move, the power of Mrann's voice was so forbidding. "The ancient laws say that you must die with your House, but we are too few and each of us is too valuable to honor those laws today. A place will be found for you, Jeryl."

With a desperate act of will, Jeryl took one step away from the Mentor. "There is no place for me," he said. He collapsed in a quaking heap at the foot of the bier.

Leaving Jeryl to his grief, Mrann climbed the steps to the clanhall. Sarah followed. Angry, petulant words drifted out to them through the open door. The Masters were arguing the fate of Jeryl's home and younglings. As Mrann entered the hall a strong, calm voice silenced the others.

"My House will foster the younglings. If you would argue their fate, then I will settle it. I am eldest among you, and have that right."

"Excellent, Torma," said the Mentor. "I knew you would be the voice of reason on my council." He looked around the table at the other Masters. "Have you disposed of all that was Jeryl's, when he was not here to express his wishes? Your intentions may be good, but your manners are abominable." Mrann's tone was sharp; few of the Masters could meet his eyes. The exception was the Healer, Viela.

"The laws have been adhered to, Mrann," said Viela. "The assassin is dead, Hladi's younglings are provided for, and the household goods have been apportioned among the other Houses. Vengeance is for you and Jeryl to decide."

Sarah could not see Mrann's face, but she heard the question in his voice. "I have no part in this vengeance."

"But you do, Mentor. Has no one told you?"

"Told me what? What news is this?"

Abruptly Viela gestured for the Mentor to sit, but Mrann refused.

"Your apprentice went out to fight the assassin," said the Healer, "and he was injured. I think he will survive, but he is not yet out of danger."

Mrann collapsed into the chair. "That is very bad news

indeed," he said quietly, his shoulders hunched like those
of an aged man. His breathing slowed, and Sarah detected a tremor in his chest.

"What of the assembly, Mrann?" asked another Master. "What is the news from Berrut?"

"Not good. The Mentors of all the clans were at the
assembly hall in Berrut, with the GuildMasters and the
leaders of the fisherfolk. Revin of Eiku filed a formal
dispute against Alu. He contends our right to make a
trade agreement with the Terrans."

Some of the Masters slapped the table with their palms,
and others sat in stunned silence. Even Viela, the most
vocal of them, was quiet.

Sarah was surprised and puzzled. The first Terran ships
to land on Ardel had touched down within the territory
of Alu, and this gave Alu clan-right over contact and
trade with the Terrans. The second landing was near Renu
Keep, and Sarah and Mrann had expected any challenge
to come from Clan Renu. Clan-right was very specific,
and its passage from one clan to another was strictly controlled; it encompassed trade, water, and grazing rights,
and even mineral rights. The challenge from Eiku was
not unprecedented, but it was startling.

Torma recovered his voice first. "I was present when
the first Terrans came to Alu Keep. Their ship landed in
Alu's part of the great wasteland," he said. "By tradition
and law Alu controls all contact with the Terrans, as the
fisherfolk control the coasts and the mountain clans control the mines. Any Terran who wishes to trade on Ardel
must do so through Clan Alu. That is why the Terran
Union sent Sarah Anders to make this agreement with
us. How can Eiku dispute our right to trade as we see
fit?"

Mrann straightened in his chair. For the first time Sarah
noticed the intricate carvings on its back, and her eyes
sought refuge there. It was a trick to control her temper.
This dispute must have something to do with Nagashimi-
BOEM and last night's assassination. But it was so con-
voluted! Why had they not just come to Alu, and offered
an alternative to the trade agreement she was drafting?
How had they drawn Clan Eiku into this? She bit her lip,

and looked around the table. She had no right to offer
opinions in this council. Though she was welcomed by a
few of the Masters, the others tolerated her presence only
because Mrann wanted her there. She listened to the
Mentor.

"Revin produced a document showing that once, a
thousand seasons and more ago, the wasteland where the
Terrans landed belonged to Clan Eiku. He disputes the
ownership of the land, and the assembly has accepted his
contention. If Revin and Eiku succeed in this dispute,
they will possess clan-right to our land and the Terran
trade."

Sarah stepped out of the shadows to stand at Mrann's
right hand. She was permitted to ask questions. "What
is this 'dispute,' Mentor? Is it a legal process of some
sort?"

Mrann looked up at her. "No," he said. "It is an
ancient ritual that has not been performed between clans
in my lifetime. It is war."

Chapter 4

Viela started as a wave of surprise touched him. He
turned to look at the Terran. A red-violet flare of shock
had erupted at the top of her aura, and was diffusing
downward into the opalescent haze that surrounded her
body. The vile color did not encroach on the streak of
emerald that snaked up and around her right side, but
surrounded it and left it unchanged. He wondered at and
dismissed the meandering green streak.

Watching her face through the aura's mottled haze,
Viela noted the sudden drop of her chin, the gaping mouth
quickly closed, and recorded them as physical manifes-
tations of her surprise. He felt her struggling to bring her
emotions back under control. She did not guard her feelings the way an Ardellan would. Viela read her emotional
state in the coloration and brightness of her aura, and

linked that to her changing facial expressions. Subtle interpretations were difficult because her colors were deeper and richer than the Masters', but she broadcast enough of her feelings so that Viela was learning to read her well. She seemed totally unaware of her aura's existence, and of the Ardellans' ability to know her emotions. The Healer used that to his advantage although he despised Terrans for it.

Viela's glance swept the table. None of the other Masters were watching Sarah, though they were not blind to the emotions the Terran broadcast. Their eyes were on Mrann, their auras reflecting surprise and shock in a much more subtle way than did the Terran's. The Alu Masters had known their clan-right might be challenged, but they had not expected a formal dispute, especially from Clan Eiku. Eiku was not an ally, but neither was it an enemy. This move on the part of Revin and his council made little sense.

Across the table, Urlla the gem cutter spoke. "How dare they dispute with us for that land!" His topaz-streaked aura sputtered, flamelike, anger mixed with acknowledged futility. Others waved agreement.

Viela was also angry, and not only with Eiku. He saw the Terran as the cause of Alu's problems. Before she came, there had been cooperation between Alu and the surrounding clans. Since the skyship brought her at high summer, the clans had begun to contend over small things like the price of rope fiber. In half a season she had disrupted the solidarity the clans had been building for a hundred years.

Torma rose, strode to the center of the table at a point opposite Mrann, and faced the Mentor. "We have held that territory for eight dozen generations, perhaps more. What right does Eiku have to dispute our ownership now?" he challenged, striking the worn stone of the table with the flat of his palm. Viela's Healer's sense showed him nerve pathways suddenly numbing from the ends of Torma's fingers to the midpoint of his arm, as that part of his aura shaded to sapphire.

Mrann's aura flared red. His annoyance was visible as it reached across the wide slab toward Torma; the edges of it brushed against Viela's shields. "Eiku has clan-right to challenge at any time. They choose to dispute with us because the trade rights are valuable. Revin has always wanted wealth and power for his clan."

"It is power that should belong to Alu," asserted Or-eyn, second-eldest on the council.

"Yes," cried the gem cutter. "The trade rights are ours. Eiku must not take them from us."

"If you want the power, we must fight for it," said Mrann. "The assembly has accepted the validity of Eiku's challenge, and we must fight, or give up the trade rights. What do you choose to do?"

"I choose to fight," said Torma, flexing his numbed fingers. "Does anyone offer an alternative?" He walked around the table, stopping behind each chair to give the Masters an opportunity to speak, but none challenged him. Once more he made the circuit, not pausing this time, but watching for any sign of objection. A third time he strode the circle, quickly, knowing none would stop him as he finished the ritual. "It is agreed, then. We fight."

Viela watched him return to his seat, aware of the masterful way he guided the council. Seasons of experience had taught Torma to judge the mood of the other Masters, to choose his words and time them so that the council would follow his lead. He brought them to consensus with little time wasted on fruitless discussion. Yet today he would resign from the council. Viela had confirmed that Torma's mate was fertile, and he must ready himself and his House for mating and metamorphosis. Even Mrann did not know that Alu would go to dispute with an untried Master leading the council.

"In two days time we meet Eiku, in the wasteland where the first ship landed," said Mrann, his voice calm and steady. The Terran's discomfort was a pulsing violet fog beside his chair, a hazy cloud that emphasized the Mentor's strength. The cloud dissipated as Viela watched, leaving the soft white aura marred only by that enigmatic streak of emerald. The extent of her control surprised him.

Torma unrolled a strip of writing cloth and began making notes with a stylus. "We will need aleps and tents, and carts for supplies. How many younglings do you wish to take with you, Mrann?"

The Mentor was obviously weary and did not want to be troubled with these details. He waved Torma's question aside, saying, "I will decide later. Choose your alep handlers and drivers, and organize the caravan now, and see me tonight about my needs."

Torma would not be put off that easily. "Who will you ask to ride out and scout the site for you? With Elver injured, you have no second."

A sudden, intense sadness colored Mrann's aura. "I will choose later," he said, pushing his chair back from the long table. "I must see my apprentice." He swept from the room in a swirl of gray fabric, and the Terran hesitated only a moment before following him.

Viela was angered by Mrann's refusal to stay and deal with the council, but he understood the Mentor's concern for his young apprentice. He had done all he could to heal the trauma of Elver's injury; his own apprentices watched over the young FreeMaster now, and would send word if there was any need for the Healer's presence. Viela went where he was needed most, and today he was needed in council, to accept Torma's resignation and initiate the new leader.

Dispute. Viela's thoughts danced around that word, and he was frightened by it. He was old, even for a Healer, yet no interclan dispute had been fought during his lifetime. Dispute meant an end worse than death for the loser, for the winning clan would swallow the other whole. Identity, tradition, independence would all be lost.

Such a fate must not befall Clan Alu. Viela looked around the table at the twenty-one occupied chairs, and the three that stood empty. The Masters who sat here represented the twenty-four original Houses that had formed Clan Alu hundreds of generations ago. Those Houses had prospered and, with the help of the Healers, had created new lines until nearly six hundred Houses filled Alu Keep. Then came the years of famine, the drought that laid waste the southland and drove all its residents north, to fill the land of the keeps. Alu's population was already as great as its land could support. The keep could take no refugees. Younglings were starving. Masters and Mothers had begun to suffer.

The Healers Guild decreed that no more lines could be created in any of the keeps, that the population must decrease to a level the land could support. Territory was given to the refugees, and they built the cities that became trade centers and homes to many guilds. The Healers kept their secret well; they would not teach anyone the method of making new Houses. Over the course of a hundred generations the keeps' populations decreased; in Alu, several dozen Houses now stood empty, their lines ended by illness, plague, or accident. The three unoccupied chairs at the council table belonged to such Houses.

The method of creating new lines and filling those Houses again was lost, or so said the leaders of the Healers Guild. Some of Viela's teachers claimed that the ancient scrolls had been destroyed by fire, while others said that the necessary herbs had not survived the long drought. None could tell Viela more than that. Yet he saw the cities growing, their guilds prospering while the clans were in decline.

The only way left for a clan to grow was to take territory and population from another clan. Revin of Eiku wanted to acquire the lands and power of Clan Alu. It was up to Mrann and the council to stop him. The Masters of the still-existing twenty-one original Houses of Clan Alu comprised the council. They governed the clan, deciding all matters that concerned the entire clan. The eldest among them was the leader, by virtue of experience and tradition. Mrann and Viela, as Mentor and Healer, advised the council, but had no vote.

Viela sat through the long discussion of the equipment and supplies needed for the dispute, making a mental list as Torma copied intricate runes onto rolls of writing-cloth. The lists were completed and passed to stablemaster Oreyn, who would organize the caravan. Viela thought it ironic that he would also be the council's new leader. He had been appraising Oreyn's skills for the past season, and found him wanting. Oreyn was practical, concerned with the material welfare of the clan, but he was not interested in preserving its traditions. This was sacrilege to the Healer, whose guild traced its beginnings to the inception of the clan system.

The high stone walls of the chamber amplified the tempered but strained emotions of the council members. Viela would have preferred a calm council, ready to reflect on the significance of the ritual that was about to take place, but this was no longer a calm time. Torma's needs, and the needs of his House, were in direct conflict with the best interests of the clan, but postponing this moment would only endanger House Kirlei. Alu could not afford to lose Kirlei, especially not after losing Jeryl's House Ratrou.

Torma rose, pushing his chair back from the table. He stepped to the side and grasped the chair by its low, curved back, turned it so that it faced away from the stone slab. "I resign," he said. "The leadership of the council passes to Oreyn, of House Natuaa. House Kirlei's place on the council is open. You must choose a new Master to fill it, and lead Kirlei."

Viela rose and strode to Torma's side, ready to play the Healer's ancient role. Sharply he drew the fingers of one hand together, making a popping sound that echoed through the chamber. The door to the hall swung open long enough to admit two younglings, one carrying a shallow, empty pottery bowl, and the other bearing a footed plate of smoldering blue smokewood. The fragrant scent filled the chamber as gray tendrils of smoke reached for its corners. Viela took the plate's knobbed handles, supporting the heavy pottery as the youngling withdrew its tentacles. Then he placed the plate in the center of the table.

The bowl was empty. Viela accepted it from the second youngling, setting it on the end of the table in front of Torma. He dismissed the younglings with a gesture, dimmed the wall sconces with a thought. It was already late afternoon, and the tall window-slits admitted narrow shafts of sunlight that danced in the smoky air.

"Torma's mate is fertile. The time has come to add a

new Master to the line of House Kirlei. Has a successor
been chosen?'' Viela asked, though he did not turn to
face Torma. He knew the answer; the question was traditional, as was the reply.

''The youngling naReill will come to Kirlei.''

''What qualifies this youngling for Kirlei?''

''naReill was born to House Mistal, and raised by
Mother Yeera and Master Urlla. It was apprenticed to
House Natuaa and, under the tutelage of Master Oreyn,
has become the clan's best animal handler. It has exhib-
ited the necessary skill by making shimmer-light. It is
qualified,'' said Torma.

Viela reached into an inner pocket of his tunic and
extracted a small wooden box. The lid was inlaid with
finely worked copper in the twin trees design of Alu. He
laid it on the table and opened it with care. Inside were
twenty-one tiles—square, flat-glazed pieces of stone-
ware, each bearing the design of one of Alu's original
Houses. There was space for three more, but those tiles
had been destroyed when their Houses perished.

With delicate fingers the Healer selected the tile of
House Kirlei. Its color was the green of new leaves, with
fine traces of blue outlining the cloud-and-feather design.
He placed it face up in the center of the bowl before he
closed the box and tucked it back into his tunic.

The room was thick with smoke, the last rays of sunlight playing on the moving particles. The fragrance, and
the light, had a hypnotic effect on those seated around
the table. They watched as Viela, his fingers spread wide
like sunbursts, lifted the bowl and presented it to Torma.

The old Master accepted the shallow dish, cradling it
in his hands. He lifted it at arm's length and produced a
soft, warm ball of shimmer-light that grew until it filled
the bowl. The blue tracery of the cloud-and-feather design flickered within the shimmer-light, settled into a
steady pattern, and began to turn slowly in the bowl. It
turned completely around three times, then began to
shrink smaller and smaller, until it disappeared from
sight. The shimmer-light shrank with it until it, too, disappeared. With a pleased inclination of his head, Torma
returned the bowl to the Healer.

"Kirlei rests in this dish, awaiting Reill," said Viela as he presented the bowl to the council. He set it before Kirlei's chair, where it would stay until the House's new Master claimed his position and rekindled the shimmer-light.

"Power shifts on the council, also." Viela untied the thong that held the elder's medallion around Torma's neck. The medallion was ancient, older even than the band of power the Mentor wore at his wrist. It was made of metal, thin wires of copper weaving circles of iron together, with crystals of sphene in varying shades of green bound in the design, floating among the twists and turns of metal. The medallion contained enough iron for several knives, and so had great value; to the council it represented continuity. It was a bridge from the past into a future that had suddenly become very insecure.

Being careful not to touch the medallion, Viela passed it over the plate of smokewood to purify it. Then he walked to Oreyn's side, and fastened the thong about his neck. "You are now leader of the council. Guide Alu well." It was the traditional blessing, but with the dispute looming before them, it sounded more like a curse.

Chapter 5

Sarah waited alone in the central chamber of the Healer's complex, tension knotting her shoulders and tightening her scalp. The sun had set; through the open doorway she could see the last streaks of amethyst dissolving into indigo sky. She paced the gloomy room, avoiding the shadows and waiting for a youngling to bring light. Whenever she looked into the darkness, she saw Elver's blinding arc of power and the laser blast that cut through it to burn him. If only she could have saved him. The puckered scar on her right shoulder ached where tightening muscles pulled at it.

That pain stirred up old angers, and memories of pre-

vious encounters with agents of Nagashimi-BOEM. Most
of the corporation's operatives were mercenaries, hired
for their ruthless resourcefulness and their ability to mas-
querade as legitimate negotiators. They used any tactics
they thought necessary to facilitate an advantageous trade
agreement, then stepped aside and allowed Nagashimi-
BOEM's resource division to complete the negotiations.
Sometimes key installations were destroyed, Terran
Union negotiators threatened, and opposition leaders
killed before an agreement was concluded.

Sarah rubbed her aching shoulder. BOEM had used
such tactics long before it merged with Nagashimi Interstellar Drives. Its operatives preferred to work on worlds
that were rated on the lower half of the Evans Tech scale,
like New Kingston and Ardel. Accidents were easier to
arrange on such worlds, and it was more difficult to investigate them thoroughly. The laser blast that had sliced
into her shoulder on New Kingston had appeared to be
an accident, but she knew that Nicholas Durrow had
wanted to kill her. He and BOEM were after the rich
copper fields of the planet's largest continent. She had
outwitted him, and concluded a trade agreement before
her shoulder healed.

Now one Ardellan was dead and another lay injured,
because she had wasted time getting an agreement approved, and let herself believe this world was secure.

A youngling, tapers twined in three of its four tentacles, came in to light the wall sconces. The light was not
for Sarah's convenience. Two more younglings followed,
supporting a third whose leg was bandaged. The injured
one hummed softly as they set it on a low bench and
began unwrapping the wound. An apprentice, two brown
stripes on its bright yellow sash denoting its level of
training, came in with a tray of instruments and several
pots of ointments and herbs. It set to work cleaning dirt
and debris from the abrasion, one tentacle wielding metal
pincers, another a brush dipped in a green solution, a
third laying strips of kwata leaf on the cleaned wound.
The youngling never stopped humming.

Sarah forgot her anger as she watched the apprentice
work. Its tentacles danced from tray to pot to wound and

back again, in a rhythm different from the one that her father's hands had followed when he tended her childhood scrapes. Charlie Begay Anders should have had more children. He had always told Sarah that a daughter was enough, for a Navaho daughter married and brought her husband home, and raised her children on her parents' place. Had he ever really understood her reasons for living a different kind of life? She had explained them whenever she visited, had told him about Mike's work and her career, and he had nodded and told her that he was proud of her accomplishments. He had known of the strain between Sarah and her mother, and he had chosen to ignore it. Every time Sarah left him she had pretended not to see the pain and loneliness in his eyes. She would always regret the years they had spent apart.

Mrann stood at Elver's bedside. The lines on his forehead deepened as he looked down on his sleeping apprentice. Elver was not yet out of danger. The wound in his shoulder was extensive, but it had pierced no irreplaceable organs, and he did not seem to have bled overmuch. He would live, if he did not develop an infection.

The Mentor picked up Elver's cloak and looked at the shoulder. The Terran weapon had burned through the fabric, leaving a gaping hole with ragged, charred edges. The blackened threads crumbled and fell to the floor when he touched them. Mrann crushed the cloak in both hands, listening to the crackle of now-brittle fibers. He was angry. He gathered the cloak into a ball and used all his strength to throw it into a corner. Then he stalked from the room.

Sarah was waiting for him. "How is Elver?" she asked. Concern had made her aura hazy, and colored it a soft topaz. It was usually a bright, sparkling white, except where the emerald streak swirled. Mrann noted the change, attributing it to misplaced feelings of guilt.

"I think he will live. If there is no infection, the wound will heal cleanly," replied Mrann. His tone was sharp; he tried to soften his next words. "You should not feel responsible, Sarah. You are not the cause of Elver's injury."

"I accept some of the blame for what happened."

"It was not your doing." Mrann watched the green streak move through Sarah's aura. It was undulating and swelling, as it did whenever she talked of the death of her "father." Mrann did not understand what relationship that alien word denoted, although Sarah had tried to make it clear to him. The structure of Terran families seemed very complex. Mrann had disregarded the explanation and concentrated on Sarah's sorrow. The depth of it touched him, for it brought to mind his own grief at the death of his mate. Sarah mourned for her "father" as deeply as a FreeMaster mourned for his lost family. That grief was a special bond between FreeMasters, even after they became Mentors. In her sorrow, Sarah Anders shared that bond.

The busy apprentice was bandaging its patient's leg. Mrann walked over and watched it. "You do excellent work," he said, patting it on the head. "Keep a careful watch on Elver, and send word to me if he bleeds or shows any sign of infection during the night.

"Come," he said to Sarah. "I want to see that weapon now."

Mrann's aura was still red with anger and frustration when they left the Healer's complex. He was glad that his companion was head-blind, since he was too tired to try to control that manifestation of his feelings. They strode without speaking along streets lit by starlight and Mrann's shimmer-light. The cold wind chilled his face and hands. He set a fast pace up the hill, and the exertion helped to dissipate his anger. By the time they reached the clanhall he felt calm.

The Mentor's quarters were on the second floor of the clanhall, and Sarah occupied a room just across the narrow corridor. Mrann led the way down the hall, his mind probing ahead for the hidden latch that kept his heavy door closed. The wood was nearly a hand's span thick, with no handle or ornament except a small wooden pull ring through which a youngling might slip a tentacle. Mrann found the latch, blinked as his thoughts tripped it, and the door swung open. He waited while Sarah opened her own door using the special handle that had been installed for her. He had tried to teach her to open the latch with a thought, but she could not manage it. He sensed that her strength was not in the physical manifestation of her power; her sensitivity and empathy impressed him. She might be a Healer of minds and a mender of broken bonds, if she ever truly came to believe in her power. He watched as she took the weapon from its hiding place in her pack, and then she followed him into his room. His thoughts closed the heavy slab behind her. The latch clicked home.

A single wall sconce was burning, illuminating a small circle of wall with its dim glow. Mrann stood in the center of the room, arms outstretched and head tilted up. He projected a bit of shimmer-light into a second sconce, and a tiny glow started there. Concentrating, he increased the flame to match that in the first sconce, and then made them both brighten until they illuminated the center of the room. The corners were still shadowed. Dropping his arms, Mrann went to the hearth. He stirred the coals, blew on them until they reddened, then added some kindling and stepped back as the fire caught. The flare lit the nearest corner, revealing Jeryl seated on the floor, legs curled under him, arms tucked against his abdomen, shoulders hunched and head down. The Mentor ignored him.

Mrann motioned Sarah to a chair, and set about making tea. He measured shredded bark into a pot of water and hung it from a hook in the fireplace to heat. The pot was ceramic, brightly glazed in a blue and green pattern, with a chipped spout. While it swayed above the flames, he took cups and a strainer from a cupboard.

Sarah sat in her accustomed place before the hearth. Mrann's chair was to her left, with a small table between them. He watched as she examined the weapon she carried, then placed it on the far side of the table, as if further contact with it was distasteful to her. The weapon's presence in his room . . . on his planet, angered him. He tried to hide his wrath from Sarah; this was not, could not have been her doing.

"Tea," said Mrann, offering Sarah a handleless cup

filled with pungent red brew. She responded by twisting her lips into the odd grimace she called a "smile."

"This smells like nutmeg and apricots. My grandmother made tea like this," she said as she took the cup. She sipped as Mrann poured some for himself.

The Mentor was tired. His bones felt heavy as he sat back in his chair and tried to straighten his drooping shoulders. He could feel tension and anger knotting the muscles of his face and scalp, making deep wrinkles under his eyes and around his mouth. He set his tea aside with reluctance and reached for the alien weapon.

"That is a powerful laser, too powerful for target practice or hunting," said Sarah quietly. Her left palm rubbed absently at the front of her right shoulder. "It's not military issue, or even a type popular for self-defense. I don't think the assassin could have gotten it by chance."

The metal felt cold under Mrann's fingers. He turned the weapon over several times, ran his palm along the smooth surface, then tapped one of the protruding studs with a fingertip. Sarah gasped and reached for the laser.

"Please don't press the controls. I made sure the safety was on, but if you accidentally disengage it, the weapon could fire."

Mrann shrugged. "Thank you for your warning." He held the laser carefully as he rose. He stood facing Sarah, eyes closed, one hand palm upward, all six fingers extended, with the laser resting on that palm. With the other hand he began to read the psychic residue left on and around the weapon by those who had handled it. He unleashed his anger and let it fuel his psychic work. His hand circled above the laser, palm down and fingers curved inward, as he sorted the impressions. Sarah Anders was its most recent holder; the traces of her handling were easily identified. "Before you touched this weapon, it was carried by a Master of Clan Eiku. That agrees with the earmark of the assassin's mount. But a Terran carried it before that." Mrann pressed the laser between his palms. "This weapon belonged to a powerful and dangerous Terran, someone who fears little and risks much. We should be wary of him." The malevolent psychic residue that clung to the weapon made him feel physically ill. He set it on the table and stepped back before he opened his eyes.

"I do not understand how an Eiku Master could obtain such a weapon," he said. "The trade agreement bans all weapons except knives."

"This is not the first time that a Terran has disregarded a diplomatic agreement." Sarah's anger and bitterness were apparent in her aura. Their ruby light was overwhelming the soft topaz of her concern for Elver. She would not look at Mrann. Instead, she stared at Jeryl, who still huddled in the corner. "What will happen to the trade agreement if Alu loses this dispute? What will happen to our plans for a spaceport, and regular trade between your people and mine?"

"The treaty will be void. You will have to renegotiate everything with Clan Eiku." Mrann sat, and picked up his cup of tea. He stared at the liquid's surface for a moment, watching the shimmering light that was reflected there, and wondered how much Sarah knew about the Terran who had owned the weapon. She would tell him, if he asked the right questions. "Why would one of your people violate our laws and bring a forbidden weapon here?"

Sarah sighed, and stared into her own tea. "Our agreement is between Clan Alu and the Terran Union, and binds all the traders who operate within the Union's laws. The laws are enforced by a branch of our government called the Authority. Not all traders abide by the laws. Some powerful businesses have combined to arrange special trade agreements, outside the Union's laws. Others operate under the laws of non-Union planets. In some sectors of space across the spiral arm other starfaring races vie with us for resources.

"In itself, this is not a bad thing. We have treaties with the starfarers that give each race its fair portion of space and worlds. The businesses operate outside those treaties. They pay a fair price for the goods and services they purchase. The agreements that they make do not include the safeguards the Union believes are necessary to protect the interests of an undeveloped planet and its people. There are no limits on the number of ships that come and go, or on contact between human personnel and natives. There are no controls to protect the ecosystem. Weapons are not regulated.

"Experience has shown the Union that these controls are very important." Sarah looked at Mrann. "My job is to make a trade agreement that will benefit both our peoples, while contaminating your world as little as possible. I must do so before agents for these businesses can make their own agreements. I believe they are already on Ardel, that they gave this weapon to the assassin, and that they are encouraging Clan Eiku in this dispute."

Mrann was balancing his teacup in his right palm. Sarah's aura showed him that she was telling the truth. She believed that her trade agreement and her Union would be better for Ardel than an independent arrangement with other Terrans. Mrann agreed. He trusted Sarah. She had never tried to lie to him, where his earlier Terran visitor had told him nothing but lies.

"There was another Terran here just before you arrived," said Mrann. "His name was Dorra, or Durro, I think, and he may have possessed that weapon for a time." He pointed to the laser. "I cannot be certain of that. He seemed to be powerful, and dangerous, and he spoke untruths as if he expected me to believe them. He wanted to negotiate for mining rights, but I refused. He was very angry when he left Alu. Perhaps he is using the misguided ambitions of the Clan Eiku to gain the rights for himself."

Sarah's sudden anger startled Mrann. "I have dealt with Nicholas Durrow before. This morning I sent a message to the commander of my ship, asking him to monitor communications to and from Ardel. I shall also ask him to begin searching for Durrow's ship.

"This has been a great tragedy for Elver, and for Jeryl and his family. I am sorry for the part my people played in it, and I vow that the person who gave this weapon to the assassin will be captured and punished," Sarah said quietly. "I wish I could do more. Building a new life after the loss of a mate must be very difficult."

Mrann set aside his empty cup. He watched Jeryl, who was stirring for the first time since they had entered the room. "The only life open to Jeryl now is that of FreeMaster. He will spend his life without mates, without younglings, without a House of his own. He can never undergo the final metamorphosis that would complete his life, making him a Mother. He is doomed to be like me, forever a Master."

"You are the Mentor of your clan, chief adviser to the other Masters. Is that not a post of honor?"

"No." Mrann tried to keep the bitterness out of his voice. "It is a position of necessity, even in peaceful times. With the challenge issued, it becomes vital. Someone must defend the clan. Eiku did not succeed in killing my apprentice, but Elver is wounded and there will be no one to second me in this dispute." He looked at Jeryl. "Someone must take my place if I should die in dispute. Until Hladi's death, Elver was the only FreeMaster in Clan Alu. Now you are free of the responsibilities of House and family, Jeryl. Your only loyalty is to your clan. Will you apprentice with me?"

Jeryl made no response. In fact, he seemed not to have heard the Mentor's question. Then, with a suddenness that belied his melancholy, he uncoiled his body and leaped up from the floor. In one long step he was at the table, his hand grasping the butt of the laser. He picked it up, examining it for a moment before he clutched it to his chest. "Let me end this dispute before it begins, Mentor. Hladi's vengeance will be the death of Revin, Mentor of Eiku."

"It would accomplish nothing, Jeryl." Mrann rose, extending his hands to take the weapon, but Jeryl stepped away from him. There was a wild, unfocused look in his gray eyes. He was a cornered animal, ready to bolt for freedom at the first sign of threat.

"If Revin was dead, his apprentice would claim the right to challenge me, and the dispute would go on." Mrann stalked Jeryl, backing him into a corner. With the fingers of one hand spread in a gesture of warding, he reached for the laser with the other. Jeryl let it fall into the Mentor's hand.

Mrann stepped back and handed the laser to Sarah. "I

have cleared this weapon of the impressions it carried. Disarm it for me, or destroy it.''

Sarah took the hand laser reluctantly. She turned it over, looking at the various studs and slides before she tucked it into her sash.

Jeryl had lost all animation, and stood defeated beside Mrann.

''Hladi will be avenged if Alu wins this dispute. I promise you that.'' Mrann looked from Jeryl to Sarah. He was going to make a suggestion that would shock the council of elders. ''My apprentice would ride out to scout the battleground for me. Elver will not be able to ride for several more days. Will you both go into the wasteland tomorrow and map the landing site for me?''

Sarah looked surprised. ''I would be glad to do this for you, Mrann. I will do anything I can to help you and Clan Alu win this dispute.''

Jeryl raised his head slowly and looked across the room. His gray eyes were focused beyond Mrann. When he spoke, his voice was quiet. ''No, Mrann, I cannot. I must avenge my mate and my House.''

Chapter 6

Arien liked the wasteland. It was bare earth and jagged rock, but it was not barren. Plants grew there, some squat, thick-leaved and woody-stemmed, others light and lacy, hiding meaty tubers in the sand. The animals were sleek and scaled, basking in the sun by day and sleeping underground by night, or furred and night-sighted, hunting or hunted in darkness.

At twilight the day's heat dissipated. A hunting bird circled, dove and came up with a bushrat struggling in its talons. It landed on some rocks, took the prey in its beak, and beat it senseless. The night breeze ruffled its feathers, and it lifted its bloodied beak and screeched a warning as Arien and Durrow rode past.

They were tired and hungry, their mounts near exhaustion. Arien searched the bottom of his saddle pouch for a crumb of nutbread, finding nothing. He and Durrow had eaten the last of their meager stores at midday. He wished he had risked Revin's anger to ask for some food and an extra water skin. Fleeing through Eiku's empty kitchen, he had grabbed a half-full skin from a peg near the hearth, but that water was gone now, shared with the Terran and the aleps.

Arien's mount drew a great, shuddering breath. The night breeze cooled its body but did not assuage its hunger and thirst. Durrow's animal labored, head down and chest heaving. The Terran weighed half again as much as any Ardellan Master. The animals plodded through the darkness, using all six of their legs to pick safe paths over the rough ground.

"If I'd had my transmitter, we'd have come back by shuttle instead of riding these damned beasts," Durrow muttered for the fifth time. Arien ignored him. He had made Durrow leave the transmitter in camp because he feared Revin would mistake it for a weapon. No one must learn that Durrow had brought Terran weapons to Ardel. Even with his camp hidden deep in the wasteland where few Ardellans traveled, they were taking a great risk.

Arien's sharp eyes scanned the horizon. It was full dark before he saw the glow of artificial light reflecting off low-hanging clouds. He said nothing, but a moment later Durrow spotted it and pointed. "Camp," was all he said.

In Arien's mind, Terran was synonymous with fool. He had worked with the first Terran Union survey crew three years before, guiding them during his second summer as a FreeMaster. He'd watched them sample sand and stone and water. They'd ignored things of great value, like the iron mines in the mountains, and wasted time gathering lumpy crystals of sphene from the wasteland. They'd paid for his services with a roll of copper wire and enough iron to make two hands of blades. It was five times the usual fee. His guildmaster was pleased.

Durrow was clever, but that only made him a clever fool. He was always in a hurry. Arien had taught him to ride, shown him how to change his mount's gait from six-legged to four-legged. Now Durrow kicked the alep behind its central limbs, and it folded those legs against its belly and ran. They pulled away from Arien, moving with reckless speed on the uneven ground.

Muttering an oath, Arien kicked his own mount into a run and pursued the Terran. In a moment he was beside Durrow, reaching for his alep's nose-strap. Durrow waved him away, but Arien was too angry to back off. With practiced hands he pulled both animals up short. The sudden stop almost threw Durrow from his saddle.

"What are you doing?" Durrow yelled, and rage billowed out around him, enveloping Arien. Instead of trying to calm him, Arien countered with the strength of his own anger.

"These aleps are exhausted," he said curtly, staring into Durrow's smoky eyes. "They may be hurt if we run them on this rocky ground."

"I don't give a damn about the aleps." Durrow's aura blazed.

Arien leaned away, frustrated. The Terran's lack of emotional control made it impossible for him to establish an empathic connection between them. They communicated in Durrow's language, using words and gestures that could not express subtleties. He wanted to make the Terran understand the need for caution, but he could not see how to do it.

"Take care of your mount, Durrow! If it twists a leg, you will walk to your camp. We still have a long distance to travel." Arien loosed the animal's nose-strap and watched it drop its central limbs to the ground. "Aleps are meant to walk six-footed on rough ground."

Ignoring the warning, Durrow kicked his mount again and pulled sharply at the rein. The animal twisted away from Arien. Legs drawn close together, back arched, it jumped high into the air. Durrow lifted from the saddle, came down hard and bounced as the animal landed stiff-legged on the hard earth. It jumped again, and Durrow held tight with knees and hands. Then it kicked out swiftly, breaking into a fast and awkward six-legged run.

Arien urged his own mount to a smoother four-legged pace, following Durrow in the darkness. Durrow's alep snorted, flinging its head from side to side. It was trying to run out from under its rider, but the Terran would not be left behind. Durrow sawed at the rein, trying to slow the animal. Instead it turned off the trail and away from the camp. It moved quickly, legs not quite tangling themselves, always on the verge of falling. Durrow clutched the rein in one hand, a piece of the animal's neck fold in the other. His tight grip kept him in the saddle, and when the alep finally made a misstep and fell, he went down under it, yelling.

When Arien reached them the alep was on its side on the ground, legs flailing. By shimmer-light he could see Durrow's torso. His thighs were pinned beneath the animal.

"Get this damn thing off of me," Durrow yelled, trying to squirm free of the alep. His movements upset the fallen animal even more, and it kicked out wildly at Arien's alep.

Dismounting, Arien led his alep off to one side and anchored its rein with a rock. Walking back, he muttered a vulgar oath under his breath. "Be still, Terran," he said. "I will free you after I tend to the animal."

Arien knelt. He stroked the alep's nose and spoke to it in a soothing voice. When it stopped struggling, his hands moved up each leg in turn, gentle fingers probing for tears in the cartilage that supported the animal. Halfway up the third leg he found what he feared—a swollen place, where his careful touch made the animal jerk. Cursing Durrow under his breath, he reached into his sleeve and drew out a slender dagger. With a swift, anguished stroke he plunged it into the animal's torso. The beast convulsed once, and then lay still.

Arien buried the blade in the sand, letting Ardel cleanse it of the alep's lifeblood. His rage could not be so easily dispelled. Slipping the dagger into its sheath, he rose and walked around the body to study the Terran. He sensed no fear in Durrow, but they both knew the human was helpless.

"Can you move your legs?" he asked, suspecting that the alep's body was not heavy enough to disable the Terran.

Durrow nodded, his gaze never leaving Arien's face.

"There are no trees in this wasteland, so I cannot make a lever. I have an alep to pull the body off you, but no rope to do it with." Arien stopped walking, and looked into Durrow's eyes. "I could ride to the camp and bring back help, but that would leave you at the mercy of the wild tols and dog packs which will soon smell the alep's blood." It was a tempting thought. By the time he returned with help Durrow would be devoured, and Arien would be free to return home.

"The animal isn't very heavy. If I help, we could lift it enough for me to get free," suggested Durrow, forgetting that Arien did not share his muscular build.

"All right. We can try that, but if it does not work I will go for help." Already Arien could hear the distant cackling of a dog pack, and the worried snorting of their remaining mount.

Kneeling behind Durrow's head, he dug away the sand from beneath the Terran's lower back. Durrow's body slipped down until most of the alep's weight rested on the ground on either side of him, and on his legs. Arien leaned forward and tested the weight of the body with his arms and shoulders. It was too much for him. Even with Durrow's help, he would not have the strength to lift it.

"I can't feel my feet," said Durrow. His voice was calm, but Arien detected apprehension in his aura. They were both aware of the threats that lurked in this darkness.

There was a way that he could free Durrow. He had the training and the power to move the alep's body with his mind. Durrow knew nothing of this, and Arien dared not let the Terran guess the true measure of his, or any Ardellan's abilities. Durrow had already learned much from his encounter with Revin. He was a fool, but he was not stupid. He would put the clues together. Right now Arien was only a guide and interpreter for the Terran; he must not allow himself to become a weapon in Durrow's fight for the wealth of Ardel.

A dog cackled, and Arien's alep wheeled, tugging at the anchored rein.

He had no choice. He could not leave Durrow to die, though he thought the Terran deserved such an end. He bent forward and positioned Durrow's palms under the alep's body. "When I begin to lift, push with all your strength," he instructed. "As soon as your legs are free, shimmy back into the hole."

Leaning back, out of Durrow's line of sight, he closed his eyes and assumed a posture of power. Crossing his arms before his chest, he spread his fingers wide, six slender, opposable digits standing out about each broad palm. He remained still for one hundred heartbeats, gathering power.

Reaching outward and leaning over Durrow, Arien positioned his hands on either side of the Terran's body. Pushing hard, he twisted with his mind, straining mentally as well as physically to lift the alep. Durrow strained and grunted below him. For a long moment they made little progress, and then the alep was levered up against its own stiff legs and Durrow dragged his feet into the hole. Arien let the body fall back to the sand.

Durrow sat up, massaging his legs and feet back to life. "No broken bones," he said. "Just some bruises. It's a good thing Ardel's gravity is less than Earth normal." Any expression of gratitude was conspicuously absent, but Arien had no energy left to dispute with the Terran over his lack of manners.

Their remaining alep was snorting louder, and pulling at its rein. The cackling dog pack was still far away. Arien suspected the scent of a wild tol had spooked the mount. He walked to the animal slowly, grasped its nose-strap, and stroked its broad forehead as he spoke to it. The alep gentled, calmed by his familiar presence, and he loosed its rein from the rock and led it to Durrow.

"You had best ride," he said, looking down at the Terran. "We should leave this place before the tol arrives. The wild ones have claws sharp as daggers and nearly as long, and they will attack anything that moves. He will make short work of this alep, and us, if we stay."

Durrow struggled to his feet, balancing with difficulty. "My feet are numb," he said. Arien helped Durrow mount the alep, but he kept the rein in his own hand, unwilling to take chances with the only transportation they possessed. He led the animal back to the trail, using his keen senses to scan the surrounding darkness for danger.

The Terran camp was set in a broad, shallow crater of undetermined origin. The crater's rim was still sharply defined, and it helped to protect the camp from the fierce winds that raged across the wasteland. Six bubble tents nestled in a semicircle below the windward rim of the crater, facing the open port of the twelve-passenger shuttle.

The sky had cleared and first-moon was setting. Arien led Durrow's mount up the outer slope toward the rim of the crater. Before they reached the top a sentry appeared, his weapon aimed at Arien's chest. The FreeMaster stopped, standing very still while he waited for Durrow to speak.

"Let us pass, Williams."

"Captain! We weren't expecting you, sir." The barrel of the weapon turned away.

"Well, I'm here," said Durrow curtly. Williams melted back into the darkness, and they continued into the camp unmolested.

The tents were dark, their occupants asleep. The shuttle's exterior lighting was turned low, suffusing the area with a glow that faded into night beyond the rim of the crater. Stopping beside the shuttle, Arien helped Durrow to dismount. The Terran was obviously stiff and sore, but he refused further aid from Arien and walked alone up the ramp into the vehicle.

Arien led his alep to the small store of grain and dried grass behind the shuttle. He was still angry with Durrow, and with himself. He should have had more control over the situation at Eiku and on the trail. Instead he had let Durrow gain the upper hand. His GuildMaster would not be pleased.

Two stakes had been driven into the bare earth behind the shuttle. Arien slipped the saddle and pad from his mount's back and tied its rein to one of the stakes. He vigorously brushed the animal's coat, then gave it extra food and water. There was no longer any need to conserve the grain—he had lost an animal and a saddle to Durrow's folly. He thought about going back for the other saddle in the morning, but knew it would be too much to ask of this mount. The animal deserved a rest. He scratched its broad forehead, and it brayed at him.

With his animal cared for, Arien could think of his own hunger. He had a store of tea and nutbread, dried fruit, and tubers in the small bubble tent that had been set aside for him, but he needed to stop at the shuttle for water. He stole up the ramp, hoping to fill his water skin and get out without being noticed by Durrow, but the shuttle's interior was brightly lit, leaving no shadows in which to hide. Trying to be unobtrusive, he stepped to the rear where the large reserve water tank was located.

Durrow sat in the front of the shuttle, talking with his pilot, Angela Roletti. Arien did not like her; she was a tiny bundle of anger with a disharmonious aura.

"FreeMaster," Durrow called, addressing Arien with unaccustomed politeness, "come and look at this."

Roletti protested, shaking her head and gesturing as she uncoiled her slender frame from the copilot's chair. Durrow ignored her objections.

Arien stoppered his half-full water skin and slipped the strap over his head. His intuition warned him that this was a mistake, but he could see no way to avoid dealing with the Terrans. Making his way down the narrow aisle, he gestured an impersonal greeting and refused the chair that was offered.

He was wary of Roletti because of her obvious anger at his presence. She was an enigma; Durrow had explained that she was a female and not to be addressed as Master, but Arien did not understand that. The pilot was an adult, working side by side with the others. An Ardellan in the female stage would be concerned only with the nurturing of young. Perhaps Roletti was not a Master, but he certainly would not call the pilot Mother.

"We don't need his help, Nick," said Roletti, tugging at her short red hair with one hand. Her fingers stabbed at rows of bright rectangles along the edge of the navigation table. "Williams and I mapped the site yesterday, while the geologists were taking samples."

Just beneath the clear surface of the table, a drawing sprang to life. The dense amber field crawled with green lines which formed groups of concentric ovoids and irregular curves. The movement made Arien's head hurt. He made a small mental adjustment and the pain faded.

"Are you sure they'll hold the dispute at the old landing site?" asked Durrow. He pointed to a place on the still-forming map. Arien saw no relationship between it and the place he knew, but since Durrow called both "landing site," they must be the same.

"The clans dispute ownership of that piece of land. By ancient law, they must conduct the dispute there," he said.

Roletti touched more controls, and shapes climbed and shifted to form hills and valleys inside the table. Arien watched, fascinated by the writhing lines.

"There are large deposits of titanium sands in that area, and in several others," said Roletti, manipulating controls to highlight several places on the map. "The geologists reported that this continent has only a few deposits of iron and copper high in the mountains, but the titanium sands are plentiful. The sands are on the surface in the desert areas, easily accessible. We could strip mine and refine right there, if we put in a small nuclear reactor for power." Blue light appeared in some of the broad, flat places, flanked by streaks of red and yellow.

"Make two copies of this map for me," said Durrow. Roletti touched a control, and the maps extruded from a slot across the aisle. "Duerst will be pleased. Nagashimi-BOEM needs more titanium, and it will be easy to ship refined metal from here."

"Has Clan Eiku agreed to give us the mining rights once the dispute is settled?" asked Roletti.

Durrow warned Arien to silence with a forbidding glance. "I'm sure Revin can be convinced to accept our proposal, after he's won the dispute. We must conclude the preliminary agreement quickly, so that our employers can take over. Someone else is negotiating with Clan Alu right now."

"Probably an attache from the Trade Commission," said Roletti. "A Terran Union ship has been traveling in and out of the system nearly as long as we've been on Ardel."

"If the attache has been here that long, she may be ready to close a deal with Clan Alu."

"Then we'll have to make sure Eiku wins," responded the pilot.

Arien was shocked. "You plan to interfere in this matter?" he cried, extending his arms in a gesture of warding against Roletti. Her aura was glowing brightly, fueled by anger and hostility. Green eyes flashed a warning as her rage expanded, but Arien defied the swirling ruby haze.

Durrow rose, stepping between them. "Roletti, stop it!" he growled, pushing her into her chair. "Free-Master, I don't require your help any more tonight. Go."

Arien stared at the Terran for a long moment, then turned and walked away from the table in silence. His dismissal was all the answer he needed. Durrow intended to interfere, to insure a victory for Eiku. The last of his illusions about the Terran were gone, leaving behind a deep, cold, dangerous anger.

2257:12/4, TERRAN CALENDAR
RECEIVED 14:28 HOURS, ARBITRARY LOCAL TIME
TO: SARAH ANDERS, TRADE ATTACHE/ARDEL
FROM: CAPTAIN SWENSON, TERRAN UNION
        INTERSTELLAR SHIP *BLACKHAWK*
    EN ROUTE TO BARTEL'S COLONY TO
DELIVER EMERGENCY CHEMICAL SUPPLIES
PER TRADE COMMISSION'S REQUEST. WILL
RETURN TO ARDEL IN APPROXIMATELY FIFTY-

SEVEN HOURS. TRUST YOU CAN HANDLE
SITUATION UNTIL THEN.

Sarah stared at the message, then did some quick cal-
culating. Nearly twenty-six and a half hours in an Ardellan day; that meant the *Blackhawk* might be back by
mid-afternoon two days from now, if nothing delayed it
at Bartel's Colony. Two days for Nicholas Durrow and
his mercenaries to carry out their plots. She wadded the
hard-copy into a ball and threw it across the room. Then
she sighed and began to strip for bed.

Chapter 7

Sarah Anders woke well before dawn, rose, washed with
chilly water, and dressed in tunic, slacks, and boots. She
smoothed the furs on her sleeping platform before sitting
cross-legged in its center. A single candle burned on the
table. A second, unlit, rested on a saucer before her.

She began with her daily prayer to Changing Woman,
mother of the ancestors of the Navaho. She had learned
the ritual chant from her grandmother, and still practiced
it because it helped her retain her perspective on her place
in the cosmos. Changing Woman was the female Earth,
fertile and nurturing, deserving of respect. She was that
part of every woman that was linked to the origins of the
race.

"In beauty it is done, in harmony it is written. In
beauty and harmony it shall so be finished. Changing
Woman said it so." Sarah closed her eyes and let the
warmth of the prayer's final lines fill her. She felt centered and powerful, ready to perform the exercise Mrann
had taught her.

She imagined the candle, cold and white, its pristine
wick standing straight. Its only purpose was to bring light
to the darkness. She imagined the wick growing warmer

and warmer, being heated by the power of her thoughts. The candle welcomed the heat, readied itself to fuel a flame. The wick became hot, approaching the temperature of spontaneous combustion. It would light! Flame burst from the tip of the wick, traveled downward quickly to almost touch the wax of the candle. It burned merrily, giving off palpable heat. Sarah opened her eyes.

The candle was cold, the wick unlit. Sarah sighed. Her meditative powers and her imagination were strong, but they were not enough to help her do what the Ardellans did with ease. She could not light the candle, she could not make shimmer-light, she could not open a door latch. Yet Mrann insisted that she had the power to do all of these things.

Sarah set the candle aside and climbed off the sleeping platform. She snagged a brown cloak from the chair with her left hand, grabbed her belt pouch with her right. As she stepped through the doorway she ran her fingers over the contents of the pouch: folding knife, dietary supplements, foil strip of water purification tablets, emergency medkit. She clipped it to her belt as she strode down the hall. Mrann had told her to be at the stable at dawn. He seemed certain that Jeryl would join her. She had doubts about Jeryl, and about her own increasing involvement in Ardellan affairs. She was here to conclude a trade agreement with these people, not to help them win a war.

The back stairway was dark, lit only by moonlight from a long, narrow window. Second-moon touched the keep's wall as Sarah descended. She stopped to watch it. Her hand brushed the ancient stone of the stairwell, and she was struck by the timelessness of this place. What difference would a few days make to a civilization which had existed nearly unchanged for centuries? One Terran could not ruin Ardel, or even Clan Alu. Then she remembered watching Elver fall, and the smell of his scorched flesh. She remembered summer evenings in her grandmother's hogan, when the storyteller came to visit from the University. He was a distant cousin, and he came at grandmother's invitation to practice his stories. He had many chants about the strength and power of the Navaho before the white men came, and many more about the changes the newcomers brought to the people's lives. Remembering them, she was suddenly afraid for herself and for Ardel.

Two more steps down, and the wall rose to hide second-moon. Gazing up from the shadows, Sarah watched unfamiliar constellations end their nightly dance. Sol was out of sight, visible only from the other hemisphere until midsummer. In the east, the sky had lightened to indigo. The sun would rise soon.

Sarah turned right, and pushed open the kitchen door. Bright lights and the smell of fresh bread and stewed fruit greeted her. She smiled at the kitchenmaster. Younglings bustled from table to washbasin, carrying dirty bowls and platters. Fire blazed in the wide hearth, warming Ortia's ovens. A huge clay pot of cooked grain was cooling on the sideboard.

The back door slammed. Three younglings came in, carrying empty sacks. One of Ortia's assistants gave them sacks full of bread in exchange for the empty ones, and they trooped out, letting the door slam behind them. Many of the Clan's four hundred and fifty Mothers baked their own bread, but some ordered what they needed from the clanhall's kitchen. The grain and all the foodstuffs were part of a communal supply. Ortia cooked for the Mentor and any guests who were staying at the clanhall, for the work details, and for the Healer and those in the infirmary. He always made plenty of food; any resident of the keep who was in need of a meal could find it in Ortia's kitchen.

Jeryl was sitting at a table, staring into a cup of steaming tea. When Sarah had left him with Mrann last night, they had been arguing about the virtues of revenge. She had not expected to see him this morning. She poured herself a cup of fragrant brew from the communal pot, and joined him. "May the sun smile on you today, Master," she said, wrapping her hands around the mug to warm them. Mrann's war seemed very far away.

"And on you, Master," mumbled Jeryl.

She almost laughed. "I am not a Master, Jeryl. Please call me Sarah."

He glanced up, but his eyes did not focus on her. He

looked through her, toward some point far beyond the walls of the keep. Pinpoints of light brightened his pupils and gave him a feverish look.

"Are you all right?"

He did not reply, but his eyes met hers for a moment. The pupils were dilated, as if he were drugged.

"Can I help you, Jeryl?" she asked, wondering if she should go for the Healer.

He turned back to his tea and took a long swallow before he answered. "No. I am all right. I stood vigil for Hladi last night. The incense has certain properties . . . a little more tea and some food, and I will recover."

A youngling brought them a tray of nutbreads and a small bowl of fruit preserves, and Jeryl ate quickly. Sarah sipped tea and swallowed a handful of dietary supplements, then helped herself to bread and fruit. The supplements provided her with vitamins and amino acids that were missing in the local fare. A time-release capsule implanted beneath her skin released a substance that gave her some protection against allergic reactions. The drug was not foolproof, but it worked most of the time. The supplements were concentrated and sometimes upset her stomach, but she preferred using them and the anti-allergy implant to eating dried rations.

They ate quietly. Behind them the door banged open and shut as more younglings came in to get rations for their work crews.

Jeryl wolfed his food, twice waving for a youngling to bring him more tea. Sarah savored the rich bread, which reminded her of muffins made with pecans and dates. The chewy, sweet substance in the bread was a nut, not a fruit, or so she had been told; on a tour of the keep's orchard Mrann had shown her the trees on which it grew. The preserves were tart, like a marmalade, and just a little bitter.

When Sarah finished her tea, she asked Ortia for a packet of his fresh-baked breads to take on her journey. Swallowing his last bite, Jeryl pushed aside the empty tray and straightened in his chair. His eyes had lost their artificial brightness, and he seemed more awake and alert. He also requested breads from the kitchen's Master, and two flasks of cold tea.

"Have you decided to scout the landing site for Mrann?" Sarah asked when Jeryl followed her through the clanhall and into the street. He strode beside her toward the stable, his pack thrown carelessly over one shoulder, tunic askew and sash twisted.

"I have little choice. The Mentor is stubborn," he said. The sky was brightening, but the light showed them shapes, and not detail. The gravel crunched and slipped beneath their feet, and Jeryl stumbled, nearly dropping his pack.

Sarah slowed her pace. She was tempted to offer Jeryl her arm, but she knew he would refuse. Mrann had been certain Jeryl would ride today. She should not have doubted him. "Mrann asked me to accompany you. Did he tell you why?"

"He did not want me to ride alone, but none of the Masters can be spared today. I am not a youngling who needs a Mother to watch over me." Jeryl was walking fast, and slipped and almost stumbled again. Sarah thought perhaps he needed a nursemaid.

At the stable, a group of younglings waited with two saddled aleps. They were a mismatched pair, one small and charcoal gray, the other black, its shoulder reaching to Sarah's chin. Jeryl took the rein of the smaller alep, slung his pack over its rump, and leaped to its back. The beast was so startled that it shied and twisted under him. The movement spooked the other animal, and it dragged a youngling halfway across the yard. The others ran after it, bouncing on stubby legs and squealing as their tentacles grasped mane and tail, saddle and rein. Quickly they brought it under control and tied its rein to a fencepost.

Jeryl was still fighting with his mount. He tugged at the rein, pulling the alep's snout to the left. It turned in a tight circle, moving fast. Sarah ran for the sheltering fence and joined the younglings straddling the top rail. Her alep spooked again, and tried to pull free of the fencepost. The rail shook, and two younglings fell backward, landing outside the corral.

Jeryl's alep spun, ears back and tail down, using all

six legs to maintain its balance. It thrust out one foreleg, kicked with the opposing rear leg, and twisted its hindquarters. The other mount brayed. Jeryl stayed in the saddle, tugging harder at the rein. The alep's snout almost touched his leg. Its mad circling slowed, and he gave the rein some slack, but when the alep tried to twist away from him he pulled it tight again. It slowed a second time. He kept the rein tight until the mount was walking sedately.

Sarah climbed down and approached her alep. naReill, the stablemaster's apprentice, was already at its head, calming it with whispered words. Sarah mounted, settling easily into the soft leather saddle on the alep's narrow back. She took the rein from naReill, tugged gently, and pressed with her left knee. The animal turned away from the fence and docilely walked across the corral to the gate.

As they left Alu Keep, the sun was rising. Sarah smiled as she thought of her grandmother greeting Sun Father each morning with a prayer, and an offering of corn meal and corn pollen tossed to the winds. It was a beautiful tradition, one she had never kept.

naReill and another youngling rode with them, clinging precariously to the back of a young alep. They twined their tentacles around knobs on the saddle, and wrapped them around each other and the alep's neck. The animals moved with an uncanny six-legged rhythm that was almost hypnotic. Jeryl was impatient and tried to increase the pace, but when their mount speeded up, the younglings bounced from side to side and squealed. They looked so comical that Sarah laughed. Jeryl slowed to a fast walk.

It was nearly midday when they rode out of the rolling hills and vineyards onto the level plain of the landing site. Three years earlier the first Terran ship had set down on this barren waste. The land was desolate, dry, with scattered outcroppings of rock and little vegetation. The few animals that lived here needed little water; they ate the juicy leaves of succulents, and each other. Piles of broken and crushed rock dotted the plain, like remnants of some giant strip mining operation.

In the distance Sarah could see the burn-scarred landing site, and beyond that, the dust of another group making its way out onto the plain. "Jeryl," she asked, pointing toward the advancing cloud, "is that a party from Eiku?"

Jeryl shaded his eyes with one delicate hand, the other tugging at the rein. "It could be wild aleps," he said, but his voice did not sound convincing. He was silent for a moment as the other group approached. "Yes, I can see a gray cloak. It must be a party from Eiku, come to scout this area with their Mentor or his apprentice."

Jeryl's face was changing as Sarah watched. His eyes were narrowing, and the bright burning pinpoints of light had returned, giving him a look of madness. Suddenly he kneed his mount forward at a canter, leaving the younglings behind.

A wave of anger swept over Sarah. She turned to stare at the approaching riders, saw them as enemies, murderers. The leader was surrounded by a red fog; it did not interfere with her perceptions of him, but added to them. His rage was nearly as deep as her own. She knew he intended to kill her—not her, but Jeryl! These were Jeryl's thoughts!

With a start Sarah pulled back from the unexpected contact with Jeryl's mind. She blinked as her view of the riders changed. The red haze vanished, along with the anger she had been feeling. She no longer felt threatened by the stranger. Instead, she wanted to keep Jeryl away from him.

Jeryl had ridden far ahead of her. She pushed her alep to catch up, marveling at its easy switch from six to four-legged gait.

She could see the other riders clearly now. A lone mounted figure in a gray cloak was surrounded by a crowd of younglings. She thought they must be from Clan Eiku. The mounted Master would be the Mentor or his apprentice. She watched as he forced his mount in a wide circle around the landing site, trying to avoid Jeryl.

As the Eiku changed direction, so did Jeryl. Sarah was worried. She kneed her alep to even greater speed and pulled out in front of Jeryl, blocking his path. The young-

ings were close behind, their bodies bouncing wildly as
their mount ran.

"Would you confront this Master, Jeryl?" Sarah cried,
trying to keep her alep dancing between Jeryl and the
Eiku.

"No," Jeryl replied, his eyes wild and his face flushed.
The wind caught his silver-blond hair and spread it about
his head like a madman's halo as he shouted his challenge. "I seek revenge for Hladi. I will not confront this
Master. I will kill him!"

Jeryl swung the head of his mount around the rear of
Sarah's alep and rode toward the Eiku Master. Sarah
turned her alep and chased him. The Eiku had left his
escort and was riding out to meet Jeryl in the center of
the burn scar. Jeryl slipped his dagger from its sheath
and held it ready, but the Eiku had no weapon. That did
not mean he was helpless. As he raised his arms in a
gesture Sarah recognized, she wished impotently for the
laser weapon she had left in her quarters.

She rode fast, the younglings just behind her, but they
had no hope of stopping Jeryl. The Eiku's hands were in
the air, sparks snapping from his fingertips. Jeryl rode
swiftly toward his target, dagger extended in his right
hand, intent on revenge. Then power shot from the Eiku's
hands, a bolt of lightning streaking toward Jeryl. He
turned his mount hard to the left, and ducked, and the
bolt sped past him. Sarah thought he would retreat, but
he turned and attacked again, the dagger held before him
like a talisman. It would not protect him. The Eiku sent
another bolt of power, and Jeryl was too close to turn
aside. The lightning touched the tip of Jeryl's dagger,
flipping him from the back of his mount. He landed flat
in the sand. His frightened alep ran on for a dozen strides
before it turned and circled back toward Sarah's snorting
mount. It brayed at Jeryl as he struggled to his feet.

By the time Sarah reached Jeryl, he was searching for
his dagger. "Are you all right?" she asked, dismounting
beside him.

He did not answer, but grabbed the reins of her alep
and started to mount. His face was more flushed than

before, and his eyes burned as he watched the Eiku ride away.

Sarah grabbed his arm, pulling him down from the saddle. "You can't go after him, Jeryl. He's a Mentor. He will kill you."

"No. I must kill him. It is Hladi's revenge!" Jeryl struck her, sending her reeling across the scarred ground. He started to mount, but naReill and the other youngling were on him, dragging him down and pinning him in the dirt.

Sarah brushed the dust from her tunic as she rose. She called softly to Jeryl's mount, which was standing ten meters away. It rolled its eyes and brayed as she approached, but it did not run from her. She opened the small pack behind the saddle and drew out a flask of tea. Kneeling beside Jeryl, she offered it to him, but he turned his head away, the wild light still burning in his eyes. A second time she made him look at her, and she offered the tea. He took it.

"Are you hurt?" she asked.

"No," he said, calming. "My dignity is shattered, but my body is only bruised. This was foolhardy. I will have better opportunities for revenge." He held out his hands, palms upward, in a gesture that asked pardon. "Did I harm you?"

"No, I'm all right. Can you ride?" She helped him to his feet.

"Yes," he replied, taking another drink of tea. His suddenly-cold gray eyes focused on the dust of the retreating Eiku party with an intensity that made Sarah shiver.

2257:12/5, TERRAN CALENDAR
TO: MINERAL RESOURCE DEVELOPMENT
         GROUP, TITAN

FROM: NICHOLAS DURROW
RE: NEGOTIATIONS FOR MINERAL RIGHTS/
             ARDEL
   TITANIUM SANDS OF HIGH GRADE AND
EASILY ACCESSIBLE, AS REPORTED EARLIER.
AUTOMATED STRIP MINING AND REFINING
WILL PRODUCE HIGH QUALITY PRODUCT. IRON
AND COPPER OF GREAT VALUE HERE.
FAVORABLE TRADE AGREEMENT IMMINENT.

Nick Durrow punched in the routing code that would
send the dispatch through to the message drop on Titan.
There, the operative who handled communications for
the bogus ''Mineral Resource Development Group''
would encode it and pass it on through other drops until
it reached Austin Duerst at Nagashimi-BOEM.

The ship that had brought their supplies was cruising
near the Ardellan system. Duerst would have it return,
with an official Nagashimi negotiator. He would wait until Durrow signaled him, and then come down to ''steal''
the trade agreement away from Durrow. They would all
go home with extra credit chips in their pockets.

Durrow had plans for those credits. He was through
handing over the sweet deals to Nagashimi-BOEM. Next
time they called him to arrange a trade agreement for
them, he would have enough money to close the deal
himself. He was going to move into the big leagues.

Chapter 8

Viela scraped the bottom of the bowl with his spoon. It
was midday and the kitchen was hot, but not uncomfort-
ably so. Through the open door he watched fluffy clouds
moving across the sky, and dancing swirls of wind-lifted
dust on the path. Before him sat a cup of tea and several
empty dishes. He scooped up the last bit of fruit and

boiled grain and ate it with relish. It was good to have enough food.

Mrann came through the archway from the main hall, his cloak hanging off one shoulder, the other arm laden with hide bags. He dumped the bags on the table.

"Ortia, these are to be filled with fruits and vegetables for the journey."

"I was going to send a youngling down to get those, Mentor. There was no need for you to bring them. Have you eaten?" asked Ortia, handing Mrann a cup of tea.

"No." He pointed to the roast fowl on the sideboard. "I will take some of that," he said. Ortia cut a large portion and brought it to him.

"Eating flesh drains your energy," commented Viela. Mrann glared at him.

"If I ate like you Healers do, no meat and no preserved foods, I would have starved to death my first winter." He set down the tea, and began stripping the meat from the bones with his fingers.

"Healers live very long lives."

"More due to the fact that they never mate than to their diets."

Viela pushed his empty bowl aside. "Your choice of menu is just another sign of your failing judgment."

Ortia brought Mrann a slab of nutbread. "Have you nothing better to argue about? I have heard this debate too often."

Mrann shrugged. "It seems that Viela never tires of pointing out my faults. What troubles you today, Healer?"

"Your continuing association with the Terran leads me to question your suitability as Mentor of Clan Alu."

"You stretch the limits of my patience, Viela. Sarah Anders is a kind and generous person who is concerned with the welfare of Clan Alu and of all Ardel. We must deal with the Terrans now that they have found us; I prefer to negotiate with one whose vision extends beyond trade and profit."

"What law forces us to deal with the Terrans? We can ban them and their ships from our lands. We need not be troubled by them any longer."

"Your naïveté amazes me."

Viela drained his mug, and stood. He and Mrann would never agree on this subject. Their discussions only served to put more distance between them. "We must continue this argument another time. I am needed at House Kirlei. There is a cocooning to be done." There was joy in his voice. Cocoonings were happy occasions, for they insured the continued vitality of the clan.

"Give my regards to Torma," said Ortia, grabbing a youngling and pointing it toward Viela's dirty dishes. Viela glanced at Mrann as he left the kitchen. The Mentor said nothing; he was absorbed in his meal.

House Kirlei was built of chiseled and fitted rock. Viela approved of its flowing curves and softly rounded edges. Most of the front was covered with a blue and green mosaic of birds soaring among the clouds. The main portal was circular, stopped with a round wooden door that swung on a single massive hinge. The door was open, and Viela entered with the ease of one who knows he is expected. Smooth stone walls defined the entryway, curving high to join the arched ceiling. There were no corners anywhere. One oval doorway opened on a large chamber where younglings worked at a loom. Torma emerged from another.

"Have you brought naReill with you?" he asked, his aura tinged green with anxiety.

"No, it was to meet me here," replied Viela. The stablemaster had told him the youngling would be released from its duties and waiting at Kirlei.

"I expected naReill to arrive before midday, but it has not come. I sent one of the younglings to the stable to fetch it, and neither has returned."

Viela hid his concern. "They will be here soon. Doubtless Oreyn has found a hand of things he wants naReill to do before it leaves. Let me examine Eenar, and if naReill is not here when I am finished, I will go to the stable myself."

They walked through a maze of tiny interconnecting rooms toward the Mother's chamber. There were few windows and no other light sources, and while Viela's

eyes adjusted to the dimness his other senses explored
his surroundings. He heard the click and slide of the
loom, and the chattering of younglings, and felt the dis-
cordance of their immature auras. Torma was a cloud of
anxiety walking before him. Sheltered in the centermost
sanctuary of Kirlei was the Mother. Her aura was like
the warmth of a kitchen hearth, the fading strength of an
old tree, the quiet acceptance of grain bending in the
wind. He followed Torma into her chamber. Gentle sunlight illuminated the room, filtered by the leaves of the
roof-vines that surrounded the skylight. The walls were
bare, rough cut stone, with a grotto carved from the far
wall. Light touched the edges of it, but its depths were
in shadow, mysterious. Jagged crystal formations projected from the stone at random, breaking the light into
rainbows. The crystals were energy reservoirs, and the
largest cluster was at the head of the platform where
Eenar rested.

Since becoming Mother, Eenar had spent much of her
time in this chamber. She had nursed her younglings and
taught them rudimentary skills, and when they were fostered out she taught her craft of weaving to the younglings fostered at House Kirlei. Viela had known Eenar
as a strong Master and an affectionate Mother; now she
was old and misshapen, her plump body wrinkled and
her teats drooping. Soon, deep inside that ancient body,
new life would stir. In the womb that was beginning to
grow in her abdomen, Torma and Reill would deposit
their seed. Younglings would grow, gathering their nourishment from her substance, draining her of strength and
life, until, with her death, they would emerge into the
world.

Before that could happen, there must be two Masters
in Kirlei.

Viela approached Eenar. He stopped before her platform and reached out with both hands, spreading his fingers to stroke her aura. Except when performing a
Healing, he would not touch a Mother. Her physical and
emotional states were highly interdependent, and he
could read them accurately in her aura. Eenar was approaching fertility rapidly—much faster than Viela had

expected. If naReill was not cocooned within the next few days, it would not complete metamorphosis before Eenar reached her critical fertile period. Without both Masters, there could be no mating. The line of House Kirlei would end.

There should have been a six-day and more to spare before the time became critical. Viela had never seen a Mother approach fertility this quickly. Her metabolism was rapid, her womb swelling, the dark stain of her excretions showing on the furs. Her eyes told him that she understood this, and that she was concerned because naReill was not with them. He wanted to calm her, to help slow the changes in her body, but it was more important to find naReill. He motioned for her to stay on the platform, then bowed and backed away, drawing Torma out of the chamber with him.

"I am going to the stable. I will be back with naReill shortly," he said.

Torma guided him back to the portal. He was frustrated and anxious, and that grated on Viela like sawgrass against bare legs. He paused in the doorway. "Make a tea of blue-flower and sweet bark. Give some to Eenar. It will calm her," Viela said. "Drink some yourself. I will be back soon."

There were many younglings working at the stable. Viela did not see naReill, so he searched for the stablemaster. He found Oreyn at the breeding pens, checking the condition of his pregnant stock. Oreyn was bent over, one arm thrown over an alep's back, his ear pressed to its side.

Viela pushed aside a youngling and strode into the pen. "Stablemaster, where is naReill?" he called.

Oreyn straightened. "naReill? It is at the dispute site with Jeryl. Were you not told?"

"naReill was to be cocooned today. Why did you send it out? You told me the youngling would be waiting at Kirlei."

"Mrann asked me to send the youngling. naReill will be in charge of the aleps and borras for the caravan and the dispute. He wanted it to see the route and the site."

Viela quietly uttered a vile oath, but Oreyn heard it. He patted the alep on the rump and walked to Viela's side.

"This dispute causes problems for all of us. I knew you needed naReill, but I could not argue with Mrann. The needs of the clan must come first."

"I understand," said Viela, but the words were empty. "I will take the issue to Mrann. Thank you for your help." He strode out of the pen.

Viela saw nothing of the keep as he walked toward the clanhall. His mind was focused on his concern for Eenar. He did not think the cocooning could wait until after the dispute. Her body was changing more quickly than had that of any Mother he had seen. He intended to demand that Mrann give him naReill, and take another animal handler to the dispute. It was true that naReill was the eldest and most experienced of Oreyn's apprentices, but there must be another youngling who could do the job as well.

As Viela approached the clanhall, its broad wooden door opened and the Mentor appeared. He swept down the wide steps, his gray cloak billowing behind him, and passed the Healer with only a cursory nod of acknowledgment. Viela turned and followed him.

"Mentor!" he called. He was angry when Mrann did not respond. "I must speak with you!"

Mrann strode across the circle, either not hearing or ignoring the Healer. Viela stalked after him, the power of his concern feeding his anger.

"Mrann!"

The Mentor turned his head, but he did not slow his pace. "I am going to the infirmary to see my apprentice. Come along, if you wish."

The Healer's complex was built on the lowest spot in the keep, to protect it from storms and high winds. Excess rainwater drained away through stone channels under the roadway, running outside to irrigate the lowland fields. Some of the Healer's buildings were older than the wall of the keep itself. They were made of dressed stone, and served as small, tidy dormitories for Viela's apprentices. The complex's newer wooden buildings included sheds for drying herbs, and the compounding rooms.

The most ancient structure stood behind the sheds. Its single story of rough-cut stone had been the first permanent construction in Alu Keep, and it still dominated the complex. It was sturdier than most of the other buildings, despite its age. Viela chose it to house his patients.

The Healer reached Mrann's side as he entered the ancient building. Viela pushed past the Mentor, leading him down the narrow passage to the central hall. A group of younglings, supervised by one of Viela's apprentices, was clearing away the remains of the midday meal. The Healer stared at them, and they bundled the last of the dishes together and hurried off.

Viela loosed the anger that was festering in him. It billowed about him in a fiery haze. "naReill was to be cocooned today. You sent him off with Jeryl, without informing me. Why?"

Mrann's gray eyes flashed. "I am not required to explain my motives to you, Healer," he said. Then he waved a hand, as if the matter was of no importance. "naReill is our best alep-handler. I wanted it to see the trail, and to choose a site for the corral."

"Any of the stablemaster's apprentices could have done that for you. naReill's metamorphosis is the future of House Kirlei. You have jeopardized that."

"Healer, the whole clan is in jeopardy. A delay of a few days in the cocooning of a youngling will not matter." Mrann shrugged dismissal, walking slowly past Viela into Elver's room. The Healer followed him.

Elver was out of bed, dressed in a robe and seated at a small table, eating. His color was bright and unnatural, but he looked stronger than when Viela had last examined him. He set down his tea when they entered.

Mrann nodded a brief greeting. "Will you be ready to ride tomorrow?" There was no concern in his voice, just matter-of-fact inquiry about the state of Elver's health.

"Ride! He is much too weak to ride. You cannot expect to take him to the dispute?" Viela was incredulous. Mrann demanded much of his apprentice, but Viela would not believe he would callously risk Elver's life.

"I must have an apprentice. Alu has no chance to win this dispute unless there is someone to second me."

"Elver will certainly die if he attempts to channel power for you. All his energy must go into healing his wound."

"Do not judge too quickly, Healer." Elver rose and pulled aside the rough brown cloth of his robe, baring his torso. There was a long burn scar running across one side of his chest, from the shoulder to just below one of the nodules that contained his dormant tentacles. The wound had been open earlier, but now it was covered with a delicate film of new tissue.

Gently, Viela laid his fingers on the wound, and sensed the condition of the injured organs beneath the surface. "You are healing quickly, but it is still too soon for you to be riding."

"I will be ready tomorrow," asserted Elver. "If I spend tonight in healing trance, there will be no danger of the wound reopening."

"Trance takes too much energy," Viela objected. "You will deplete yourself; the dispute will burn you out."

Elver was obstinate. "Mrann risks the same fate. I will not let him go alone."

"You will allow him to do this?" remonstrated Viela, looking to Mrann for a denial that he feared would not come.

"Yes. It is necessary."

The Healer threw up his hands in futile protest. "If you insist on the trance, I will stay with you tonight. But I do not believe you will ride tomorrow without endangering your life." Viela wanted to order Mrann from the room, but he did not dare. Instead Viela left, constraining his anger until he was out of Elver's sight. He was angry with Mrann, not with Elver, and he did not want Elver's recovery affected by his anger.

When he descended on the younglings in the outer hall, they scattered like leaves before the wind. Only the apprentices stayed to face his obvious wrath. He gave them short, sharp orders, sending one for more food for Elver, and another to prepare a potent herbal tea that would give him additional strength.

Mrann joined him in the central chamber, looking tired and pale. Viela guessed that he had transferred some of his own energy to his apprentice. Under other circumstances he would have offered the Mentor a restorative potion, but he was too angry. Instead he took up an attack stance, arms spread wide and aura expanding. He was determined to confront Mrann with the problems of House Kirlei.

"Mrann." The name was a low-voiced challenge. "Eenar is reaching fertility faster than any Mother I have ever ministered to. There is no time to spare. naReill must be cocooned tonight."

"No." Mrann turned away, head bowed, one shoulder drooping. "There is too much at risk."

Viela grasped Mrann's arm. He felt the jolt as their energy fields intermingled. The Mentor pulled away, trying to break the contact, but Viela moved with him. Energy flowed from his body to Mrann's, like water flowing from a high place to a low one. He was still angry, but he could not let the Mentor walk away exhausted. He maintained the touch until their energy levels settled and the interchange between them was an equal flow in either direction.

"Take another youngling to the dispute," Viela said.

With a costly expenditure of power, Mrann broke the contact and walked away.

Chapter 9

Sarah sat at the big table in the clanhall, flanked by Mrann and Oreyn. Jeryl's map was spread before them. "The plain is wide and barren. There is no place to conceal people or weapons except among these rocky outcroppings. It would be safest to stay away from them." She searched for words for snipers and spies, and found none. "Someone might hide there, and do you harm. This open area near the Alu trail would be a better place for your

camp.'' She traced the place with a finger, aware of
Mrann's friendly gaze on her, and of the inexplicably
hostile glance of Oreyn. The hairs on the back of her
neck bristled. Oreyn had been one of her allies on the
council. He supported the trade agreement, and often
talked of the prosperity it would bring to Clan Alu. Now
he was angry and resentful, and she did not know the
reason.

"I prefer to be near the rocks, where we can shelter
the tents from the night wind," said the Mentor. "Where
did naReill decide to put the corral?"

Sarah pointed to a crosshatched area of the map.
"naReill wanted to keep the animals away from the
rocks. It is afraid the aleps would climb into them and
run away."

"A sensible precaution."

Oreyn's fingers drummed an irritating tattoo on the table top. "Where is Jeryl? He was sent to scout this area.
Why does he not make the report?"

Sarah stared at him. Was he resentful because she made
the report in Jeryl's place?

"Jeryl stood vigil for Hladi last night, and was exhausted after the day's ride. I sent him to rest," said
Mrann, his eyes still on Sarah and the map. The drum-
ming stopped.

"I am the leader of the council, Mrann," complained
Oreyn. "Jeryl must answer to me. Is it not enough that
I must deal with the first dispute that involves Clan Alu
in two hands of generations? Can we not adhere to protocol until this is finished?"

"You are newly-made leader. I am Mentor of Alu, and
have advised the council for many seasons. Trust me to
do what is necessary to preserve Clan Alu. You and the
others of the council will not risk your lives in this dispute. My apprentice and I will fight for you." Mrann
took the map and rolled it around a wooden rod. "You
have served long enough on the council to know that in
times of emergency, you may have to relinquish some of
your authority to me. Jeryl is acting for my apprentice. I
will direct him as I see fit."

Oreyn rose. He did not seem to be bothered by Mrann's

reproof. He rested a hand on the Mentor's shoulder, leaned forward and spoke softly near his ear, but Sarah heard. ''Viela came to the stable today, seeking na-Reill,'' he said.

''That is not your concern, Oreyn. I will discuss the matter with the Healer. You must have the caravan ready to leave by mid-morning.'' He rose and left the hall, taking the map with him. Oreyn stood beside the table, one hand in the air, the other dangling by his side. His mouth opened, but no sound issued from it.

Sarah followed Mrann, thinking about having a snack of dried fruit and protein bars from her small cache of supplies, and then heading for her warm and comfortable bed. She was stiff from the ride and wanted a hot bath, but the Ardellans had no such amenities. She would have to settle for a quick wash at the basin in her room, and a rubdown with a heavy cloth.

''Sarah.'' She had reached the stairs when Mrann turned back and called to her. ''Come to my room for tea.''

She almost refused, but there was something impera-tive in his tone. She nodded, then realized that the ges-ture did not mean agreement to the Ardellan. ''I'd be glad to join you.''

They were halfway up the stairs when the clanhall's heavy door slammed.

''Mentor!''

The voice was insistent. Sarah turned and saw Viela in his ceremonial blue Healer's robe, a single tongue of shimmer-light flickering above his head. The dark wood of the door was a somber backdrop, the stonework around it framing him in soft gray.

''I want the youngling, Mentor.''

''You cannot have it.'' Mrann's voice was calm, and full of power.

The flame that floated above Viela's head brightened, steadying to an intense blue-white glow. It shed more light than the wall sconces, and cast stark shadows throughout the hall. Oreyn was standing in the doorway of the meeting room, watching the confrontation.

''You are endangering House Kirlei.''

Mrann walked down a few steps and stood between Sarah and the Healer, one hand raised in a gesture of warding. "The fate of the clan rests on this dispute. Would you have me take less than the best Alu has to offer? If the battle is lost, it will not matter whether the youngling was cocooned."

Viela's eyes were shadowed in spite of the shimmer-light. Sarah was afraid of his power, but she could not force her eyes away. He raised his hands to cup the glowing ball above his head and his sleeves fell back, baring arms spiraled with lines of blue dye.

"Promise me you will bring naReill back safely. It is not to be one of the sacrifices."

Mrann's voice rang through the hall. "I cannot promise that, Healer, but I will not order naReill to stand behind me unless I have no other choice."

The shimmer-light was extinguished, and the wall sconces. In the darkness Sarah heard the big door open and close again, and then the sconce at the top of the stairs began to glow. Dazed, she wandered up to the landing.

"Come," said Mrann, walking past her. "You will feel better after you have some tea."

She watched him perform the ritual of preparing tea. He behaved as if the encounter with Viela had never happened. When the tea was ready he handed her a cup, and she sipped it, grateful for the warmth of it in her hands. Before half the cup was gone, her trepidation had dissipated.

Mrann sat quietly sipping his tea for a long time. Sarah finished hers, and he poured her a second cup before he broke the silence.

"What occurred on that plain today? Jeryl was not merely tired when he returned with the map."

"We met a scouting party from Eiku. Jeryl," Sarah paused, choosing her words with care, "tried to exact vengeance for Hladi's death." She watched Mrann's face, but she saw no reaction. He waited quietly for her to continue.

"We saw the dust of the other party. Jeryl rode toward them. I felt his anger touch me, and then I was seeing the others as he saw them, and feeling his emotions. The rider was surrounded by a red haze; I could tell that he was enraged and wanted to kill Jeryl.

"That frightened me, and shattered my contact with Jeryl. I could see that the Eiku Master wore a gray cloak. I rode after Jeryl, tried to stop him. I almost succeeded, but he broke away from me. The Eiku could have killed him easily, I think, but he only knocked Jeryl from his mount and split his dagger." She slipped the damaged weapon from her tunic and set it on the table. "naReill found it in the sand and gave it to me."

"Was the Eiku young, or very old?" asked Mrann, turning the dagger over in his hands.

"Youthful, I think, though I didn't get a close look at him."

"It was probably Barnn, the apprentice. I do not think the Mentor would have shown such restraint. He angers easily, and is not known to be merciful." He put the dagger back on the table, and poured hot tea into their cups. "How do you feel about your contact with Jeryl?"

"Frightened. A little confused. I don't like losing control."

"You have more control over this than you believe," Mrann assured her. "Next time it happens, remember that you can break the contact at any time you choose."

Sarah did not feel confident about that. She had been shaking after she broke free of Jeryl, and it was not all due to the immediate crisis of his attack on the Eiku. She had no idea how she would handle this if it happened again.

Mrann interrupted her thoughts. "Do you have anything else to tell me?"

"Yes," Sarah replied, wondering how he knew there was more. "There was something that even Jeryl did not notice. I saw signs of a recent landing by a small ship, a shuttle perhaps. Have you been contacted by any other Terrans in the past few days?"

Mrann looked surprised. "You are the only Terran I have seen since you came to Alu Keep. I know of no landings since then except the patrol ship that brought your supplies at midsummer, and it landed just outside the keep's front gate.''

"These were definitely landing tracks, and very recent. The sand was almost undisturbed. I think they were no more than two or three days old." She was certain it was Nick Durrow's shuttle. He must have been surveying the wasteland, searching for the titanium deposits. Had he also maneuvered Clan Eiku into fighting with Alu?

"You will have to be especially careful in this dispute, Mrann. Expect the unexpected, be surprised at nothing. The Eiku have already proved themselves to be devious in the way they killed Hladi and injured your apprentice."

Mrann rose, planting his hands on the table between them, and leaned over Sarah. "Do you tell me how to conduct dispute, alien? I am Mentor, Terran, and I have powers you cannot imagine."

Sarah was suddenly contrite. She was becoming involved in local events, interfering in them even as she tried to prevent others from interfering. She rested her hands on the table, palms upward, in the Ardellan gesture that asked forgiveness.

Mrann straightened. "Forgiveness, Sarah. I should not have lost my temper. You have been a good friend, and I know that you are trying to help." He sat down again as though no anger had passed between them, and reached for his tea. "You called your own ship. When will it arrive?"

"I expect it by mid-afternoon tomorrow, if it is not delayed. It may be able to keep Durrow from interfering further with your affairs."

"Alu must fight this battle alone, and if Revin is an honorable Mentor, Eiku will also fight without aid. Will you ride with me tomorrow, to observe the dispute?"

Sarah was startled. Her position on Ardel depended on the outcome of this dispute. She wanted to witness the fighting, but she had feared Mrann would not allow an outsider to be present. "I would be honored," she said, excited and a little afraid.

"Jeryl rides with us, also. Hladi was cremated today, and his lust for revenge will increase. That may be useful.'' Mrann offered Sarah a bowl of nutmeats, which she declined. ''Elver's condition is greatly improved and he will be my second, but he is weak, and Jeryl is the only other Alu who stands alone now. The other Masters will stay here, and lend what aid they can.''

''Why won't the other Masters fight with you?'' asked Sarah. Mrann had never explained the conduct of a dispute to her; she was puzzled that the Masters would not help to defend their clan.

''We are expendable—those of us who no longer have mates. Younglings are expendable, also, because the clan has more younglings than it can ever metamorphose into adults. But Masters and Mothers are the heart of the clan, and their lives cannot be risked.''

''Then the fate of the entire clan rests on the shoulders of the younglings and the Mentor?''

''Not really,'' replied Mrann. ''The younglings do not fight. They are the tools of the Mentor. Only the Mentor does battle for his clan, aided by his apprentice. The surviving Mentor or apprentice is the victor.''

Personal combat to the death to resolve a dispute between clans was an elegant alternative to war. It was certainly less barbaric than the many types of mass warfare Terrans waged. No destruction, few deaths, just a quiet passing of power to the clan of the victor. Its cold-blooded practicality made Sarah shudder. ''I must go, Mrann. We both have much to think about, and much to do before morning, and I need sleep if I am to ride with you.'' He waved his hand in dismissal and unlatched the door with a thought.

The corridor was cool and silent, and her room with its padded sleeping platform was inviting. She stepped inside, picked up her journal, and realized that she was not ready to put her thoughts on paper. The message light was blinking on her com-unit. She pressed the retrieve key, waited for the hard-copy to print.

2257:12/5, TERRAN CALENDAR
RECEIVED 18:12, ARBITRARY LOCAL TIME
TO: SARAH ANDERS, TRADE ATTACHE/ARDEL

FROM: CAPTAIN SWENSON, TERRAN UNION
      INTERSTELLAR SHIP *BLACKHAWK*
DELAYED AT BARTEL'S COLONY. EXPECT TO
ARRIVE AT ARDEL WITHIN SIXTY-SEVEN
HOURS. PLEASE REPLY WITH UPDATE ON YOUR
STATUS.

Sarah cursed. The *Blackhawk* would not reach Ardel
until the day after the dispute. She was on her own. She
pounded out a quick message describing the current situation and warning them about Durrow's group. The mineral survey map was hanging on the wall above the com-
unit; she checked the coordinates of the dispute site and
added them to the message. If the *Blackhawk* could break
away sooner, perhaps it could meet her at the dispute.

She was feeling too frustrated to sleep. Instead she wandered through the clanhall's deserted passages, stopping
once to stare absently at an intricate wall hanging. Finally
she slipped outside, to walk along the great wall of Alu
Keep and order her thoughts.

The large lavender moon was high in the sky, its small
white sister just rising. The mourning wall was a brooding
presence behind the clanhall. Sarah felt a tingling in her
body as she walked beside it. The skin on her right shoulder pulled painfully at an old scar, and she massaged it.
The wall was high, at least half again as tall as she, and
small niches in its inner surface held carved stone urns.
They contained the ashes of dead Mothers, and a few Masters whom Mrann had said died before their time. Below
each burial niche were carved the swirling designs of ancient runes. Sarah had asked Mrann about them once, and
he told her that survivors carved them, as a tribute to the
deceased.

Sarah moved out of the moons' bright light and into the
shadow of the clanhall. As her eyes became accustomed
to the dimness, she saw a Master leaning against the wall
ahead of her. She did not want to disturb his meditations,
so she turned back. Her foot kicked a pebble, and the
Master jumped.

"Who is it?" he asked.

"Jeryl?" replied Sarah, recognizing the voice. "What

are you doing here?'' she asked as she came closer, her tone hardly above a whisper. She could just make out the fresh niche in the wall, with a new urn in it. The stone below it was smooth, with none of the curled and swirling runes carved into it.

"Sarah." Jeryl slumped against the wall. "I came to pay my last tribute to Hladi, but I have nothing to write. Her death had no meaning."

Sarah felt his despair. It reached into her mind and threatened to take hold of her thoughts and emotions, but she forcefully pushed it away. "Then write of her life, Jeryl."

"If there is no meaning in death, how can there be meaning in life?" he asked bitterly. He was openly using the wall for support, and Sarah doubted if he could stand unaided. "So much that I do not understand is happening to me. I can feel things now that I never felt before. I see things that were closed to me, I know things that I was never meant to know, things that only the Mentor knows."

"Have you spoken to Mrann about it?"

"No. I will not." Jeryl tried to stand, and fell back against the wall. "He wants me as apprentice, but I do not want the mysteries and powers that he holds. I want to be only Jeryl, Master of Clan Alu."

Sarah stepped close to him and offered her hand in support, but he brushed it away. "Mrann wants you to ride with him tomorrow, Jeryl. Your clan may need your help. Will you do it for Alu, if not for your Mentor?"

Jeryl looked up, and Sarah could see pinpoints of light burning in his eyes again. "I will ride, for Hladi and for Alu," he said.

"Good. Then you need to rest." She slipped her arm around his back, and this time he did not resist. "Let me help you to your room." Jeryl did not say a word, just moved with her toward the clanhall.

Chapter 10

Viela sat naked in the sand pit in his room, his legs crossed and folded under him. Moonlight played across the chamber, stealing in through the skylight to illuminate the center and leave the walls in murky shadow. His ritual implements rested in the sand beside him: a flat disk of copper, its surface embossed with a design of intertwined tentacles beneath the green corrosion; water, in a fine black-lined pottery bowl, the Alu tree design etched in the baked green clay; a piece of smokewood. Slender blue snakes of dye glowed on his arms, spiraling from hands to shoulders, meeting in a kiss at the back of his neck. The sand was his connection to the earth, for there was no floor under the pit; the unobstructed moonlight his channel to the heavens. He felt energy flow through him from earth to sky and back again, slowing his breathing, clearing his mind.

Staring into the water, he considered the events of the last two days. Hladi's death and Elver's injury at the hands of the assassin, and then the assassin's unspeakable death, and his own part in it; the news of the dispute; Torma's resignation from the council; naReill's aborted cocooning. All were events of disruption and change, and his consciousness was fighting changes, trying to maintain the rigid limits of his existence. The patterns of a lifetime were changing, and from fear and distrust he was striking out against those he saw as the instigators of change—Mrann and the Terran.

Life is change. Viela understood that with his mind, but in his soul he was afraid. He could let that fear rule him, and in time lose his power and position in the clan. Instead he chose to conquer that fear through intellect and ritual. He wanted to accept the changes, to learn to grow with them and become a more powerful leader and a more effective Healer. His anger and resentment were interfering with his work. He could not safely guide Elver's healing trance unless he put them aside.

He needed to cleanse his aura of negative emotions. The teachers had given him many methods for doing this, but he almost always chose this ritual. With a carefully channeled thought he kindled the smokewood, and watched the faint blue haze rise from it. The smoke was pleasantly aromatic. He breathed deeply, centering his concentration.

With slender fingers Viela grasped the copper disk, and held it before his eyes. He stared at it for a long time, then brought it down and touched it to his chest. He felt the anger and resentment that were the root of his fear, and when the emotions were clear and vibrant, he focused on the disk. He extended his arms, holding the copper with his fingertips and allowing the feelings to flow into it. The metal grew warm. Still he pushed, drawing all of the negative emotions out of his aura, sending them into the copper disk. It vibrated with the energy he was forcing into it. He could feel it pulsing against his fingertips. The energy threatened to flow back through his arms, but he held it at bay for a long time. Then he plunged the metal into the bowl of water. A cloud of steam rose, though the disk was not warm enough to vaporize the water. The steam mixed with the smoke and created a fog that took moments to clear. The dish was empty, save for the now-bright copper disk. Viela touched it gingerly, then picked it up and returned it to its place in the sand.

With precise motions Viela extinguished the smokewood and gathered up the implements. He had accomplished his purpose. His aura was clear, the anger and resentment that had colored it having evaporated with the water. Now he could safely guide Elver's trance.

Viela knew the theory behind trance healing. In trance, a Master could draw upon the biochemical energy stored in his body to speed metabolic processes such as cell growth. Torn cartilage in an arm or leg could be healed in days. A punctured organ could be knit together again overnight. But the trance used vast amounts of stored energy, consuming the body's reserves of nutrients at an alarming rate. The healing trance was dangerous, because if it was not carefully monitored, the body could consume itself.

There were several factors in Elver's favor. Because of the nature of his wound, he had lost very little of his precious body fluids. The damage to his internal organs was significant but no longer life-threatening. He was young and strong, and he had survived the post-trauma shock very well. But he had a serious disadvantage. He was much too slender. His body carried little in the way of excess fat, and even muscle tissue was not overabundant. He would not have much reserve to draw upon in the trance.

Younglings had been feeding Elver all day. Viela had ordered special foods that were easily digested and would provide large amounts of energy. He also sent teas and potions made from an assortment of roots, flowers, and leaves and brewed in a ceremonial iron container. He wanted Elver to store as much energy as it was physically possible to acquire in one day.

Despite these preparations, Viela was apprehensive when he walked into Elver's room. Healing trance was a dangerous state. Viela had witnessed it only a handful of times in the forty years since he had taken his Healer's vows. Some of his teachers maintained that trance should not be allowed under any circumstances. It was dangerous to the Master in trance, because it could drain his resources until his body could not survive without outside support, and it was dangerous to the Healer who witnessed it. The Healer could be drawn into the trance, to provide power and energy for the failing patient. Some Healers did not return from that journey.

Viela had never allowed himself to be drawn into another's trance. The trance healings he had witnessed had sometimes been complex, but they had never been hurried. In each case the patient had had time to store energy, and had been able to work slowly in the trance, coming to consciousness often enough to keep his resources replenished.

Elver would have to do it all in one night. The damage he had to repair was not minor. The nerve bundles lead-

ing to his dormant left tentacle were severed, and would
need to be regenerated. Nearly half of the great organ
that cleaned wastes from his body fluids had been destroyed. The muscle damage was not as serious, and
could be allowed to repair itself in its own time, but the
other things, once started, must be seen through to completion. It would be fatal to stop this trance once it had
begun.

Elver's room was darkened, muffling draperies hiding
the window. Viela pulled another drapery across the
doorway, to prevent light and sound from entering the
room. With few outside stimuli to disturb him, it would
be easier for Elver to maintain the trance. Viela banished
all the younglings and even his young Master apprentice
for the night.

Elver was in the early stages of trance. Viela sat on the
edge of the bed. He could sense the deepening and pulling inward of the young FreeMaster's aura as Elver turned
all his attention toward the nurturing of his damaged
body. The aura receded from Viela's field of contact, and
the Healer had to actively seek it out, following it into
the uppermost levels of Elver's mind. This was where the
danger began for Viela, or any Healer—pursuing that elu-
sive life-spark as the trance deepened, and being tempted
to feed it and nurture it until the Healer lost himself and
followed the trance-worker into death, or back up into
life.

Viela could ''see'' Elver tracing the paths of broken
nerves, assessing the organ and muscle damage, choosing where to expend energy first. Fluids were moving
through his body at an accelerated rate, putting an added
burden on damaged organs, but nerve regeneration was
critical, and Elver chose to facilitate that. Carefully, he
traced the severed bundles back to the nearest branching
point, and there began regrowth. His body disassembled
the nonfunctioning bundles, dissolving the raw materials
back into the fluid system and drawing out the building
blocks it needed to generate healthy new fibers.

How long the process took, Viela could not guess. His
sense of time was lost; his sense of a world outside El-

ver's body was dim and unreal. All that existed was the event of Elver's trance.

At last the nerve bundles traversed the scar left by the wound, and joined the healthy nerves that extended into Elver's dormant tentacle. It stirred within its nodule, sensation and function restored. Elver was weaker, his reserve depleted. He still had much work to do.

Organ regrowth was the most energy intensive form of trance-healing. Organ function could not be suspended during regeneration. If the rebuilding was slow, it would not affect the work load of the organ overmuch, but Elver had neither the time nor the reserves for slow regeneration. He must push his system to work at top speed, increasing his metabolic rate and forcing all of his body's systems to operate at the dangerous level of overload.

Viela "followed" Elver down into the wounded organ to assess the damage. The laser blast had burned away more than half of it, though enough essentials were left to keep it operating. If it had been wholly destroyed Elver would be dead, but enough of it still functioned to keep him alive until the rest regenerated. The major circulatory vessels were untouched, but there was much damage to repair among the smaller ones.

With meticulous care, Elver began the rebuilding. First, he cleared away the cauterized flesh bit by bit, sealing off leaking vessels and exploring damaged nerves. When the area was cleared of dead material, he began regenerating. Structure by structure, he directed his body to grow, to follow the existing pattern and reconstruct the pieces that were missing. He drew nutrients from his circulatory system, and when they did not appear as quickly as he needed them, he pushed his metabolism to function faster. The fluid coursed through his body, bringing nutrients and taking away waste materials at a frantic rate. The stress on his system was increasing. Waste products accumulated more quickly than his damaged organ could remove them.

Viela saw the poisons in Elver's body approaching toxic levels. Elver was strained beyond safe limits, burning with excess heat, and his organs were beginning to suffocate in their own wastes. The damage was still reversible; soon it would become permanent, and life-threatening.

The Healer was bound into Elver's trance, and now he must begin to function as a Healer rather than an observer. He could slow the disastrous rush of Elver's body toward self-destruction, but only by endangering himself. By using his own body systems to monitor and control Elver's, he risked being drawn into the destructive spiral that had captured his patient. Yet he was a Healer, and his ethics would not let him watch Elver die without attempting to aid him.

For the first time he touched Elver, placing one hand on the top of his head and the other just below his wound. With sensitive fingertips he searched out the nerve channels and tapped into them. He attuned his body to Elver's so that any changes he might induce would be gradual and would not precipitate shock. Draining off the excess heat was his first priority, for that would damage Elver's body even faster than the toxic wastes building in his system. He accepted it into his own body, bringing their two systems into equilibrium, and then began to dispel it through his skin. He was warm. He longed to remove his robe, but would not break the contact with his patient.

The regrowth was still going on, but at a reduced rate. He dared not stop it completely, or even allow it to slow too much, for the only way to clear Elver's system of the poisons was to filter them through the damaged organ. Elver had passed the point of no return—damaged as it was, his organ could not remove the poisons as quickly as they were building up. But with every bit of new growth, the organ's capacity would increase, and it would be able to do its job more effectively. If Viela could keep Elver alive until his body could begin to cleanse itself, they might both survive.

Viela had never been so warm. This was not an outside heat, but a warmth that came from within his body. He could not escape it. His exposed skin radiated heat, and his robe kept it close against his body. In the blackness of the room, he saw himself and Elver as two points of bright light, brilliant flares that might burn themselves out at any moment.

It was a long time before he felt a positive turn in
Elver's condition. The first sign was that the heat stopped
increasing. Elver's body temperature did not drop, but it
stabilized at a level that would not permanently damage
tissue. The shortage of mass in his body became critical.
He needed material to construct the new growth, and he
needed it quickly. When his reserve was gone, the need
for more raw materials would force him to cannibalize
muscle and soft tissue, weakening his body still further.

Viela, as Healer, could pass energy to Elver, but he
could not give him the raw materials he needed. The
most he could do was direct the destruction of existing
tissue, and keep the damage to a minimum. To do even
this he must stay in deep trance with Elver, risking his
own life by keeping his body's systems closely linked
with those of his patient.

He had made his choice when he first touched Elver.
He would not withdraw now. With concentrated effort he
guided Elver's circulatory system, forcing the fluids to
move more quickly through areas where the damage
would be felt least, and to destroy only slowly around
the vital organs. The poisons were still building in Elver's
system, further complicating Viela's job, but the damaged organ was healing quickly and taking over its natural function.

Immersed in the ongoing processes of his patient's
healing, Viela had no concept of time. His only measure
was his own exhaustion. His body was dehydrated, his
skin and his robe soaked with perspiration. His legs
shook. It was not until Elver passed the critical stages
and began cleansing his system of the accumulated poisons that Viela realized these things. He guided Elver to
a safer level of trance. Finally, still unsure whether he
and Elver would awaken, the exhausted Healer drifted
from his own trance into sleep.

Chapter 11

Sunrise was Sarah's favorite time of day. She had watched many sunrises in New Mexico with her grandmother; now she made a point of watching at least one sunrise on every planet she visited. Few events approached the spectacle of Sol rising on Terra, where dust and pollutants in the atmosphere produced intense colors without obscuring the view. On Benardi, the haze was so thick that day was only slightly brighter than night, and the sun was a faintly luminescent spot in a muddy sky. Regass' white dwarf rose in a clear sky, but was so bright it could only be viewed through dark lenses that hid all color.

Ardel's sunrise was gorgeous, thanks to a pair of active volcanoes in the far south, beyond the wasteland. Sarah stood outside Alu Keep's main gate and watched the eastern sky. Clouds hanging low on the horizon reflected light in pools of amethyst and rose, slowly brightening until the colors ran together and the sky lightened. As the rim of Aer's disc appeared, she whispered the words of the Sun Father greeting chant. She wished for the offerings her grandmother had given to the winds each morning—a pinch of cornmeal for sustenance, and a pinch of corn pollen for fertility. For the first time since she'd left Mike, she longed for the safety of her grandmother's hogan and the comfort of the old woman's counsel.

A loud exclamation inside the keep brought an abrupt end to Sarah's contemplations. She turned back and strode through the gate to see what was wrong. The caravan was forming, stable hands pulling loaded carts into line along the road. Viela and Mrann were arguing next to the corral. Between them, a pallid Elver leaned against the wooden rail.

"He is too weak to travel!" exclaimed Viela.

Looking at Elver, Sarah did not doubt the Healer's

statement. She was amazed to see Elver up and about. A wound like his would have kept a Terran near death for a week or more. Mrann had told her of a trance Ardellans used to heal themselves; this was the first evidence she had seen of it. Elver appeared thinner than he had a few days ago, and his skin had none of its usual golden tinge. His forehead was damp, his hair matted, his eyes yellowed and the lids drooping. Viela did not look much better. He was not as wan, and did not appear emaciated but his unkempt hair and the deep creases above his eyes testified to a night of little sleep. Neither of them looked healthy enough to ride.

Elver laid a steady hand on the Healer's arm. "I am fine," he protested. "My wound has healed. I do not care to sleep and eat in the safety of the keep while Mrann fights Alu's battles alone. I will ride with him."

"The decision to go or stay is Elver's. He is weak, but he is recovering quickly. You can advise him of the dangers of travel," admonished Mrann, facing down the taller Healer, "but you cannot tell him how to choose. Look to yourself, Healer. You are nearly as exhausted as your patient. Will you stay behind?"

Viela seemed determined to make Elver stay at Alu Keep. "You need sleep. A six-day of rest, and food to restore your strength. If you try to travel now, you endanger your life." Viela was vehement about this. He stood firm against the Mentor, extending a hand in a warding gesture as he spoke to Elver. "You are too weak to be of any use at the dispute."

"You are wrong," said Elver, in a voice that was quiet but indomitable. "Mrann tested me this morning. My capacity to channel energy is adequate, and improving. He trained me well. I will stand with him at the dispute." Elver straightened up from the rail and walked away, his pace slow but steady.

"You will die!" shouted the Healer. He turned to Mrann. "You must not ask him to do this. Take someone else, someone who is healthy and strong. Take Jeryl!"

"Elver has the training and experience to aid me. Jeryl has strength, but is untrained and unwilling. There are no other FreeMasters in Clan Alu. I have no choice,

Healer. I use what resources I have." There was bitterness in Mrann's voice. "If you believe Elver is too weak to sit a mount, he can ride in the cart with you."

Viela slammed his right forearm against the top rail of the corral, startling an alep. He muttered something under his breath, then turned to stalk away. He ran headlong into Sarah.

"Watch your path," he said as he stepped around her.

"It is you who should watch your path," said Mrann. "The Terran has been standing there for some time. Were you not aware of her aura so near yours? Perhaps it is you who needs to rest."

Viela favored him with a withering glance before he walked away.

"I didn't mean to upset Viela," said Sarah. "He doesn't approve of my presence in Alu Keep. I don't want to antagonize him."

Mrann shrugged. "Do not concern yourself with the Healer's feelings. He is too accustomed to having things his own way. It is time he learned that the continuance of the clan may necessitate the sacrifice of an individual or the breaking of a tradition. In some things, Elver is much wiser than Viela." He turned to look at the caravan. "Have you seen Jeryl?"

"Not since last night."

"Then I must send someone back to the clanhall to find him." Mrann clapped, and a youngling appeared at his side.

Sarah waved the youngling away. "Let me go. I met him at the mourning wall last night, and helped him to his room. He was restless, and I sat with him for a while. He could not sleep, but he said he would stay there and meditate until it was time to meet you."

"There is no need for you to go. A youngling can fetch him," said Mrann.

"I want to go. There is nothing for me to do here. I feel a kinship with Jeryl because of my own loss." Sarah frowned as she thought of her father's death. She should have been with him; she should have taken him home to New Mexico, where his ghost could have roamed the ancestral lands.

Mrann dismissed her with a gesture, and she started up the long graveled roadway toward the clanhall. It was bustling with normal activity—Masters shouting orders, apprentices opening the fronts of workshops to the morning light, and other younglings, less mature and not yet wearing the sash of apprenticeship, clutching tools and packets of food in their tentacles. Their round, short-legged bodies jostled one another in their haste to reach the fields and gardens outside the keep. Sarah smiled at their awkwardness. They reminded her of a very large litter of mongrel puppies she had played with when she was a child.

She threaded her way through the crowd of ungainly younglings and past the shops to the residential part of the street. A few of the Masters and apprentices noticed her and waved. They were accustomed to her morning strolls through the keep, and did not expect her to stop and chat. Sarah nodded and waved back, but kept walking.

Sarah rounded a corner and found Viela standing in the roadway, staring at her. She knew that he was angry; she could feel his rage pushing at her. Instead of turning aside, she chose to confront him.

"What angers you so, Healer?"

When he did not answer, she stepped closer and raised her hands, palms up and fingers spread. It was a gesture asking for forgiveness, an expression of her wish for peace between them. He did not respond. She took another step toward him, close enough so that her fingers almost brushed his chest. Suddenly his hatred became a part of her. She understood his rage at her intrusion into the life of Clan Alu. Her presence had brought about Hladi's death and Elver's injury, and the dispute. She was killing his clan, transforming it into something he did not choose to accept. He feared her, and that fear was being transformed into hatred and anger.

Sarah's hands had begun to shake. She pulled them back, and was relieved to feel the invading emotions slip away. Viela stared at her for a moment longer, then turned and walked away, leaving her trembling in the roadway.

* * *

The broad circle in front of the clanhall was empty. Sarah stopped and stared about in surprise. The heavy granite roadway showed no imprint of wheels or animals' feet, and there was no sign that they had been dragged from the circle. Sarah had seen no machinery capable of moving anything so heavy. The stones had been there, that was indisputable. She suddenly realized that she had never learned how they had gotten there in the first place. Now they were gone, and she had no time to investigate the mystery.

She pushed open the clanhall's imposing door and ran up the wide steps two at a time. Jeryl was staying in the guest room next to hers. She knocked, and when there was no answer she pushed the door. It was latched.

"Jeryl! Mrann is waiting for you," she called. He did not answer. She heard a dull thud, like something falling. Was Jeryl in trouble? Closing her eyes, she slowed her breathing and concentrated as the Mentor had taught her, trying to open the latch. She had practiced a hundred times, and never succeeded. It seemed nothing would happen this time, either. She would have to find someone to open the door for her. Then she felt a sudden release as the latch clicked and the door swung inward.

"I helped you open it; you could not manage alone." Jeryl's voice was expressionless. He sat at a table in the center of the darkened room, a small wooden carving on the floor at his feet and a ball of weak shimmer-light floating above his head. His hair was disheveled, his cloak wrapped about his shoulders with the sleeves hanging empty.

Sarah flushed. "The caravan is waiting for you, Master."

"Tell Mrann that I am not going with him."

"I am not your errand runner, Jeryl. Carry your own messages to the Mentor." She turned away, then looked back at him over her shoulder. "What of Hladi's revenge? Last night that was very important to you. Has it ceased to matter?"

Jeryl's shimmer-light flared and then disappeared. Sarah waited; when he did not move, she walked to the

door. She was about to pull it closed behind her when he
rose, adjusting his cloak.

"I will come," was all he said, but his voice conveyed
the blackest of futures for any of the Eiku he might meet.

Jeryl's eyes were closed through the entire journey.
Sarah could not tell if he was asleep or in trance, or how
he stayed in the saddle. The caravan traveled slowly, and
did not reach the chosen site until sunset. Then Mrann
halted abruptly and Sarah had to turn Jeryl's alep to keep
it from running into the Mentor.

"I am awake, Sarah," Jeryl said irritably, sitting up
straighter in the saddle. "Mind your own concerns and
let me be."

Sarah bit back a sharp comment. Jeryl's dilated pupils
reflected bright pinpoints of light, and his skin was pale.
He had not had a proper night's rest since Hladi's death,
and Sarah feared he would not sleep until he exacted
vengeance from Eiku.

The Eiku were already at the landing site, their camp
set up in the shelter of some rocks on the far side of the
plain. Two figures in gray cloaks rode out to greet the
Alu column, trailed by a score of younglings. Elver clambered down from the Healer's cart and mounted one of
the spare aleps. The caravan pulled aside, but Mrann and
Elver, followed by a few younglings, rode out to greet
the Eiku delegation.

Without conscious volition, Sarah's hand slipped to her
right hip. Concealed under her tunic, tucked carefully
into the waistband of her slacks, was the laser pistol that
had killed Hladi. It was forbidden to carry such a weapon,
and she risked much smuggling it out of Alu. Yet with
Durrow stirring up trouble, she would not go unarmed.

It was difficult to see any great distance in the dust,
but Mrann's white mount and the silver cloaks of the
Mentors and their apprentices were visible. Sarah
watched, fascinated, as Mrann and one of the Eiku faced
each other in the center of the great burn scar. Their
apprentices rode in slow circles about them. Mrann lifted
his arms in a gesture of power, which was echoed by the
other. Sparks flew between them, and the circle was lit

as bright as day. It looked like a ritual challenge. Mrann and the Mentor of Eiku, old, white-haired Revin, were clearly visible for a moment. Then they dropped their arms and the light died. In the sudden darkness, both Mentors and their apprentices were hidden.

Sarah blinked and looked toward the circle once more, and saw Mrann riding out of the darkness toward her. Behind him was Elver, looking exhausted. As he passed Sarah, the apprentice slipped in the saddle and almost fell from his mount. She reached out to steady him, turning her alep quickly so that she could ride beside him. Jeryl rode up to support him on the other side.

The younglings had already erected a temporary corral, and were setting up tents in the sheltering ell of rocks. That disturbed Sarah. Leaving Elver to Jeryl's ministrations, she rode off to find Mrann.

The Mentor was walking back from the corral when Sarah met him. Dismounting, she greeted him abruptly. "It would be better if we did not camp so close to the rocks, Mrann."

"Rocks cannot harm us, and they provide shelter from the wind," replied the weary Mentor.

"They also provide cover for anyone who wishes to attack the camp." Sarah knew she was exceeding her influence with the Mentor, but she was concerned for his safety, and the well-being of the entire party.

"Who would attack us?" Mrann stared at her.

Sarah sighed. "I fear that Durrow and his crew will come. They must have provided Hladi's assassin with the laser weapon. I'm sure they have more weapons and will try to aid Eiku in the dispute."

Mrann was shocked. "Eiku would allow no such interference!"

Forbearing to mention the attack against Hladi and Elver, Sarah tried another tack. "Off-worlders have ways of getting what they want, without regard to your customs. The titanium ores that are abundant here are a powerful enticement, perhaps powerful enough to encourage interference in the dispute."

"No. Revin would not permit it. The camp will stay

where it is." Mrann's voice brooked no argument, but Sarah would not retreat."

"Let me post a watch, then. Three younglings to stand through the night. All right?"

Mrann sighed in resignation. "If it will make you feel more secure, yes. Now go, and let me rest."

Sarah walked her heavy-footed alep to the corral, and turned the tired animal over to the stablers. On her way back through the camp, a familiar youngling hurried past her. She reached out and tapped it from behind, rapping it sharply between the eyestalks which barely reached to her shoulders. She had often seen Masters attract a youngling's attention this way. Turning to see who had accosted it, the youngling tripped on its feet, which seemed too large for its slight body.

Sarah tried not to laugh at the youngling's comical lack of coordination, and almost choked. It was a moment before she could speak clearly. "naReill? What are you doing here?"

The youngling crossed its eyestalks. "Why should I not be here?"

"You are pledged to Torma's House, to become a Master."

"Yes, but I am needed here, to care for the aleps and to help the Mentor."

"Can you do something for me?" asked Sarah. "Mrann has given me permission to post a watch in the rocks behind the camp tonight. Will you choose two other reliable younglings and meet me at my tent?" naReill dipped its eyestalks in assent, then turned and disappeared into the night.

Sarah walked through the camp, past the open canopy that provided shelter for the younglings, and past the smaller kitchen tent. The party was fasting tonight, but younglings were already preparing a large, pre-dawn meal. Beyond the busy kitchen, there was a cluster of five smaller tents. The first, occupied by Mrann, was already sealed, but the Healer's tent was open. Sarah paused at the door, wondering whether to enter and inquire about Elver. She heard him speaking to someone in a soft, clear voice.

"It is all right, Jeryl. The receptivity you are experiencing is normal."

"How can this turmoil be normal?" asked Jeryl.

"When Hladi died, many powers locked within you were suddenly unleashed. Normally it happens only when you are in metamorphosis, ready to become a Mother. The death of your mate when she gives birth releases the blocks. You would need these powers to understand and meet the needs of your newborn younglings."

"Am I becoming a Mother, then?"

"No," replied Elver. "You are becoming like me, like Mrann—a master with extended powers and abilities. You could be Mrann's apprentice, or you could challenge him . . ."

The Healer approached the tent entrance and glared at Sarah. She turned away, unwilling to face him.

naReill and two other younglings were waiting at her tent. Sarah motioned for them to follow her into the rocks behind the camp. The night was dark. The two moons had not yet risen, and a scattering of feathery clouds obscured the stars. Sarah and the younglings picked their way over the boulders, until they reached the highest point where they could still be concealed from view.

"Stand here tonight," Sarah instructed naReill, showing the youngling where to hide among the rocks. "If you see any movement on the plain, or anything unusual in the Eiku camp, send one of the other younglings to fetch me." Then she took the others down into the rocks, and set them to watching the perimeter of the encampment.

Sarah made one last circle around the camp. All was quiet except for the kitchen, and she saw nothing unusual. Chiding herself for being overly cautious, she returned to her tent and tried to sort out her thoughts. She dug through her pack until she found her journal. She punched the buttons of the combination lock and the cover opened. The tiny reading lamp, controlled by a self-contained light sensor, brightened to full illumination.

She stared at the page of spidery handwriting for a moment, then closed the cover with a snap.

Stripping off her over-tunic and boots, she settled down
to rest with the forbidden laser pistol tucked within easy
reach. Her last thoughts as she drifted to sleep turned on
Elver's enigmatic words to Jeryl—"You could be Mrann's
apprentice, or challenge him . . ." What did he mean?

Chapter 12

Arien sat in the sand beside his tent, head bowed and
eyes closed, deep in power-gathering meditation. A fleet
of ponderous clouds rolled overhead, obscuring the light
of the rising moon. Arien felt the moons' presence. He
drew energy from the winds that pushed the clouds about
and from the infinitesimal movements of the sand beneath his body, storing it against time of need.

For two days he had been waiting, and observing the
Terrans. For two days the Terrans had gone about their
business. None of them had disturbed Arien, but he was
always watched.

Tonight was different. Durrow had posted sentries on
the ridge, and called the rest of his people into the shuttle. Arien was alone. His skin tingled with anticipation.
Power coursed along his nerves, but his muscles were
relaxed. Slowly he raised his head and opened his eyes.

The crater was lit only by the dim exterior lights on
the shuttle. The sentries stood far from Arien, looking
out across the wasteland.

Arien turned and crept behind his tent, then scrambled
on hands and knees up the slope toward the crater's edge.
Sand slipped under his palms and stones bruised his
shins. He pressed his belly to the ground as he approached the rim, then sidled over the ridge and down
the other side.

His alep made a low sound when it smelled him. He
climbed to his feet and stroked the animal's snout to quiet
it. The saddle waited on the sand, with a pouch of feed

and a half-filled water skin. Arien bent to pick up the saddle.

"Don't touch that!"

Brilliant light blinded Arien. He straightened up, shading his eyes with both hands. The alep squealed and tugged at its rein.

"I should kill you and that stinking beast right now."

Arien recognized the voice. It was Roletti, Durrow's pilot. How had she come so close to him? He should have sensed her presence. He closed his eyes, dropped his hands, and took a step toward her.

"Stay where you are."

The light turned the insides of his eyelids red-gold. He heard fear and anger in her voice. Beyond that he sensed little. Her usually agitated aura was subdued and difficult to discern. Arien stopped moving and offered his hands with flattened palms turned upward. Roletti dimmed the lantern. He opened his eyes.

"I told him you would try to run," she said.

"I came to tend to my alep." Any Ardellan would acknowledge the half-truth and not press the matter.

"You lie," spat Roletti. She stepped closer, and Arien saw the laser weapon in her hand. "You were going to warn your friends about us, weren't you?"

Arien slowly raised his hands, turning the palms toward Roletti. He drew power upward from the earth along the nerves of his feet and legs, preparing to kill her.

"Pilot!"

The shout startled Arien. When Roletti slipped her weapon into its holster, he dropped his arms and channeled the energy back to earth. Then he looked over his shoulder. Williams, one of Durrow's security people, was standing atop the ridge behind him. "Captain wants you at the shuttle, Roletti. You, too, FreeMaster."

"Watch for me," Roletti said as she pushed past Arien. "I will kill you."

Williams, a burly man with dark skin and limited patience, waited for Arien. He stood quietly, his annoyance a bristling shield, while Arien calmed his alep and gave it food and water.

Arien was angry. He dared not refuse Durrow's sum-

mons. He wanted to ride away from the camp, but he
knew that Roletti and Durrow would track him and kill
him. If he could not warn Revin, he must find another
way to keep the Terrans from meddling in this dispute.
Perhaps he could use their own methods against them.
He had seen Durrow tell lies, expecting them to be believed. Yet Roletti had not believed his lie about the alep.
Could he convince Durrow he would do one thing when
he was really planning to do another? He gathered up the
edges of his anger and bundled it away to hide it from
Durrow. He cleared his aura out of habit, though he knew
the Terrans could not see it, and followed Williams across
the crater.

"FreeMaster!" called Durrow, beckoning to Arien.
His tone was too friendly, and the broad distortion of his
facial features that was called a smile made Arien shudder. He sensed deception, and approached the Terran
cautiously, trying to project disinterest across the gulf
that separated their races.

"FreeMaster, I need you to translate for me. We are
going to visit Revin, and I must be sure he understands
what I offer him."

Arien stared at him, wondering if the Terran had lost
his reason or his memory. The Eiku Mentor's threats were
as real as his rage. Another visit to Eiku would surely
mean death for both of them.

"Master Durrow," he said darkly, "if you return to
Eiku, you will not leave the keep alive."

"We aren't going to Eiku, FreeMaster. We will meet
Revin on neutral ground—in the disputed territory." The
false smile had disappeared. Durrow spoke like someone
accustomed to being obeyed.

Arien was shocked by Durrow's boldness. "The dispute is between Alu and Eiku. You have no right to become involved in it. Revin will be greatly angered by
your presence."

"Revin will listen to what I have to say, FreeMaster.
He wants to win this dispute, to bring his clan the riches
and honor that are rightfully theirs."

The anger Arien had taken care to hide flooded into
his aura. Durrow's disrespect for Ardellan customs en-

raged him. Again he thought of fleeing, but that would not prevent Durrow from confronting Revin. Durrow might take armed men with him, and that could result in death for Terrans and Ardellans. Arien's presence would inhibit Durrow to a small extent. If this was the interference Durrow planned, he might be able to thwart it.

Roletti and Williams were already aboard the shuttle with several other crewmen, standing before the open armaments locker. Durrow hurried Arien past them, shoving him into the navigator's seat and taking the co-pilot's chair himself. Arien fumbled with his safety harness, looking back over his shoulder. Roletti slammed the locker door and tripped the lock, then climbed into the pilot's seat and began her preflight check.

Arien held his breath and closed his eyes when the shuttle lifted off. His body was pressed against the seat, his head pushed back and his chest constricted as if a ribbon-snake was squeezing it. His hands gripped the armrests, crushing the life from an imaginary opponent. He hated riding in the shuttle. A moment later acceleration slowed and the pressure eased. He took a ragged breath and opened his eyes.

One of Roletti's aerial maps covered the navigation table. A fluorescent yellow circle marked the site of the dispute. At the back of the shuttle, the crewmen laughed and talked together quietly, but tension undercut their joking. Intrigue and deception danced between Durrow and his pilot. Arien wondered if Roletti had given the men weapons from the locker. He was being used, and it angered him, but he had no recourse now. The map offered him a temporary refuge. Focusing his eyes on the yellow markings, he let his mind drop to a deeper plane and began a power-gathering exercise.

The shuttle landed with a gentle thud. Arien was so deep in trance he did not notice the landing's effect on his body. Durrow touched his arm, and for a moment he thought they were back at camp. Then he recognized the shuttle. He fumbled with the awkward harness, followed Durrow to the port. Roletti flicked a switch, plunging them into darkness, and Durrow hit the controls with the flat of his hand. The inner door parted as the ramp slid into place. Before them loomed a rocky hill.

Arien and Durrow climbed in silence. The sky was overcast and the night dark, though both moons were high. The clouds diffused their light, making the sky a shade brighter than the land. The Terran and the Ardellan reached the crest of the hill, and looked down on Eiku's torchlit camp on the other side. Dark shapes moved among the tents, occasionally silhouetted in the torchlight. Arien also saw the flickering torches of the Alu camp far across the plain.

With Arien close behind him, Durrow descended the rocky slope and strode toward Eiku's camp. They encountered no guards. There were many younglings about, but they ignored the visitors.

Steeling himself for the battle that was to come, Arien pointed Durrow toward the lighted cluster of tents. Before they could move, a shadow separated itself from the darkness and greeted them.

"Depart," it said, blocking their path with outstretched arms. "If you disturb the Mentor, you will surely die."

The warning came too late. One of the tents began to glow, and then the flap was thrown open and Revin appeared. A ball of shimmer-light rode the wind above his head as he approached the intruders. The phantom, Revin's apprentice, returned to the shadows.

Durrow had never seen shimmer-light before. He was fascinated by the ball of brightness which hung, unsupported, in the air above the Mentor and followed his every move.

"Terran!" Revin spat the word like a curse, and his aura glowed with ruby fire. Arien was fearful of the Mentor's strength and power, and he stepped to Durrow's side with great apprehension. "Your life is forfeit to me now, Terran, and your death will give me great joy," called the Mentor across the gulf of sand and rock that separated them.

Durrow leaned toward Arien, and spoke softly in his native tongue. The Terran's aura was calm and steady in the face of such great power. He stood unmoving, defying an energy that could burn and blacken his body in an instant.

Arien raised his hands toward the angry Mentor, fingers spread wide in a gesture of protest. "The Terran points out that this is not Eiku land, Mentor. This territory is claimed by Alu and Eiku, and is therefore neutral ground. If you are honorable, your curse cannot touch him here."

Revin's anger grew. Arien took an involuntary step backward, grabbed Durrow's arm and tried to pull him back, too. The Mentor raised his arms above his head, supporting the shimmer-light with his palms. His aura flickered with power. For a moment Arien thought the Mentor would burn Durrow where he stood. Then Revin's hands moved apart, and the shimmer-light increased until it engulfed his head, hiding his features. A voice projected from the light, a voice of command that allowed no contradiction. "It saddens me to see you still in the company of this Terran, Arien. I will no longer listen to your words. Tomorrow this will become Eiku land. If you intend to live longer than that, you will leave now. I have no matters that bear discussing with either of you."

Again Durrow whispered to Arien, and Arien stepped forward to stand between him and the Mentor. "The Terran wishes only to offer his aid, Mentor. He believes he can help Eiku win this dispute. He offers some of his men, and the power of their laser weapons, in exchange for the mineral rights. Eiku will be well paid, Mentor. So the Terran claims."

As Arien spoke, the shimmer-light continued to grow, to a ball of greater size than any he had seen before. The energy Revin was expending was mighty indeed. Finally the ball engulfed the Mentor entirely, and still it grew. Arien was frightened. He stepped back, bumping into Durrow. All about them younglings gathered to watch the spectacle.

Arien whispered, "The Mentor will not deal with you, Terran. I fear he is angered enough to forget his honor, and kill you now. There is no profit in staying here." He pushed Durrow toward the hill, through the throng of younglings. The Terran did not protest.

They climbed quickly. Arien fell as he scrambled up the slope, and heard his tunic tear. He was relieved when they reached the top and could see the bulky shadow of the shuttle. He risked a quick look back at the camp. Revin was still standing in a huge ball of brilliant light. Arien shoved Durrow, and they tumbled down the far side of the hill and then sped up the ramp without looking behind them. The engines were on standby, purring softly, and the shuttle lifted almost before Arien reached his seat.

This time Arien welcomed the momentary pressure of lift-off. An instant later they were safely airborne, though they were not yet out of Revin's reach. Their brief meeting with the Mentor had accomplished nothing; in fact, it had angered Revin more. He would never deal with Durrow, no matter what wealth the Terran offered him.

Arien let his consciousness wander through the shuttle. He touched Durrow's feelings, expecting to encounter anger and disappointment, and sensed satisfaction instead. Roletti, too, was pleased. He reached for the other Terrans, and touched—nothing. A glance toward the back of the shuttle gave unnecessary confirmation that only he, Durrow, and Roletti occupied it now.

The meeting had been a diversion. Arien remembered the open locker, and knew the Terrans were armed. He had seen the weapons demonstrated when a pack of wild dogs passed near Durrow's camp. The lasers were deadly, and the crewmen were expert shots. He shuddered. There were plenty of rocks for them to hide in near the Eiku and Alu camps. They had only to wait for daylight, and their powerful weapons could kill any of the Ardellans. And there was nothing he could do to stop it.

2257:12/6, TERRAN CALENDAR
TO: NICHOLAS DURROW
FROM: MINERAL RESOURCE DEVELOPMENT
         GROUP, TITAN
RE: NEGOTIATIONS FOR MINERAL RIGHTS/
         ARDEL
   MESSAGE RECEIVED AND FORWARDED.
CONTINUE AS PREVIOUSLY ARRANGED.
CONTACT CODE 217AR/12, STANDARD
FREQUENCY.

Durrow smiled. This was going to be a sweet deal. His people would make certain that Clan Eiku was victorious tomorrow, and that Revin would not survive the fight. Then it would be a simple matter to arrange a trade agreement with Barnn. He could easily manipulate the apprentice.

Durrow would be glad to be free of this backward planet. He and Roletti were heading for Sol system with enough credits in their pockets to trade this old shuttle in on a larger ship. He had contacts and backers now. He was through being a hired boy.

Chapter 13

"It was a shuttle, Mrann. I'm certain of it." Sarah Anders stood beside the makeshift feast table, one hand on her hip, the other rapping the planks to emphasize her words. Viela watched her over the rim of his mug. The flickering torchlight lit half of her face, but left the rest

131

in eerie shadow. "The younglings saw it land behind the
Eiku camp, and woke me. I watched it lift off."

"If it left, it cannot present a threat to us," said
Mrann. He added a slice of nutbread to a plate overflow-
ing with roasted fowl, vegetable stew, and fresh scarletberries. Gathering his cloak close about his legs, he sat
on the bench beside Viela.

"You can't assume you are safe because the shuttle is
gone. It may return."

Viela put down his mug and poured tea for Mrann.
Sarah's presence at the dispute angered him. He pretended to ignore her, but he was aware of her frustration.
Her aura was a mottled, churning haze of green and yellow, turbid with agitation. The strength of the emotional
pressure she brought to bear against Mrann surprised
him.

Sarah's arm swept out to point to the great piles of
rocky debris on the plain. "The shuttle could have left
someone behind. There are many places to hide here.
One person with a laser weapon like the one used to kill
Hladi could kill everyone in the circle."

"No." Mrann set aside his knife and began to tear the
fowl apart with his fingers. "Revin would not allow it."

"Revin might not have been consulted," said Sarah.

This suggestion was more than Viela could tolerate.
"Adults do not hide from one another. That is a youngling trick."

"Terrans will hide if they have something to gain."
Sarah was angry. She stood with hands on hips and head
thrown back, glaring at Viela.

"They could not disguise their auras. We would be
able to sense them." Viela kept his voice calm and measured, and watched the green streak of irritation in Sarah's aura brighten.

"Then probe the area, Viela. Tell me that no one is
concealed in the rocks," she challenged.

"This discussion is not productive," said Mrann, still
dissecting his meal. "I want it ended now."

"You are ignoring a real danger," protested Sarah.

Mrann put down the fowl and reached for the runestaff
that was leaning against the end of the table. His fingers

closed around the knobby headpiece. As he charged it with the energy of his anger, the wood began to glow. He spoke in a tone that demanded obedience. ''You presume too much, Terran. You will not speak to me of this matter again.''

Sarah's aura swirled with frustration. She leaned forward, planting both palms on the table, and the plank tilted precariously. Hot tea splashed from Viela's mug. Sarah, her jaw set, brow furrowed, and eyes flashing, stared at Mrann. Her mouth moved, but she made no sound. Finally she straightened and stalked off toward the corral.

Viela was elated. The compulsion Mrann had laid on her forced Sarah to be silent, at least on this matter. Her foolish fears made Viela wonder about the sanity of humans. Adults could not hide from one another. No one would practice the kind of deceit she suggested. Then he remembered the scorch marks on Hladi's body, and Elver's burns. He shuddered. That was the work of a deranged individual. It could not happen again. Could it? He stared after the retreating Terran. Her kind had already caused his people much pain. Now she warned of greater danger to come. The only way to safeguard Ardel was to be rid of all the Terrans, forever. When this dispute was over, he would see that they were forced to leave Ardel.

The Healer had other matters to think about. Elver was walking slowly toward the table, supported on one side by Jeryl. A night of rest had not banished his weakness. His aura's color was pale, its shape nebulous, and his face was flushed in the torchlight. Viela feared he could not ride into the dispute and survive.

Jeryl helped Elver to a seat opposite Mrann. He poured tea for Elver and himself, but he did not take any food, and neither did Elver. The apprentice sat slumped on the bench, his long arms lying on either side of his empty plate. He did not touch the mug of tea.

That was all the evidence Viela needed. If Elver did not have the strength to eat, he had no strength to fight. A bristling in his tentacle nodes signaled the tension the

Healer felt as he addressed Mrann. "Mentor, I need to speak with you about your apprentice."

"Speak, then." Mrann did not look up. "We have little time before dawn calls us to the circle."

"Elver cannot attend that circle. He is much too weak to fight by your side." It was said; now he must deal with the Mentor's anger at being directly opposed.

Mrann put down his knife and looked at his apprentice. His eyes were piercing; Viela could almost see him stripping away layers of aura to reach the carefully shielded core of Elver's being. The apprentice met his eyes, never flinching.

"What say you, Elver? Do you have the strength to join me this morning?" He rested one hand on the top of the runestaff, his fingers stroking the smoothness of the wood.

Elver did not speak. He touched the staff, then took possession of it as Mrann let his hands fall away. Pulling it to his side, Elver let his other hand stray up and down the wood, tracing the delicate runes with a fingertip. His actions spoke for him. He would carry the staff into the circle for Mrann. He would fight.

Viela could not let Elver give up his life without protesting. There was one other who could carry the staff, who could aid the Mentor in Elver's place.

"Jeryl."

The FreeMaster had ignored most of the proceedings, his attention on his tea. Now he looked up, and Viela saw the fire burning deep in those icy gray eyes. Jeryl had needed his Healing as much as Elver had, but he had ignored Jeryl. Preoccupied with the obvious wounds, he had failed to see the deep emotional injury Jeryl had suffered.

He knew it was too late to help Jeryl now. The FreeMaster was deep in the throes of vengeance-fever, and would have to find his own way through the compulsion to a healthy existence. Perhaps aiding Mrann in the dispute, actively fighting Eiku, might help to banish his need for revenge.

"Will you fight in Elver's place, Jeryl?" Viela asked,

one hand toying with his cup. "You have the strength
and the will to channel power for Mrann."

Jeryl set his mug down. The fire in his eyes burned
brighter, but his words were cold and hard. "Hladi's revenge is a private matter. I will not sully it by confusing
it with this dispute." He rose and left the table, following
the Terran toward the corral.

"I am trained to do this, Healer," said Elver. His voice
was an open challenge though there was not much power
in the words. Sparks of ruby anger bristled from his aura,
especially near the crown of his head, but the rest of it
was dim and hazy.

"Let them be, Viela. It is too late to train Jeryl, and
Elver is the only apprentice I have. Give us your blessing,
or leave us alone."

There was a finality in Mrann's tone that made the
Healer shiver. A vision came to him—burnt forms scattered in a circle of blasted earth. He slammed his mug
on the table. It cracked, spilling tea across the planks.
Some of it dripped onto his feet. Before younglings could
be called to clean up the mess, he rose and fled to his
tent.

Pulling the door flap shut behind him, Viela folded his
legs and crawled to the thick center pole. He was afraid.
The terrible vision would not leave him. With swift hands
he made a depression in the sand and sat in it, legs
crossed and back supported by the pole. He closed his
eyes for an instant, touched the flame at the heart of his
being, and brought part of it forth to shine as shimmer-
light above his head. He faced away from the door flap,
for he would feel the presence of anyone trying to enter
there. He concentrated on the images that decorated the
far wall of the tent.

The Healer's tent was a large circle of tightly-woven
cloth, supported by a center pole that reached to his
shoulders when he was standing. The perimeter was
staked to the sand, except for a section that formed the
bottom of the triangular door flap. The tent was simply
protection from rain and sun; more elaborate shelters
were used for longer periods of time. For traveling and

short stays, the flat-circle tents were convenient and easy to carry.

A colorful triangular mural covered one third of the tent's wall, its tip touching the top of the center pole and the wide part anchored at the tent's bottom edge. The design was partly woven and partly embroidered, worked on bits of cloth sewn to the tent fabric. It was a symbolic representation of the journey that is a Healer's life. Parts of it were still incomplete.

Viela sought out one of the unfinished segments and concentrated on the ideas that might fill it in. He was trying to flush from his thoughts the vision of charred bodies, but his mind wove blackened forms into the mural, until he tore his gaze away in frustration.

The sand offered him refuge. Gazing at it, he sent his mind questing for peace in the beauty of the coming dawn, but again he saw charred forms sprawled on blackened ground. Recoiling in fear and disgust, he pulled himself back to reality long enough to search out a carved stone box filled with herbs. He took two leaves in his hands, one green and the other mottled brown, and crushed them between his fingers, letting the oils mix. He breathed the vapors deeply, savoring their bitter tang, and let them carry him into trance. The herbal oils helped expand his consciousness beyond the limits of his body. As long as the aromatics circulated in his system, he would be unable to use his body.

The trance took him. It was like a living thing, with an existence and a will of its own, and it carried him to places he had not explored before. He soared high into the air and looked down, but he did not see the physical world below him. Instead he read dynamic energy patterns. He watched them dance across the ground, forming, separating, and rejoining as the beings that were those patterns interacted. His time sense was distorted; he might have been there only a moment, or for days.

The wasteland was a good place to watch the patterns. There were few living things to clutter the energyscape. The power-lines of the planet made a grid that defined the area, giving him a reference. He picked out the energy vortex that was Mrann, and the two that were Jeryl and the Terran. Elver was weak. The Eiku masters were unfamiliar.

Letting himself flow with the power of the herbs, Viela spread his consciousness in thin wisps above the camp. Watching the movements below, he allowed the drug to dull his emotions. He did not want to feel the pain and fear that would come with injury and death. There would be pain enough when the trance and the dispute ended. The combatants would have no need of his services until then. In this kind of fight, injuries were either minor, or fatal.

As he ranged above the field, watching new patterns form where the younglings gathered outside the circle, he touched another mind. Startled, he pulled back, coalescing his consciousness into a form that was more defensible. The other seemed equally startled, for he also pulled away. After a few moments he came seeking Viela.

This energy vortex was familiar. It was a pattern that Viela had touched before. He searched his memory, and remembered a young FreeMaster who had shared his home many seasons ago, after the tragic deaths of his mates. Arien was his name. He had walked out of Alu one night and disappeared, and Viela never knew where he had gone.

Arien was angry. Viela felt that anger, and believed for a moment that it was directed toward him. Then he realized that Arien was beckoning him, trying to lead him toward something that was the source of his rage. With trepidation, Viela allowed his consciousness to disperse again, to flow outward in the direction Arien indicated.

In the rocks that overlooked the circle, he touched someone . . . alien.

Chapter 14

Sarah's alep tugged at the rein. She tugged back, but it swung its head low and nipped at a passing youngling. She slapped its neck hard as the youngling yelped and trundled out of reach. Pulling back on the single strap attached to its halter, Sarah turned the alep's head so she could glare into one of its eyes. She thought it unfortunate the Ardellans had never developed the bridle and mouth bit.

"This animal is more than I can handle," she said to Jeryl. Unlike the blocky, lumbering mounts she had ridden before, it was mountain-bred, sleek and fast, and the way it shifted its weight from side to side made her uneasy. When it turned to watch the other animals in the corral, its powerful neck muscles almost pulled the rein from her hand.

"You will have no problem controlling it," said Jeryl, sidestepping his smaller alep close to hers and tapping it between the ears. "It is restless now, but when the dispute starts, it will behave."

As if to contradict him, the alep lowered its head and nipped at his mount's foreleg. Jeryl's alep bared its teeth and danced aside. Sarah muttered a curse.

"I really think it would be better if we traded mounts. Yours is much more docile."

"Mine is also much smaller. It would not support your weight."

That was probably true. She had grown used to the lower gravity here, and often forgot that she massed more than all but the most rotund Ardellans.

Mrann and Elver walked toward the corral, their cloaks ominous shadows billowing in the pre-dawn breeze. Jeryl pointed to them. "Be glad that you are allowed to ride. Mrann and Elver will fight on foot."

"They should take the mounts, then, and let us stay on the ground."

"Dispute is always fought on foot. The only people allowed to go mounted at a dispute are the guards. It is a ceremonial role, since there is no one here to guard against, but Mrann has asked us to perform this service. We should respect his wishes and ride."

The sky was beginning to lighten in the east, but to the west, where Eiku had its camp, all was still dark. Sarah peered at a jagged patch of deeper blackness towering near the enemy camp. Was there really nothing to guard against? A shuttle had landed behind that mound of boulders. She was suddenly glad of the strength and speed of her mount, and the laser pistol she had smuggled out of Alu. It pressed hard against her stomach, and she slipped a hand under her tunic to adjust it. The weapon felt cold to the touch, despite the warmth it absorbed from her body.

If Durrow had placed armed mercenaries among the rocks, Mrann and the others would be easy targets. She intended to watch for the glint of sun on metal, a movement among the boulders, anything that might give away the location of an ambush. She was a good shot, but she must disable them quickly. If they knew about her, she would be as much a target as Mrann and the others. She could testify against them at a board of inquiry, even force them to face an interstellar tribunal for their illegal activities here. They would not let her leave the field alive.

She had not felt personally threatened in many years, not since the "accidental" shooting on New Kingston. The danger was exhilarating and frightening, or perhaps the exhilaration frightened her. She took a deep breath, and centered her mind on the task before her. Touching the sash tied to her upper arm, she whispered a prayer to Changing Woman.

Mrann stopped before her mount, his cloak settling slowly against his body. Elver paused one step behind him, planting the runestaff in the sand and leaning against it. A youngling carrying a torch passed by, and Sarah had a fleeting glimpse of Mrann's features. Lines etched his face deeply, and silver wisps of hair stood out about his head, but his eyes flashed with life and power. She could not tell if he was still angry with her. It would be futile to warn him again of the danger in the rocks. He raised one hand and touched the nose of her alep with his palm.

"Whatever happens, do not enter the circle. Power will not leave the boundaries we draw, so you will be safe outside the circle. I cannot protect you if you violate the sacred space." His voice was stern. A gust of wind lifted the bottom of his cloak. Elver leaned into the breeze, head down and shoulders swaying.

Mrann touched his palm to the snout of Jeryl's mount. Jeryl answered with the same palm-outward gesture, like a silent blessing. The Mentor dropped his hand, pulled his cloak close about his body, and turned toward the circle. Elver lifted the staff and followed him.

The plain was awash with the glimmering topaz light of dawn as they approached the circle and met the pair from Eiku. There was only one outrider for Eiku; he wore Healer's colors. The wind died suddenly, and in the stillness the four silver-gray cloaks of the combatants shimmered with an eerie light. The apprentices, Elver and Barnn, stayed behind each of their Mentors. They lifted the runestaffs above their heads, holding them with arms spread wide. Elver faltered once, and then stood steady.

Striding toward the center of the burn scar, Mrann and Revin raised their right arms. The metal bands of their office glinted on their wrists. They stopped six pace apart. Sarah watched them and the rocks, her eyes moving quickly around the circle. She saw a line of power stretching between the Mentors, extending outward to the staffs held by their apprentices. A blink, and the line was gone. As Aer's disc climbed above the horizon, the green and gold sphene and beaten copper of the wristbands sparkled, offset by the dull gleam of iron. Every detail in the circle was sharp and clear.

The runestaffs still held high, Elver and Barnn paced clockwise around the Mentors, redefining the circle they had traced the night before. They each walked one and a quarter times around, and stopped counterpoised to the Mentors. The four figures formed a square inside the boundary of the sacred circle. Sarah looked away, and saw an afterimage of a shining wheel, with slender spokes extending from Mentor to Mentor and staff to staff. She turned back to look at Mrann and the wheel disappeared.

Jeryl nudged his mount toward the circle, halting just outside it behind Elver. Sarah stopped her alep beside his, her back to the Alu camp. The animal was easier to control since Mrann had touched it. It moved carefully under her weight, using its central legs for extra support, and she guided it with her knees. Her right hand clutched the butt of her weapon under her tunic.

The Eiku guard stopped his mount on the opposite side of the circle, behind Barnn. His hood was drawn up, his face shadowed.

A dozen younglings from Alu formed a line behind Mrann. The first was one of the younglings who had accompanied naReill to stand watch last night. It was standing on the edge of the circle. A dozen younglings from Eiku stood behind Revin. An oppressive silence settled on the circle. No one moved.

"Why are the younglings gathering behind their Mentors?" whispered Sarah. Her gaze flicked over the rocks and the Eiku camp.

"They will provide energy for the Mentors to fight with," replied Jeryl without turning to look at her. "Legends say that once, the whole clan stood behind its Mentor at dispute. Now only the most expendable offer their lives."

"Offer their lives? Do you mean they will die?"

Jeryl ignored her. She reached for his arm, but a change within the circle caught her attention.

The air around Mrann and Revin was glowing. Clouds of subtle color that could barely be seen flowed downward from their upraised hands. The colors shimmered like a rainbow of jewels as they cascaded—amethyst . . . sapphire . . . aquamarine shading to deep emerald . . . topaz, and finally ruby—moving faster and faster until they blurred into a continuous spectrum. Each Mentor stood in the center of a shifting, glimmering rainbow cloud.

With one slow motion the apprentices extended their runestaffs into the center. The carved headpieces touched, sending out a shower of sparks; the circle was filled with blinding white light.

Sarah lost sight of the Mentors. The light was too bright; she could not look at them. She turned away, blinking tears from her eyes. Bright spots clouded her vision. She felt the coldly deliberate anger with which Mrann and Revin struck at one another in the midst of that ball of light. They were no longer in her world. They had created their own special place to do battle.

She had to block the light with a hand in order to see the rocks and the Eiku camp. Yet her mount did not shy from the blinding light, or try to turn its head away. Neither did Jeryl's alep.

"Do you see the light?" asked Jeryl, leaning toward her. "The aleps and the younglings do not see it. Only an adult can see the auras, and only someone with the potential to become Mentor can see the energy that they use against each other."

Sarah stared at him. She knew her mouth was hanging open. The Ardellans' simple door locks had frustrated her. She could not unlatch them without help. She could not make the shimmer-light that even a youngling must make before it could undergo metamorphosis. Yet she had felt Jeryl's rage when he faced the Eiku two days ago, and she had also touched Viela's anger. Now she saw the light. And what did he mean, the potential to become Mentor?

The light surrounding Mrann and Revin was swelling, brightening. Suddenly a line of power leaped out from it, touching a youngling at the edge of the circle. The youngling fell back, eyestalks shriveling and body scorched almost beyond recognition. The bones of its rib cage and spine poked through smoldering flesh. Sarah gagged. It was naReill's companion. naReill ran from the corral to the smoking corpse. As it bent over its friend, the body flamed once more. naReill fell back, wailing, waving a blackened tentacle in the air. Other younglings

ran to help it. Sarah jabbed her mount hard with one
knee, turning it away from the circle. Exhilaration had
turned to horror. Her stomach revolted, and she swallowed bile.

"Master Anders, look!" naSepti was bounding across
the sandy plain, its tentacles extended for balance and
eyestalks pointing toward the rocks behind the Eiku
camp. Sarah turned, but she could see nothing but the
light in the circle. Guiding her mount with her knees,
she drew her weapon. She heard Jeryl follow. Rounding
the far side of the circle, she saw it—the glint of sun on
polished metal. Pulling her alep to a stop, she raised the
pistol and aimed.

A sudden flash blinded her as her mount stumbled.
Belatedly her ears registered the whine of a laser rifle's
discharge. Then a second whine, but her alep was falling
and she had no time to think of anything but getting free
of the saddle. She freed her right foot from the stirrup
loop, stood high on her left leg and pushed, throwing
herself out onto the sand. Her ankle twisted beneath her,
and something tore. She smelled more burned flesh, and
this time could not hold her gorge. Then tentacles
grabbed her under the arms and pulled her to safety as
the alep came down, its forelegs almost severed. Blinking away tears and bright images, she tried to stand but
collapsed. The pistol was still in her hand. naSepti
dropped to the ground beside her, pulled Sarah's sash
free, and began to bind her ankle with it.

The pure white light that had surrounded the Mentors
was gone. Four figures were visible through an opalescent shimmer that slowly shrank to enclose only Mrann
and Revin. The apprentices stood near the edge of the
circle, facing each other through the opalescent haze.
Across the field the Eiku guard was down, his alep struggling on the ground.

Jeryl rode just outside the circle, trying to keep the
body of his mount between the assassin and Mrann.
When Elver was free of the field, he also moved to protect his Mentor. At that moment, Revin struck. Sparks
of power arced straight toward Mrann. Elver leaped forward, throwing himself into the haze. Thrusting his staff

between the Mentors, he intercepted the destructive charge meant for Mrann and channeled it through his own body. Light flared to twice Elver's height. His body was too weak to absorb the power. It charred, his cloak burning with a bright flame. He fell in a heap of ash and scorched flesh, the runestaff landing unharmed on the sand.

"Sarah, give me the weapon," shouted Jeryl as he rode away from the circle, leaving Mrann standing with neither apprentice nor guard.

Power flashed from the Mentor at that instant, angry scarlet rills cascading from his upraised hands and flowing over his body like blood. "No! I fight this dispute alone!"

Leaning far off his mount, Jeryl pulled the weapon from Sarah's hands. She recognized the fanatical light of vengeance in his eyes. Then he swung his mount away from her, kicking up a cloud of dust and fine sand as he rode toward the rocks.

The three combatants in the circle formed a triangle, with Revin and Mrann exchanging bursts of power and Barnn using his staff to counter Mrann's attacks. Mrann was weakening, his once pure white aura fading to a blue glow. Sarah was afraid that the battle would soon be over. Revin's apprentice moved slowly along the edge of the circle toward Mrann, interposing his staff closer and closer to the Alu Mentor. Each time Mrann attacked, he intercepted the power and tried to turn it back against its originator. Behind him, more younglings burned.

Revin's aura flared red as Mrann's hands produced strong white power and sent it directly against Barnn. In an instant the apprentice was a charred smudge on the sand, while his Mentor's aura guttered impotently.

Jeryl stopped just short of the rocks, and he called out a challenge that Sarah did not understand. Raising his weapon with both hands, he waited for an answer.

High in the rocks a Terran appeared, and before Jeryl could take aim, Sarah heard his weapon discharge. Then Jeryl fired, and the whine became a scream before it exploded with a violence that left a crater in the pile of stone.

Victory echoed in Sarah's mind, but she felt no joy in it. Turning back to the circle, she saw Mrann's blasted body on the sand. The laser shot had destroyed his legs and part of his torso. She turned away, retching. The victory belong to Eiku. All her arrogance, all her fine plans had come to naught. She had failed to save Mrann from the assassins.

"No!" The scream was vocalized, but Sarah scarcely heard it. The emotions that accompanied it overwhelmed her. She lost herself in Jeryl's anger as he rode past her. With a derisive gesture he hurled the laser pistol toward her. He vaulted from his mount and was into the circle in two long strides, kneeling beside the burned body of the Mentor. Lifting Mrann's right arm, he slipped the wide wristband from it. Then he stood, his own arm upraised, and faced the Eiku Mentor.

"I CHALLENGE." His feelings were as distinct and powerful as words spoken aloud. "I HAVE THE RIGHT."

Reaching high above his head, Jeryl slipped the copper band onto his wrist. The hues of power began to flow down his body, amethyst giving way to sapphire, aquamarine, and emerald, followed by brilliant topaz and the ruby red of anger. The red manifested longest, but then it, too, flickered and he glowed white as Mrann had done.

Revin raised his arm once again, accepting the new challenge, and he began to glow with the force of his thoughts and feelings. Fatigue caused his power to flicker, but he had the advantage of experience.

The two figures stood on opposite sides of the circle, brilliant white light glowing around each of them. Sarah struggled to her feet, leaning on naSepti. She wanted desperately to watch this contest, but the blinding light made that impossible. When she closed her eyes to shut out the brilliance, the circle became clear in her mind. The combatants resolved into two poles, one a ruby-red fire of vengeance, the other pure white righteousness. Sarah touched the other watchers, too, the Masters of Eiku and Alu who felt the conflict in their clanhalls, Viela, and with him a solitary mind whose pattern she did not know. She felt their strength flowing past her to the combatants, and watched the Mentors' auras increase in power.

Something cold and hard was pressed into Sarah's hands. It was a distraction, and she pushed it away. "Please take it, Master." naSepti's words were soft and quiet, but insistent. "It is necessary. We have seen others moving above in the rocks."

It did not occur to Sarah to open her eyes. She turned her mind toward the pile of rocky debris behind the Eiku camp, and felt among the stones for things that did not belong there. It was a simple task for her to find the two surviving Terrans. Their fear was a beacon as bright as the dawn, and she traced it down through the stones until she touched them.

Words were outside her capabilities, but emotions were not. She reached into the minds of the humans, searching out their vulnerabilities. When she touched their weakest parts, she closed on them, twisting and turning the foundations of their minds until they retreated from her in panic and collapsed into unconsciousness.

Jeryl and Revin still faced each other in the circle, and Sarah turned her mind back to them. She was afraid for Jeryl. He bent low to the ground, reaching for something she did not recognize. Revin extended his arms to strike. Choking down a shout, knowing that it would go unheard, Sarah prayed that Jeryl would be able to counter Revin's power in time.

Jeryl's fist closed on the object he desired. It was the runestaff. He lifted it high in his left hand, grasped the other end with his right, and held it horizontally above his head. The wristband of his new office flashed with Revin's reflected power.

The force loosed by the Eiku Mentor was arcing across the circle toward Jeryl. Sarah detected streaks of emerald and sapphire in Revin's attack, and realized that he was weakening. Jeryl knew it, too, and countered with the strength of the runestaff. Holding it like a quarterstaff, he intercepted the arc of power an arm's length from his head and threw it back across the circle toward the other. Behind him, four younglings sacrificed their life energies to give him strength.

A howling cry rose from Jeryl's throat, washing over Sarah and making her shiver. His thirst for revenge welled around him, deepening the color of his aura. One last bolt of power arced outward from his hands and the staff before his tall frame collapsed.

Murmurs of victory began again, but Sarah was afraid. Her mind no longer perceived either Jeryl or Revin. Slowly, with great trepidation, she opened her eyes to look at the circle.

The earth was charred black, blacker than the original burn scar. Five bodies were scattered about the circle, three of them burned beyond recognition. The gray heaps that were Revin and Jeryl showed no sign of movement, and Sarah feared they were both dead. She started toward the circle, pulling away from the youngling who supported her, but her ankle gave out and she collapsed onto the sand. Her head struck a rock, and pain took her.

Chapter 15

Viela's consciousness floated above the battlefield. He looked down on devastation. Burnt bodies were scattered on the sand. Around the circle, the power-lines of the planet were warped, bent by the awesome energy that had been channeled into this spot. The circle itself was intact but fading, with no one left to give it power. One of the aliens who had hidden among the rocks was dead, the others unconscious. Viela felt no sorrow. Anger and hatred filled him.

With a Healer's skill he touched each of the bodies inside the circle. A single ember glowed among the charred husks. One life continued, weak and faltering. Viela's training asserted itself, urging him back to his body so that he could nurture that life.

His consciousness was still twined with Arien's. They shared rage and an urge for vengeance. He could not tell which feelings were his and which were the Free-

Master's, as he began to disentangle himself from the other's mind. The drug-induced trance was ending, and he felt himself pulled downward toward his resting body in the Healer's tent.

Arien was withdrawing, too. His body was calling him. It took much energy to keep physical and mental forms functioning at such great distances from one another, so much that sometimes the unwary or careless died in trance. Arien's anger and hatred were dissipating his strength. If he did not return to his body soon, there would be one more death added to the cost of this dispute. Viela felt him withdraw, and hoped he could reunite mind and body in time.

The bit of life within the circle grew neither stronger nor weaker. Viela watched it as he worked his way back to his body. He drove his mind downward, becoming aware again of the physical part of himself. His organs cleansed the drug from his system, and he pushed them to work harder, faster, so that his physical senses would begin to function again. He explored inward, reawakening his body, making first the small muscles move, and then the larger ones. His time sense returned. In moments he had enough control to stretch and crawl out of the tent.

The devastation in and around the circle was awful. Blasted husks that were once younglings littered the ground. One of the aleps was mortally wounded, blood oozing from its damaged forelegs as it thrashed and rolled in the sand. Viela shuddered at its agony. He rose and strode to its side. Muttering an ancient blessing, he knelt and pulled his dagger from its sheath. A single swift stroke stilled the alep's heart and ended its pain.

The Terran lay nearby, unconscious, but life was strong in her. He walked past, leaving her to the ministrations of a youngling, and entered the circle.

Ignoring the charred bodies of Mrann and Elver, Viela strode to the place where Jeryl lay facedown in the sand, his arms outstretched, his hands still clutching the runestaff. Beyond him were more burnt husks—Revin and his apprentice, and Eiku younglings.

Jeryl lived. Viela squatted beside him and took the

runestaff from his burnt and blistering hands. He placed
his own hands above Jeryl's head, palms open and fingers
spread, not quite touching him. With slow stroking motions he drew his hands down Jeryl's body, following the
circulatory system, tracing the major muscles and organs. He encountered strained muscles and bruised flesh,
but no serious injury other than the burned hands. His
palms hovered above the blistered flesh as he felt Jeryl's
pain, and explored the damaged nerves and muscles. The
hands would heal, scarred but not stiff.

Jeryl's life force was nearly depleted. He had put all of
his power into that last killing blow, and it might yet
cause his death. Viela's hands traced an elaborate pattern
in the air over Jeryl's torso. He centered his thoughts on
the power of the planet beneath him, and began to draw
that power upward into his body. Placing one hand on
Jeryl's brow and the other on his chest, Viela let a controlled stream of energy flow through him and into the
FreeMaster's weakened body.

It was a technique any Master could use, but only a
Healer would dare to use it on an unconscious patient. It
took skill to regulate the flow of power, to give the patient enough energy to survive without putting him into
shock. Viela fed the power to Jeryl slowly, monitoring
his nervous system to make sure there were no block-
ages. When the energy built to a dangerous level in his
arms because the burnt hands would not permit it to flow,
Viela coaxed new pathways around the damaged nerves.

When he could do no more, Viela rose and called his
apprentice to his side. "Take him to my tent," he said.
"Wrap him in blankets and put heated stones at his feet.
Make an infusion of knobby bark and scarletberry flowers, and swab his hands with it. Call me if he wakes."

Mrann and Elver lay where they had fallen, grotesque,
misshapen corpses sprawled on the sand. Viela walked
to Mrann's side, stood looking at the blackened wrist that
had worn the Mentor's bracelet. "I warned you," he
whispered. "Elver was not strong enough to fight. Jeryl
should have been your second." He touched the scorched
hand in benediction, then waved a crew of younglings
into the circle.

"Wrap the bodies in linen," he told them. "There is a bolt of it in my cart. Put them carefully into the cart. Then gather the dead younglings into a pile, and burn them. We will return to Alu today."

There were three-hands-plus-two dead and injured younglings, no great loss except for naReill. Viela found it sitting beside the body of its dead friend, keening and rocking. One of its tentacles was burnt and shriveled, damaged beyond all possible healing. naReill was now an imperfect specimen; it could not undergo metamorphosis. No one could predict how the malformed tentacle might manifest when the youngling emerged from the cocoon. Torma was waiting in vain for this youngling to be his mate. Another would have to be chosen. The cost of this victory was too high. Mrann, and Elver, and if the new youngling could not be chosen and cocooned soon enough, Eenar and Torma's House, which would go into oblivion.

Eiku younglings were removing the bodies of Revin and his apprentice, and gathering their dead to be burned. Their Healer was down outside the circle, obviously injured and attended by his apprentice. Viela strode toward them, intending to offer his help, but the apprentice waved him away. He turned back, saw the runestaff, and went to pick it up. The heavy wooden staff vibrated with power, but it was undamaged.

Walking back to his tent, he passed Sarah and naSepti. She was still unconscious, sprawled on her back in the sand, one arm caught beneath her body, her tunic torn and her sash wrapped about her ankle. Viela believed that she and her trade treaty were the cause of this dispute, but as a Healer he was obligated to help even her. He tossed the staff to a passing youngling and knelt at her side.

"Unwrap the ankle," he ordered naSepti as he explored the back of her head with his fingers. There was a large, hard swelling there, but he sensed only bruising, no bleeding under the skin. The injury to her ankle was more serious. The ligaments were stretched, and torn in one spot. The ankle would have to be kept immobile until they healed. Her weight and skeletal structure meant that a splint would be necessary. He had no knowledge of her regenerative powers; she might heal in a day, or several six-days.

"Get someone to help you carry her to her tent." He would bind the ankle there. He had one task to complete first. There were two Terrans alive and asleep in the rocks. If he could capture them, he might prove to the council that Terrans could not be trusted.

Viela climbed the rock pile, arms and legs spread wide as he searched for secure footholds, his splayed fingers gripping rough spots on the boulders. He had climbed for pleasure as a young Master, but that was many seasons ago. He was too old for the climb to be easy. He reached upward, cut his palm on a jagged piece of crystal, clung tightly with his other hand as he searched for a safer hold. His blood made the rock slippery. The center pad of his left foot was bruised and cramping. He should have stayed below, and sent the younglings up alone.

Behind him a hand of younglings scaled boulders, climbing on one another until one of them found a secure position and turned to help the others up. Their tentacles found holds on the rock more easily than did Viela's fingers, but their short legs gave them no purchase. One of them slipped, and was left hanging by a tentacle over open space until the others managed to pull it to safety.

Viela was not concerned about the younglings. He had to reach the top before the Terrans regained consciousness. A violent explosion had blown a crater in the rock pile, destroying one Terran and his weapon, but if the others had weapons that were functional, they could kill him in an instant.

Climbing steadily, Viela kept as much rock as possible between himself and the crater. He reached a point where he had to come out into the open, but he sheltered behind a boulder for a few moments first, one arm lodged in a crevice. He had sure footing, and he relaxed the cramped muscles of his foot, willing more blood to the affected area.

Peering over the boulder, Viela could see into the crater. There was nothing left alive there, though the stone that had not been blown away was energized and vibrant. There were gobbets of flesh and splinters of bone splattered among the broken rocks.

Two Terrans were alive, somewhere beyond the crater. No movement betrayed them to the Healer. He sensed the vitality of their bodies, though their minds were still. With care he circled the crater, motioning the younglings to follow him, and trod a narrow path along the top of the rock pile. He found the ropes the Terrans had used for climbing, fastened to the rock with small metal darts.

The Terrans were crumpled over their weapons. Poking and prodding did not rouse them. Viela helped the younglings to bundle each of them into a rope sling, and to lower them down the back of the rock pile using their own ropes. They would be cramped and bruised when they awoke.

Viela was unwilling to touch the alien weapons. He slipped out of his tunic and wrapped them in it, tying the bundle to his sash. Then he followed the younglings down.

Viela tried to control his rage as he climbed back down. He wanted to wreck these Terrans, to make them suffer in payment for the damage they had done. So many lives lost, and the traditions of the clan violated. Nothing he could do would be sufficient vengeance. He stored his anger, knowing it would help him to see the survivors, and the dead, back to Alu.

Chapter 16

The sleeping furs were heavy, and too warm. Sarah threw them off, and shivered as the cool night air penetrated her light shift. The furs covered her again of their own volition. She opened her eyes, but the world was out of focus. She smelled wax burning, saw a flickering point of light. She blinked, and saw a candle; blinked again, and recognized the stone walls of her room in Alu Keep.

Something warm and soft brushed her chin. She turned her head. A throbbing pain began at the back and circled around to her forehead, reminding her to move slowly. A youngling arranged the furs, tucking them under her chin.

"You must rest, Master," it said. "The Healer has ordered it."

Sarah stretched, pushing the furs away again. The cold air felt invigorating. The pain in her head was receding. She tried to sit up, and the room spun. Squeezing her eyes shut, she lay down again. Pain lanced through her skull when her head touched the bed. She moaned.

"Are you unwell, Master?" asked the youngling. "Shall I get the Healer?"

"No," she said softly, opening her eyes. "I'm all right. Have I been unconscious long?"

"All day, Master. Since you fell this morning and hurt your head."

Breathing deeply, eyes closed, Sarah sat up slowly and leaned against the wall. The youngling pulled the furs up around her shoulders. Gratefully, she snuggled into them. Probing the back of her skull with gentle fingers, she found a bump that was large and solid, but no broken skin. She diagnosed bruising and a mild concussion, but no fracture.

"You're naSepti, aren't you? You were at the dispute." She closed her eyes and tried to remember. "You pulled me out from under my mount when it fell."

"Yes, Master."

"How did I hurt my head?"

"You fell on a rock. Do you not remember?" asked the youngling.

Sarah thought. She remembered the laser blast, Mrann's death, blackened bodies in the circle, and Jeryl's challenge. Jeryl fell . . . "Jeryl!" She opened her eyes to banish the vision of his motionless body sprawled on the scorched earth. "Is Jeryl all right?"

"Yes. His hands are burned, but otherwise he is uninjured. He is very weak. The Healer has ordered him to

rest in the Mentor's chamber.'' naSepti took a flask from
the table and offered it to Sarah. "The Healer left this
potion to help you rest. He said that you should drink it
when you woke."

She shook her head, and grabbed at the wall as nausea
and vertigo flooded through her. The sound of her heart
pounding filled her ears. She took a deep breath and
swallowed, and let the room right itself. When the vertigo subsided, she opened her eyes.

"I have potions of my own, naSepti. Do you know
where my pouch is?"

"I put it on the table, Master. Shall I bring it to you?"

"Please." Her transceiver beeped once, the signal that
it had received and stored a message. She looked at it,
and saw the blinking yellow light on the automatic monitor. "How long has my machine been making that
noise?"

"Since we returned from the dispute," said naSepti.
It trundled to the table and came back with her pouch.
"What does it mean?"

"There is a message waiting for me."

"The Healer said you should not move. Can I bring
the message to you?"

"No. I'll get up." She had suffered concussion once
before; it had not kept her immobile. She pulled out her
medkit and spread it open on the bed. The vial of analgesic tabs was nearly full. She popped the top, shook out
two of the coated tablets, and swallowed them without
water. Then she moved slowly to the edge of the bed,
lowering her feet to the floor. Her left leg was heavy and
stiff below the knee. The ankle throbbed. She bent over,
saw the leather splint that bound it, and remembered
twisting her ankle.

Her medkit contained splinting material and joint-
wrap. Her first aid training suggested flexible wraps for
sprains and stiff wraps for broken bones and torn ligaments. She thought back to the accident. It was unlikely
that she had broken anything, but she might have torn
some of the ligaments. The splint on her ankle was well-
made, probably the work of Viela. "Did the Healer tell
you how badly my ankle was injured?"

"You stretched the muscles and tore something. He said you must wear the splint until it heals."

She lifted the ankle back onto the platform and began untying the thongs that fastened the splint. "I have some material in my medical kit that will make a lighter, better splint," she said when naSepti protested. She peeled back the layer of stiff leather and pulled away the soft batting that lined it. Her ankle was swollen, and purple on the outside beneath the joint.

"I have a larger pack in the cabinet. It is this same color." She pointed to the orange medkit. "Can you bring it to me, please?"

naSepti rummaged in the cabinet for a moment, found the heavy pack and dragged it across the floor to her. Sarah leaned over, but straightened quickly when her head began to spin. "There is a blue bag in the pack. Will you hand it to me?" It contained her chemical cold packs. She chose the medium-sized one, twisted it sharply to break the seal and mix the chemicals, then pressed it against her ankle as she felt it grow cold. It would stay cold for thirty minutes. That would be more than enough time for the analgesics to take effect. The message could wait that much longer; it had not triggered the red priority light. She leaned back against the wall and closed her eyes.

Sarah's ankle was numb from the cold, and her head had stopped throbbing. She chose one of the ultra-thin stiff-wraps and formed it to her ankle and the back half of her foot. It was lined with knit cotton to prevent chafing. When she had it fitting as tightly as she wanted it, holding her foot and ankle in a comfortable walking position, she pressed the seal closed. She pulled out the tube of hardener and painted the chemical onto the bandage. It began to harden immediately.

In ten minutes she was able to walk on her wrapped ankle. It throbbed as she lowered it to the floor. Gingerly, she rose, trying not to jar her head, and keeping most of her weight on her right leg. Leaning on naSepti, she pulled the furs close about her shoulders and limped to the table. She stabbed at the keypad of her transceiver with her index finger, watched as the printer produced a hard-copy, then touched the reset control.

naSepti brought her a chair. She sat, and reached for the twisted lump of black metal that lay beside her transceiver. She turned it over and over in her hands. "What happened to this laser pistol?"

"It is the weapon you took to the dispute," said naSepti. "When you touched the Terrans in the rocks, you damaged their weapons, and this one."

Sarah gave the youngling a disbelieving stare. "I could not do this. The controls are melted and the power supply is fused. It would take great heat to do this much damage."

"There was no one else who could have done it," naSepti assured her. "Your mind has great power. The Masters have felt it. It was you."

Her fingers trembled as she set the deformed weapon on the table. Much that she had experienced at the dispute seemed like a dream now. Perhaps it had all been a fantasy. She might have imagined the blinding light, the visible bolts of energy. Logic told her that was not possible. Her body was injured, and the damaged weapon lay beside her. But she could not accept the idea that she had destroyed the laser.

Her hand strayed to the message. The *Blackhawk* was on its way back to the Ardellan system. It would be within range of voice contact tomorrow, and expected to make planet-fall early the next day. She would finally have some support against Durrow; she hoped it was not coming too late.

"Will your people come and take away the two Terrans who are in the storeroom?"

Sarah frowned at the youngling, puzzled by its question.

"The two you touched in the rocks. The Healer had us bring them back and put them in the storeroom, but the Masters do not know what to do with them."

"I don't understand, naSepti. How did I 'touch' them?"

The youngling bounced over to stand in front of her, its tentacles twining together in gestures she could not interpret. It was distressed and excited, and that made it inarticulate. "You just touched them, Master, their minds . . . You made them sleep. More than sleep—the Healer could not wake them. We found them in the rocks, next to their weapons, and they could not hurt us."

It made no sense to Sarah. She remembered knowing that there were Terrans in the rocks, probably Durrow's mercenaries, but after that she had no memory of them. The Healer might be able to explain what this youngling could not express in any way she understood. She did not want to think about it now. She would see Viela and the council leaders in the morning. She started to rise, but the youngling rushed to her side and settled her back into her chair.

"What is it you want, Master? I will get it for you. The Healer does not want you to walk on your foot."

She wanted to see Jeryl, to make certain he was all right, but she could not tell naSepti that. "Tea. Tea, and perhaps some bread and preserves."

"I will bring it right up," the youngling said as it dashed out the door.

Sarah waited until the hall was silent before she thumped her way to the door and across to the Mentor's chamber. One swift glance told her that Jeryl was not there. Guided by intuition, she moved as swiftly as she could to the main stairway. She clumped down the steps, pain jarring her ankle, her head throbbing. A moment later she was through the last hallway and slipping out the back door of the clanhall.

Ardel's twin moons were hidden by clouds and the keep's great wall was all in shadow, but Sarah knew dawn was approaching. She felt Jeryl's presence near the dark stone. Hobbling along, her left arm begging support of the ancient wall, she made her way toward Hladi's resting place.

The night air was chill, and she was glad of the fur clutched about her shoulders. She took each step deliberately, placing her bound foot on the stone with care. Once she slipped on a pebble and almost fell. Smothering a cry of pain, she stumbled against a warm, yielding, motionless object and clutched at it for support.

"Jeryl," she said as she righted herself, and she was not surprised. The cloaked figure lifted its hands from the wall and turned to look at her. Sarah pushed his hood back, her right hand tracing the line of Jeryl's hair, brushing it away from his face. "You should be in bed, Mentor. Come back to the clanhall with me." In memory she saw him striding to the center of the circle, his arm upraised and the Mentor's wristband glinting in the sunlight. Now his blistered hands glistened with salve.

"Do not call me Mentor!" Jeryl's voice was low and insistent as he turned back to the wall.

Sarah leaned forward in the dimness and her hand brushed Hladi's burial urn. The soft stone felt warm and smooth, almost alive. "You do her no good if you kill yourself. Come back with me," she pleaded.

"No. I cannot rest until this duty is done." A pinpoint of light appeared at the tip of one of his fingers, and he traced it in flowing, swirling designs on the stone. The rock glowed red with heat where the light touched it. When he finished, he slumped forward against the wall, and Sarah pressed close to him.

"What does it say, Jeryl?" she asked, tracing the runes with a fingertip.

"That Hladi's death was the price of Clan Alu, for without it there would have been no one to challenge Revin, and Alu would have been lost to Eiku."

"Alu demands a heavy price," said Sarah. But if the assassin had not killed Hladi, Elver would not have been injured, and he could have been more help to Mrann. Who knows what the outcome of the dispute might have been? Hladi's death was not the price of Clan Alu, it was the price of involvement with Terrans.

"Alu demands more than I can give." Jeryl sagged against Sarah, and she put her arms around his slight body and supported him. She pulled him away from the wall. They leaned on each other as they walked back up the path to the kitchen door.

Chapter 17

Viela met dawn on the shadowed streets of Alu. He was trudging uphill toward the clanhall and breakfast, when the sun's rays struck the great stone bier. He stopped, gazing at the shrouded bodies of Mrann and Elver. Suddenly he had no appetite. He remembered their blackened forms lying in the circle, and hoped their souls had fled before the flames destroyed their bodies. A peaceful death kept the soul near the body until cremation, but this violence was more than any soul should have to bear.

Their sacrifice had won victory for Clan Alu. Eiku was vanquished and subject to Alu's will, but Viela foresaw many problems. Alu's council must govern Eiku, but the council's new leader had no experience. And Torma, who had experience enough to guide two clans, had retired to his House. He waited there for Viela, and for the youngling who was to be his mate.

Viela turned away from the bier, and strode back down the hill toward House Kirlei. A chill wind ruffled his hair. He shivered, tucking his hands into the sleeves of his heavy cloak. Younglings bustled past him, but he did not see them. His thoughts were filled with Torma and his mate Eenar. He dreaded telling them of naReill's injury, and its unsuitability for metamorphosis. They had waited long for his cocooning, and now they would have to wait again, while another youngling was selected by the council.

He did not notice the intricate mosaic fronted entrance of House Kirlei. He passed through the port and the first chamber like a trancewalker. When he became aware of his surroundings, a youngling was taking his cloak. Another offered a bowl of hot water to warm his hands. Viela dipped his fingers and dried them on a soft cloth, while his higher self wandered the house in search of Eenar and Torma. He found the Mother awake but qui-

escent, reclining in her chamber. Torma stood just outside the door, his aura fluttering with anxiety. Viela went
to him.

There was no gentle way to break the news. "naReill
was damaged in the dispute. It is no longer eligible for
metamorphosis."

"Mrann promised me that naReill would not be one
of the sacrifices. He said that he would keep the youngling safe for House Kirlei!" Spikes of sickly green fear
erupted in Torma's aura; gouts of ruby and milky amber
speckles testified to his anger and distress.

Viela understood, but he had no words to calm the
Master. Quick motions of his hands drew the symbolic
shields around them, preventing Torma's aura from spilling into Eenar's consciousness. Then Viela reached out,
touched the Master's chest with one hand, and gave his
arm a sharp quarter turn. His spread fingers contacted
nerve centers, calming Torma without interfering with
his awareness.

"The Mentor did not lie to you," he said to Torma.
"naReill's burns were an accident. It ran to the aid of a
fallen companion, and gained nothing for its compassion
but a shriveled tentacle. Its friend was already beyond
help."

"What are we to do? Eenar is nearly fertile. I must
cocoon a youngling soon."

The Healer shared Torma's concern. Eenar was fast approaching the point of fertility, when she must mate or die
without reproducing. If she died, Kirlei would be lost forever. Torma would complete his life as a FreeMaster, without
House or home. Alu could not afford to lose another House.
A youngling must be found to take naReill's place.

Torma's control was returning. He no longer broadcast
panic. Viela removed his hand from the Master's chest
and cleared his own aura. He maintained a single thread
of contact with Torma's aura, to monitor it. "I must see
Eenar," he said, and Torma gestured assent. He led the
Healer into the Mother's chamber, but stayed in the shadows, out of her sight.

Eenar was resting on the platform, two younglings sitting beside her and stroking her, a tray with a pot of

medicinal tea and a bowl of herbs set nearby. With gentle
psychic nudges Viela explored her aura. Things were not
as bad as he had feared. They still had time—Eenar's
progress toward her fertile period had slowed. If they
could locate a youngling and cocoon it today, the new
Master would emerge in time to join Torma for the mating. Kirlei could be saved, if they worked quickly.

Turning, the Mother reached for her mate. She was a
sensitive; she knew Torma was in the room even though
she could not see him. If his control broke and he let her
sense his distress and fear, she would panic. Viela stepped
between them, one hand behind his back motioning
Torma to leave the chamber. For a long moment there
was no sound. He feared that the Master would not obey
his command, but then he heard the shuffle of feet, and
the door opened and closed again.

The Healer went to Eenar, and settled her back on the
platform with gentle hands. His fingers hardly touched
her person, but his aura infiltrated hers, soothing the rip-
ples of concern he found there. He searched through the
bowl of herbs, finding snikgrass and wonder-leaf. These
he twisted together to release and mix their oils. He
dropped the little tangle into the tea, stirred it with a
finger, and poured a cup for Eenar. She would sleep, but
not too deeply. They would awaken her for the cocooning.

"We must see Jeryl, and have him choose a youngling
to take naReill's place," said Torma as the Healer
emerged from the Mother's chamber.

"That is more properly done by the council," replied
Viela, taking the Master's arm and guiding him away from
the chamber, and Eenar. If Torma lost control, it must
happen as far away from his mate as possible.

"There is no time to have Oreyn call the council. The
choice must be made now, and the cocooning done today." There was an urgency in Torma's voice that penetrated the Healer's exhaustion and awakened his
sympathy. "Jeryl is Mentor now. In times of dire need
he can act for the council."

"The Mentor is adviser to the council and protector of

the clan. You allowed Mrann to take a more active role in the governing of Alu because you trusted his experience and his judgment. Jeryl has neither experience nor judgment. He is Mentor by default, and by the strength of his drive for revenge. I do not believe Oreyn and the rest of the council will trust him with decisions that are rightfully theirs to make.'' As they left the House, Viela looked toward the clanhall and the biers, and he mourned for Mrann, a leader he had admired and respected, even though they had not always agreed on the path Alu should take.

Torma shrugged. ''What you say is true, but I cannot stand by and wait for the council to make this decision. Kirlei must have a youngling today. I will force Jeryl to make a choice. The council may censure me later, but Kirlei will be safe.''

The walk up the hill was cold, though Torma did not seem to notice. His aura bristled with purpose. His life, the life he had always looked forward to, depended on the coming confrontation with Jeryl. Viela understood. He had once made a choice between that life and the life of a Healer. Torma had no choice. If a youngling was not cocooned in time, he would lose Kirlei, and all that it meant to him.

When they passed the biers, with their burdens shrouded in gray cloth, Torma paid no attention, but Viela nodded once in acknowledgment of the Mentor who had been his friend and rival. Then he followed the Master up the steps and into the clanhall, throwing open his cloak to accept the warmth the building offered.

Jeryl was on the staircase. His face was flushed, his hair disheveled, and his tunic looked as if he had slept in it. One hand brushed the wall, seeking support or guidance. He was not wearing the Mentor's wristband.

''Mentor!'' called Torma, waiting at the bottom of the stairs. ''We need your guidance. Will you come down and help us?''

''Leave me alone, Torma.'' Sharp, angry words echoed in the open hall. ''I do not wish to be Mentor.''

''What you wish to be has little to do with what you are, Jeryl. When you took the badge of office from

Mrann's wrist you became Mentor of Clan Alu. You agreed to protect and defend the clan, to advise the council, and to be the spiritual leader of Alu. If you were not prepared to accept those responsibilities, you should not have put the band on your wrist. Where is it now?'' asked Viela. A Mentor never removed his wristband.

"It is in Mrann's room. Wear it if you like, Healer."

The contempt in Jeryl's voice made Viela cringe. If the new Mentor of Alu would not discharge his traditional obligations, Alu had more problems than the Healer had thought.

"I give the band to you," said Jeryl. "It means nothing to me. I have a death to avenge." He stumbled on the sixth step but recovered and came down the last few with a semblance of dignity.

"I cannot wear it," said Viela. "You accepted the power of Mentor when you fought in the dispute. You must also accept the responsibilities of that post. Torma has a request to make of you."

"Yes." Shocked by Jeryl's words and attitude, the old Master had forgotten for a moment the purpose of this visit. "My House is fertile, Jeryl. I am in need of a mate."

"That is a matter for the council," replied Jeryl, dismissing them with a gesture. He turned down the hall toward the kitchen, and Torma and the Healer followed. The warm, bright room was filled with the fragrance of fresh-baked bread and hot tea. Ortia, the rotund kitchenmaster, was busy at the ovens, and Sarah was drinking tea at one of the long tables.

"The council chose naReill, but it was injured in the dispute, and is now deformed. We would ask Oreyn to reconvene the council and have it choose another youngling, but we have no time to spare. You must appoint a youngling to be cocooned today. This is Torma's request, and he will bear the censure should the council be angry."

From the sleeve of his cloak, Viela pulled a strip of writing-cloth coiled about a wooden rod. "This is the council's list of eligible apprentices. I have removed the names of those who died in the dispute, but there are still

more than a hand to choose from.'' He offered the list to
Jeryl. Jeryl would not take it, so Viela laid it on the table
before him.

A youngling bustled in, a tray of mugs balanced on
three of its tentacles. Jeryl grabbed one, filled it with
tea, and cut a large slice of bread before sitting next to
Sarah. He gestured at the bowl of preserves. She passed
it to him.

"May the great sun smile on you this morning, Healer,
Master Torma.'' Her greeting was formal, demanding
a formal reply, but Viela was too angry with Jeryl to both-
er.

"You are Mentor of this Clan by your own actions,
Jeryl. Accept the duties that are part of the position.''
He pointed to the list of younglings. "Make a choice.''

Jeryl glanced at the intricate runes. Each designation
identified an individual by name, House of birth, and
apprenticeship. No qualifications were listed. A youngling could not reach this stage of the selection process
unless it was capable of making shimmer-light and had
proved itself competent as an apprentice.

"naSepti, please bring me some more tea,'' called
Sarah, and the youngling trundled to the hearth to get the
pot.

"There, Torma, you have your mate,'' said Jeryl,
pointing to naSepti. "This one is on the list, and is as
good a choice as any.'' He seemed amused, though Viela
could not be sure if it was humor or irony.

"There is another duty the Mentor must perform, Jeryl.
There are two Masters of Alu outside on the biers, waiting to be cremated.''

Jeryl looked up from his breakfast. "No,'' he said, and
his aura became hard and cold and difficult to read. "I
will not accept that responsibility. Take back the wristband, Healer. Perform the rite yourself.''

"I cannot. The band of power is yours until you die,
Jeryl. You knew that when you put it on. Accept your
fate, and perform your duty to Mrann and Elver.'' He
took naSepti by the sash and led it from the room, with
Torma following close behind.

* * *

The Mother's sanctuary of House Kirlei was bright with midday sun, shining through the leaf-covered skylight. Eenar lay in a pool of light. The crystals projecting from the wall above her head were also touched by that brightness, and beginning to glow with the energy they were storing. These crystals were violet, and delicately shaped with many small projections. A gentle touch could break them, but they had survived for generations in this sacrosanct room.

Torma pulled the heavy stone door shut behind them, and set the wards that sealed it. No one would enter or leave the chamber until the ceremony was over and naSepti was safely cocooned, or dead.

The youngling was unafraid. This metamorphosis, if it was successful, would give it a new life as a Master, with the privileges and responsibilities that went with a House. If unsuccessful, naSepti's life would end, but that ending held no fear for the youngling. Worse would be the fate that befell so many of its companions—a life working in the fields or as a servant, with no chance of reaching maturity. Becoming an adult was every youngling's wish.

Viela guided naSepti to the platform where Eenar lay, pushed the youngling down to squat in the sunlight, and then stepped back. He had no duties in the ceremony, except as witness. It was sufficient that Torma wanted him here. He had witnessed many cocoonings at Alu, though never before had he been present at a second in the same House. Viela was old, but only with this set of cocoonings would he pass the bounds of his first generation. Torma was the first he had known as a youngling whom he would see become a Mother.

Torma came to kneel beside naSepti, raising his arms above his head and cupping his hands to the energy that streamed in through the skylight. He was still for a long time, but the increasing intensity of his aura testified to the process going on in his mind and body. The nebulous, glowing form that surrounded him grew, and merged with the aura of his mate. Then, in a dance that was almost too slow to see, the energy form enveloped naSepti, welcoming it into Kirlei.

The youngling was in the beginnings of trance. With a

gesture of blessing, Torma brought his hands down to caress Eenar. The puddled secretions of her reproductive glands stained the coverlet. Dipping his fingers into this sacred moisture, Torma anointed naSepti. The liquid activated dormant glands in the youngling's body, and naSepti collapsed a moment later, as the metamorphic processes began.

Gathering naSepti into his arms, Torma carried the ovoid body to a shallow grotto in the rock wall of the sanctuary. He propped the youngling in the grotto, letting the rotund body sink back against the stone. Already glands in his arms were producing soft white silk, and he spun it out through two opposing fingers, anchoring the threads to the rock and weaving a soft, protective covering over naSepti's form.

Closing his eyes, Viela let himself sink into awareness of the youngling. With skill honed by years of use, he touched naSepti's mind and felt the soft silk covering its body. The delicate fibers enveloped it, binding its tentacles to its sides. It should have been frightened by its inability to move. Instead it was calm, protected and nurtured within the safety of its new House. The silk continued to cover naSepti, climbing slowly toward its face; the stone of the wall behind it gave it warmth and support. It was no longer naSepti. It was part of Kirlei, and soon its already-changing body would make it Master of the House.

Chapter 18

Sarah still sat in the kitchen, sipping her third cup of tea. She lounged with her back to the fire, letting the heat soak into her strained muscles. Her splinted ankle was propped on a stool, the injured area resting on a chemical hot-pack. She had learned much about first aid from her father. One of the first things he had taught her was that strains and sprains should be treated with cold-packs for twenty-four hours, to keep the swelling down, then treated with heat to improve circulation and speed healing. Sarah sighed. The ankle had stopped throbbing, and the warmth was soothing.

Jeryl sat at a table, eating slowly. His blistered palms were covered with pads of soft cloth. Sarah thought he looked tired, but stronger than when she had found him at the mourning wall. Perhaps he had slept. He was still angry; Sarah could feel it from across the room. His rage had not died when he killed the Eiku Mentor. Perhaps that was why he refused the title of Mentor, and the responsibilities that accompanied it: he could not accept any of it until he purged his anger.

She missed Mrann. He had been her friend, the only one she had made on Ardel, and she mourned him. His death was more than a personal loss; it negated their work on the trade agreement and the spaceport plans. All that time wasted haggling over details, and the hurried transmissions to Sandsmark to get Commission approval of the changes! The agreement could be renegotiated, but without Mrann to back her, the council was not likely to cooperate. The Healer and many of the older council members wanted nothing to do with Terrans.

If Jeryl took up the Mentor's wristband, she might convince him to support her. Perhaps he would have some influence with the council. But what could convince him to accept the role of Mentor?

Sarah finished her tea, and felt the beginnings of pressure in her bladder. That meant climbing the stairs to her room, and another awkward battle with the sanitary facilities. She struggled to her feet, limped to the back stairway. The outer door stood open. Sunlight danced along the top of the mourning wall, but the burial niches were shrouded in shadow. She saw hundreds of urns in every shape and color—round urns of milky green stone, angular ones of violet crystal, slender ovals of a shiny black substance. Intricate, spidery runes were carved beneath each one. If she could read them, they would tell her the history of Clan Alu.

Soon two more urns would rest there, bearing the ashes of Mrann and Elver. Their runes would tell the story of Alu's dispute with Eiku.

First there must be a funeral. She was surprised how important this was to her. Her bond with Mrann had been strong enough to need the resolution provided by a parting ceremony. She did not adhere to the Navaho belief that the ghosts of the dead wandered about, haunting those who spoke their names aloud. A funeral would not appease Mrann and Elver, or put their souls to rest. She did not know the significance of a funeral to the Ardellans. Until she had heard Viela speak of the cremation, she had not known there would be a ceremony.

"Why won't you perform the cremation of Mrann and Elver?" she asked.

Jeryl ignored her question, so she hobbled to the table and stood in front of him. Playing on the anger Jeryl could not disguise, she covered his cup with one hand, pinning it to the table just as he reached for it. "Mrann and Elver gave up their lives for Alu. You owe them the dignity of cremation and burial in the mourning wall."

"No," said Jeryl, rising. "Alu owes them cremation and burial."

"What frees you from the obligations of Mentor?"

"I am not Mentor. I never accepted those obligations." His voice was harsh, his eyes flashing.

"You used the power when it was to your advantage. Now you would deny the duties that go with that power." Jeryl moved toward the door, but Sarah stepped in front of him again. "You can't run away from this, Jeryl. Mrann performed Hladi's cremation; you owe him the same in return."

Jeryl stopped. He stood silent for a long time. When he looked up, Sarah thought she saw fear in his eyes, but she knew this for her own projection. Whatever was there was too alien for her to understand.

"If I do this, I accept it all—the power and the obligations."

"You accepted it when you took the band from Mrann's wrist," said Sarah, but Jeryl gave no sign that he heard her.

"Master Anders!"

She turned to see who called her. Oreyn had entered through the back door, hair flying and cloak flapping.

She lifted a hand in greeting, and turned back to Jeryl. He was gone.

"I must speak with you, Master Anders," said Oreyn.

"May the sun smile on you today, Master Oreyn." He was the new leader of the council. Sarah accorded him the same respect she had always given to Torma and Mrann. "How can I help you?"

"Viela brought two prisoners from the dispute. They are Terrans. We have imprisoned them in a storeroom, but we do not know how to dispose of them."

"Prisoners?" Sarah smiled. Perhaps Nicholas Durrow was locked in that storeroom. She would certainly like to "dispose" of him. "I would like to see these Terrans, Master. I must go to my room first, but when I return, would you take me to them?"

"Yes, but you must be careful. They are very dangerous."

Sarah came down the stairs from her room with the portable recorder from her transceiver in her pocket, and the rolled survey map clutched in one hand. She followed Oreyn through the clanhall to a narrow corridor under the back stairs. It ran past a row of storage closets. The last door at the end of the hall was open. Two Masters sat on stools in the corridor, one on either side of the open doorway.

Oreyn stepped aside so that Sarah could peer into the tiny, windowless room. Light from a single torch illuminated the corner where two black-clad Terrans lounged. When they saw her, they scrambled to their feet.

The woman was of medium height and build, with muscular arms and legs showing through her tight coverall. Her dark hair was clipped short. Her companion was male, taller, well-muscled with the same short haircut and an extra pad of fat on his belly.

Sarah took a step forward, and was stopped by a barrier she could not see. Nothing physical touched her; her leg simply would not pass beyond a certain point. She looked from one side to the other and realized that she could not pass the seated Masters. Stepping back, she turned to Oreyn.

"I would like to talk with the prisoners. Is that permitted?"

Oreyn gestured to the guards. "Open the room, please."

The Masters shifted almost imperceptibly, and Sarah walked into the room unimpeded. Again the Masters moved, and she sensed the barrier closing behind her, making the room an effective prison. The Ardellans did not realize that a closed door, latched and barred on the outside, would be enough to hold the Terrans.

"Names," she commanded.

They looked at each other, and the woman nodded.

"Gresch," said the man, "Howard K. Gresch."

The woman's voice was soft and musical. "I am Elizabeth Arnaud."

"This is an informal interrogation," said Sarah. "Depositions will be taken aboard the *Blackhawk,* which will take custody of you when it arrives later today or tomorrow. Until then, you will be held here. You are not required to answer any of my questions.

"Who are you working for?"

They exchanged another glance. Elizabeth spoke. "We are employed by Captain Nicholas Durrow, as security guards."

"Why did Captain Durrow come to Ardel?" Sarah asked. Gresch stared stoically at the wall. The woman pursed her lips but remained silent.

Sarah tried another subject. "Where is Durrow's camp?"

This time Gresch spoke. "We camped at an old crater in the wasteland. I can show you the location, if you have a map."

Arnaud glared at him. He shrugged. "Durrow abandoned us. Why shouldn't we tell her where he is? He'll have moved on by now, anyway."

Sarah unrolled her map and pressed it against the wall. The corners automatically adhered to the stone. She handed Gresch a marker and watched as he marked a place in the wasteland. The map showed it to be a wide crater, created by the impact of an astral body innumerable years ago. He made no comment; neither did Arnaud.

"Why were you at the dispute?" asked Sarah.

Neither one of them answered.

"How were you captured?"

Fear clouded Gresch's eyes. He looked at his feet, shuffled them, then threw his head back and looked into Sarah's eyes. "Something attacked my mind," he said. "It knocked me out." Arnaud nodded.

For an instant Sarah remembered "seeing" them high in the rocks, letting her thoughts reach out and touch them, hurting them. . . . The memory was gone. She was responsible for their capture, and their fear, but she did not know what she had done. She might never know.

It was midday before she left the prison. Arnaud refused to answer any more questions, and Gresch only answered those that would not implicate him in any wrongdoing.

Sarah was warming herself in the kitchen when Jeryl came in, his hair disheveled and his cloak dusty. For the first time since the dispute, he was wearing the Mentor's wristband.

"I will conduct the cremation of Mrann and Elver now," he said to her. "You may witness it."

She smiled. Apparently Jeryl had made a decision about his place in the life of Clan Alu. She clambered to her feet and followed him through the clanhall, limping. A youngling opened the wide front door for them. At the bottom of the steps, bright afternoon sun drew sharp shadows across the shrouded bodies of Mrann and Elver. No one waited in the circle. She touched Jeryl's arm. "Where are the mourners?"

"There are no mourners. Whom did you expect to see?"

"I thought the council members and Viela would be here," Sarah said, even as she realized that she was imposing her Terran standards on this very different society.

"They mourned when they felt the death cries of Mrann and Elver. Today we only dispose of their physical bod-

ies. There is no need for anyone else to be present.''
Jeryl went down to the granite bier.

Sarah stayed on the steps, leaning against a post. A
pair of younglings trundled across the circle, carrying a
heaping basket of laundry between them. The life of the
clan moved on.

The charred and blackened bodies of Mrann and Elver
lay on the cold stone, covered by soft gray cloth. Between them, bright and unscarred by the dispute, rested
Mrann's runestaff. At the foot of the bier, where Jeryl
stood in silent meditation, was a beautifully crafted urn.
It was round at the bottom, very full of body, swirling
up to a narrow triangular neck. Carved of stone, it was
utterly black, absorbing all the light that touched it and
returning nothing.

"Only one urn?" she asked.

"They died together in dispute," replied Jeryl. "It is
tradition to place them in the same urn."

After a time Jeryl leaned forward and reached for the
runestaff. It glided effortlessly toward him, moving in a
graceful but impossible arc from the bier to his hands.
Grasping it with both hands, he raised it above his head
and held it parallel to the ground as he walked around
the bier. He stopped at each corner of the great granite
platform, leaning forward to touch the staff to the shroud.
The gray cloth seemed to change color when he touched
it, but the effect was so brief that Sarah could not be
certain.

His circle complete, Jeryl stood at the foot of the bier
with his back to Sarah. After leaning the staff against the
bier, he picked up the urn. He removed the lid, setting
in on the ground, but the body of the urn he placed in
the center of the bier between Mrann and Elver. Then he
took up the staff again, and walked to the head of the
bier.

Jeryl raised the staff above his head once more, standing very still. The wooden runestaff began to glow. Sarah
was mesmerized by the sight of it. Then Jeryl extended
the staff, touching the end of it to the urn which burst
into flames. The gray cloth ignited, but Jeryl stood where
he was, the runestaff still in his hands. Startled, Sarah

backed toward the safety of the clanhall. Flames engulfed the entire bier, hiding the urn and the staff in the conflagration. She could see Jeryl's face through the flames. He never moved.

The fire lasted only moments. The flames died, leaving the staff unharmed in Jeryl's hands. The urn glowed with heat and an odd, shifting color, but nothing remained of the cloth or the bodies. The top of the bier was smooth and clean, unscarred by the fire.

Jeryl laid the runestaff on the bier, and carefully settled the lid on the urn. Then he turned and walked away.

Sarah stumbled down the steps. Surely she had just witnessed magic. She held her hands over the bier, testing for radiant heat, but the granite was cool. She touched it. It was clean, dry, cold. She walked to the head of the bier, where the glowing urn rested. The urn radiated warmth. On the stone beside it lay the Mentor's wristband.

2257:12/8, TERRAN CALENDAR
TO: MINERAL RESOURCE DEVELOPMENT
         GROUP, TITAN
FROM: NICHOLAS DURROW
RE: NEGOTIATIONS FOR MINERAL RIGHTS/
         ARDEL
   CONCLUSION OF TRADE AGREEMENT
DELAYED DUE TO UNANTICIPATED SHIFT OF
POWER AMONG ARDELLAN REPRESENTATIVES.
NEGOTIATIONS CONTINUING. FAVORABLE
RESULTS EXPECTED WITHIN A FEW DAYS.

Nick Durrow laughed as he punched in the routing code for Titan. The message would eventually find its way to Austin Duerst's desk. Long before that it would be intercepted by the communications computer on board the

Nagashimi ship that was waiting nearby. Duerst's official negotiator would learn of the delay in less than an hour. It pleased Durrow to think of him pacing in his room, impatient to be about his job and concerned about the delay.

Meanwhile, Durrow wanted to break camp, and dispose of some excess baggage. It was time to get rid of Arien. The Ardellan knew too much about Durrow's part in the dispute. Roletti wanted to kill him. Nick was tempted to let her do it, but he had learned from his experience at Eiku Keep. Ardellans knew when one of their number died. These FreeMasters were a close-knit bunch. They would come looking for Arien's body, and if they couldn't find it, they would know whom to blame for his death. Durrow shrugged. He was going to Berrut to negotiate with the GuildMasters there; he did not want Arien's guildmates asking questions and causing problems. Nor did he have time to arrange an "accident." There were other ways to be rid of inconvenient personnel.

Chapter 19

Angela Roletti was a good pilot. That was why Nicholas Durrow employed her. She brought the shuttle in over the trees at a low angle, scanned the meadow to be certain it was empty, and set down easily in its center. They were less than a kilometer from Ardel's largest city.

Durrow was in a hurry. He was out of his seat and at the shuttle's port as soon as they touched ground. Roletti barely took time to power down the engines before she rushed after him.

"Captain!" She reached for his arm, but dropped her hand when she saw his expression. She lowered her voice. "Take me with you."

"No. Stay here with the others." He nodded toward the four geologists, who remained in their seats. His voice was a husky whisper. "I've already lost three people. I don't want to risk any more."

Roletti's hand dropped to her laser weapon. "I can take care of myself."

"That's why I want you to stay here. We can't leave those four alone. They don't know how to handle weapons." He could not tell her that she would be a liability in Berrut. "If I'm not back by nightfall, take the shuttle back to the wasteland. Rendezvous with me here at noon tomorrow."

"At least take a communicator . . ."

Durrow remembered his previous meeting with Starm of the Messengers Guild. The old GuildMaster had coveted the copper and iron that Durrow carried, but was suspicious of the powered tools. He had warned Durrow not to bring them back to Berrut.

"No. It might be mistaken for a weapon." Roletti began to protest, but he waved her to silence as he stalked down the ramp.

Too many things had gone wrong with his plans. It should have been easy to make a trade agreement with one of the clans. He offered iron and copper in exchange for the titanium ores that were abundant in the wasteland. Clan Alu refused to deal with him, and Clan Eiku was defeated. Now he would trade with the GuildMasters of Berrut. They were businessmen, they would understand the advantages he offered.

No one must ever know that he had interfered in the dispute between Alu and Eiku. The cost of that action was already much too high. Arien told him all three of his people had died, killed by the explosion of a malfunctioning weapon. That was a blessing; if they had been captured and turned over to Terran Union officials, they could testify against him. They were good people, but they were mercenaries. Their loyalty was purchased, and lasted only as long as they were paid.

Now the only person who knew of his treachery was Arien. He had abandoned the Ardellan in the wasteland with only one alep and no water. Dehydration would kill him before he could reach the mountains.

Durrow's new plan was dangerous, but he was used to

playing dangerous games for power. He was good at it.
And this time he would depend only on himself.

Berrut was not much of a city, by Durrow's standards.
It was a sprawling village of wood frame buildings, graveled and stone-paved streets, and open gardens. Revin
had claimed that more than ten thousand adults lived here.
Most of the Masters lived in the guildhouses near the
center, the Mothers and younglings in crèches on the outskirts, surrounded by gardens and orchards.

The streets were laid out like the spokes of a wheel,
extending inward toward a large court at the hub. Durrow
passed inns, shops, and crafthalls, interspersed with tree-
filled parks. He was conspicuous in his form-fitting black
coveralls, but he had been seen in Berrut before. Starm
had told him that the Union survey team had spent days
here, talking with the GuildMasters and visiting the shops
and crafthalls. The Ardellans had become accustomed to
seeing Terrans in their midst. The younglings and Masters who crowded the street paid little attention to Durrow. Still, there was always a clear path for him to walk,
opening before him and closing behind him. He strode
toward the center of town, past workshops and guildhouses bustling with early morning activity. He saw little
to differentiate this street from one in Eiku Keep, except
that most of the construction here was of wood rather
than stone, and it was much more recent.

Durrow reached the hub of the wheel. In the center of
the court, looking like an overgrown child's puzzle, was
an ancient stone building with new additions of wood and
brick springing up all around it. It was the seat of Ardel's
ruling council. The most important guildhouses ringed
the court, and it was one of these he sought—the Messengers Guild.

The great green door was closed. Durrow took a deep
breath before he raised his hand to the knocker. He raised
the weight, let it fall once, and a skew-eyed youngling
wearing the green sash of the guild opened the door and
stepped aside, gesturing for him to enter. It did not care
that he was a Terran. He was a customer, and this guild
was a business, like any other.

The first floor of the guildhall was one large room,

divided by a wooden staircase into eating and working areas. To the left stood long tables and a wide hearth where younglings prepared the day's food, and to the right were arranged ranks of desks and a wall of cubbyholes filled with rolls of writing-cloth.

GuildMaster Starm sat at the front of the hall, a little apart from the apprentices who copied runes at their desks. Durrow waited for a gesture of recognition before he approached. The Messengers Guild, charged with maintaining communications within the city and between the widely separated keeps and fishing communities, was the most powerful guild on Ardel. Through his messengers, GuildMaster Starm effectively controlled the loosely-organized government by monopolizing the spread of news and information.

Starm was an old Master with white hair and cold gray eyes. The lines of his face were harsh, and Durrow was wary of him. He motioned the Terran to a chair and offered tea, which Durrow refused with what he thought was a polite nod. He waited for the GuildMaster to refill his own cup before he began to speak. The words he had rehearsed tumbled through his mind, the phrases tangled and confused, and for the first time he felt uncertain.

"Master, I bring you bad news," he said, halting over some of the Ardellan words. He hoped Starm would think any inconsistencies in his story were due to problems with the language. "The dispute between Alu and Eiku is over, and both Mentors are dead." This much was truth, as Durrow knew it.

The apprentices at the closest desks stopped working to watch the GuildMaster, but his expression did not change. "How do you come by this information?" he asked.

"FreeMaster Arien observed the dispute, and told me."

"Where is the FreeMaster? Did he not come with you?"

Now the dangerous work began. Durrow wove a net of lies, hoping there would be just enough truth in it to deceive the GuildMaster. "Arien left me to return to his guildhall. He seemed very upset by the results of the dispute.''

''And of Alu and Eiku, did either of the Mentors' apprentices survive the battle?''

A strand of truth: "No, Master, they did not." He paused.

A half-truth, carefully constructed: "FreeMaster Arien told me that someone interfered with the proper conduct of the dispute." Durrow kept a tight rein on his emotions, trying to present a neutral front to Starm. The alien might misinterpret any gesture he made; better to make none. He tried to quiet the heavy thudding of his heart.

"Who would interfere in a dispute?" Starm's words were stern and unbelieving.

"A Terran."

The GuildMaster watched him intently, and Durrow dared not let his eyes drop, because now he spoke the essential lie. "The Terran who was trading with Alu used a forbidden weapon to kill Revin of Eiku."

All of the apprentices stopped working, their attention on the pair at the front of the room. Durrow felt Starm's gaze slice through him, but he did not waver. Intuition told him that a mistake now would cost him his life, forfeit for lying to a messenger. He was a gambling man and he played the bluff well. The tension between them was a palpable entity, but Durrow did nothing to lessen it, and finally Starm looked away.

He made a loud clapping noise, and several of the apprentices rushed forward. "Call the messengers," he ordered. A youngling bounced up the staircase, and a moment later it returned, followed by a score of Masters wearing the bright green tunics of the guild. Starm beckoned three of them to his side, but the others arrayed themselves before the GuildMaster, ignoring Durrow. An apprentice passed among them with a basket of small tiles. Each messenger selected one and examined it before dropping it in the pocket of his tunic.

"The Mentors of Alu and Eiku are dead, and Alu stands accused of treachery. Ride to the clans and the waterfolk," Starm commanded. "Inform the Mentors and the GuildMasters that the assembly will meet on the day after Festival, to demand an account of the actions of Clan Alu.''

There was glee in Durrow's heart, but he stamped it down, and tried to project concern and neutrality. He watched the messengers file out, wondering how many of the Mentors would come for the assembly. The key to his plan lay with the GuildMasters, who might be bought with promises of trade goods from beyond the sky.

Starm turned to the three messengers who stood beside his chair. He held three more tiles, which he distributed among them one at a time. ''Ride to Alu Keep and inform the Healer that he is summoned to testify before the assembly. Do the same at Eiku Keep. Ride to the FreeMasters' guildhall in the mountains, and tell FreeMaster Arien that he must come to testify. The tiles will be their passes into the great hall.''

The last name was like a cold knife in Durrow's chest. Adrenaline rushed through his system as he thought of Arien. When that messenger reached the guildhall and learned that Arien was not there, FreeMasters would be sent out to search for him. They might find him, and bring him to Berrut in time to testify. Durrow had to keep the FreeMaster away from Berrut. Arien knew the truth about the dispute, and could destroy all his plans with a few words.

The messengers left. Starm turned back to Durrow. ''You will testify, also,'' he said, and his tone left no room for disagreement.

''Certainly,'' responded Durrow. ''I would also like to meet with some of the GuildMasters, regarding the possibility of a trade agreement with my people. I would appreciate any introductions you can give me.''

''That would be . . . interesting,'' said Starm. ''You may stay at the guildhall. It is preferable to an inn.''

''Thank you. I would be honored.'' Durrow was thinking fast. ''I must return to my ship, to get some maps and things I will need. I will return before sunset, if that is agreeable.''

''I look forward to you joining me for dinner,'' said Starm.

* * *

"That messenger must not reach the FreeMasters Guild." Durrow looked up from the navigation table where he was sorting maps, selecting the ones he would need in Berrut. "I can't have Arien here, damaging my credibility with Starm and the assembly."

Roletti laughed, a short, sharp sound. "It would be easy to kill Arien."

"No. It would take you too long to find him in the wasteland, and his people would feel him die. They have some sort of psychic connection with one another." Durrow shook his head, but did not look up. "It'll be better to stop the messenger. If the message is never delivered, the FreeMasters won't go looking for Arien." He folded the maps and slipped them into his pouch, along with a small communicator. This time he must take the risk, so that he could recall the shuttle when he needed it. He would keep the device carefully hidden. "Detain the messenger, and be sure to get the tile he carries. It'll be in his tunic pocket. I'll need three days, maybe four, to arrange the trade agreement. Then we'll contact Duerst's negotiator. He can offer the GuildMasters a better deal, and I'll conveniently disappear. We'll kill the messenger, dump his body in the wasteland, pick up our credits, and be on our way."

Chapter 20

Arien woke with cramped legs. Refreshed but stiff, he opened his eyes to the midafternoon sun, rose, and stretched. The long power-gathering meditation had strengthened his mind, but his body needed food and water. He hoped Durrow would not require him soon. He wanted to make a hot meal.

He turned, and froze. The crater was empty, the little community of tents spirited away as if it had never been there. For a moment Arien doubted his sanity. Then he saw the pile of refuse near the ridge, and the shuttle's landing marks. Sand was already drifting across them. In a few days they would be invisible, but the garbage would remain, a Terran legacy.

Arien examined his belongings. His sleeping furs and supplies were tossed in a pile, and the tent was gone. His mount drowsed on its tether line, its legs bent and propped against each other at strange angles to give it purchase on the slope. The Terrans had fled, leaving him nothing that was not his own.

With a sudden realization he dove for the water skin, his hands digging quickly into the sand where he had buried it to keep it cool. It was still there. Pulling it from the earth, he saw it was more than half empty. He cursed long and loud, startling the alep. He should have filled it before he settled into trance. The nearest water was two days away, near the FreeMasters guildhall. Two days on a fresh mount, with a second animal to carry his gear.

Durrow had stranded him, knowing he would have no choice but to leave his equipment and most of his supplies and ride for the guildhall. He had plenty of food, but that did him no good without adequate water. In the dry heat of the wasteland, he and the alep would need much water. He hefted the skin speculatively. Carefully rationed, there was enough to get them home.

Arien considered making psychic contact with the guild. He could have them send a party to meet him with extra water and mounts. The contact would take time and much energy—more of each than he could spare right now. Even if they could set out at once, it would take them two days to reach him. In that time he and his mount would die of thirst.

It was clever of Durrow not to have killed him out-of-hand. His death cry would have brought the other FreeMasters into the wasteland to search for his body. Led by the echoes of his psychic presence, they would have found his remains quickly, and then gone in search of the Terrans.

He wondered where the Terrans were, and what they were doing. Alu and Eiku would be wary of them, but they might find refuge with Clan Renu, or among the guilds in Berrut. Obviously they wanted him occupied so that he could not ruin their plans, whatever those might be.

Muttering a string of foul oaths under his breath, Arien began sorting his gear. He kept a small amount of food for himself and his mount, and his extra dagger. The rest he wrapped in the sleeping furs, laying them in a sheltered spot. Perhaps one of the other FreeMasters would ride back with him in a few days to retrieve them. Of course, that assumed he would reach the guildhall, which was not a certainty.

His hot meal forgotten, Arien saddled his mount. Gathering up his water skin and food pouch, the spare dagger tucked in his sash, he set off toward the mountains and home.

Messenger Chemi held his mount's rein in one hand, twined through his fingers in a casual grip. The other hand fingered the tile in the pocket of his tunic. The intricate rune burned into its smooth surface told him his destination—the FreeMasters guildhall, a half-day's ride into the mountains. This was one of the shorter trips, and he counted himself lucky for drawing it twice in his last three assignments. He was getting too old to ride long distances. His last trip to the sea had left his body tired and aching for a six-day. Next mating time, he would retire to the nursery and Motherhood, passing his green tunic to his apprentice, naLiiss. Until then, he would hope for the short trips.

He was riding his usual mount, a big gray. Beside him naLiiss rode a small dappled alep. The youngling had been his apprentice and companion for nearly seven seasons, even longer than he had had the gray alep. He would not admit to feeling affection for naLiiss, but there was a strong attachment between them. Chemi had no doubt that when the time came, the youngling would be a fine messenger.

A forest of scarlet conifers skirted the edge of the great plain and climbed the mountainside, reaching for the sun. Chemi and naLiiss rode close to the trees, in the shadow of the great mountain, and watched the wool-deer that grazed on the lush pasture of the plain. Once a fuzzbird trilled at them from the top of a thorn-bush, and Chemi pointed to it. "Listen to the song," he said to his apprentice, "for it will warn you of danger on the trail. The shriek of a fuzzbird once saved me from the claws of a hungry tol."

It was late afternoon when they found a trail that turned away from the pasture and led up between the trees. They climbed through forest for a time, and then the path crossed a long, narrow meadow. The near end was almost level, but the far end curved up the mountain and was hidden by a grove of trees. The grass was short, for the season was early and the nights still cold. When the weather warmed, the herders would bring their wool-deer here to graze.

Chemi and naLiiss were alone in the meadow, except for a cascade of tiny yellow flowers in the sunniest part of the valley. No birds flew overhead. No small animals darted through the grass. The only sounds were the plodding and snorting of their mounts. The silence made Chemi uneasy. He scanned the trees, wondering what predator had frightened the meadow's residents.

The trail was in deep shadow when they reached the trees and began climbing again. Chemi conjured a ball of shimmer-light to float above his head, to frighten the night hunters. They were near the pass to the Free-Masters guildhall. It was safer to keep traveling than to stop and make a fire for the night.

A branch snapped. Something large was moving in the forest. Chemi's shimmer-light flared. A fuzzbird shrieked. Light flashed. A high-pitched whine hurt his ears. He twisted in his saddle to look at naLiiss, but his alep stumbled and fell. Its front legs were gone. naLiiss was on the ground, a black figure leaning over it. Chemi scrambled away from his dying mount and ran for the forest. Something grabbed his tunic. He kept running, felt the tunic tear. He tripped, and fell headlong into blackness.

Chemi woke slowly. He lay naked and bound on a cold, hard surface. He kept his eyes closed while his mind explored the condition of his body. His wrists were bound behind him, his arms twisted and the cartilage aching at the joints. His legs were bound and almost immobile. He could turn from side to side, if his hands did not get caught beneath him, but any other movement was impossible.

His mind reached out to explore the space around him and found life, but not the warm, comforting presence of other Masters. He touched strangeness and drew back in fear, setting barriers to protect himself from the unknown. With his shields in place he could sense nothing outside himself, so he opened his eyes to look for naLiiss.

The room was unlike any other he had seen. Flat panels set in the ceiling and along the walls glowed with a harsh light, driving out shadows. The floor beneath him was metal, its dull gray sheen and cold touch unmistakable. He rolled, trying to see more, and brushed against something soft and yielding. With a single twist he rolled over, closing his eyes as pain shot through his arms. When he opened them again, he saw naLiiss. The youngling was naked and unconscious, its tentacles bound to its body with wide strips of white cloth.

Chemi rolled again, and saw rows of padded, contoured chairs lining a central table. An open door admitted cool night air and the sound of discordant voices. The language was alien to him. The voices sounded like the Terran's, the one who had been with Starm.

Someone stepped into the room, a small slender person in black clothing that fit like a second skin. The being was not Ardellan. Its hands were strangely formed, like the Terran's. Its body was all curves and bumps, its hair the color of copper. It had a loud and strident voice.

Other strangers followed the first. Chemi counted five in all. They each had oddly-shaped hands and form-fitting clothing, but the colors of their skin and hair and the shapes of their bodies varied. They spoke a cacophony of meaningless syllables that beat against Chemi's shields.

naLiiss stirred, moaning softly. Chemi rolled against the youngling, hoping to silence it with his touch. He moved quietly, not wanting the strangers to know that he was conscious, but one of them heard and came down the aisle. A grotesque hand seized Chemi's arm, and pain flooded his mind, washing away his defenses. Chemi struggled, trying to break the contact as the other's fear and anger penetrated his psychic armor.

The messenger had nowhere to hide. The stranger's emotions invaded his mind, bringing with them confusion and a deep sense of violation. His instinctive reaction was to close down, to retreat to the innermost recesses of his soul, where no one but a mate might reach him. Such a retreat would be suicide, and unforgivable. This thought roused his anger, and he tore his arm from the stranger's grip, irreparably ripping muscles and tendons.

The invading emotions receded to an endurable level when the physical contact was broken. The other stood watching as Chemi's blood puddled on the metal floor. The Ardellan turned away, concentrating to seal vessels and staunch the flow. When he looked up again, the rest of the strangers had gathered, standing about his feet in shocked silence. The copper-haired one moved toward him, reaching out, and he twisted away from its hand.

Chemi blinked, and a small, flickering sphere of shimmer-light appeared above his head. The strength of his anger fueled it, driving back the strangers. Most of them fled down the aisle. He closed his ears to their discordant voices, keeping his eyes on the tall one who stayed to watch him, and ignoring the others.

Chemi felt the floor move. He glanced about, startled, and saw that the whole room moved with it. He feared his mind had tricked him and nothing had moved. Sensing that the shimmer-light was his preservation, he fed it with the energy of his fear. The floor moved again, and Chemi fell back, crowded against the body of his apprentice.

Arien relaxed in the saddle while his mount picked its way over the rocky terrain. Their path was well-lit by the twin moons and the night air was cool. They could travel far tonight and take their rest tomorrow, hiding from the harsh midday sun.

The night was still, except for the soft plodding of the

alep's steps. Arien listened to the gentle click of pebbles beneath the animal's feet, felt the smooth action of its muscles and the pulsing in its heart, which beat just a bit faster than his own. He spent a long time trying to find peace in the simple movements of his mount.

There was no peace for him. Anger coiled and twisted through his mind like a sandsnake, and would not let him rest. He came as near to hatred as he had ever come in his life—hatred of Durrow and all that was Terran. The alien possessed no honor, no sense of integrity. Arien rued the day he left the FreeMasters guildhall in Durrow's company.

Where was Durrow now, and what was he doing? That question nagged Arien, worrying at the corners of his thoughts. He was sure the Terran had a plan, and was executing it now, but Arien was powerless to intervene.

A low, rumbling sound crossed the vast wasteland to touch Arien. The noise startled his mount, and with a single misstep they both went down. Arien landed in a prickly thornbush. He looked up to see the Terran shuttle circle lazily overhead before it moved out across the wasteland.

Muttering epithets, Arien struggled free of the thornbush. His mount was slow to rise, and lame in one leg. The damage might not be permanent, but the alep could not carry a rider now. The day's journey to the guildhall had become three days, walking. The nearest water was in the mountains, two days away, and Arien's water was almost gone.

The FreeMaster cursed his ill fortune and the Terran who was the cause of it. By shimmer-light he unsaddled his mount, discarding everything but food, water, and a dagger. He was alone and impotent in the midst of the wasteland, while Durrow was free to wreak havoc among the clans. He had failed his guild and himself.

Chapter 21

Sarah rode with Jeryl into the wasteland. Her ankle was stiff in its binding, and throbbed a little. She had slapped a pair of patches against her calf before she laced up her boot. One dispensed a long-acting analgesic, the other a drug to keep her ankle from swelling. Her head still ached, and the analgesic was helping that, too. She was determined that Jeryl would not pursue Durrow alone. She could not bear another death between Ardellans and Terrans.

There had been too many deaths already, and she knew that she might have prevented some of them. If she had been more vigilant, instead of letting herself be lulled by the peace of Clan Alu, she might have forestalled the dispute and saved Mrann's life. She could have insisted on keeping the *Blackhawk* in-system, and she could have questioned Mrann about other Terrans visiting Alu Keep. She did neither, until it was too late. Now Durrow ran free among the Ardellans while she waited for the *Blackhawk* to return. How much more damage would Durrow cause before he could be captured?

Sarah had built such an attractive picture of the Ardellans' simple lives: a primitive agrarian society, supplemented by trade and craft guilds. Individuals who had mastered a few psychic tricks—minor telekinesis, empathy, healing. She behaved like an amateur, observing only the surface and naively accepting that as reality. Her analysis of their culture was simplistic, but she treated it as valid because it filled her own needs. She saw what she wanted to see.

She was ashamed. Her training and education had not been faulty; she knew how to analyze an alien society, and how to maintain her objectivity while negotiating a trade agreement. But her judgment had failed in the face of her desires. She used the Ardellans, tried to make their society a place where she could feel at home. She denied their alienness in a desperate attempt to belong. She avoided mentioning their psychic powers in her reports to Sandsmark, instead dwelling on what she perceived as their similarities to Terrans.

It took Hladi's assassination and the dispute to strip away her misconceptions. She did not know these people. All she had were questions, and the realization that their lives, their technology, and their society were much more complex than she had been willing to admit.

So she followed Jeryl into the desert. She carried her pocket transceiver with her for the first time since she had arrived on Ardel. It was her link with a reality shehad tried too long to ignore.

The morning sun was warm on her shoulders. She threw back her hood and let the wind lift her hair. The air smelled clean and dry, and the soil was sandy beneath her mount's pads after they left the fields and orchards of Clan Alu. Her mount plodded along beside Jeryl's alep. The pack animals followed, their leads tied to the back of Jeryl's saddle. They carried bedrolls and water and provisions for six days.

Jeryl had not spoken to her since they left Alu Keep. Sarah was glad of the silence. She could not bear to hear him speak again of revenge.

At midday, she watched him fish a packet of food from his saddle pouch. He used his hands gingerly. His palms were nearly healed, the blisters replaced by tender pink scar tissue.

Sarah was searching her own pouch for food when an electronic beep pierced the silence. Her alep started and began to run, folding up its central legs as it headed across the sand away from the trail. She still had the rein in one hand, but it was slack and she could not bring the animal's head up quickly.

Suddenly Jeryl was beside her, using his mount to turn hers aside. He pushed his alep's shoulders forward and swung its head to the left, forcing her mount to slow and turn to avoid a collision. They rode in a wide circle as both animals slowed their pace. Jeryl had loosed the pack animals before he pursued Sarah. When she had her alep under control, he rode back and recovered them without a word.

Sarah pulled her transceiver from her sash and thumbed the call button. "Anders here."

"Interstellar scout ship *Blackhawk* at your disposal, Commander." The rank was a formality. On Ardel she had authority, but aboard the *Blackhawk* she would be a civilian.

"Put me through to the Captain," she said.

"Jan Swenson here, Commander. Sorry that it took us so long to get back. What's the situation down there?"

"It's not good, Captain Swenson. We have an independent negotiator attempting to conclude a trade agreement with some factions of the native population. It is alleged that he has meddled in local affairs, and that he supplied the weapon used to murder an Ardellan a few days ago. He has been identified as one Nicholas Durrow. Sector authority has an extensive dossier on him. It is suspected that he is employed by Braddock-Owen Extraterrestrial Mining, but the connection has never been confirmed."

"There is a Nagashimi ship cruising the system," offered Swenson, "and the duty master at the communications routing station reports a lot of chatter between it and Nagashimi-BOEM headquarters."

"They're probably waiting for a signal from Durrow. He usually sets up the trade pact, then conveniently disappears. An official Nagashimi-BOEM representative shows up with an agreement identical to the one Durrow set up, and finalizes it with the natives. We're left out in the cold. This time we've disrupted his plans. Two of his people were captured with weapons that the local government has forbidden us to bring planetside. They are being detained at Alu Keep."

"Do you want us to pick them up?" asked Swenson.

"Yes, but not yet. I want Durrow and the rest of his people in custody as soon as possible."

"I can call for a light cruiser to back us up. Will we need reinforcements?"

"We can't wait that long," said Sarah. "Durrow has a very small group here, with only one shuttle. His activities usually border on the felonious; this time I think we can prove that he's gone over the line. His friends from Nagashimi-BOEM will probably cut and run when they learn that we have arrested some of his people. They don't want to be publicly involved in anything grossly illegal."

"Understood. Where can we find him?"

"I have a possible location for his camp. I'd like you to overfly the area, see if Durrow is still there or if he has moved on. If he is still camped, do whatever you need to do to keep him there." She gave Swenson the coordinates, and Gresch's description of the crater. "Contact me when you reach the area. Anders out."

"Aye, Commander. Please adjust your homing beacon. *Blackhawk* out."

She locked the beacon onto the *Blackhawk*'s frequency before she tucked the transceiver back in her sash. Jeryl watched her.

"I did not understand everything you said. *Blackhawk*," he pronounced it "blackhoke," "is the ship you sent for?"

"Yes. I sent it ahead to the crater, to see if the shuttle is still there," she explained.

He scanned the skies with a sweeping gaze. "How is it that you can speak at such a great distance through that little box, but you cannot light a torch or open a latch with your mind?"

She hoped it was a rhetorical question. She did not want to give him an answer.

Sarah took a long drink from her water skin. She looked at the sun, guessed they had about two hours of daylight left. Her tunic was damp under the arms, and sweat trickled down her leg to wet the lining of her ankle splint. She would have to remove the splint and apply a new one when they made camp. She wanted a shower.

They had been following a well-marked trail since they left Ardel's farmlands. Sarah would not call it a road. Occasionally it intersected other paths, but the one just ahead was the widest, most well-traveled trail they had seen.

Jeryl was riding ahead of her. He stopped his mount

where the trails met. "We are near the crater now. This is the road from Eiku Keep," he said, unrolling the map.

"We will follow the Eiku road this far." Jeryl pointed to a spot near the circle Gresch had used to mark the crater's location. "Then we turn off toward the crater. We should reach it before sunset."

Sarah nodded. She was hoping the *Blackhawk* would find Durrow's shuttle at the crater. She set off down the new trail, scanning the horizon. Scattered debris caught her eye.

"What is that?" she asked, pointing.

"Bones," said Jeryl. "A recent kill." He rode ahead to investigate.

The bones of an alep were strewn across the sand, picked clean by scavengers. Jeryl dismounted and picked up a torn leather pad. It was the remains of a saddle.

"This alep was killed within the last few days," he said, nudging a bone with his foot. "The tracks are covered by blowing sand. I cannot tell which direction the rider came from, or where he went."

A large blue beetle crawled through the eye of the skull. Sarah shivered. Then her transceiver beeped. It startled her more than it did her mount. She grabbed the box, thumbed the control as she took a deep breath.

"Anders here."

"Commander, this is the *Blackhawk.*" She recognized Swenson's voice. "We located the crater. It's empty. The shuttle was there, but it has moved on. Do you want to set up a search pattern?"

"Yes, but I also want you to take custody of the prisoners at Alu Keep." She felt uneasy about the mercenaries. They could cause a lot of trouble at the keep if they escaped confinement. Viela and Oreyn were expecting the *Blackhawk* in the morning, and would be happy to give up their prisoners. "Land outside Alu Keep's main gate at first light, and send a messenger to the stable inside the gate. Have him ask for Oreyn, leader of the council. Oreyn will transfer the prisoners to your custody." She gave him the coordinates of the keep.

"We can start a search pattern tonight," suggested

Swenson. "If we're lucky, we'll locate the shuttle before first light."

"Start immediately. Contact me if you find the shuttle." She looked at Jeryl. "My companion and I will camp at the crater tonight. Anders out."

Jeryl dropped the useless saddle and mounted. "They did not find Durrow," he said, turning his mount back to the trail. "Perhaps we can find some sign to tell us where he went."

The crater was small and shallow and, on a planetary scale, recently made. To Sarah it felt immensely old. Bedrock lay exposed on the windward side, but sand was piled high against the opposite rim. It was empty, save for footprints and the drifted imprints of a shuttle's landing gear, a pile of empty tins and containers crawling with beetles, and an unnatural heap of sand near the rim.

They staked their aleps beyond the edge and gave them water and grain before they walked into the crater. The footprints were mostly Terran boots, but the clearest set were broad and circular—Ardellan. They overlaid many of the other prints, and nowhere were Terran prints superimposed on them, so the Ardellan must have been the last to leave the crater. At one spot his prints were muddled with an alep's, and trailed up and over the rim.

Sarah hobbled up the sandy slope, her ankle throbbing. The alep's trail led toward the distant mountains. Jeryl followed her, but stopped to investigate the heap of sand just under the crater's rim.

"Sarah!" He was unwrapping a bundle of furs. He spread them on the sand, sorting through the store of food and personal articles inside.

"Why would he leave these things?" she asked.

"There are tracks of only one alep. He had no pack animal to carry them." Jeryl looked at the mountains. The light was fading, the first chill of darkness coming on. "It is not safe to travel the wasteland alone, with only one mount. The nearest water is almost two days' ride from here, at the foot of the mountains. There are many dangers to pass between here and there."

"He may be well armed, and have plenty of water with him."

"If not, his life is in danger. We can put his things in our packs, and follow him at first light."

Sarah nodded. If the Ardellan were traveling across the wasteland without water, he might well become another casualty of his people's encounter with Terran greed. She helped Jeryl bundle the belongings into the furs and carry them down to a sheltered spot on the floor of the crater. The sun set as Jeryl brought their own furs and packs. Digging through her bag for a battery-powered lamp, Sarah cursed the darkness. Suddenly the area was bright again, as if someone had switched on a lamp. She looked up, saw a ball of shimmer-light floating above Jeryl's extended hands. She smiled, holding up her lamp.

"I won't need this, will I?"

"What is it?" he asked.

She flipped the switch and the translucent plastic shield glowed with diffuse light. "A lamp."

The shimmer-light disappeared as Jeryl reached for the lamp. He turned it over and over in his hands. She showed him how to turn it on and off and take it apart, but when he asked her why she could make light only in the little box, she hesitated to answer. How could she explain the difference between electric light and shimmer-light, when she did not understand shimmer-light?

She put her lamp aside, depending on Jeryl's light to make camp. The ball floated above his head as they spread their furs and made a cold supper. There was no fuel for a fire, and it would be a cold night. Sarah limped over the rim to relieve herself, taking the lamp with her to check on their mounts. The animals were quiet, the grain Jeryl had put out for them consumed.

Returning to the crater, she found Jeryl repacking their things. "I want to leave at first light," he said, pointing to the pouches of food and water skins he had ready. Tugging his own robe close against the chill air, he handed another to Sarah.

"The moons are rising," he said. The huge violet sphere hung just above the crater's rim. Shimmer-light still danced above Jeryl's head, and he let it dissipate as he settled onto the furs.

Sarah removed her boots and took out her medkit. She parted the front seam of the splint with a tiny tool. It opened easily and peeled away from her ankle. She cleaned the skin with a treated wipe. The area under the ball of her ankle was still dark purple and very tender, but she could flex the ankle without too much pain. She applied a fresh stiff-wrap and sealed it. Then she lay back and propped her ankle on her pack.

Jeryl lay an arm's length away, staring at the sky. "See how swiftly second-moon rises? Tonight it will pass first-moon before it reaches zenith. In a few more days, it will rise before first-moon, and we will celebrate the Festival of Overtaking."

Sarah was puzzled. "Why are they called first-moon and second-moon, if they do not always rise in that order?"

"Is not the first always the largest, and the most powerful?"

"In my language it can sometimes mean that. Most commonly it means the one which precedes all others."

"You confuse first with eldest, which means the one that comes before. We do not know which moon is eldest. Our storytellers say they are siblings. Ardel is their Mother, and the sun is Master of their House."

They lay in silence for a while, watching the moons and the stars, and listening to the small noises of the night. Sarah thought of Mrann and Elver. She realized that blaming herself for their deaths was as conceited and egotistical as was her earlier, simplistic view of the Ardellans. She was an observer here, and perhaps a student. She was not a god, to direct their lives. These people made their own choices, for good or ill. She was not responsible for them, any more than they were responsible for her. She could not have prevented their deaths any more than she could have saved her father. It was time to let go of the guilt.

"Can you teach me to make shimmer-light, Jeryl? Mrann tried to teach me to light a torch, but I couldn't do it. Is making shimmer-light more difficult?"

"It uses more energy, but it is not difficult at all. Sit up and face me." Jeryl sat, crossing his legs, the robe wrapped about him like a small tent. "No one can teach another to make shimmer-light. All younglings are born with the potential, but not all discover how to use it. You have it, too. I can guide you to it, but only you can bring it out. You must close your eyes and concentrate. Deep within yourself you will find a tiny flame. Reach for it, touch it carefully, and do not mishandle it. Coax it into your hands."

Sarah closed her eyes, and turned her concentration inward. She took three deep breaths as her grandmother had taught her, and centered her thoughts by envisioning the dancing, leaping blaze of a campfire. Then she searched within herself for the flame Jeryl described. She did not find it.

She sighed, and opened her eyes. "It is not there, Jeryl. I do not have the flame."

"That is not true. I have seen the fire within you. You will not be able to touch it until you truly believe it exists."

"I have no proof of its existence."

"You have as much proof as I had before I made shimmer-light for the first time. A youngling cannot be chosen for metamorphosis until it makes shimmer-light. Many younglings never learn to do it. Some of them are blocked by their own fears, and others simply do not believe in themselves. I was afraid."

"What did you do?"

"I went alone to an ancient ruin, and became lost in the maze of tumbled buildings. When sunset came, my fear of darkness overshadowed my other fear. I convinced myself that I could make shimmer-light. I believed, and the shimmer-light appeared."

"I think belief will not come so easily to me," said Sarah.

Jeryl shrugged. "It does not matter. Now we should rest."

They stretched out in the furs once again. Sarah stared up at the stars and thought about shimmer-light. Her professional training had given her a veneer of scientific ra-

tionalism. Beneath that she was still a daughter of the
Navaho, trained by her grandmother in the ways of the
People. At a young age she had learned that not everything is what it seems to be. She had made a vision quest
the summer of her puberty rites. The next winter her
grandmother had died, and Sarah's mother never let her return to New Mexico. She wanted to raise her daughter in
the sterile modern world of her city. Sarah had never
lost the discipline she had learned from the old woman.
Could she now call upon it, and set aside her disbelief?
The light that Jeryl described was an Ardellan thing. She
was human. Did she truly have the spark within her?

Sarah thought of the enhanced vision she had possessed during the dispute. The things she saw had never
before been seen by a human being. If she had not seen
them herself, she would not have believed them to be
possible. She shuddered, remembering how Revin's mental power made Elver's body burn like a torch. Yet the
bright energy that had surrounded Mrann and Revin had
thrilled and excited her.

She remembered being inside Jeryl's head as he rode
toward the Eiku apprentice when they were surveying the
landing site. She had felt his anger as her own. She also
remembered feeling Viela's hatred and fear as the Healer
stared at her on the morning they left the dispute. She
had never experienced that kind of rapport with another
person, even when her psychic powers had been their
most active. What was happening to her?

For the first time she remembered using her mind to
seek out and disable the Terrans hidden among the rocks.
She could have killed them with only a little more effort.
That realization frightened her. She thought of the fused
laser weapon that naSepti claimed she had destroyed. If
she had the power to do these things, she must have other
abilities that she had never explored. Shimmer-light was
real. She could produce it, but only if she believed in her
own power.

She closed her eyes and turned her thoughts inward.
Again she visualized the campfire with its dancing, leaping flames. She concentrated on a single, flickering point
of fire. As that flame became more and more real to her,

the rest of the campfire ceased to exist. She began to see the tiny flame dancing within the shadowy outline of her body. She built up the body, made it substantial. The fire flickered, threatened to go out. She visualized fuel, fed the fire, made the flame burn steady and hot. Then she began to move it outward from the center of her body. She saw herself holding out a hand with the flickering tongue of fire resting in the palm. She felt its heat, but it did not burn her.

"Sarah," whispered Jeryl, leaning close to her ear. "Open your eyes slowly."

Her heart pounded with a sudden rush of adrenaline. She opened her eyes. She was dazzled by a bright pinpoint of light that disappeared almost before she had registered its presence. She looked at Jeryl in amazement.

"Was that . . . shimmer-light?"

"It was."

Sarah smiled in the darkness.

Chapter 22

Viela stood at the foot of the bare stone bier, looking at Mrann's burial urn. It held more than the ashes of Mrann and Elver. For Viela, it held the ashes of the old ways. He touched it with first one hand and then the other, stroking the dark smooth surface. The stone warmed under his hands. He remembered the day he had come to Alu, his new Healer's cloak a proud testimony to his station. Mrann had been Mentor then, young and eager, and had welcomed him as a colleague and friend. When had they become rivals?

He took his hands from the urn. He had no time for memories, or for regrets. Mrann was gone, and there was a new order in Alu. The Mentor's wristband lay on the bier beside the urn, where Jeryl had left it after the cremation. Two nights and a day it had lain there, forlorn testimony to the new Mentor's character. It was forbidden

for anyone but the Mentor to wear it, so Viela fastened
it to a thong and slipped that over his head. The jeweled
band dangled against his chest, bumping his Healer's token.

The urn gleamed in the early morning light, a myriad
of colors shifting across its surface. The stone was almost
translucent. When Viela looked at it, he felt his gaze
drawn beyond the polished exterior into the depths of the
stone. The simplicity of its design, from the narrow pen-
tagonal base to the wide shoulder and tricorn lid, testified
to the skill of the carver and the beauty of his chosen
material. Viela admired it as art, and as a reflection of
Mrann. His own urn was very different—soft and round,
carved of green stone. It rested in a corner of his sleep
chamber, waiting.

He used both hands to lift the urn from the granite
bier. Hugging it to his body, he carried it up the steps
and through the open door of the clanhall. The hallway
was dim. He smelled fresh bread and roast wool-deer.
The urn was heavy, and he held it tightly as he walked
down the hall. The kitchen door was open. One of the
apprentice cooks began to follow him as he passed
through the kitchen. When Viela reached the back door,
the kitchenmaster called the youngling back to work.

The burial niche had been prepared, the runes for
Mrann and Elver etched into the stone below it. The niche
was a hand's span deep, a semicircle carved into the stone
with a flat bottom shelf and an arched top. Settling the
urn into it, Viela brushed away a few stray grains of sand.
No one had carved runes describing the lives of Mrann
and Elver; they no longer had mates to perform that service. With their deaths, their Houses were truly gone,
their lines ended forever. He did not care to write about
their deaths. It was Jeryl's place as the new Mentor to
complete the record.

There was nothing more he could do for the dead.
Turning away from the wall, he climbed the steps to the
kitchen. At the hearth, Ortia was haranguing his apprentice, listing all the unpleasant duties that would fall to
the youngling if it did not keep to its work. He took time
to gesture to Viela and point to the large kettle he kept

by the fire, but Viela waved a refusal. He had no time for tea. Torma was waiting for him.

The clanhall's door was still open. Viela walked down the hallway toward the rectangle of sunlight, and saw two figures silhouetted against the morning sky. He recognized Oreyn, but the energy pattern of the other person was alien. Viela turned back toward the kitchen, hoping to avoid them, but Oreyn had already sensed his presence.

"Healer," he called, striding down the hallway. "I sent a youngling to find you. This is Captain Swenson of the scout ship *Blackhawk* come to take away the Terrans." He hesitated over the Terran words, his aura flickering with insecurity. He and Torma had studied the language with Sarah, preparing for trade meetings with other off-worlders. Viela had studied the language also, but he refused to speak it. He preferred that the Terrans feel free to speak in front of him, not knowing that he could comprehend much of what they said.

Swenson strode forward and made a little bow, just a momentary dip of head and shoulders. He was short and slender, dressed in blue clothing that accentuated the shape of his body. Four more Terrans of varying shapes and sizes, wearing identical clothing, followed him into the clanhall. Their auras formed a seething conglomeration of emotion that made Viela's skin crawl. He backed away from them.

Swenson spoke, and Oreyn attempted to translate. Viela listened to the Terran's words, and understood them.

"I regret the difficulties caused you by the Terrans you hold, sir. If you will remand them to my custody, my government will see that they are punished. Also, if you will file a report with Commander Anders, you will be reimbursed for any damage they have done."

Reimbursed . . . damage! What reimbursement could repay the lives lost, and the changed future of Alu? The Captain's words were stiff and pompous, like a carefully rehearsed speech, but his aura negated their effect. Viela saw a swirling combination of sadness, regret, and anger, and for a moment he believed this man might compre-

hend the damage already done. He dismissed that
thought. "Just take the Terrans from our storeroom. We
want no more from you." He heard Oreyn soften his
words in translation.

Viela led them to the storeroom, listening to Oreyn and
the Terran discuss trade possibilities. Though Oreyn offered many proposals, the Captain was careful to make
no commitments.

"We have fine cloth to trade—our weavers are the best
in any clan," claimed Oreyn, pulling off his patterned
cloak and offering it to Swenson. "The thread is made
from the fleece of our own wool-deer, and is spun and
dyed by Alu craftsmen."

"I can see the quality of your weaving," said Swenson. He did not touch the cloak.

"We also make pottery, and fine stone carvings. We
would like to trade these for iron and copper."

"I am certain there is a market for your cloth, and for
your pottery and carvings. You must arrange the details
with Commander Anders. We have many things of value
to offer you. Why do you want iron and copper?"

"Sarah has told us that these metals are plentiful on
other worlds, but here they are rare. We need iron for
knives and tools, and copper is the best conductor we
have found for energy work."

"What is 'energy work'?" asked Swenson.

Viela interrupted before Oreyn could reveal any more.
"Here are your prisoners." The door to the room was
open, but two Masters sat outside it, generating an energy field across the doorway. Viela could see the field
as a shimmering, luminescent wall. He gestured to the
guards, and the field died.

Swenson entered the room with two of his four crewmen. They had no visible weapons, and Viela did not
think they could conceal any under their tight-fitting
clothing. They did carry pairs of metal cuffs that they
used to bind the prisoners' hands together behind their
backs. One of the prisoners tried to speak, but the Captain silenced her. "You will be questioned and allowed
to record a statement on the ship. Until then, keep quiet,

and remember that if you escape, you have nowhere to run.''

Dismissing the Masters who had guarded the door, Viela pulled Oreyn to one side to let the Terrans pass. The four crewmen fell in around the black-clad prisoners, moving ahead of their Captain down the corridor. Viela and Oreyn followed Swenson.

''Take care how much you reveal to these Terrans,'' whispered Viela, his voice sharp with warning. ''There is no need for them to know how important copper is to us, and what use we put it to.''

''If they will give us copper, how will it matter what they know or do not know? We will be free of the tyranny of the mountain clans and their puny mines. What a power Alu could be with copper to use and trade!''

''Do not believe that to be true, Master. If we accept copper and iron from the Terrans, we will be in their power. We will only trade one tyranny for another.'' The blue-clad guards moved out of sight around a corner, but Swenson paused and looked back over his shoulder. Viela gestured for him to follow the others. ''Giving power into the hands of these aliens is dangerous. We do not understand their minds or their motives. Already they have changed the paths of Alu and Eiku, while protesting that they would not interfere in our lives.''

''Eiku's greed brought those changes, Healer.''

Oreyn was angry; Viela could see it in his aura. ''What of your own greed?'' he goaded. The other was silent as he hurried after the Terrans.

The street outside the clanhall was sunny. Viela, Oreyn, and the Terrans walked together, strolling down the main road to the gate. There were younglings about, rushing to the workshops and fields. For the most part they showed no interest in the Terrans, but one of them, a fieldmaster's apprentice by its yellow sash, stopped to gawk.

In two strides Viela was in front of it. ''House,'' he demanded.

''Arlein,'' said the youngling.

''Name.''

''naBriln.''

"Your Master shall hear of your conduct. Go." Viela
waved dismissal. He would not talk with the Master of
House Arlein; pointing out the youngling's error before
its fellows was punishment enough. It would pay attention to its duties in the future, instead of gawking at the
activities of adults.

The *Blackhawk* was waiting in the meadow beyond the
gate. Viela had seen the little shuttle that the survey crew
used when they were making their maps. This ship was
much bigger, nearly as large as the clanhall. It seemed
impossible that such a thing could fly like a bird.

Like the shuttle, this ship was made of metal. The
Blackhawk contained more metal than the mountain clans
could mine in two hands of seasons. The shell was made
of iron, mixed with other metals that Viela did not recognize. Threads of pure copper ran throughout the ship.

As Viela watched, a hatch opened, sliding back under
the skin of the ship. A ramp unfolded to touch the sand.
The rectangular opening was flooded with bright light,
silhouetting the broad figure of a crewman. His footsteps
sounded with a hollow clang as he walked down the ramp.
Oreyn stepped back, a gout of fear disrupting his aura,
but Viela stood his ground.

"Take the prisoners aboard, Schimmel. I'll be up
shortly." Swenson turned back to the Ardellans. "I would
like to offer you a tour of my ship," he said, "but we
have duties to perform for Commander Anders."

Oreyn talked with the Captain, but Viela did not listen.
He was exploring the aura of the ship. A made thing
could not live, but this one did. Power surged through its
copper threads, ordered and disciplined, different from
the energy of the Terran minds. Sarah insisted that the
Terrans built these ships, but Viela did not believe her.
They lived inside the metal skins like parasites, existing
on the bounty of something stronger than themselves.

The clatter of the Terrans' footsteps on the ramp echoed off the wall of Alu Keep. Viela shuddered. So much
metal in one place made him uncomfortable. Without a
word he turned and walked back into the keep. Oreyn
was still speaking with Swenson and their voices drifted
after him, but he ignored them.

It was nearing midday. Mothers would soon be bringing their younglings out to romp in the gardens. The
Mothers would bask in the sun and gossip as the little
ones climbed trees and chased one another. Viela was
tempted to go and watch them. His morning had been
filled with death, and the mysterious nonlife of the Terran
ship. Life was meant to be the focus of a Healer's energies. He had seen too much injury and death these last
few days.

Viela felt a need to renew his commitment to Alu and
the future of his people. He walked toward House Kirlei,
thinking of the new Master that was growing there. Septi
would be mature soon, and would emerge from his cocoon to mate with Torma and Eenar. Kirlei would continue. Viela knew that as he neared the House.

Eenar had been beyond sleep for several days. She lay
awake most of the time in spite of Viela's potions, waiting for Septi to emerge from his cocoon. Torma waited
with her, his anxiety so intense that it became like a
separate entity that shared their House. Viela sensed it
as he entered the front portal. The cloud and feather design that graced the far wall of the main chamber did not
have its usual restful effect on him. The blues and greens
seemed to clash rather than harmonize, but he knew the
reason for that was the ambience of the House.

Torma met him, one tiny youngling perched on his
shoulder and another dangling from his arm, its tentacles
locked in the intense grip of the very young.

"You have taken up Mothering a bit early. Hladi's
younglings?" Viela asked, reaching for the one perched
on Torma's shoulder. The youngling snaked its tentacles
around the Master's head, refusing to be moved. "They
seem healthy enough. Are they adjusting well to Kirlei?"

"The runt is giving me some trouble. It will not eat
unless Eenar feeds it, and she has no energy for that now.
It may die." He said it without emotion. Younglings often died from disease or defect; there was no point in
becoming attached to them. Only adults were generally
considered worthy of affection.

"How is Eenar this morning?"

"Come and see her. She was asking that you monitor

Septi. She is anxious to know how the metamorphosis is progressing.'' Torma plucked the youngling from his arm and deposited it on a bench where two others were playing with a torn piece of cloth. ''She no longer eats or sleeps. I hope she will improve after the mating.''

''No doubt she will, although you do not need to be concerned. She is strong, and will bear a healthy litter even if she never eats another meal.'' Viela heard a noise behind him, and turned to see his eldest apprentice standing in the open portal.

''Healer!'' called the apprentice.

''What is it?'' Viela's words were terse. He did not like to see such uncontrolled excitement in his apprentice.

''A messenger, Healer. Come from the council in Berrut to speak to you.''

Viela did not let his voice betray excitement or apprehension, though he felt both. ''I will see him when I am finished here.''

''He said you were to come immediately, Healer.''

The messenger's presumption angered him. ''Not even a messenger can order a Healer away from his duties. I will come after I have seen Eenar.'' He dismissed the apprentice with a wave.

''Perhaps you should go, Viela.'' Torma was unwrapping tentacles from his neck.

''No. It will only take a moment to see Eenar and check on Septi's progress. The messenger can wait.'' He was tempted to extend his visit just to annoy the messenger, but that was the sort of game he objected to the Masters on the council playing with each other. He would do what he had come to do, and then speak with the messenger.

Eenar was looking well, though he sensed her energy level was low. Torma had been feeding her, and giving her the teas and potions Viela recommended. Her body mass was good, great enough to support the younglings that would soon be growing inside her. The only difficulty was that she could not, or would not, sleep.

More important, Septi's metamorphosis was progressing well. The outlines of his body were visible through the white silk of the cocoon. The plump oval was collapsing in on itself, becoming wrinkled and pitted as the tissue redistributed to the legs and arms. The tentacles were already dormant, withdrawn into nodules in the chest. When he emerged from the cocoon in a few days, he would be no taller than he had been as a youngling, but he would be a functional adult. For the next few seasons he would grow until he reached his adult height.

There was nothing Viela could do to hurry the process along. Torma and Eenar would have to wait for Septi to emerge and mate in his own time. After reassuring Torma about Eenar's condition, the Healer took his leave and went with his apprentice to meet the messenger.

"You are requested to appear before the assembly in Berrut on the day after Festival." The messenger stood at the gate, his alep's rein held tightly in one hand.

"Who believes he has authority to make such a request?" Viela's anger was cold and hard. He let some of it show, hoping to intimidate the messenger.

"Starm, GuildMaster of the Messengers. He calls the assembly to meet because there have been reports of improper conduct at the dispute between Alu and Eiku. You are to be a witness." The messenger was well-trained, cool, and impersonal. His aura showed no sign of his feelings about the message.

Viela was enraged. "Whose conduct was improper? And who makes the accusations?"

"I do not know, Healer. You must come to Berrut to find out."

Out of habit his hand sought the Healer's token on his chest, and encountered the Mentor's wristband. Alu had no Mentor to defend the clan to the assembly. Jeryl was gone, off on a foolish quest with the Terran. Oreyn could stand as council leader, but he was inexperienced. Torma dare not leave Eenar long enough to attend the assembly.

Viela knew he must go, must do his best to be an impartial witness for the assembly and still defend his clan. He grasped the wristband, and with a convulsive jerk tore it from the thong and threw it to the ground.

Chapter 23

Durrow woke at dawn in a room above Starm's guildhall. His right hand was resting on the haft of his favorite knife. He broke his fast alone, disdaining an invitation to the guild's kitchen. Ration bars from his pack and water treated with purification tablets satisfied his body's needs. He washed in the little basin in the corner, combing his hair and cleaning his nails before he put on his black jumpsuit.

He hated waiting. He paced across the stone floor of the room, kicked a small hand-worked rug and sent it sliding to bunch against a wall. Trying to quell his impatience, he sat in a chair beside the bed. He put his feet up, soiling the furs with his boots. The dusty boots annoyed him. He cleaned them with an embroidered table covering, then tossed it on top of the rug. He began to pace again.

When Starm came for him, Durrow's mood was as black as his clothing. He bit back a sharp reply to the GuildMaster's formal greeting, and strode out of the room before Starm could see the disarray. It had been a mistake to stay at the guildhall. He should have taken a room at an inn, where his actions would not be so easily observed. Here Starm would know his every move.

He was dependent on the GuildMaster for information, and for introductions to the other GuildMasters of Berrut. This gave Starm power over him. Durrow disliked feeling dependent. He was aware of Starm's power, and it irritated him. Only the thought that Roletti would have captured Starm's messenger by now, and would prevent him from reaching the FreeMasters Guild, enabled Durrow to smile at the GuildMaster.

Starm led Durrow out of the guildhall and clockwise around the circular court where Berrut's main streets met. Each street was paved with flat stone in a different color,

and the stones came together in the court to make an
intricate spiral around the old hall in its center. The Messengers' guildhall was at the entrance to green street.
They passed three other roads and then turned left into
red street.

Their destination was the Metalsmiths' guildhall, a
long, low building that dominated red street. Its wide
gates opened on a walled courtyard, separated from the
guildhall by a long veranda. The courtyard was filled with
tables and workbenches and scurrying younglings. Apprentices in hide aprons struggled with heavy tools of
hardwood and iron.

Forges and water troughs filled the center of the court,
clustered around a huge anvil. Three smiths moved in an
intricate dance, working heated iron on the anvil in ro-
tation. The GuildMaster was working at a forge, instruct-
ing apprentices in its operation. He was short for an
Ardellan, barely a hand taller than Durrow, and almost
as broad in the shoulders. Muscles rippled in his bare
forearms as he handled the heavy tools. Seeing Starm,
he called for another smith to continue the instruction,
and went to greet the visitors.

"May the great sun smile on you, Masters."

"And on you, Reass," replied Starm. "This is the
Terran, Captain Nicholas Durrow. He would like to speak
with you."

Reass was expecting them. He led them past a table
where several Masters were engraving intricate runes on
ornate gold tableware, and into a dark, cool hall. There
was no hearth in the room. Water trickled down one of
the stone walls in steady rivulets, disappearing into a
small channel where the wall met the floor. Instead of
the long tables and benches of the Messengers' guildhall,
there were clusters of small, round tables and stools. Reass
motioned them to a table near the dripping wall, and
brought mugs of foamy cider from the sideboard.

"You are interested in the working of metals, Master?" he asked as he sat beside Durrow.

"Yes, though not in the same way you are." Durrow
was suddenly aware of his inadequate knowledge of the
language and his faulty pronunciation. He had to enun-

ciate clearly to be understood over the steady trickle of the water. "I have been told that your supplies of iron and copper are limited, but I see many iron tools in your courtyard."

"We cannot put a value on those tools. There are no others like them. It took three years to produce enough iron to make the anvil." Reass drained his mug. It made a hollow thud when he set it on the table. "Almost all our metalsmiths live and work here, where they can use the tools owned by the guild. There are a few independent smiths among the clans, but their work is limited because they cannot afford many tools."

Durrow nodded. "I have been told that the metal you possess makes your guild the wealthiest and one of the most powerful in the city," he said. He brought out a crystal-studded rock and a small pouch filled with sand, and handed them to Reass. "My employers are interested in mining these crystals, and gathering the sand. Both are plentiful in the wasteland, and your people do not use either one."

The smith examined the rock, then set it on the table. He ignored the sand. "We sometimes use the crystals for household ornaments. The gem cutters do not like to work with them, because they are brittle and shatter easily. What use can you have for them?"

"There is a metal trapped in those crystals and in the sand. We know how to release the metal and work it with special tools to make the hulls of our ships." There were other places where Durrow's employers could obtain titanium, but they were all regulated by the Terran Union. An unregulated, untaxed supply of the metal would be invaluable. "We would like to trade for sand and crystals."

"There is no metal that our forges cannot work." Reass spoke with the certainty of ignorance. Touching the ore, he said, "The crystals do not belong to our guild. Why do you come to me?"

Starm pushed aside his empty mug and answered the question. "Trade rights belong to Clan Alu, but there is a question of treachery in the dispute between Alu and Eiku. The assembly will hear the testimony, and if it decides Alu acted improperly, trade rights will revert to Eiku.''

"You wish my support in the assembly."

Durrow nodded. "I am prepared to offer your guild a stable supply of high-quality metals in exchange for your support." He brought a fine steel knife and a small coil of copper wire from his pouch and gave them to the smith.

"You would no longer be dependent on the mountain clans for your metals," said Starm. "The guild would be able to produce more tools, and support more smiths."

Reass stroked the steel blade, testing the edge with a finger. Then he uncoiled part of the wire, breaking it off and winding it in a tight spiral. "The copper is pure, but the iron is not," he said.

"The iron is mixed with carbon to make it stronger and more resistant to corrosion," said Durrow. "We can provide it like this, or as the pure metal."

"The Metalsmiths Guild will prosper with a steady, economical supply of metal. You might even become as powerful as my guild," added Starm.

"And in exchange, you want only the crystals and the sand?" questioned Reass.

"Yes, just the crystals and the sand," said Durrow, smiling.

Starm and Durrow visited the Leatherworkers Guild, offering the GuildMaster a limitless supply of metal tools and fittings in return for his support. At the Stonecutters Guild, Durrow produced his carbon steel blade and offered hammers and chisels of the same fine metal to the GuildMaster. Their help was less certain than that of the smiths, but Starm was confident that they could be swayed to Durrow's side.

Shortly before midday they traced their way back through the central court to gray street, the avenue of the merchants. It was not a market, though anything could be bought or sold there. The street was lined with peaceful shops, separated by clusters of trees and stone benches. A small walled park stood between two low buildings, one showing tapestries in the window, the other boasting a row of stone urns. Across the street was an inn.

The great blue door of the inn was propped open, revealing the bright and cheery dining room within. Durrow followed Starm through the doorway. The far wall was an ingenious arrangement of sliding doors that opened onto a private garden. The doors were pushed to one side, letting sunlight and fresh air into the room. There were many small tables, set well away from the hearth where a small fire kept several pots steaming. Along one wall was a wide shelf, laden with platters of meats and bowls of fruits and vegetables. Plates and utensils were stacked at one end. A Master was helping himself to the food.

Stepping up to one of the occupied tables, Starm greeted the Masters who sat there. "May the great sun smile on you, GuildMasters. I bring someone to speak with you—a Terran, Master Durrow."

"We greet you, Master," said the one in the gold tunic. The one in blue offered a quick, palms-up gesture. Even to Durrow's unschooled eye, they looked very much alike. "This is Harra, of the innkeepers, and I am Mikal, the merchant. Not knowing the customs of your people, we have waited our meal for you. Will you join us?"

Before Durrow could reply, Starm made a sweeping gesture. "Yes. We have not eaten."

The two GuildMasters rose and walked to the counter, gathering up plates, bowls, and utensils. Starm followed, and so did Durrow, imitating their actions. He eyed the platters of food, trying to identify some of it. He preferred to eat the rations he carried in his pack, but he did not want to offend the GuildMasters.

Starm tore a leg off a roast fowl and dropped it on his plate. Durrow took the second leg. It pulled away from the carcass easily, but it was greasy. He looked around for a napkin to wipe his fingers. Finding nothing that would serve, he blotted them on his handkerchief. He recognized a bowl of yellow tubers as something Arien had eaten often, and he spooned some onto his plate. The nut cakes looked innocuous, so he took one of them, also. When he came back to the table his plate was almost bare, while the others carried platters laden with many varieties of food.

Being forced to eat native food put Durrow in a black mood. It suited him well that the others kept silent while they ate. He picked at the food. The tubers were sweet, but coarse in texture, and the fowl was gamy. The nut cake was acceptable, and he washed it down with cold tea while the Masters finished their meal.

A youngling cleared the dishes away and wiped the table, and another brought mugs and a pitcher of cider. Mikal poured.

"The Terrans wish to trade with us," said Starm, a cluster of crystals cupped in his palm. His fingers turned it around and around. "They offer us iron and copper in exchange for these crystals and the sands of the wasteland."

The GuildMasters were silent. Durrow moved the pitcher to one corner of the table, and brought out his maps. "The organization I represent is interested in building a mining and processing facility here," he pointed to the location of the largest ore deposit. "We want to dig out the sand, and change it to a form that we can transport on our starships. We will pay well, in iron and copper of the highest quality."

"We have heard that there is a dispute over the trade rights," said Mikal. Harra concurred.

"That is a matter for the assembly to settle," replied Starm. "If Alu's actions are found to be improper, the assembly can confiscate the trade rights and make a trade agreement that will benefit everyone."

Durrow's right hand swept an arc over the map. "If we are granted trade rights, we will bring in Terrans to construct a port for our starships. They will need food and supplies, and they will have money to spend on arts and crafts. And when the spaceport is completed, there will be the refinery to build, and other Terrans will be needed to keep the equipment in the mines working properly."

"You offer us a new market for our goods, and in return you ask us for . . . what? To stand against Alu in the assembly?"

Starm's voice was low and cold. "We ask you to listen to the testimony, and to judge fairly."

Something that might have been a smile touched Harra's lips. Mikal offered Durrow more cider. They reminded him of carrion eaters dancing about a dying animal. He had no doubt they would back his cause when the assembly met.

Chapter 24

Arien stared at the holes in his boots. He was disgusted. After almost two days of walking on sand and rocks, the soft tol-hide soles had worn through. Stripping the ragged remnants from his ankles, he tossed them at a sun-basking lizard. The broad pads of his feet were blistered and tender. He wrapped them carefully with strips of cloth torn from his tunic, cursing Durrow under his breath.

His mount had fared little better. The animal walked with a shuffling gait, its injured leg held gingerly above the ground. Its central limbs were down, supporting the main weight of its body, but its movements were slow and clumsy. Arien did not know whether it would ever be a suitable mount again. He added another debt to the Terran's account.

Arien had finished the water before midday, and had discarded the empty skin. He was exhausted; every bit of extra weight slowed him down. He still carried dried meat and bread, and grain for the alep, but without water the food would do them no good. The meat would make him thirsty, and the grain would clog the alep's intestines. He was tempted to discard it, too, but if they reached water, they would want to eat.

He was angry. He used that to keep despondency at bay as he trudged through the heat of the day. Thoughts of the guildhall's shaded grounds were replaced by visions of Durrow's burnt and blackened body sprawled on

the sand. The images left him feeling satisfied and revolted at the same time.

His thirsty mount nibbled on a cluster of chubby succulents, and Arien cuffed it between the eyes and dragged
it away. The succulents were filled with water, but it was
brackish and would make the alep ill. He found a thicket
of thornbushes. They often protected young plants with
their dense, thorny branches. He hacked away some of
the dead lower growth, and found some tiny green shoots.
Digging, he followed their thick stems down to plump,
moisture-laden tubers. His hands were scratched by the
thorns and covered with dirt, but that did not matter
when he held the tubers. He peeled them quickly, gave
one to his mount and bit into the other himself. The yellow flesh was sweet and tangy.

Arien decided to walk through the night. The tuber had
slaked his thirst, the air was cool and clear, and the starlit
sky was beautiful. He strode with a sureness that belied
the distance he still had to travel. Feeling at one with the
world around him, he forgot for a time that the wasteland
could kill him.

He was still walking when dawn brightened the tops of
the distant mountains, illuminating the scarlet forest that
covered the steep slopes. The pass to the FreeMasters'
guildhall was a dark gash in this living tapestry. It twisted
upward from the narrow strip of lush pasture that skirted
the mountains, to disappear behind one of the smaller
peaks. It was the path home, and Arien rejoiced to see
it. His alep smelled the pasture and its tiny stream of
fresh water. It stumbled forward, tugging at the rein.

Triumph lit Arien's face. He had foiled Durrow's pilot.
Before nightfall he would be home, eating and drinking
his fill at the big table in the guildhall. He would tell the
GuildMaster of the Terran's treachery, and they would
plan his downfall together. He quickened his pace, rev-
eling in his victory.

They moved toward the mountains with single-minded
determination. Sharp stones cut the tender pads of Arien's
feet, but he ignored the wounds. His alep grew tired and
stubborn, and stopped to nibble another succulent. Arien

slapped its nose. The animal brayed its frustration, but it followed him.

At mid-morning they reached water. Shouting, Arien splashed into the little stream. His exuberance startled a school of tiny fish. He drank his fill, and dug fleshy tongue-roots from the bank with his dagger, munching some himself and feeding the rest to his alep. The animal stood in the water, letting it splash against its belly as it ate grain from Arien's hand.

They followed the winding stream for a distance, until it turned away from the pass. Then they crossed the narrow strip of grassland to the forest's edge. The trail to the guildhall was wide and well-marked, and Arien saw the spoor of two aleps. They walked through the false darkness of deep forest, until they broke out into the sunshine of a narrow, flower-spattered meadow. The alep stopped to graze, and Arien sprawled on the sweet grass and napped.

He did not sleep long. The sun was still high when he rose, stretched, and tugged the alep back to the path. They left the meadow and continued climbing through the forest. Arien was hungry. He watched for plants that had edible roots, and for last season's nuts. A scrap of bright green fabric tangled in the scarlet needles of a conifer caught his attention. He pulled it free, examining the dark stains that discolored it. It was messenger green, and from its fine weave, part of a tunic.

The frightened braying of his alep startled Arien. The animal tugged at the rein, trying to run back toward the meadow. Arien patted and soothed it, then tied the rein to a tree before he walked ahead to investigate. He clutched the knobby hilt of his dagger tightly.

Around the bend the path was strewn with twisted and broken cartilage and bone, the remains of several animals. Scavengers had stripped the bodies, leaving behind only what they could not digest. Arien saw two alep skulls as he picked his way through the carnage. He found the rest of the messenger's torn tunic beside the burned cartilage of an alep's forelegs. He had seen burns like that before, caused by the Terrans' laser weapons.

Arien collapsed on a patch of laser-scorched ground,

bunching the tunic in his hands. His triumph was false. He recognized Durrow's role in this destruction.

Anger spread like a ruby shield around him, inhibiting some of his perceptions but increasing the sensitivity of others. His hand closed on a little tile that was wedged between two rocks, and he felt the emotions of the Master who had touched it last. With sensitive fingers he traced the rune of the FreeMasters Guild, and knew the messenger's destination. He cupped the tile between his palms and concentrated on it, but the message eluded him.

A gentle touch drew Arien back to the world. He saw an arm clad in dusty brown, a tunic of Alu weave and cut, then looked up into the care worn face of a young Master. He sensed a second presence and shot to his feet, flinging the tattered green tunic aside.

"Terran!" Arien cried, and his anger lashed out, knocking the alien to the ground.

"Hold, Master." Jeryl grabbed Arien's shoulder and spun him about. The tile fell from Arien's hand. "If you challenge the Terran, you challenge Jeryl of Alu," he declared.

Arien slipped to the ground, fighting exhaustion, anger, and frustration. He wanted to fight, to drive the Terran away. He needed time to gather power. Jeryl stalked past him to look at the carnage that littered the trail. The Terran stayed with her mount, well out of Arien's range, but the alien presence aggravated him. He watched through slitted eyes as Jeryl picked up the messenger's tunic, hoping he would not see the tile that lay near it.

"Messenger green, Sarah," called Jeryl, holding the torn tunic above his head. "Someone surprised the messenger and his apprentice, and killed them or took them away."

"Those burn marks are from lasers," said Sarah quietly. She had climbed to her feet and was waiting with their mounts. "If we check the far end of the meadow, we will probably find evidence that the shuttle landed there."

Jeryl nodded, tucking the tunic into his sash. "Keep-

ing a messenger from his mission is a death offense," he
said.

Behind Arien a single beep sounded, a noise that was
totally alien. He turned to watch the Terran, saw her take
a small box from her sash.

"Commander Anders, this is the *Blackhawk.*"

The transceiver was smaller than the one Arien had
seen Durrow use. Sarah nestled it in one hand and spoke
into it. "Yes, *Blackhawk.* Have you located the shuttle?"

"Negative, Commander. We are widening our search
pattern."

"Contact me as soon as you locate the shuttle. Do not,
repeat, do not attempt to approach the shuttle without
contacting me. I have reason to believe that they have
kidnapped one or more of the natives."

"Message received and understood, Commander. I
will inform the Captain immediately. *Blackhawk* out."

"Thank you, *Blackhawk.* Anders out." Sarah pock-
eted the transceiver and left the mounts, coming to stand
with Jeryl. She silently surveyed the destruction.

Arien climbed to his feet. He pretended to stumble,
picked up the messenger's tile and slipped it into his
pocket. Ignoring Sarah, he hailed Jeryl.

"The one who did this owes me a life-debt," he said.
"I will seek him out, if you will lend me a mount. Mine
is lame."

"Life-debt?" laughed Jeryl. "He abandoned you in
the wasteland, and you think he will honor a life-debt?
Do you have a name, fool?"

"You challenge a FreeMaster." Arien stepped toward
Jeryl, his arm outstretched in a gesture of warding, and
spoke in a threatening tone. "I am Arien, and I have
power."

"I have not tracked you for two days to fight with you."
Jeryl pointed to the pack animal that carried Arien's furs.
"We found your belongings at the crater."

"We can spare a mount for you," said Sarah. "Do
you know where Durrow is now?"

Arien ignored her.

"We search for the people who did this," said Jeryl.
"Do you know where they might be?"

With a sweeping gesture, Arien indicated the waste-land. "I saw the shuttle two nights ago, out there. What business do you have with Durrow?" He would not look at Sarah. She seemed familiar, but he did not know why.

She stepped forward, challenging him. "He has bro-ken Terran laws. I want to detain him, to keep him from creating further devastation among you. If he has kid-napped some of your people, I want to return them to their homes, unharmed."

"He has already done more damage than you could know," cried Arien. Then he realized that she did know the harm Durrow had done. "You were at the dispute! You killed Durrow's assassins!"

"She killed no one," said Jeryl, stepping between them. "I killed one Terran, and the others are Alu's pris-oners. They directed us to the crater camp."

Struggling to maintain his defenses, Arien looked from one to the other. He would not, could not, trust a Terran. What of Jeryl, who seemed to trust the alien? When nei-ther made a move toward him, Arien stared belligerently at Sarah. He focused his anger and resentment on her, and was startled to see her expression change. She backed away from him. She was not as head-blind as Durrow; she must be able to feel his rage.

"My guildhall is near here," Arien offered. He did not try to conceal his animosity. "You may come with me and rest there, if you wish, Jeryl."

"I will not come without Sarah."

"Terrans are no longer welcome in the FreeMasters' guildhall."

"Is that the decision of your guild, or your own prej-udice?" asked Jeryl. "Commander Anders controls the fastest method we have of locating the other Terrans."

Arien considered this, his fingers seeking the little tile in his pocket. He wanted to find Durrow. "You are both welcome," he said. Under his breath he added, "for now."

2257:12/10, TERRAN CALENDAR
TO: AUSTIN DUERST, VP/RESOURCE
        DEVELOPMENT, NAGASHIMI-BOEM
FROM: GLENN ELSNER, CAPTAIN, NAGASHIMI
        INTERSTELLAR SHIP *WHITE CRANE*
  SUDDEN INCREASE IN TERRAN UNION
ACTIVITY OBSERVED IN VICINITY OF ARDEL.
UNION SHIP CURRENTLY RUNNING PLANET-
WIDE SEARCH PATTERN, PERHAPS HUNTING
RENEGADE TRADERS OR SMUGGLERS.
  EXPECTED OPPORTUNITY FOR TRADE TALKS
HAS NOT MATERIALIZED. UNION TRADE
REPRESENTATIVE SEEMS FIRMLY
ENTRENCHED.
  WILL REMAIN IN ORBIT AND CONTINUE TO
OBSERVE SITUATION. PLEASE ADVISE
IMMEDIATELY SHOULD YOU DECIDE
WITHDRAWAL IS ONLY OPTION.

Chapter 25

It was late afternoon when Viela and his companions
reached the outskirts of Berrut. He and Oreyn had ridden
in silence since midday, but Urlla the gem cutter had
spent the afternoon complaining about being away from
his mate at Festival. The Healer had heard enough; he
let his aura flare, making his displeasure obvious to Urlla.
The sudden show of anger startled the gem cutter, but it
only silenced him for a moment.

"You do not understand," Urlla asserted. "You have never had a mate. To be apart at Festival . . ."

"Urlla!" Oreyn was angry. "I brought you to Berrut so that you can observe the assembly. Some day you will lead Alu's council. You will have to set aside your personal interests and do what is best for Clan Alu."

Viela damped his aura. "I do understand, Urlla. More completely than you will ever know." He was remembering a spring day much like this one, many seasons ago. He had been a youngling then, apprenticed to the Healers Guild in Berrut. The time of choosing had come. He faced two doors, one leading away from the Healers' compound, back to the clan of his birth and a normal life with his siblings, the other opening into the sacred courtyard and the mysteries of the guild.

naViela chose the mysteries, and found itself cocooned with a hand of other younglings in a secret ceremony that it did not understand. Only one Mother was present. The younglings were anointed with strange oils and decoctions, and wrapped in silk. They emerged from the cocoons as Masters, ready to mate, but the Mother had left the courtyard. The new-made Masters were alone and frightened. Before them stretched extended lives, and the knowledge that they would witness the deaths of their littermates, and of their littermates' young. They would study secrets and learn the mysteries, and always be alone and lonely. Nothing would mark their passing except the records of their deeds.

He had never regretted his choice. Sometimes, at Festival, he wondered what his other life might have been like. By now he would be a Mother, with younglings nearly grown and fostered out. The thought was nearly as foreign as the Terrans' tales of travel from star to star.

Which brought him back to the reason for this summons to Berrut. Terrans! Viela wanted to curse them all. Instead he guided his mount off the main road and down a long, tree-lined path. Oreyn and Urlla followed in single file. The fields on either side were fenced with thickets of close-growing thornbushes, meant for keeping tame animals in and wild animals out. Aleps grazed in one pasture, borras in another, the young frolicking while their mothers rested. At the end of the path was a stable, large and well-appointed, with a stone barn and several paddocks.

Younglings scurried about the yard, hauling water and grain in wooden buckets. Two of them coaxed a recalcitrant team of borras to pull a small cart loaded with bundles of straw. Another, wearing an apprentice's sash, trundled over to meet the riders.

"We need lodging for our mounts for at least two days," said Viela. He pulled out his money-string, unfastened a single iron ring, and offered it to the apprentice. "This should insure that they get a private paddock and plenty of grain."

The youngling slipped the ring into a pocket in his sash, and accepted the rein from Viela as he dismounted. Oreyn also dismounted, but Urlla stayed in his saddle.

"What is this?" asked the gem cutter. "We are not in the city, are we?"

"Certainly not," replied Viela, forgetting that Urlla had never visited Berrut. He pulled the pack from his mount's saddle and slung it over one shoulder.

"Why should we leave our mounts here? Is it not better to stable them at the inn, where Oreyn can care for them himself?"

"There is no stable at the inn," said Oreyn. "These younglings are competent to care for our animals."

"No one is allowed to ride in the city." Viela reached for Urlla's rein, but the gem cutter held tight to it, refusing to dismount.

"I will not walk. I am a member of Alu's council, and will not be seen walking into the city like a youngling."

"No one is allowed to ride in the city," repeated Viela. He had run out of patience. With a deft tug he pulled Urlla from his saddle, setting him on the ground with a thud. "We walk from here to the inn."

The walk was silent but not peaceful. Oreyn strode beside Viela, his pack slung over one shoulder. Urlla followed them, carrying his own pack, shifting it from side to side more often than its weight warranted. He glowered and sulked, the ruby haze of his aura brushing Viela's calmer topaz shield. The flares that erupted when their auras collided made Urlla and Oreyn flinch, but Viela ignored them.

The Healer fingered the Mentor's wristband that once again hung against his chest, and wondered where Jeryl was and what he was doing. His absence had made it necessary for Oreyn to be Clan Alu's spokesman before the assembly. When this crisis was over, Alu's council would have to send to the FreeMasters Guild for a new Mentor. That is, if the assembly allowed Alu to remain autonomous.

"In a few days it may not matter that you were once a member of Alu's council," said Viela to the angry gem cutter. "If the assembly finds Alu guilty of misconduct, the trade rights will pass to Eiku, and Alu's council will be dissolved."

That statement brought Urlla out of his sulk. "Dissolve the council? They cannot do that!"

"The assembly can do anything it chooses to do," said Oreyn.

"How could it enforce such a decision? Alu is a powerful clan. It would take more than a declaration of the assembly to dissolve our council."

Oreyn turned to look at Urlla. "You have much to learn, young one." The term was not one of affection. "If none of the clans and guilds will trade for our cloth, and the mountain clans refuse to send us metal, how long will Alu remain powerful? We rely on the other clans for too many things: bark for tea, borras, almost half of our grain, raw jewels for the gem cutters, dyes for the weavers. Alu can survive without these things, but we cannot hold power."

"Then we must make certain the assembly does not have reason to censure Alu. Viela's testimony will show them the truth of what happened at the dispute. If they accept what he says, they will know Alu is blameless." The bravado in Urlla's voice was not supported in his aura.

Viela shrugged. "Jeryl took up the Mentor's wristband in the circle, and challenged Revin. By law he is Mentor of Alu, and should be here to represent the clan. Eiku's supporters will ask where he is, and why he is not with

us. They will use his absence to spread suspicion about
our motives and to cast doubt on my testimony.''

They walked in silence for a long time. Then Oreyn
said, ''Viela and I must stand together before the assembly. I will support his testimony. I can testify about the
Terrans that were captured after the dispute. We need
only tell the assembly that Jeryl is pursuing the other
Terrans. Urlla, you must not discuss Jeryl's absence with
anyone. Viela will keep the Mentor's wristband hidden
under his tunic. No one will know that Jeryl does not
have it. They will know that we do not tell everything,
but they will not be able to find fault with what we say.''

''That is wise. It means that the three of us cannot be
seen arguing,'' cautioned Viela. ''Disagreement between
us will cause the assembly to doubt our testimony. We
must present a united front, a show of strength to make
up for our missing Mentor.'' He tried to project confi-
dence, but he had grave doubts that they could convince
the assembly of Alu's integrity unless Jeryl should appear
and testify.

Viela had not visited Berrut in many seasons, since
before his littermate Reass became GuildMaster of the
Metalsmiths. The streets were dirtier and more crowded
than he remembered. Festival always brought visitors
from many clans, come to exchange younglings for fos-
tering and to trade in the market. Many others had come
to attend the assembly. The visitors strolled the avenues,
enjoying the spring sunshine. A group of fisherfolk in
bright clothing haggled with a street vendor for sweet
cakes and early fruits. Urlla was watching them; he collided with a veiled crèche Mother wearing a cloak of Alu
weave. He bowed and excused himself, but she strode
past, ignoring him.

''I wish my mate was with me,'' complained Urlla,
watching the Mother. ''We should be together for Festival. It is important to mark the Overtaking together, to
utter the prayers and read House Mistal's scroll of names
in the moonlight. We have many past Mothers to honor
in our House.''

''Your mate is at home with her younglings, where she

belongs. Clan Mothers do not traipse about public streets at Festival," admonished Oreyn. "It will not harm either of you to be apart. Think of Alu instead of your own pleasure."

Rebuked, Urlla ducked his head and followed Oreyn and the Healer. The avenue widened as it approached the central court where the main streets met. It was shaded by tall trees with broad, flat, many-lobed leaves that rustled in the breeze. Two of the trees stood in front of the Inn of the Blue Door, their lowest branches brushing the roof.

Viela opened the door. The inn never changed. With the fair weather, the doors to the garden were thrown open and the first floor was filled with sunshine and the sweet smell of trees. Food was set out so that patrons could serve themselves. Harra, the innkeeper, sat near the door, collecting coins and assigning rooms.

Viela stepped inside and surveyed the room. The tables were crowded with representatives of many clans. Most of them would be attending the assembly. He recognized a few of the Mentors, but there were many he did not know. He had hoped to see more Healers among the crowd, for as a senior member of the guild he had some influence with them.

Leaving Oreyn and Urlla at the door, Viela stepped up to Harra's table. He offered the innkeeper two iron rings.

"How many rooms?"

"Two," said Viela. "A corner room, if you still have one."

"The corner rooms were taken before midday. I can give you one opening on the garden, if you wish."

"That would do."

Harra picked up a stylus. "Names?"

"Viela of Alu, Oreyn of Alu, and Urlla of Alu."

Shaking a hand in Oreyn's direction, Harra said, "Please ask your companions not to block the doorway."

The door swung open, and Urlla had to jump aside to avoid being hit. Three Masters entered. Viela recognized two of them: Starm, of the Messengers Guild, and Kaalu, the Eiku Healer. The third was younger, and wore a

council leader's emblem and the insignia of Eiku. Starm
kicked Oreyn's pack aside and strode toward Harra.

Stepping forward to block their path, Viela confronted
the newcomers. "May the great sun smile on you," he
said, making a formal gesture of greeting. Before any of
them could reply, he continued. "It is good to see you,
Starm. We have much to discuss before the assembly
meets tomorrow."

Starm looked from Viela to Kaalu and his companion,
wisps of topaz polluting the sapphire calm of his aura.
The Alu Healer pressed his advantage.

"You have been discussing the meeting with these representatives of Eiku, have you not? Alu would also like
an opportunity to consult with you, considering your tra-
ditionally neutral position in the assembly."

"The GuildMaster allowed us to visit his guildhall, to
observe the operations of the Messengers Guild more
closely." Kaalu did not tell a lie, but his aura showed
that he had not revealed the whole truth. Viela suspected
collusion between Eiku and the Messengers Guild, some
attempt to throw the assembly vote to Eiku. He motioned
for Oreyn to join him.

"We would like to make such a visit, if it is possible.
Could you find the time to accommodate us this evening,
GuildMaster?"

"I am afraid not. I have already taken too much time
away from my duties. Perhaps tomorrow, or the next day,
if you will be in Berrut that long." Starm's aura clouded,
the sapphire and topaz blending into a murky green. Viela
knew he was concealing something.

"We shall be in Berrut for several days, but we should
like to talk with you before the Assembly meets, as these
others did."

"That is impossible. Come to the guildhall tomorrow
afternoon, and bring your attendant with you," said
Starm, looking at Oreyn. "I have business to complete
at the guildhall. Please excuse me. I shall see you all in
the assembly hall tomorrow morning." He nodded to the
two who had come in with him, and to Viela, and then
he swept past Urlla and out the door.

Viela was angry. He gave a cursory nod to the two

from Eiku, and turned back to the Innkeeper. "Which rooms?" he asked.

"Green room and blue room, second floor," replied Harra. "Enjoy your stay."

Viela did not answer him.

The rooms were small. Viela took the one with the green door and a window on the garden. It had bare wooden walls and a sleeping platform, a stool, and a small chest for clothing. He dropped his pack on the chest, hung his cloak on a peg beside the door, and crossed the hall to the other room. Urlla was standing at the window, cloak thrown over his right shoulder, pack still trailing from his left hand, gazing at the court and the assembly hall. He seemed mesmerized by the city. Oreyn had already emptied his pack and was placing his neatly-folded clothing in the cupboard.

"I have some friends to visit, people of influence who may help us tomorrow. Would you come with me?" Viela asked.

Urlla turned slowly, tossing his pack onto the bed. "Yes," he said, "I would like to see more of the city. Will we visit any of the guildhalls?"

"I think it best if you remain here," said Oreyn. "I will accompany the Healer." He ignored the flare of anger in Urlla's aura and followed Viela through the door.

"We go first to the hall of the metalsmiths. I have not seen my littermate Reass since he became GuildMaster there. We were good companions when we were younglings," mused Viela.

Viela closed the door to his room and set the mental seals on the latch to guard against intruders. It was an unusual precaution, but Viela was disturbed by his encounter with Starm. He wanted to be certain his belongings were not touched.

They walked down the stairs and through the crowded dining room, past Harra at his table, and through the blue door. Viela led Oreyn across the court to red street, to the metalsmiths' compound. The stone wall that surrounded the guildhall was high and forbidding, but the wide wooden gate was thrown open in welcome. They

stood in the gateway, watching the workers while they
waited for a greeting and an invitation to enter.

The work yard was filled with metal. There were tools
and knife blanks strewn across tables, wooden buckets
filled with iron fittings, thin copper plates stacked waiting for the engravers. Each time Viela visited Reass over
the years, he saw more metal in the hands of his littermate's guild. Metal was wealth, and, properly adminis-
tered, wealth was power.

Reass was working at the forge. He was clad in shorts
and a heavy apron, and beads of moisture shone on his
shoulders as he hammered a length of iron into a knife
blade. The hypnotic ring of metal striking metal filled
the courtyard. Viela let the sound wash over him, watched
the easy, fluid motion of his littermate's arm. Reass had
been the strongest of their litter. Viela was the runt, and
Reass had protected him, made sure he had enough food
to survive. They had been chosen for apprenticeships at
the same time, Reass to the metalsmiths and Viela to the
Healers. There had been no guarantees that they would
become adults, but they had both been accepted into their
guilds and became Masters. Somewhere they had three
littermates, all younglings still.

A journeyman approached them, his hands raised in
greeting. "Welcome," he said. There was a black stripe
cutting diagonally across his apron where hot metal had
scorched it. "How may we serve you?"

"We wish to speak with your GuildMaster," said
Viela. "When he finishes his work, tell him that the
Healer Viela has come to see him."

"I will tell him." He gestured to a bench set in the
shade of an old tree. "Come in and rest. The Guild-
Master should be finished soon."

Viela sat on the bench, but Oreyn wandered among the
worktables, talking with the journeymen. He fingered
knife blanks and stroked plates of copper while he asked
questions. Viela knew he was dazzled by the sight of so
much metal. The workers took him for a customer, and
answered him politely.

Viela liked to watch Reass. The heavy muscles of the
smith's arms and shoulders rippled as he swung the ham-

mer, using heat and pressure to shape the metal into a fine blade. Other smiths worked beside him, but none had his grace and precision. Their strokes were short and choppy, their movements irregular, and they heated their pieces more often than he did. Reass worked the red-hot metal quickly. When he was satisfied with the blade, he plunged it into a tub of water. Steam billowed up, hiding his face. When the air cleared, he was looking at the Healer.

"Viela!" called Reass as he strode across the yard, one hand raised in greeting. "Your presence brings grace to my guild."

Viela rose and made an answering gesture. "Your hospitality honors me," he replied.

Oreyn heard the greeting and joined them. "I am Oreyn, leader of Alu's council," he said.

"Welcome!" Reass' eyes were on Viela. "Come, join me for a refreshing drink. We have much to talk about. I have not seen you in . . . two summers?"

"Three," said Viela, following Reass toward the guildhall. "It is good to see you again, but this is more than a pleasure visit. We have important business to discuss with you."

"I know of your reason for being in Berrut," said Reass. "You will testify before the assembly tomorrow, concerning the dispute between Alu and Eiku."

"Yes," said Oreyn. "Once that problem is settled, we want to discuss trade possibilities with you. The trade agreement between Alu and the Terrans is almost completed, and we will soon have Terran iron and copper for sale."

Viela's anger was a ruby streak in his aura. Alu would not trade with the Terrans if he could prevent it. He would drive them away from his clan and his people, but first he must clear Alu's reputation. "Alu has been greatly wronged in this matter. The accusations brought by Eiku are unfounded, as my testimony will prove."

Reass led them into a cool, dark hall. "Eiku did not accuse you, though its leaders agree with the accusations. The charges were voiced by Starm, on behalf of a FreeMaster named Arien. So the rumors say."

"Arien! I do not believe that!" exclaimed Viela. He had suspected Starm's complicity, but Arien had watched the dispute. He knew the truth.

"A messenger has been sent to the FreeMasters Guild, to bring Arien to the assembly," said Reass. "You can confront him yourself, tomorrow."

Chapter 26

Sarah Anders stood before the great hearth on the first floor of the FreeMasters' guildhall, a mug of hot spiced cider cupped in her hands. She hunched over the mug, shivering though the room was not cold. The afternoon's events had left her exhausted, physically and emotionally, but her anger with· Durrow kept adrenaline surging through her body. Visions of the laser-wreaked carnage on the trail haunted her.

Jeryl sat at the other end of the hall, nursing a cup of tea in silence. An untouched bowl of stew was at his side. Sarah walked over, reached out to touch his hand. He drew away.

"Do not come so close," he pleaded. "Your rage is a heat that surrounds you. It burns me."

She stepped back, hand falling to her side, head turned aside. "I'm sorry. I didn't mean to hurt you. I want you to know how much I abhor what Durrow did. I'm angry with him, not with you."

"I know that."

She rushed on. "He will be punished for what he's done, for killing Mrann and interfering in the dispute, and for harming that messenger." She needed to make Jeryl understand that, as much as she needed to believe it herself. Her objectivity had fled in the face of her rage.

"Are you certain the messenger is still alive?" she asked.

"I have ·not felt a death-cry," Jeryl said.

Sarah nodded. Knowing her presence gave Jeryl pain, she walked back to the hearth.

At last Arien came down the open staircase, dressed in a clean tunic and boots. An older Master, wrapped in a blue cloak, followed him. His weather-worn features reminded Sarah of Mrann, and a sudden sorrow drowned the remains of her anger.

The older Master gestured greetings to Jeryl. "The guild thanks you for the aid you gave my apprentice, Master. I am Malin, leader of the FreeMasters. What is your keep?" The questions seemed a polite formality.

"Alu. I am Jeryl, and this is Sarah Anders." He motioned for her to join him, pointedly making no reference to her Terran origins.

Sarah nodded politely at the GuildMaster. "Favor, sir," she said in Ardellan, and was pleased when Malin could not hide his surprise. "The hospitality of your guildhall honors me."

The words were a formal greeting to which there was only one polite response. "You honor us with your presence, Master."

Arien snorted. It was a harsh, bitter sound. "This is a Terran, Malin. Why are we honored by the presence of one who brings death and destruction among us?"

Jeryl opened his mouth to reply, but Sarah silenced him with a glare. "Durrow and his cohorts are Terrans, but their actions are not condoned by Terran authorities. What they have done here violates our laws, as well as yours. They will be punished."

"If I find Durrow, he will be dead," said Arien.

"FreeMaster!" Malin's reprimand was sharp, his expression shocked. "I will not have threats in my guildhall on the day of Festival."

Chastised, Arien gave a stiff nod of acknowledgment to his GuildMaster before leaving the room. Malin turned to Jeryl and Sarah. "You are welcome to celebrate the Festival of Overtaking with us." The invitation was coolly polite.

Sarah looked questioningly at Jeryl.

"Tonight second-moon will rise before first-moon," he said. "The Festival of Overtaking will be celebrated

in the keeps with prayers for the continuation of the
Houses. Each Master will stand in the moonlight and
read the names of all the Mothers who lived and died in
his House. Then the Mothers will carry offerings to the
mourning wall. Tomorrow they will feast with the younglings.

"This would have been my first Festival with Hladi. I
would rather not spend it alone. These FreeMasters have
all lost their mates and Houses; their ritual will be different from the one I have witnessed. Will you attend it
with me?"

Sarah thought of Hladi's graceful funeral urn, set into
the mourning wall years before its time because of Terran
greed. Her people owed Jeryl and Clan Alu a debt that
could never be repaid. Yet Jeryl offered her friendship
and trust. She could not refuse him. "I would be honored, Jeryl."

They followed Malin out into the dusk, to the courtyard where the other Masters were gathered. Sarah felt
uncertain about joining their circle, but when she tried
to stay back, Jeryl grasped her arm and drew her gently
to his side. As they stood silently together, the night sky
deepened to indigo and the stars began to appear. In a
few moments the tiny white moon climbed over the eastern peaks to claim sole possession of the sky.

Malin faced the rising moon and lifted his hands high.
Sarah gasped. The gesture brought to mind another circle, and flashes of power that killed. No energy streamed
from Malin's palms. He was surrounded by a golden light
that kept the darkness at bay.

"We are FreeMasters," he said. "Our freedom is a
twin-edged blade. We have lost our mates, our families,
our clans, our Houses. The dreams we had, of metamorphosis and Motherhood, can never be realized. In exchange, we have gained power and long life. Most of us
do not consider it an equitable trade.

"Tonight we mourn that which we have lost. We celebrate the Overtaking not with prayers for the continuance of our Houses, but with cries of sorrow and pleas
for forgetfulness. We walk in pairs that we may share one
another's pain and ease one another's loneliness. We wash

away the past with moon-kissed water, and pray for peace of mind and strength to face another dawn.

"So it is; so it must always be among the Free-Masters."

Malin lowered his arms. A tiny flicker of shimmer-light appeared in the darkness, floating above his head. Soon a hundred flames danced in the air, weaving intricate patterns as the FreeMasters broke their circle and began to move across the compound. They moaned as they walked, and some cried out, making sounds that tore at Sarah's heart.

She watched Jeryl, studying his solemn features. They were barely illuminated by the delicate light that hovered a hand's breadth above his head. His hair gleamed in the shimmer-light, but his eyes were lost in shadow. His mouth was pressed tightly closed, and he did not make a sound. She let her hand brush his, felt the warmth of his skin, the wiry strength of his fingers against hers. This time he did not push her away.

The Masters were pairing off. Couplets of shimmer-light moved through the darkness toward the other side of the compound. Arien approached, his arms twined about the shoulders of another FreeMaster, the flames above their heads bobbing and weaving in a private dance. Seeing Sarah, he turned aside, stepping off the path to avoid her. Other pairs followed, but they were engrossed in the ceremony and ignored the strangers in their midst.

As the last of the couples passed them, Jeryl turned to follow. Sarah hesitated, but he tugged at her arm and drew her along the path.

They followed the procession of delicate flames on a winding path through the compound and around the clan-hall, to an open garden of ghostly trees and hedges. Here the couples formed another circle around a small reflecting pool, and joined in a soft, melodious chant. The single moon was visible in the pool, until a couple came forward and knelt at its edge to dip their hands in the water. They anointed each other with the moisture as the surface of the pool rippled, disturbing the reflection. Then they rose and stepped aside, and another couple took their place.

Jeryl shuddered. Sarah reached for his hand, felt her
skin tingle as their fingers intertwined. A wave of sadness
flooded into her. She thought of Hladi, lying composed
on her bier, and of her own father, buried far from his
homeland. Tears filled her eyes and constricted her throat.
Jeryl pulled her forward, knelt beside the pool and tugged
her down beside him, dipped her hand into the water.
Her throat relaxed. The tears stopped flowing from her
eyes. Jeryl touched her face with his wet hand, then rose
and disappeared into the darkness, his shimmer-light
snuffed out. She climbed to her feet and followed the
small sounds of his rustling clothing.

She found him in the guildhall, warming himself before the great hearth. Jeryl stared into the fire, his shoulders hunched and his hands extended toward the flames.
Sarah watched him, and shared his loneliness. She
wanted to touch him, to offer him her friendship and support, and more. She felt the same special kinship with
Jeryl that she had shared with men who later became her
lovers. That disturbed her. She retreated to the open
doorway and watched the couples in the garden. As each
couple left the pool and the now-silent circle, the lights
above their heads coalesced into single entities, and the
pairs melted into their own private places in the darkness.

The larger moon rose. The last pair of Masters was
gone, and the pool's surface was still again. The garden
was shadowed and silent. Sarah stared at the moons' reflections on the water until a cold gust of wind lifted her
cloak and made her shiver. Then she closed the heavy
wooden door and walked to the hearth. There was a pot
of tea by the fire, next to a tray of mugs. She filled two
mugs and handed one to Jeryl. She watched the fire,
afraid to look at him. He took the mug from Sarah's hand
without touching her.

Standing before the fire with Jeryl, she realized how
empty her life was. She had few friends and saw them
rarely; she hardly knew her children. If she died tonight,
who would write her death message? Would anyone
mourn for more than a moment? She was alone, just as
Jeryl was alone. For years she had used her work to hide
her loneliness.

That work had served her well until she came to Ardel. Here it had betrayed her. The walls she had so painstakingly built were tumbling down. The friendship and mutual respect she had shared with Mrann, the reawakening of her psychic powers, and this strange and frightening attraction she felt for Jeryl had broken through her defenses. Now she knew how long she had been alone and how lonely she truly was.

Jeryl took an earthenware flask from the mantle and pulled out the stopper. He offered the flask to Sarah, holding it above her mug. His gaze caught hers.

"We have shared snatches of each other's thoughts and feelings," he said. "This will make us more open to one another."

Sarah's hand trembled. She willed it to be steady as Jeryl poured some of the flask's syrupy contents into her mug, and then into his own. She sipped the tea slowly. It tasted poignantly bittersweet, and brought unexpected tears to her eyes.

The room was altered subtly, but Sarah could not say how. She stood very still because she was afraid to move. When Jeryl took her mug and set it beside his own on the hearth, she made no objection. Taking her hands, he held them with fingers that did not mesh with her own, pressing his palm to hers. With his touch the room was suddenly transformed. The material world faded, and she was confronted with a world of brilliant colors and flowing energy patterns. Her body appeared to be a shimmering, changing web of forces. Jeryl was a net of energies very different from her own, yet there were points of contact where power flowed from one to the other and back again, increasing in intensity as it flowed through them.

The depth of the colors that surrounded and invaded them grew, reflecting the increasing energy of their emotions. Power cascaded between them, lighting the room with its strength and making Sarah tremble. She felt her will slipping away, becoming lost in the intricate webbing of energy that was Jeryl. For the first time she felt that she was capable of touching the soul of another being. The feeling frightened her. She wrenched her hands away from Jeryl's, and the room returned to a reality she could accept.

She felt a sudden, profound sense of loss, and in her weakness she sat on the wide hearthstone. Jeryl stood before her, his face open and inviting. He extended his hands, waiting, but he said nothing. Sarah stared into the depths of his gray eyes. She was afraid, and she was fascinated. She lifted her hands and laid them in his, in spite of her pounding heart.

A persistent beeping woke Sarah long before dawn. Disoriented, she groped through the darkness, one hand rummaging among her piled clothes to locate the transceiver. She was naked, sprawled on a platform and covered with furs. She had no idea how she had gotten there, or when.

She found the insistent piece of technology, pulled it out and palmed the switch. "Anders here," she croaked. Her throat was dry.

"This is Captain Swenson of the *Blackhawk*, Commander. We have located Durrow's shuttle. Repeat, we have located the shuttle."

Sarah was suddenly alert. "Where, Captain?" she queried, reaching for her tunic.

"Three kilometers southwest of your location, Commander. Shall we move in?"

That would take them down the mountain toward Berrut. It was not far. If she mustered Jeryl and some of the FreeMasters, they could reach the shuttle before dawn. "No. Repeat. No. Do not move in. Hold your position until I contact you. I will organize a ground party. Anders out." She stumbled to the door, wondering how to find Jeryl, and was surprised to see him standing in the hall.

"I heard the signal," he said. "Have your people found Durrow?"

"They've located his ship." She suppressed an urge to reach for Jeryl, to find a physical expression for the psychic connection they shared. He was with her, whether she touched him or not. She straightened her tunic, tugging it down over her thighs. Others were coming from their rooms, wisps of shimmer-light floating behind them. Jeryl lit a sconce. They were on the second floor balcony, overlooking the great hall. Malin appeared, wrapped in furs, with Arien close behind.

"We can reach Durrow's shuttle before first light, if we leave immediately. Any of you who wish to come are welcome. I want to be there when the *Blackhawk* captures the shuttle."

"Blackhawk!" exclaimed Arien. "What has your ship to do with this? We have had enough trouble from one Terran ship. We do not want another."

"Do you propose to stand against Durrow's lasers yourself?"

"I do."

"His weapons will burn you before you can harm him," protested Sarah.

Malin shrugged, the fur slipping from his shoulder. "We are capable of defending ourselves against Terran weapons."

Startled by their certainty, Sarah looked from one to the other. "You cannot keep the shuttle on the ground. They will just raise ship unless the drive is disabled. Can you do that with your thoughts?" she challenged.

"We can try."

"Do not be foolish," exclaimed Jeryl. "With the help of the Terrans, we can take the ship quickly. Perhaps we can keep them from killing the messenger."

Arien stalked toward the stairs. "I will not trust one Terran to stand against another," he said.

Jeryl followed the FreeMaster, extending his arms above his head. Power surged around him, audible cracklings in the air. His fingers wove strange patterns of force as his eyes followed Arien.

The other turned, but before he could accept the challenge, Sarah stepped between them. Her eyes met Malin's and pleaded with him for help, but she could discern no reaction there. "You waste your energy, arguing with each other," she said. She tried to keep her voice calm and persuasive, but she knew they could detect her fear. "We have a common enemy. Working together, we can defeat him."

Malin stepped forward, baring his wrist to show his band of office. "The Terran is correct," he said. "We must ride. Now."

Chapter 27

Sarah's injured ankle throbbed. She had changed the splint hurriedly, wrapping it tightly and putting on extra hardener to keep the ankle from moving. Then she pulled on her clothing and ran to the stables with Jeryl and Malin. They took the first mounts they found, not caring whose aleps they were. Arien, the Healer Lirra, and two other Masters joined them. Younglings ran back and forth with saddles and reins. In a few moments they were riding quickly down the mountain, with shimmer-light and the great moon illuminating their trail.

Arien claimed to know the meadow where Captain Swenson had found the shuttle. He led them on a twisting trail through dense woods. The homing beacon on Sarah's transceiver was active, and the *Blackhawk* was following their progress. If they strayed too far from their destination, Swenson would contact her and give her a new vector. After two kilometers the terrain leveled and the trail widened. Arien quenched his shimmer-light and slowed their pace, then rode ahead to scout the meadow.

"The shuttle is there," he said when he returned. His mount was snorting and blowing. The thin saddle was soaked with sweat. "There are two sentries with large laser weapons outside the port, and the external lights are dimmed."

"If we approach from the sunward side, they will have difficulty seeing us against the dawn," suggested Jeryl.

Malin agreed. "We must move quickly, to be in place when the sun rises."

The sky brightened slowly. Sarah rode beside Jeryl, following Arien and Malin. They made a wide loop around the meadow, deep in the sheltering darkness of the trees. On the far side they stopped and dismounted. Sarah swung her bad leg up and over the saddle, made a quarter turn, and slid to the ground. She expected to land on her good ankle, but slipped and jarred the injured one. She yelped in pain, and Lirra rushed to her side, throwing an arm around her waist to support her.

"Sit," he insisted. "You should not walk on that ankle. Let me examine it."

She pushed him away. "It's fine," she said. "The splint is tight enough to hold it straight and keep it from swelling. It will support me." She slowly put weight on it. It ached and throbbed, but the hard wrap kept it from twisting. It would hurt like hell and probably swell when she removed the splint, but she had no time to worry about that now.

Lirra stayed with the mounts. The others approached the meadow on foot, creeping through the unheeding conifers in a straggling line. The sky behind them turned rosy with the approaching dawn, and they could see each other as moving shadow shapes. Walking between Jeryl and Arien, Sarah was conscious of the strain between them. Her ankle ached, but she ignored it. Berry bushes crowded the edge of the forest, offering them cover. They knelt to look at the shuttle.

It squatted in the clearing like an enormous metal beetle. Sarah could make out few details in the gentle glow of its dimmed exterior lights. The port was open, one sentry patrolling outside it, weapon dangling casually from his left hand. The other leaned against the shuttle. The craft was small, but equipped with jump capability. Sarah had seen such small ships at the space stations, and knew that daring pilots made routine jumps along the shipping lanes, but she could not imagine taking to deep space in one of them. They were useful for survey work and hopping about a system, but usually dependent on a larger ship for interstellar transport.

It was time to contact the *Blackhawk*. Sarah pulled her transceiver from her sash. Arien crouched beside her. His hand grasped her wrist, keeping her from lifting the transceiver to her mouth. Sarah tried to shake him off, but he held on tight. His fingers were strong. Her hand shook, the fingers tingling. She stared at him. ''Mateless orphan!'' she muttered, the most foul insult she knew. Her fingers numbed and lost their grip, and the transceiver slipped to the ground.

Suddenly Malin was between them. Arien dropped her arm. Malin scooped up the transceiver and gave it to Sarah, glaring at Arien. ''She may call her ship,'' he said. He turned to Sarah. ''Tell them only to keep the shuttle on the ground. They may use no weapons, and may not land without permission.''

His tone left no room for argument. ''Agreed,'' she said as she palmed the control. She spoke quickly. An instant later the dark shadow of the *Blackhawk* fell out of the sky to circle above the meadow.

The leaning sentry spotted the *Blackhawk* immediately. He shouted something to his companion, but the other was already crouching at the foot of the ramp, eye to his rifle sight. The noise of the *Blackhawk*'s engines filled the clearing. The first sentry scrambled up the ramp and ducked into the shuttle. He reappeared at the port, firing sporadically at the *Blackhawk* to cover the retreat of his companion. The shuttle's engines powered up with a low drone. The ramp lifted and the port snapped shut.

Sarah could feel the vibrations where her knees touched the earth. Jeryl put a hand on her shoulder, shouted something at her, but she could not hear above the noise of the ships. He pointed. Malin and the others were standing, fighting their way through the bushes. She followed.

The *Blackhawk*'s circling produced a violent wind in the treetops. Needles and small branches rained down around the edge of the meadow. Some larger branches began crashing through the trees. One struck the shuttle, bouncing across the roof. Another came down between Malin and Arien. They ignored it.

The shuttle raised power as the *Blackhawk* spiraled lower. It started to lift, looking for a way to dodge past the bigger ship. The shuttle was more maneuverable than the *Blackhawk*, but the meadow was small and the tall conifers hemmed it in. The *Blackhawk* filled the sky, an immense predator stalking its prey.

The FreeMasters stood in an arc along the edge of the forest, facing the shuttle. Malin took the central place, flanked by two guild members on his left and Arien and Jeryl on his right. Sarah stood behind Jeryl. She wanted to be a part of this. She could guess at the energy they would raise, and the power that would be expended against the shuttle. Her heart pounded, her ankle throbbed, fright and exhilaration and anger forced adrenaline into her bloodstream.

The FreeMasters touched hands, palm to palm, with the outer two holding their free palms toward the shuttle. Sarah had seen Mrann and Elver practice power transference and energy channeling. Malin was doing the same thing, using his companions to draw and focus extra energy on the shuttle.

The shuttle's engines strained as the pilot looked for an opening. The *Blackhawk* moved in tight circles, her engines whining. The shuttle bounced, settled to the ground, bounced again. Its engines faltered and sputtered. It lifted once more, started to turn, but the engines died and it landed heavily.

The *Blackhawk* pulled up, moving in wider circles that were easier on the ship. The FreeMasters still stood in their semicircle, hands joined, watching the shuttle and waiting.

The ramp extended and the port opened. Two crewmen with laser rifles appeared, crouching just inside the opening and firing at the *Blackhawk*. Their effort was useless. The larger ship climbed out of range, continuing its lazy circles. They still fired at her, wasting time and power attempting to drive her away.

The sun rose, its first rays tentatively poking over the trees. The FreeMasters stood in shadow at the edge of the forest, watching the shuttle. Malin edged forward with small steps, his hands still touching the other FreeMasters'. They followed him, and the two on the ends also followed, turning the arc inside out to form a wedge.

They advanced toward the open port, disregarding the laser fire. Sarah walked behind them, holding her breath as she watched the flashing energy bursts. If the sentries saw Malin and his people, they could destroy them in a few seconds. The sentries stopped firing at the *Blackhawk* when they realized that it was out of range. The heavy, throbbing drone of the engines was fading, and the whirlwind had ceased.

Malin stepped out of the shadows into the sunlight three meters from the end of the shuttle's ramp. He raised his hands in a gesture of power. "Surrender!" he called.

Sarah wanted to rush forward, throw Malin down, shield him with her body. The sentries saw him, brought their rifles up to take aim. Time slowed. She felt her fear and rage growing, watched the Terrans touch the weapons to their cheeks and gaze through the sights, saw the power Malin was gathering between his hands.

The sentries' fingers moved on the pulse triggers. Sarah closed her eyes, saw the bright streak of energy that was Malin, the dimmer spots that were the Terrans. Dazzling pinpoints of energy stood out beside them—the power packs of their lasers. Her rage heightened her senses. She heard the clicking of the triggers, heard the whine of energy building. She reached in, blocked the release of that power, let the energy back up until it forced its way through another channel.

The Terrans screamed. Sarah opened her eyes, watched Malin's power strike the side of the ship and disperse. Her extended senses showed her that he had overloaded the ship's electronic systems. She had overheated the weapons, melting their mechanisms and turning them into junk.

Arien and Jeryl ran up the ramp. Sarah followed, saw Arien kick a smoking rifle out of his way. Its heat scorched the side of his boot. The sentries were sitting on the floor inside the port, nursing burnt and blistering hands. Jeryl grabbed them, shoved them down the ramp toward Malin and the others. He went through the shuttle, dragging people from their seats and pushing them outside.

They found the messenger at the back of the shuttle. A tiny flicker of shimmer-light floated above his head, but he was unconscious, burning with fever. Sarah helped to cut away the tape that bound his naked body. Dried blood from a festering shoulder wound stained the floor beneath him. Arien muttered a vile oath, and Sarah answered with one of her own.

"Durrow will pay for this," she said.

Arien ignored her.

Jeryl came to help them move the messenger. He struggled when they lifted him. In the shadows behind him they found the crumpled, lifeless body of a youngling.

The shuttle stank of scorched insulation and melting synthetics. The control panel was fused, the computer was a molten mass of metal and plastic and silicon. The weapons locker was red-hot. Sarah slipped past it, looking for the navigation station.

With the computer destroyed, she could not access the log. The navigation circuitry was burnt out, the display down and the equipment useless. She found some maps and charts, mylar overlays generated by the computer and used by the geologists to mark survey data. Crew rosters, logs, rendezvous times, all vital information was locked in inaccessible memory behind the fused boards.

She rolled the charts and took them with her. The shuttle was junk. It would never lift again. The metalsmiths could send someone to salvage the iron and copper, if anyone would work in the thing. They had no equipment to dismantle the titanium alloy hull. The Union fleet would detail a crew to cut it apart and ship it to the nearest reclamation center.

She stood on the ramp and surveyed the Terrans. Malin had them grouped in the center of the meadow, where he and another FreeMaster could watch them. They stood quietly, nursing their hands. They wore the same black coveralls as the two captured at the dispute. Nicholas Durrow was not among them.

"I want Nicholas Durrow," she called as she strode toward them. They looked at her, but no one said a word. "I am Sarah Anders, and I represent the Terran Trade Commission. At this time, I am the Authority's representative on Ardel. Elizabeth Arnaud and Howard Gresch are already in custody aboard the patrol ship *Blackhawk*.

You will join them soon. The other member of their party is dead. His body has not been recovered.''

"He said they were all dead!" exclaimed a tall woman. The arm of her coverall was torn and her wrist was badly burned. She held it in her other hand.

"Quiet!" The short, red-haired woman pushed her way to the front. "Don't say anything."

Sarah pushed her advantage. "I want Durrow, and I will get him, with or without your help. You can make it easier on yourselves if you cooperate with me. Where is Durrow? He abandoned Gresch and Arnaud in the wasteland to die or be captured. Do you believe he will do any better by you?''

The tall woman started to say something, but the redhead glared at her and she shut her mouth.

"Berrut." He was a thin man, not much taller than the redhead, and he glared back at her as he spoke. "He's in Berrut. We left him there two days ago."

The redhead punched him in the face, hard enough to knock him down. She howled, a mixture of anger and pain, and before Sarah could grab her she was running across the open field toward the forest. Two of the FreeMasters chased her into a bramble thicket. Sarah tried to follow, but she could not run on her injured ankle.

"Do not be concerned," said Malin. "There is nowhere for that one to go."

Arien joined them. "The rest of these," he pointed to the remaining Terrans, "are sheep. That one, the pilot Roletti, is the dangerous one. She surprised me at Durrow's camp. I did not sense her presence until she was behind me. She threatened to kill me."

"I don't think she is very dangerous without weapons," said Sarah.

"She has the cunning of a lizard." Arien walked away.

Sarah asked the crew more questions about Durrow, and about the messenger. They would not answer her. The thin man avoided her eyes, and the woman stared at the ground. They were afraid of incriminating themselves. Finally she gave up in disgust and left them with one of the FreeMasters. She could no longer hear the redhead and her pursuers crashing through the forest. Would they catch her?

Sarah crossed the meadow to talk to Jeryl. He stood with Arien, watching Lirra attend to the injured messenger.

"How is he?" she asked.

"He may lose the use of his arm," said Arien. His voice was bitter and angry.

"The *Blackhawk* could transport him to the guildhall," Sarah offered.

"No! We will not put him in another Terran box. Lirra can treat him here. Malin has already sent for a cart." Arien turned his back on her.

She would not argue with him. He had sound reasons for hating Terrans. She looked down at the messenger sprawled on Lirra's cloak, at the angry red welts crossing his body where they had removed the tape. The Healer was cleaning his shoulder, using wet cloths to soften the dried blood. The messenger tossed and moaned, but his eyes stayed closed.

Arien could stay with the messenger; she needed to get to Berrut. "Jeryl, Durrow is in Berrut. How soon can we reach the city?" she asked.

"By midday, if we ride hard."

Malin joined them. "You go to Berrut?" he asked. "What will we do with the prisoners? I do not want to take them to the guildhall."

"Two others are already aboard the *Blackhawk*," said Sarah. "Captain Swenson could take custody of this group . . ."

"No!" Arien was angry. "There has been too much Terran interference here. These are our prisoners. They have broken our laws. We will keep them, and we will punish them!"

"You have no authority," Malin reminded him. "Their crime is against the Messengers Guild. The GuildMaster must say what is to be done with them."

"If we give them to the Terrans, they will never be punished," said Arien.

Malin looked at Jeryl. "You have lived with this Terran. Is her word good? Arien claims the Terrans tell untruths and use them to trick others. Is that your experience?''

Sarah remembered Mrann, and the perfect trust they had had in each other from the beginning. He never questioned her word. Did Jeryl trust her as well? They were close now, in ways she did not understand. If last night's sharing had any meaning, he would support her. She looked into his eyes.

"It is my experience that this Terran is truthful," he said. "Ask her what will become of the prisoners."

She felt Malin's stare as she spoke, and knew she must not break her word. "Captain Swenson will bring them to Berrut, and give them to the GuildMaster of the Messengers to be punished. If the GuildMaster wishes it, they will be returned to Terran Union Authority and imprisoned."

"That is sufficient," said Malin. "Call your ship."

Arien was furious. "This is a mistake. Terrans have no honor."

Lirra interrupted him. "I care nothing for Terran honor," he said. "The messenger is awake. He is trying to speak."

Malin knelt beside him. "Chemi," he said, touching his hand. "Have you a message for me?"

Chemi opened his eyes. "GuildMaster," he said. He closed his eyes and moaned. "Starm sends for Arien. Clan Alu is accused . . ."

Jeryl and Sarah bent closer, trying to hear.

"Alu is accused of treachery. Assembly meets . . . after Festival." He grimaced as Lirra began to stitch the torn muscles of his shoulder together. "Arien . . . testify." He passed out.

"Away now," Lirra said sharply. "You have your message. Let me work."

Sarah pulled out her transceiver. "Durrow has something to do with this," she said.

"Alu is unjustly accused," cried Jeryl, looking at Malin. "I must go to Berrut to defend my clan."

"You are not Mentor," chided Malin. "If you do not wear your clan's wristband, the Assembly will not allow you a seat."

"The Assembly called me to testify," said Arien. "I observed the dispute, and I know of Durrow's interference. Alu was not at fault."

"The *Blackhawk* can get us to Berrut quickly," suggested Sarah. "Are you willing to ride in the patrol ship?"

"No!" Arien was adamant. "I will not set foot in a Terran ship again."

"If we ride, can we get to Berrut before a judgment is made?" asked Sarah. She would call the *Blackhawk* to pick up the prisoners, and to wait for the FreeMasters to bring in the redheaded pilot.

"Chemi said the Assembly is meeting after Festival. That might mean today, or tomorrow," said Malin. "If we ride quickly, I can take my place as a GuildMaster, and Arien can testify. Perhaps we can expose Durrow's manipulations."

Sarah palmed the button on her transceiver and hailed the *Blackhawk*.

"Quickly," urged Jeryl. "We may already be too late."

2257:12/11, TERRAN CALENDAR
TO: AUSTIN DUERST, VP/RESOURCE
         DEVELOPMENT, NAGASHIMI-BOEM
FROM: GLENN ELSNER, CAPTAIN, NAGASHIMI
         INTERSTELLAR SHIP *WHITE CRANE*
WITHDRAWING FROM VICINITY OF ARDEL
IMMEDIATELY. ALTERCATION BETWEEN
TERRAN UNION SHIP AND UNIDENTIFIED
SHUTTLECRAFT HAS RESULTED IN DISABLING
OF SHUTTLE. CREW IS IN CUSTODY ABOARD
UNION SHIP *BLACKHAWK*. CAPTAIN AND PILOT
ESCAPED AND ARE BEING SOUGHT BY LOCALS
AND UNION REPRESENTATIVE.

SITUATION TOO DELICATE TO BEGIN TRADE
NEGOTIATIONS NOW. SUGGEST YOU CONSIDER
FURTHER ACTION AND ADVISE AS SOON AS
POSSIBLE.

Austin Duerst tore the hard-copy in half and dropped
both pieces in the recycler. Then he dictated a recall
message to the *White Crane*. Nick Durrow and his crew
were a lost cause—they had made some mistakes, and
now they would pay the price. Durrow was the only one
who knew that they were working for Nagashimi-BOEM,
and he was smart enough to keep his mouth shut if the
authorities ever caught up with him.

Duerst sighed. He would almost rather take his chances
running with Durrow, than go up to Jim Nagashimi's office and explain how they had lost their chance at all that
titanium.

Chapter 28

Viela stared at the great door to the assembly hall. It was
half again his height, and twice his width. A hand's span
thick, it swung on hinges the length of his forearm. It
was crafted of wood, three different grains and colors
fitted together in a pattern of diminishing rectangles. A
green-sashed youngling stood beside it, checking the cre-
dentials of each Master who approached. It passed them
through the great door in silence, one at a time.

GuildMaster Reass arrived, his leather apron replaced
by a formal red tunic. A copper disk engraved with the
hammer and anvil of the metalsmiths was pinned to his
chest. His aura was murky, guarded, confusing. He
passed Viela without acknowledging him and stopped before the door. The youngling touched the metal emblem
with a tentacle and allowed Reass to enter the chamber.

Viela followed Reass. He was wearing his best tunic,
and his Healer's medallion. Mrann's wristband nestled

between his tentacle nodules, suspended by a thong and hidden under his tunic. It rubbed against his chest when he moved. He dared not let the Assembly know that Jeryl denied the role of Mentor and refused to wear the wristband. Oreyn walked beside Viela, proudly wearing Alu colors and the emblem of the council leader. Viela was gambling that the emblem would be enough to admit Oreyn to the Assembly. If they would not accept him as Jeryl's proxy, Alu would have no voice on the council.

They stopped before the door. Viela still had the ceramic tile the messenger had brought him at Alu. He pulled it from his pocket, and gave it to the youngling. They waited in silence while the youngling examined the twin trees design. Apparently satisfied, it snaked out a tentacle to trip a hidden control. The heavy door swung open.

Viela stepped up to the doorway, and looked into the assembly hall. He saw a huge, bowl-shaped room with tiers of benches forming concentric rings about a sand pit. The ceiling was arched, unsupported by beams or pillars. Clumps of rock crystal jutted from the polished stone walls, glowing and sparkling in the shimmer-light. He took a step into the hall. Hearing a muffled grunt behind him, he turned.

The door was closing. Oreyn was struggling with the youngling, trying to step through the doorway. The youngling had wrapped two tentacles around his arm and was pulling him back. Viela stepped forward, left shoulder braced against the wall, right arm outstretched to hold back the door. With his free hand he grabbed the youngling's sash and tried to pull the youngling aside.

The youngling was only as high as Viela's chest, and weighed half what a Master weighed, but it was persistent. It wedged its body between Viela and Oreyn, and slipped a tentacle free to work more hidden controls. The massive door pressed forward, bending Viela's arm. He tried to pull Oreyn past the youngling and into the chamber, but the youngling was immovable. The door forced his arm down. He could step out of its way, either into the hall or out of it, or he could stay where he was and be crushed. The youngling would not permit Oreyn to

enter. As the door touched his shoulder, Viela stepped
back into the hall. The door closed with a hollow thud.

Viela was angry. He turned toward the center of the
hall, and saw Reass standing in the aisle below, watching
him. Four-hands-and-two Masters sat on the bottom tier
of benches, shimmer-light floating above their heads.
None of them noticed the disturbance at the door. After
a moment Reass turned and went down to the circle,
choosing a seat next to Harra, the innkeepers' Guild-
Master. He stared placidly into the sand pit with the others.

Spurts of ruby streaked the amber of Viela's aura. He
forgot that he had ever doubted Oreyn would be admitted
to the hall. The Assembly had no right to deny Alu representation. He stormed down the steps toward the Masters, broadcasting his anger. Spikes of rage bristled from
his reddening aura as he searched the circle for Starm.
He saw him on the opposite side of the sand pit.

When Viela reached the bottom tier of benches, a cor-
don of fine copper cable kept him from stepping onto the
sand. The Masters were seated around the circle, hands
touching the wire and feet in the sand. He tried to slide
past them, but they were oblivious to his presence and
did not clear a path for him. Frustration added fuel to his
anger. Finally he climbed to the second tier of benches
and strode around the circle to Starm's place. The
GuildMaster ignored him until Viela touched his shoulder. Then he turned, and gestured to the cable. Viela
leaned forward and touched it with a fingertip, and his
mind connected with the group-mind of the Assembly.

The tangled web of power was woven from Master to
Master around and across the circle. It hung above the
sand, suspended from the copper cable. Dense knots of
energy pulsed where lines intersected.

The Assembly was discussing whether to admit Oreyn
as proxy for Alu's Mentor. Disjointed comments flitted
about the fabric of the unity, bouncing from one element
of the mind to another. Viela perceived them, and tried
to broadcast comments and rebuttals, but his thoughts
were not permitted to merge with the unity. He was an
observer, but not a participant.

(Oreyn is proxy for Alu . . .) (. . . Mentor of Clan Rais was ill, Selph was his proxy . . .) (Selph was apprentice . . .) (. . . Clan Alu has no Mentor . . .) (. . . offer Oreyn Alu's seat . . .) (. . . said Jeryl is Mentor of Alu. Where is he?) (Alu is accused of treachery . . .) (. . . seat an unqualified member of Alu?) (. . . does not have the objectivity of a Mentor . . .) (Oreyn cannot judge his clan's fate . . .) (Jeryl should be here to take the seat . . .) (. . . Oreyn should not be admitted . . .) (Oreyn will not be admitted . . .)

Viela released the cable and touched the Mentor's wristband hidden under his tunic. The decision was final. There would be no appeal. He sensed that an open display of rage would harm Alu's cause. Concentrating with a Healer's skill and control, he forced aside his anger and cleared his aura.

Most of those seated around the circle were Guild-Masters. The guilds usually sided against the clans on matters of policy, so Viela assumed they were unfriendly to Alu. Mikal of the Merchants Guild was sitting beside Starm. He wore three blue-green proxy bands on his arm, representing the fishing communities. Usually their proxy was held by Clan Renu, but apparently they had changed allegiance. The Terrans had disrupted more than the peace of Alu and Eiku.

Eiku did not have a Mentor. In that, Eiku and Alu were evenly matched. The most distant clans had not had time to send their Mentors, but Rais and Renu were there, across the circle from Starm. Rais wore the brown proxy band of one of the mountain clans.

Eiku's Healer, Kaalu, sat to the left of Starm. None of the energy lines led to him. He was a witness, not a member of the Assembly. Beside him was Teila of Clan Sau, wearing three proxy bands on his arm. Viela stared. One of them was Eiku's. The council permitted Eiku a representative, but denied the same to Alu! This was unfair. He touched Starm's shoulder again, trying to lodge a protest, and received a backlash of psychic power that jarred his mind. The Assembly would not permit him to interfere.

There was nothing to do but accept their decision, for

now. His testimony would convince them that Alu was blameless, and then he could dispute their treatment of the clan. He closed his eyes and touched the cable again.

Starm was explaining the charges against Alu. His thoughts moved quickly through the network, with an undercurrent of comments from the other Masters. Viela caught snatches of the accusations, muddled by other thoughts. (. . . allegedly used Terran weapons containing independent power sources . . .) (. . . interfered in the legitimate dispute between the rival Mentors, Mrann and Revin . . .) The words were damning. Starm told the Assembly that three witnesses had been called to testify—Viela of Alu, Kaalu of Eiku, and FreeMaster Arien. Only Viela and Kaalu were present. No message had come from Arien, and the messenger sent to notify him of the Assembly had not returned.

The Assembly called Kaalu to testify first. Viela wanted to sit down. He climbed over the bench between Starm and Mikal and sat there, planting his feet in the sand and wrapping two fingers around the cable. Neither of the GuildMasters acknowledged his presence.

Kaalu's testimony began. Viela was in the wasteland again, at dawn on the morning of the dispute. Mounted on a small alep, he was watching the circle from the wrong side, the Eiku side. He saw Mrann and Revin face each other through the eyes of Kaalu, riding guard for Revin.

Barnn and Elver traced the circle on foot, runestaffs held above their heads. The Alu apprentice was weak and walked slowly. He almost stumbled once. How could the Alu Healer let an injured Master take part in a dispute? Viela's reputation spoke better of him, but he was getting old, thought Kaalu. Perhaps his judgment was impaired. He was not riding guard for Mrann. Two strangers filled that role, and one of them was Terran.

The sacred wheel was drawn, and the four Masters quartered the circle, apprentices to the left of their Mentors. Younglings from Alu and Eiku took their places at the edge of the wheel. The Mentors began to channel power, drawing energy from the earth. Then the rune-staffs touched in the center of the circle, and the wheel was transformed into an energy network.

Revin struck first, sending a pulse of power across the circle toward the energy nodule that was Mrann. It struck high and to the left, splintering. Part of it was lost against the rim of the wheel, channeled back into the earth, but Mrann absorbed the rest. Behind him, a youngling burned. Mrann gathered up the energy and sent it back across the circle toward Revin, and Barnn tried to intercept it with his staff.

A bright flash lit the other side of the field, and the Terran's alep fell. There was a second flash, closer, and Kaalu felt himself falling, too. His mount screamed in agony. Kaalu hit the ground hard, felt cartilage tear in his chest. He struggled to get away from the thrashing beast. Each breath hurt more than the one before, but he had to move before the animal rolled on him. Younglings were running toward him, shouting. One of them waved a dagger. It ran toward the alep's belly, dodging its powerful legs, and stabbed the beast with one swift stroke. Blood spurted, spattering the youngling. Kaalu lost consciousness.

The scene of the dispute vanished. Viela jerked as he began perceiving the sensory input of his own body again. He was no longer Kaalu, observing a violent conflict in the wasteland. He was the Healer Viela, and soon he would relive that conflict for the Assembly. He released the cable and opened his eyes.

The dispute had looked different from Kaalu's vantage point. Elver was so weak . . . but Viela had not sent Elver into combat. He had tried to keep Mrann from taking his apprentice to certain death. His protests had not stopped the Mentor, or Elver. Nor had he been able to keep the Terran away from the dispute. It was all beyond his control. If Mrann had listened to him, Alu might not be facing a hostile Assembly. Viela closed his eyes and grasped the cable, reaching for the group-mind.

(. . . alien weapon disrupted the dispute . . .) (. . . Terran witness . . .) (Mrann chose the alien as a guard . . .)

(Who directed the weapon?) (. . . the Terran was struck down first . . .) (. . . energy beam from someone hidden in the rocks . . .) (. . . interference . . .)

The Assembly thought Alu condoned the aliens' interference! Viela could not let them believe Alu had had any part in the disruption of the dispute. His testimony would prove Alu blameless. He began to project his memories of that morning, taking the Assembly back with him to the pre-dawn feast.

"It was a shuttle, Mrann. I'm certain of it. The younglings saw it land behind the Eiku camp and woke me. I watched it lift off," said Sarah.

"If it left, it cannot present a threat to us," replied Mrann.

Sarah pointed to the great piles of rocks on the plain. "The shuttle could have left someone behind. There are many places to hide here. One person with a laser weapon like the one used to kill Hladi could kill everyone in the circle."

"No," said Mrann. "Revin would not allow it. You presume too much, Terran. You will not speak to me of this matter again."

Angry, Sarah stalked off to the corral. Her place at the feast table was taken by Jeryl and Elver.

"Mentor, I need to speak with you about your apprentice," said Viela.

"Speak, then."

"Elver cannot attend the circle. He is much too weak to fight by your side."

Mrann placed one hand on the runestaff. "What say you, Elver? Do you have the strength to join me this morning?"

Elver reached for the runestaff, took it from Mrann's hand and pulled it to his side. It was the only answer he needed to give.

Viela fled to his tent. He prepared to witness the dispute by entering trance, letting his mind range above the circle where Revin and Mrann would fight. There he encountered another watcher, Arien, and Arien led him to the aliens hidden among the rocks. He wanted to run from his tent, to tell Mrann of the danger, but his body was locked in trance and the dispute was beginning.

Elver and Barnn paced the circle, setting the energy barrier that would confine the Mentors' power. They extended the runestaffs into the center of the wheel and touched their tips to each other, turning the circle into a glowing half-sphere. Revin struck first, sending a bolt of energy against Mrann, but he was only partially successful. Most of the power dissipated harmlessly against the sphere. Mrann gathered up what power he could, added energy drawn from the earth and from the younglings behind him, and sent it against Revin. Barnn intercepted much of it with his runestaff, channeling it into the earth.

Sarah was riding guard with Jeryl. She reached under her tunic and pulled out a piece of metal—a weapon. She extended it toward the rocks where the aliens were hiding, but before she could fire, a bolt of energy swept down and severed the forelegs of her alep. A second shot brought down the Eiku guard.

Revin gathered power and sent it toward Mrann. Elver intervened with his runestaff. He tried to earth the energy, but he was weak and could not control it sufficiently. It burned him, scorching his body with a sudden, brilliant flare of power.

Outside the circle, Jeryl rode to Sarah's side. He bent down, grabbed the weapon, and wrenched it from her hands.

Mrann pulled in all the energy he could control. Behind him, three younglings died. He directed the power toward Revin, but at the last instant sent it against Barnn. The apprentice died in a blinding flash of light.

Jeryl aimed the weapon into the rocks. He fired, and the rocks exploded with suddenly released power. In the circle, Mrann died.

Starm wrenched control of the tableau away from Viela. Angry thoughts ricocheted about the energy net of the Assembly.

(. . . the Terran brought a forbidden weapon to the dispute . . .) (Mrann betrayed Alu and Eiku by asking the Terran to witness . . .) (. . . knew about the aliens

hiding in the rocks . . .) (. . . Jeryl used the weapon . . .)
(. . . condemn Jeryl's actions . . .) (. . . Revin may
have known the aliens were watching . . .) (Alu is not fit
to govern trade with the Terrans . . .) (. . . Eiku is un-
fit . . .) (. . . condemn Alu and require the clan surrender its power . . .)

"No!" screamed Viela. "You have not seen all of my
testimony! You do not understand. Let me finish!"

The Assembly did not acknowledge him.

Chapter 29

Sarah's alep snorted. It stopped beside Jeryl's mount,
dropped its head and nosed the grass. Sweat made runnels down its forelegs. Sarah shifted in the damp saddle,
pulling clammy trousers away from her thighs. Perspiration trickled down her spine, soaking the waistband of
her trousers. Her mount's shoulders steamed in the midday sun. Sarah's breath came as fast and heavy as the
alep's. She stroked its neck, and felt the throbbing pulse
of its heartbeat.

Arien had led them to Berrut at a furious pace. Malin's
tunic was wet, Jeryl's hair plastered to his forehead.
Arien still wore his cloak, the front thrown open and the
hood back, the wide bottom tucked behind him. The important question on all their minds remained unasked.
Would they reach the Assembly before a decision was
made? Aleps were forbidden on the city streets, and it
was a long walk to the assembly hall. Sarah's ankle
throbbed as she thought of trying to cover that distance
quickly on foot. Jeryl started to dismount, but Malin put
a hand on his arm to stop him.

"We can ride into the city," Malin said. "There is a
cart road near here, used by the merchants to bring goods
to their shops. They may assess a fine if we use their
road, but it will be small. The cart track will take us
almost to the assembly hall."

The road was rutted and narrow, enclosed on either side by high walls broken occasionally by gates. Arien led again, pushing his mount to its fastest six-legged pace. They rode in single file, Sarah behind Malin, and Jeryl bringing up the rear. No wind except the breeze of their passing stirred the air between the walls. The wet ground steamed, and the place smelled of mud and borra dung.

It was midday, mealtime for the merchants, and the road was empty of carts. Sarah rounded a curve and saw Arien nearly run down two younglings who were gathering dung. They threw down their buckets and spades and ran for the wall, climbing to get away from the thudding feet of the aleps. The younglings clung to the stone, tentacles snaked into cracks and crevices, toes curled around outcroppings, and they hid their faces as Sarah rode past.

She thought of her own children, living their lives on distant worlds. If they saw her now, would they know her? This world had changed her, far more than she'd ever expected any place to affect her. She had lost her objectivity, her distance, her perspective. She was bonded to Jeryl in a way she accepted but did not understand. The only thing that mattered, she realized with surprise, was convincing the Assembly to let her stay on Ardel.

The road opened up before them, long and straight and rising out of the mud. The ruts disappeared, and Arien kneed his mount to a four-legged run. Malin, and then Sarah, did the same. Sarah bounced in the saddle, her damp trousers rubbing her inner thighs raw. Arien leaned forward. His cloak worked free and billowed out behind him, flapping in the eyes of Malin's alep. The animal stumbled and screamed, crashing into a wall. Sarah pulled her mount up short, turning it half around as she tried to avoid Malin. Jeryl was behind her, and his alep's shoulder brushed her mount's hindquarters. Reined in tightly, the animals pranced and twisted in the restricted space.

Arien turned his mount and rode back, shedding his cloak on the way. Malin was scrambling out of the saddle. His alep favored its right front leg, holding it high off the ground while standing on the other five. Sarah had all she could do to keep her mount under control, but Jeryl jumped to the ground and ran to Malin's side. Arien stopped his mount in front of Malin's alep and slid from the saddle. He brushed past Malin and bent to look at the alep's leg.

"Are you hurt?" asked Jeryl.

Malin rolled up the leg of his trousers, showing a long scrape where his leg had brushed the wall. He touched it gingerly. "My leg is scraped and bruised, but not bleeding. That is my only injury," he said.

Arien straightened and looked at Malin. "The alep's injury is not permanent, but it should not be ridden until the leg heals. You will have to double with one of us."

"My alep is the largest," said Sarah. "You can ride with me."

"No. You weigh more than any of us, and your mount has carried you far today. Malin will ride with me," said Arien. His words were neutral, but Sarah felt his anger at her presumption. He gave Jeryl the injured alep's rein.

"The end of the road is just past this rise," said Malin, pointing ahead to a low hill. "We will have to leave the aleps there and walk to the assembly hall."

Jeryl and Arien helped him to mount Arien's alep. His scraped leg was already stiffening, and he winced with pain as he threw it over the saddle. Arien followed him up, and Jeryl led Malin's injured mount.

Half a kilometer, thought Sarah as she turned her mount to follow Arien. Would they reach the Assembly in time for Arien to testify, or would they find that Alu was already condemned, and herself along with it?

The assembly hall was sprawling and ugly. The original building might have been beautiful, but the patchwork additions were warts that robbed it of grace and charm. It was surrounded by a court paved with multicolored stones, each an arm's-length broad, cut to fit together without mortar. The soft pieces were deeply worn and the harder sections just weathered smooth, making the footing uneven. It made no difference to Arien and Jeryl. They ran around the hall toward the main door, the broad,

flexible pads of their feet giving them sure footing. Sarah
followed slowly, hobbling beside the limping Malin. Her
ankle was throbbing again, and her toes were swollen
below the splint. She would have to remove it soon, and
soak her foot in warm water. Right now she would trade
her saddle for a good walking stick!

"Durrow!"

The shout sounded like a challenge. Malin tried to run,
succeeded only in limping around the corner ahead of
Sarah. She stubbed her toes on a raised stone, muttered
an oath as the impact jarred her ankle and made her toes
tingle, turned the corner, and ran into Malin's back. The
collision sent him sprawling.

Jeryl bent to help Malin to his feet. Sarah was mesmerized by the sight of Arien, arms spread wide, hands
raised above his head, palms forward and fingers spread
in challenge.

"You owe me a life-debt, Terran," cried Arien. "I
claim compensation."

"I owe you nothing," replied Nicholas Durrow. His
accent was terrible, his grammar little better than pidgin.
He sat on a bench in the shadows, black against black,
the whites of his eyes gleaming.

"I claim compensation!" Arien shouted the ritual
challenge, energy crackling between his fingertips.

Durrow rose and walked into the light, a sharp-edged
dagger in his right hand. He was short and broad-
shouldered, with thick arms and dark skin and a cap of
curly black hair. He nodded to Sarah, though his eyes
never left Arien. "Nice to see you again, Commander
Anders. Had I known you were the Union negotiator, I
would have come calling earlier. Or do you still hold a
grudge about that incident on New Kingston? I assume
your shoulder has healed well."

Arien's hands moved, and Durrow's knife flashed in
the sunlight as he threatened the FreeMaster. "I didn't
expect to see you here, Arien. I relish a fight with you,
only with equal weapons." He brandished the knife
again. "You have one of these?"

Sarah reached into her tunic pocket, touched the metal
Terran Union ID with the Sector Authority seal. A few

steps and she could be between Durrow and Arien, shoving the ID into Durrow's face and demanding that he surrender his weapon. It was a ludicrous idea. He would not, could not, recognize her authority, and she had no weapon to force his cooperation. She could call the *Blackhawk* . . .

Malin stepped between the antagonists. He turned his back on Durrow, and faced his apprentice with one hand raised in a gesture of warding. "Arien! I forbid . . ."

"No, Malin. You are my teacher, and I have learned well." There was menace in Arien's voice. "I am stronger than you. If you challenge me, the FreeMasters will have a new leader."

With the wisdom of the long-lived, Malin stepped aside. Jeryl was not so wise. He came forward and stood before Arien.

"There is no time to do this now!" he cried. "You must testify before the assembly. This challenge can wait until you have cleared Clan Alu!"

"Do not be a fool. I will not testify until this matter is settled!" Arien lowered his arms and slipped his dagger from its sheath. He stepped to the side and began to circle around Durrow, drawing the fight away from Malin and Jeryl and Sarah.

Durrow lunged for his opponent, feinting with his right hand as a second dagger slipped from a hidden sheath into his left. He slashed diagonally across Arien's belly. The FreeMaster jumped back and twisted out of the way, slashing downward with his knife as he turned. He finished the pirouette with a kick to Durrow's right forearm. Durrow grunted but held onto his knife. He lunged again, coming in low and driving upward with his left hand. Arien stepped back and to the left, swung his knife low and slashed across Durrow's arm.

Durrow yelped. His blade clattered to the pavement. Blood dripped from a gash in his arm, staining the stone. The fingers of his left hand would not clench. He backed away, eyes on Arien, left arm pressed tight against his midsection, right hand holding his other knife defensively.

Arien slid forward and kicked the fallen dagger out of

the way. He crouched low, circling cautiously, moving toward Durrow's left side. Durrow moved away from him, trying to keep the building to his back. A crowd was gathering, defining the sphere of the fight. Malin and Jeryl conversed in low tones, but Sarah watched. She had sworn to let Durrow do no more harm here. She must stop the fight before someone was killed. But how?

Durrow's blood puddled on the pavement. His clothing was soaked with it, his boots spattered with dark droplets. Arien danced toward him, teasing him with the blade, trying to draw him out. Durrow did not react. His eyes were glazed, his movements sluggish from loss of blood. Arien slipped closer, extended his arm too far. With an unexpectedly quick and agile lunge Durrow thrust his dagger at Arien's chest. The FreeMaster jumped aside, but Durrow's blade slashed his arm. Fluid spurted from the wound to mingle with Durrow's blood and seep between the stones.

They were both crippled, fighting for their lives in a circle of silent voyeurs. Arien transferred his dagger to his left hand, and tucked his injured right arm into his sash. Durrow circled to the right, his movements slow and deliberate. Arien jumped forward, thrusting viciously with his dagger. It stopped a hand's breadth from Durrow's shoulder.

"No!" Arien cried, thrusting again. He looked from side to side across the circle, from Jeryl and Sarah holding hands, to Malin, who stood opposite them. "You have no right to interfere!"

Durrow was also stabbing at the air, his dagger glancing off an invisible shield. Sarah touched the invisible barrier with her left hand. It felt like the wall of force that had kept the Terrans in their makeshift prison in Alu Keep. She closed her eyes and looked at the energy pattern. The shield stretched from Jeryl to Malin across the circle. Malin had enlisted Jeryl's aid to stop the fight.

Sarah loosed Jeryl's hand and slipped around to Durrow's side of the wall. Jeryl offered her his dagger, but she waved refusal.

"He owes me a life-debt," cried Arien, advancing on Malin. "Remove the barrier!"

Malin raised his wrist and held the copper band of his office before Arien's face. "You can challenge me," he said, "but you are wounded and I will not fight with you. Put away your dagger. The Assembly meets now. You are needed in the hall."

Durrow watched Arien. The Terran's feet were planted wide apart, but his upper body swayed from weakness. He held his knife loosely in his right hand. Sarah circled behind him, favoring her ankle and trying to be silent. She could not slow the panicked thumping of her heart. Durrow frightened her. He would not hesitate to kill her if he had an opportunity.

She was an arm's length away when he turned. He tightened his grip on the knife and aimed for her belly, but he was weak and slow. Adrenaline surged in Sarah's blood. She grabbed his forearm in both hands, lifted her knee, and brought his wrist down on it hard. The dagger flew from his fingers. Bones cracked audibly. Durrow fell against her as he passed out, and Sarah let him slide, facedown, to the ground.

"We shall talk of this again, Malin," said Arien, sheathing his dagger. He was only three paces away, but he ignored Sarah and Durrow.

Jeryl waved to Malin and walked toward him. Sarah followed, striding through the space where the barrier had been. The fight over, many of the watchers were drifting away. A few clustered around Arien. Sarah and Jeryl joined them. Malin was bandaging Arien's arm with his sash.

"Jeryl!" Two of the watchers pushed their way through to Jeryl's side.

"Oreyn! Why are you not in the assembly hall?" exclaimed Jeryl.

"I was not permitted to enter. They would not accept me as proxy for Alu." Oreyn wore a bright new tunic in Alu colors, with a torn sleeve. Urlla stood beside him, carrying Oreyn's cloak.

"Viela is in the hall," said Urlla. "He entered without trouble, but the door almost crushed Oreyn's arm. No one has entered the hall since then."

"Only Mentors and GuildMasters are allowed into the

Sarah stepped between them, clutching at Jeryl's hands. His rage surrounded her. She wanted to get away from its suffocating presence, but if she ran, Jeryl would burn Durrow to a cinder.

"He will be punished, Jeryl. The Assembly . . ."

"He wronged my House; vengeance is mine." Jeryl tore his hands from her grasp and shoved her aside.

"Captain!"

The thudding of aleps' feet on flagstones accompanied the shout. Sarah spun around, saw Durrow's red-haired pilot astride one alep and leading a second. She rode up the middle of the narrow street. Angry pedestrians waved and shouted as she passed.

"Here, Roletti!" Durrow struggled to his feet, then fell back against the wall, panting, his bandaged arm cradling his broken wrist.

The pilot stopped her mount two meters from Durrow. "Can you ride, Captain?"

Sarah laughed. It was an unpleasant, cackling sound. She recognized Roletti's desperation because it echoed what she was feeling herself. "He has a broken wrist, pilot. If you could get him onto the alep, where would you take him? Your shuttle is useless."

Jeryl stepped between Roletti and her captain. His voice was soft; it sent shivers up Sarah's spine. "Do not move, Durrow, or I will kill you."

"No!" A dagger appeared in Roletti's hand.

"I'm coming, Roletti. Help me mount that beast." Durrow used his cut arm to push away from the wall, grunted with pain as he staggered forward.

Roletti slid from her mount's back, brandishing her dagger to keep Jeryl away from the animal. Durrow shuffled toward her.

"You are under arrest. Stay where you are." Sarah pulled out her identification card and waved it at Durrow and Roletti. She felt foolish and ineffectual. A crowd was gathering, watching silently. No one tried to stop Durrow.

"Move away, Sarah."

Jeryl's voice was cold, hard, distant. The watchers stepped back, giving him room to work. Sarah shuddered, dropped her ID card. It clattered to the paving stones, forgotten as she reached for Jeryl's arm.

She touched him, and in that moment of deliberate contact Sarah sank into rapport with Jeryl. Instead of the gentle ecstasy of their last contact, she was assaulted by the full force of his anger and hatred. It flooded her perceptions, transforming the world into patterns of energy and bright, shimmering colors. She struggled to maintain her self-awareness, to keep a part of her mind separate from his destructive rage.

She could feel Jeryl gathering power to strike. He raised his hands in a gesture that was all too familiar.

Sarah broke her contact with Jeryl, shouted a warning to the other Terrans. Durrow stood up straight, planting his feet firmly and raising his bandaged left arm. He kept his right arm tucked against his belly as he faced Jeryl.

"You do not have the power to harm me," he shouted. "Revin of Eiku could not hurt me, and neither can you!"

"Durrow, do not challenge him," cried Sarah. It was already too late. She smelled scorched flesh before her brain registered flaming clothing and burning hair.

"No!" screamed Roletti. Her dagger clattered to the flagstones, forgotten as she raced toward Durrow's smoking body.

Chapter 30

Viela released the cable, withdrawing from contact with the group-mind. Anger and frustration extruded ruby spikes from his aura. He had never felt so powerless. He was Healer, he had spoken the sacred oaths . . . yet the Mentors and GuildMasters would not listen to him. They believed Alu condoned the actions of the Terrans, even conspired with them to defeat Eiku. Even his littermate Reass spoke against Alu.

There was nothing more he could do. They were already talking of forfeiting Alu's trade rights to Eiku. Eiku had no Mentor, so the Assembly would appoint a new Mentor from the ranks of the FreeMasters, and would administer the trade rights until the Mentor completed his training. The Assembly would make the treaty with the Terrans, and all the greedy GuildMasters would have an opportunity to enrich their guilds. The Terrans would become an irrevocable part of Ardellan life. Viela shuddered. His worst fears were coming true.

There was a noise at the top of the hall, behind him. He turned to see the great door close behind a pair of disheveled Masters. One limped, leaning on the arm of the other as they descended to the sand pit. Their clothes were torn and dusty, their unguarded auras were shifting agglomerates of anger and apprehension. The limping one wore the wristband that named him leader of the FreeMasters. They stopped behind Starm, and the other touched the Messenger's shoulder.

Starm released the cable, separating himself from the group-mind, and looked at the newcomers. "Welcome, Malin," he said to the one that limped. "You may take your place in the circle. Who do you bring with you?"

The younger Master offered his hand palm-upward. A small tile rested in it. "I am Arien, of the FreeMasters Guild. I was called to testify before the Assembly."

Starm took the tile and examined it carefully. "Who gave you this?" he asked.

"I found it," said Arien. "I did not know its meaning then, but when we rescued the messenger, he told me what to do with it."

"Rescued a messenger? How? Where?" asked Starm, his aura sputtering with little topaz gouts of surprise.

"The answer to that is long and involved," said Malin. "It is best if you let Arien testify. He can show the Assembly all that transpired."

"We are ready to experience your testimony now. Are you prepared?"

"I am," replied Arien. He and Malin sat beside Starm on the curved stone bench.

Viela touched the cable and reconnected with the group-mind. Starm joined them, followed by Malin and Arien. The exchange of thoughts and ideas slowed, and

Viela waited for the jolt that would transform his perceptions, letting him see events through Arien's eyes.

Arien slipped from his tent and crawled around the edge of the crater, hiding just below the rim. In the shadow of the shuttle, he watched as Durrow and his crew practiced firing their laser weapons. They aimed at the red lizards that basked on the rocks, slicing them into neat cauterized chunks. They slaughtered two hands of them while Arien watched, revulsion constricting his throat.

Laril's death cry woke Arien when it swept through Eiku Keep. He followed Durrow down the stairs, watched Revin shout his rage at Durrow. Arien intervened, or Revin would surely have killed the Terran. They fled from Eiku Keep in darkness, racing into disaster. Because of Durrow's haste an alep was hurt, and Arien stained his dagger with the animal's blood. He thrust the blade into the soil to cleanse it, wishing he could thrust it into Durrow's body.

The night before the dispute, Durrow came to Arien. He wanted to speak with Revin. Arien accompanied him, and only when it was too late realized the confrontation was a diversion. Durrow left three of his crew at the site of the dispute, armed with laser rifles. Arien could warn neither Eiku nor Alu of the danger. He watched the dispute in trance, saw the Terrans cut down Mrann, and Sarah Anders destroy them in turn.

Abandoned. Left alone in the wasteland after the dispute, with one mount and little water, Arien rode, and then he walked, until he found the messenger's dead mount. Carnage was spread across the trail. He saw two dead aleps, killed by laser weapons; a tunic of messenger green; and a little tile bearing the emblem of the FreeMasters Guild. He picked up the tile and slipped it into his pocket.

The FreeMasters and Sarah Anders attacked and defeated Durrow's crew. Fearing the worst, Arien ran up the ramp into the shuttle. He saw the fused controls and the smoking navigation computer. Jeryl pushed past him, dragged Terrans from their seats and shoved them out the door. Arien turned toward the back of the shuttle, and saw shimmer-light flickering weakly in the corner. He found the messenger on the floor, his naked body bound with tape, the floor stained with his blood. The messenger's dead apprentice lay behind him. Sarah helped carry the messenger out of the shuttle, helped cut away the tape that bound him.

With a shock Viela came back to awareness of himself. This time he did not separate from the group-mind. Anger beat at him from all sides, but he and Alu were no longer its target. He let the rage wash over him, and listened to the words of the Mentors and GuildMasters.

(. . . kidnapped a Messenger!) (. . . wanton disrespect for life . . .) (Terrans speak untruths . . .) (Arien did not denounce them when he saw their weapons . . .) (. . . stayed with the Terrans to try to control their actions . . .) (. . . Terrans willingly destroyed aleps and a youngling . . .) (. . . abandoned Arien . . .) (Durrow owes Arien a life-debt . . .)

The memories Arien had shown them were powerful. They confirmed Viela's worst fears about the Terrans. The positive actions of Sarah Anders could not negate the damage done by her fellow Terrans. Viela wanted to drive them from Ardel, to rescind the offer of trade and place the planet under voluntary interdict.

He heard Starm voicing the same thought. His angry words streaked across the web from mind to mind, pounding at each Master who sat in the circle. The Terrans had imprisoned one of Starm's messengers, and killed an apprentice to his guild. If Durrow survived his dispute with Arien, Starm would seek retribution. He intended to kill Durrow, not with the flash of power a Mentor would use, but with a knife.

Many of the GuildMasters wanted the advantages trade with the Terrans would bring them. They envisioned abundant supplies of copper and iron, and new markets for their wares. They fought Starm's rage, calling for moderation in dealing with the Terrans. Reass pointed out that Arien's testimony absolved Alu, and that Sarah Anders had aided the FreeMasters in capturing Durrow's crew.

(Alu should keep the trade rights . . .) (. . . let Alu decide whether to make a treaty. Alu has clan-right . . .) (. . . drive them all from Ardel. They pollute our energy . . .) (Durrow belongs to Arien and Starm. Let Alu choose what to do with the rest . . .) (They speak things that are untrue . . .) (. . . break our laws . . .) (. . . destroy our property . . .) (. . . interfered in a dispute . . .) (. . . cannot be trusted . . .) (Send them all away . . .) (. . . away . . .)

Viela was pleased.

Viela followed Starm from the hall. Arien and Malin walked beside him. They found Jeryl and Sarah waiting with Oreyn and Urlla in the courtyard. Pushing past the others, Viela hurried to Jeryl and drew him aside.

"I have the Mentor's wristband," he said quietly. "Will you wear it?"

"I will," replied Jeryl.

Viela slipped his hands under his tunic and untied the wristband from its thong. He cupped it in his palm so that no one could see it, and slipped it to Jeryl. "If you wear this now, you are Mentor of Alu. You cannot walk away from that duty again."

"I am already Mentor of Alu," said Jeryl as he placed the band on his wrist.

"Terran!" Starm's voice echoed from the high walls. Viela turned, and saw the Messenger confront Sarah where she stood holding the arm of a smaller, red-haired Terran. Starm stood with palms together to emphasize the authority of his words. "You are not welcome here. The trade agreement you arranged with Alu is rescinded. Gather your belongings and leave, or face the judgment of the Assembly."

"Rescind the trade agreement?" exclaimed Jeryl, striding to Sarah's side. "The Assembly has no right to interfere in clan affairs. The agreement stands until Alu decides otherwise.''

''Let it be, Jeryl,'' said Arien, laying a hand on his arm. ''The censure has been lifted, and Alu is absolved of treachery. Is that not enough?''

''No!'' Jeryl tore his arm from Arien's grasp, and turned on Starm. ''I am Mentor of Alu,'' he said, holding up his wrist to display the Mentor's band, ''and I challenge the right of the Assembly in this matter. Which of you will dispute with me?''

None of the GuildMasters came forward. Jeryl stared at each in turn, and they returned his glare, but none accepted the challenge. One by one the Mentors came to stand behind Jeryl, lending their support to the cause of clan autonomy. Viela saw his victory slipping away, undermined by the Mentor he had just empowered.

''Does the Assembly still dispute Alu's right to make a trade agreement with the Terrans?'' asked Jeryl. ''Will anyone accept my challenge?''

''I will.'' Arien stepped forward, wrists crossed before his chest and fingers spread like sunbursts. ''I will meet you at dawn, in the garden near the Inn of the Blue Door.''

''Arien!'' Malin's aura spouted gouts of ruby anger. ''This is not your fight.''

''But it is, GuildMaster.'' He stared at Jeryl. ''Where is Durrow?''

''Dead. Burned to a cinder to avenge the death of my mate!''

''Durrow owed me a life-debt, and you have robbed me of my chance to collect it,'' shouted Arien. ''I cannot punish the Terran who harmed me, but I will see that no Terrans remain on Ardel.''

Chapter 31

Sarah touched Jeryl's arm, looked into his eyes. She wanted to cry aloud, "No! You must not fight!" but the words would not come. She had no right to interfere.

If Jeryl understood her silent plea, he gave no sign. She left him in the courtyard, arguing with Mrann and Arien.

Fear turned Sarah's thoughts inward. She took a room at the Inn of the Blue Door, and sat at the window for a long time, staring into the garden. Everything she had come to value—Jeryl, Clan Alu, the whole of Ardel—was slipping away from her. She had considered giving up her career in a wild gamble to stay with Jeryl at Alu Keep. Now she saw that that possibility had existed only in her own mind. She was not, and would never be, an Ardellan. The loss of her dream saddened her; what Jeryl might lose in his battle with Arien terrified her.

She found only one solution to the problem. In the morning she would call the *Blackhawk,* and she would leave Berrut. She would rescind the trade agreement, and recommend that Ardel be placed under interdict.

Then she would resign and return to Terra.

It was early evening when Sarah found Jeryl drinking tea at a corner table in the inn's main hall. He had washed, and had borrowed a clean tunic. The sleeves were too short. His wristband showed whenever he lifted his cup. The grieving Master she had met at Alu Keep was gone. Jeryl was a strong, confident leader.

"May I join you, Mentor?" she asked. She wanted this to be formal, a meeting of government representatives instead of friends.

"Sit." Jeryl waved for a youngling to bring an extra cup. When it came, he poured for her.

They sipped in silence for a while. There was much

Sarah wanted to say. She did not dare tell Jeryl how much she cared, how much she wanted to stay with him.

"Is it necessary for you to fight tomorrow?" she asked.

"If I do not fight, or if I fight and lose, you will be forced to leave Ardel. There will be no trade between our worlds."

"That would not be such a terrible thing."

"Whether it would be or not, I cannot allow the Assembly to dictate what Alu will do. The clans must remain autonomous." Jeryl set his cup down and stared at her. "What is it you want to do?"

"I want to rescind the agreement," said Sarah. "There will be no trade between Ardel and the Terran Union. You don't need to fight."

"It is too late, Sarah. This dispute cannot be stopped. If you have courage, come to the garden tomorrow and watch." He rose and started to walk away, but looked back over his shoulder at her. "If I cannot hold the trade rights for Alu, what will be the meaning of Hladi's death?"

Sarah sat alone for a long time. Masters came and went, eating their evening meals and sharing murmured conversations, but no one disturbed her. She was not hungry. She finished the pot of tea, and sent the youngling away when it offered to get her another.

Just before sunset, when they were closing the wall to the garden, a Master appeared at her table. He was short, his broad shoulders were crammed into a too-tight tunic, and a large mug of cider seemed lost in one huge hand. He looked familiar; perhaps she had seen him outside the assembly hall.

"Master Anders," he said, "I am Reass, GuildMaster of the Metalsmiths. I have come to ask you about Durrow. May I sit?"

Sarah shrugged. "There is nothing to say. Durrow is dead."

"I know that. He gave me gifts, and made promises . . ." Reass sat on the bench opposite her and pulled some things from his pocket. He laid a small knife and a coil of copper wire on the table. "He said the Terrans could provide my guild with refined metal."

"I am not responsible for Durrow's promises. If Clan Alu retains the trade rights, you can make an agreement with them. We will supply the metal if Alu asks us to, but you must deal with them."

Reass slipped the blade and the wire back into his tunic. "Many of the guilds wish to see Alu victorious," he said. He drained his mug, and stood. "We do not want the Terrans banished from our world."

Sarah watched him walk away. She understood his plea, but it did not sway her. If Jeryl and Arien fought in the morning, either Jeryl would die and Terrans would be barred from Ardel, or Arien would die, and she would have another death on her conscience. She could not bear either outcome. There had been too many deaths in her life these past weeks. Charlie Begay Anders, Hladi, Mrann and Elver, Durrow's mercenary and Durrow himself had died. There was nothing she could have done to save any of them, but she could save Jeryl and Arien. She must find a way to stop the dispute.

Angela Roletti was resting in a room on the second floor of the inn, guarded by two messengers and a FreeMaster. Sarah stopped at the door, then decided she was too tired to confront Roletti and instead walked on to her own room at the other end of the hall.

She left the shutters open so that she could watch the moons rise. She pressed the seam on her splint and peeled it off, then stripped off her soiled clothing. She hopped across the room to the sunken basin and sat on its edge, letting both legs dangle in the warm water. The bruises on her ankle had faded to an ugly yellow. She washed, then struggled to her feet and put on a sleeping shift. Mindful that she might have to rise quickly during the night, she wrapped her ankle in a fresh splint.

The sleeping platform was padded with wool-deer skins and covered with a silver-furred tol-hide. Sarah sprawled on it and stared through the window, looking at the same stars that she had stared at two nights previously, when Jeryl had taught her to make shimmer-light. That wonderful, exhilarating, frightening ability was the only thing of Ardel she would take home to Terra.

She closed her eyes, took three deep breaths, and envisioned a flame. It danced and flickered within her chest,
at the center of her being. She watched it for a time,
basking in its warmth and brightness. Then she began to
make the flame smaller and move it outward. It reached
the shadowy wall of her chest and, when she tried to push
it farther, it wavered and died.

Sarah began again, this time building the flame more
carefully, making it larger and hotter. She envisioned it
spreading down her arm to her hand, and then tried to
move it outward through her skin to rest in her palm. She
did not succeed.

Once more she envisioned the flame, feeding it, nurturing it, giving it strength. This time she sent it down
her arm, straight to the palm of her hand and outward,
to rest above the cradle of her fingers. She kept her eyes
closed, and remembered the way it had felt that night
under the stars with Jeryl. Her fingers grew warm, her
palm tingled, and when she opened her eyes she saw the
flame nestled in her cupped hand. It lasted only a moment, but it was real.

Sarah slept little. She rose well before dawn, washed
and dressed, but did not eat. Jeryl had chosen to hold the
dispute in a walled garden across the road; she walked
over in the pre-dawn light, ignoring the younglings who
scurried through the street. The garden was peaceful,
filled with the morning sounds of birds and small animals. Reflecting pools peeked from among the trees and
shrubs. A miniature waterfall bubbled and splashed, its
pool surrounded by blooming plants. The flowers were
furled, awaiting sunrise. Sarah's footsteps sent foraging
night-mice scurrying to their burrows under broad-leaved
vines. Her lips curved in a small, sad smile at their an-
tics.

Five gates were spaced asymmetrically about the wall,
with curving stone paths leading to the central circle.
Sarah sat on one of a dozen stone benches scattered
among the paths. Crystals in the stone paving sparkled
in the dim light, but she could identify neither color nor
design. The garden was much too beautiful to be the
scene of a deadly conflict.

Dawn came. Streaks of amethyst and rose brightened the sky as Starm and a retinue of green-clad messengers entered the garden. The first carried a funeral urn carved of moss-green stone. Sarah's breath caught in her throat as she realized it was meant for the conflict's loser.

Starm placed the urn in the circle, at the point where the spiraling paths met. When Sarah looked at it she saw another urn, resting between the shrouded bodies of Mrann and Elver. Her throat tightened, muscles pulled at the scar on her shoulder, sweat slicked her palms. Somehow, she would make sure this urn left the garden empty.

Malin preceded Arien through one of the side gates. He strode to the edge of the circle, then stepped aside. Arien entered the circle alone, a wraith in a shimmering white robe. The elongated, open sleeves flowed behind him as he walked. Bare feet peeked from beneath the hem, and when he bent to touch the funeral urn, Sarah saw the bandage on his forearm. He stood in the center of the circle for a moment, eyes closed and head bowed, then walked to the edge and stood on a patch of blue stone.

The five paths divided the circle into five unequal parts. The colors were visible now—azure where Arien stood, then white, rose, green-gold, and lavender. It was a giant pinwheel, the segments spiraling to meet the urn at the center.

Sarah's heart leaped when Jeryl entered the garden. He followed the rose-colored path, walking between Viela and Oreyn. Urlla followed them. She wondered what service they performed that she could not. Jeryl looked strong and fearless, his deep blue tunic bound by a leather girdle and covered with a Mentor's gray cloak, his pale hair confined by a braided thong. His feet were bare, the broad pads spreading on the stone. Sarah stared, willing him to meet her eyes.

Someone grabbed her shoulder. She jumped to her feet, turning quickly as her right hand reached for a weapon. The dagger was in her hand by the time she faced her assailant.

It was Starm, standing angry and belligerent between two messengers. "I ordered you to leave Ardel, Terran."

"I am here at Jeryl's invitation."

"Dispute is a private matter, not for the eyes of an outsider. Mrann made a grave error when he permitted you to be present." He waved his hands, and his companions began to circle the bench and approach Sarah. She stepped back, brandishing her blade.

"Hold!" Jeryl took her arm, and suddenly she was in his mind. She saw his fear and his strength in the fleeting moment before he released her. "Sarah will be permitted to watch."

Starm glared at him. "The Assembly has already banished the Terrans. Unless you win this dispute, you have no say in this matter."

"False," cried Jeryl. "Alu is autonomous. The Assembly has no jurisdiction over Alu."

"Let the Terran stay." Arien's quiet voice echoed Jeryl's position. "I want her to see her friends defeated."

Starm looked from one to the other, then turned away and walked to a bench on the far side of the garden. The messengers followed him. Jeryl turned also, but Sarah stayed him with the touch of her hand.

"I have little to give you," she said as she untied the sash from her waist. She laid it across her palms and offered it to him, using the gesture that asks forgiveness. He took it without a word, and tied it over his leather girdle. His mind opened to her, less completely than the other times, but enough to enable her thoughts to accompany him into the circle.

Arien waited. Sarah looked at him through Jeryl's eyes, and shivered.

The ritual began. Jeryl and Arien paced clockwise around the circle, defining the area where they would fight. They moved with the oppressive slowness of intense concentration. When they returned to their original positions on opposite sides of the circle, they drew their daggers. Facing outward, daggers held at arm's length, they circled again, stopping before each gate to draw an elaborate figure in the air. Sarah sat outside the circle, but part of her was inside it with Jeryl, watching him seal the gates with glowing emerald runes, binding them to the stone of wall and archway. Arien's seals were aquamarine, and slightly different in shape. Together they ensured that no one would enter or leave the garden until the dispute was resolved.

Arien returned to his place on the azure stone, and Jeryl to the rose quartz. They drew more figures in the air, muttering incantations as they paced the outer edge of the circle. The glowing runes hung like neon sculptures, guarding combatants and audience.

Their circle completed, Arien and Jeryl sheathed their daggers. Arms at their sides, bare feet spread, they took each other's measure. Then, in concert, they clapped their hands, and a shining dome of topaz energy enclosed the circle.

Sarah was afraid. She had enough contact with Jeryl's mind to understand what was happening, but she had no control. She could observe, but she was not a participant. Suddenly Jeryl raised his right arm, and his cloak fell away from the blue sleeve of his tunic. His copper and iron wristband shone brightly in the sunlight, the green and yellow jewels sparkling. Arien answered by raising his own arm, his white sleeve sliding down to reveal his bare wrist. Jeryl had the strength of Clan Alu to support him, but Arien was older and more experienced. They were a good match, and no matter the outcome, Sarah knew she would lose. The funeral urn would not let her forget that.

Jeryl conjured his first weapon, a glittering ball of energy that he hurled across the circle toward Arien. It struck Arien's shining aura and fragmented, sending out a shower of brilliant sparks and engulfing Arien in slowly dissipating red mist.

With swiftly moving hands, Arien began a series of arcane gestures. He flattened his feet against the stone path, drawing energy from the copper bound in the azurite. A glowing blue sphere grew quickly, pulsing with power between his palms. He released it, and it flew across the circle at Jeryl.

Sarah watched the energy ball approach, her heart pounding in her chest. That sphere was as deadly as any laser blast. If it touched Jeryl, it would burn him. She tried to move his body aside, but her efforts accomplished nothing.

The energy ball struck Jeryl's aura squarely over his heart, and exploded into bolts of ruby and sapphire power that flew in all directions. One threatened Jeryl's thigh, but he intercepted it with his left hand. Sarah felt the agony of seared flesh, new burns over recent scars. Her hand curled in her lap as her brain confused Jeryl's body with her own.

Jeryl ignored the pain. Power flowed upward from the earth through his feet, channeling along his spine and then down his arms and through his palms. He used it to create a pair of shimmering topaz lightning bolts. They hung in the air before him, glowing brighter and brighter. Vile green streaks of pain swirled through Jeryl's aura. Sarah winced at the throbbing in his burned hand, her own curling tighter in response.

Jeryl was growing weaker even as he hurled the first lightning bolt. Arien jumped forward, turned, thrust one arm out and deflected it before it could do any damage. The second bolt was already near. It struck Arien's leg, sending its power directly into his body. His robe flamed and died, but his leg flared brightly for a long time, long enough to burn flesh and sear nerves beyond repair. He was sorely injured, but he still managed another attack.

Jeryl's aura could not deflect the sapphire sphere. It struck him in the chest, and his cloak flamed, then crumbled into charred bits. Sarah gasped as Jeryl fell to the ground, his wristband clattering against the stone. The pain was more than she could bear. From shoulder to knee, her left side was agony.

Jeryl climbed slowly to his feet, leaning heavily on his good right hand. Sarah felt every tortuous muscle contraction, every excruciating tug on seared skin. She looked across the circle, watched Arien scuff bare feet across the azurite. Pain contorted his face whenever he moved his burned leg. Both his aura and Jeryl's had lost their brilliance. They stood in clouds of muddy green pain.

Sarah wanted to stop this dispute now, before Arien or

Jeryl died. Did she have the power to do so? Last night, alone in her bed, she had barely been able to make shimmer-light. How could she intervene here?

Arien was trying to protect his body with a web of aquamarine energy strands that stood like a shield between himself and Jeryl. A similar net appeared before Jeryl, but Sarah could tell it was illusion. Behind it he conjured a sparkling ruby sphere of energy. He formed it quickly, and released it before Arien's shield was set. Sarah cried out as it shattered Arien's shield, striking and discharging into his injured arm. The sleeve of his robe and the bandage on his knife wound burned with a bright flame, while Arien's face convulsed in agony.

Jeryl was very weak. His hands shook with exhaustion as he readied one last attack. Shield forgotten, Arien spent his energy creating a glowing blue sphere to throw against Jeryl. Sarah knew this was the time. If they launched these weapons, they would both die. Neither could withstand another attack.

Sarah thought of all the impossible things she had seen and done since she came to Ardel. There was shimmer-light, and Mrann's dispute with Revin, the laser weapons melted into slag, shields and psychic energy that she could see, and especially her connection with Jeryl. She had shared his anger and his sorrow. She had been linked to him at Festival, and she was linked to him now. Whatever had made it possible for her to create shimmer-light, to destroy the hand laser, to neutralize Durrow's mercenaries, perhaps would help her to stop this dispute. Eyes closed, thoughts centered on the circle, she willed herself into its heart. The protective dome obstructed her, but she released control and let herself flow with it, matching the resonance of its power. Three heartbeats and she was through, standing between Jeryl and Arien.

Time slowed. For a moment she felt the sharp triumph of success, but her work had just begun. Arien's blue sphere moved toward her, rolling slowly through the air. It was powerful enough to kill Jeryl in his weakened condition, but she could stop it, she could ground the energy. She stepped toward the sphere, reached out to touch it with both palms, concentrated on letting the power flow through her into the stone beneath her feet. She felt a tingling in her hands and arms, a sudden searing flash of pain as the energy passed through her body. Then it was done.

Now Jeryl was safe, and Arien would not die. She would contact the Trade Commission and abrogate the trade agreement, and have the Union lay interdict on the planet. She would make Sandsmark keep other Terrans away, but she would stay. She would find a way to stay with Jeryl. She would become an Ardellan!

She turned to look at Jeryl, smiling, her arms extended in victory. And saw another sphere of power, glowing red and malignant as it flew across the circle—Jeryl's energy ball. Suddenly she was afraid. Channeling the energy from Arien's sapphire sphere had not been easy. Her skin still prickled and her muscles twitched from the power's passage through her body. She was tired now. She needed to rest, but there was no time. She must act, or step aside and let Arien die. She lifted her arms, centered her thoughts, readied herself for the sudden jolt of energy. She spread her feet as the tingling began, preparing for the pain.

Someone shouted. She heard it with a small corner of her mind, but could spare no concentration to understand the words. Her focus was the energy ball, glowing as it engulfed her fingers, her hands. She felt the sudden flow of power in the nerves of her arms, readied for the searing flash of pain. But this time the power burned as it coursed through her, and the agony did not end.

Chapter 32

"Nooo!" shouted Jeryl as the Terran's hands began to burn. Viela sprang to his feet, but the flames were already climbing her arms and igniting her tunic. The Healer ran toward the circle, hit the protective dome and bounced back.

Arien reached Sarah, knocked her down and rolled with her to extinguish the flames. He was too late. Bits of charred clothing powdered to ash on the stone. Her aura faded as the spirit fled her stiff and lifeless body.

Jeryl was still rooted to his place, crying "No!"

There was nothing any of them could do. Arien dismantled the circle, and Viela went to Sarah. He had avoided her for so long, he could not bring himself to touch her even now. The last bits of her aura dissipated as he knelt. Running his hands above the scorched body, he sensed only death.

"She is gone," he said, looking up at the others. "The power was more than she could bear. I can do nothing for her." Rising, he dismissed Sarah from his thoughts. His concern was for the living. Jeryl's aura, and Arien's, were dulled by pain. The damage to their bodies was plainly visible. He signaled a youngling to bring his medicine bag from the bench. "Sit. Let me dress your wounds."

Jeryl waved his uninjured hand in a gesture of negation. "See to Arien first. His burns are more serious than mine." Kneeling, he slipped off the remains of his cloak and used it to cover Sarah's body. His right hand stroked the sash she had given him.

Arien stepped behind Jeryl and laid a hand on his shoulder. "I did not wish her harm."

"I understand. She made a free choice, though I do not believe she knew it would cost her life."

"She could have stepped aside and let your weapon destroy me."

Jeryl looked up at Arien. Viela could see the anguish spreading through his aura. "That was not her way. She could not let either of us come to harm. Her conscience would not bear it."

Starm stalked into the circle. "The dispute is not resolved," he said, his gray eyes dark and his aura seething with ruby anger. "Capitulate and accept the decision of the Assembly or continue the fight."

"Neither of them can fight," said Viela, spreading salve on Arien's burned arm. "They have no energy left."

Arien pushed the Healer away and turned on Starm.

"GuildMaster, you have no say in this matter. I called challenge because of a life-debt owed to me by a Terran. Sarah Anders has satisfied that debt with her own life."

"The Assembly will not accept this outcome!" cried Starm.

Jeryl raised his hands in a gesture of power. "Do you wish to take Arien's place in the circle? Challenge me!"

Starm shrugged and backed away, his hands held carefully at his sides.

"The dispute is resolved," said Arien, showing his hands to Jeryl palms-upward, begging forgiveness. "I withdraw. The dispute is yours, Mentor."

Jeryl touched his palms to Arien's in a gesture of acceptance. The amethyst flash as their auras met signified more than a temporary bonding. "Leave us," he said to Starm. "The Assembly can no longer interfere with Alu. The clan will deal with the Terrans as it chooses."

Viela's aura clouded. It seemed that he was to lose, also. What Sarah Anders had not been able to do in life, she accomplished with her death. More Terrans would come to Ardel, to change the lives of his people. Clan Alu would never be the same.

Starm bent to retrieve the funeral urn. Jeryl's hand stayed him.

"The urn is hers now," he said. "Leave it."

"I would go with you to Alu Keep," said Arien the next morning, facing Jeryl but looking past him at something very far away. He held his alep's single rein in one hand.

"Why?" asked Jeryl. He was waiting for a youngling to bring his mount. Across the stableyard Sarah's body, wrapped in a fine shroud, was being loaded into a cart. The funeral urn already sat in the front of the cart.

"Alu is my clan. I have not visited the keep since my mate died. It is time I return home."

Jeryl shrugged. "We must meet the *Blackhawk* first, and give Angela Roletti into the custody of Captain Swenson." He had used Sarah's transmitter to call the *Blackhawk* and had arranged to rendezvous with the ship outside Berrut. "The *Blackhawk* must also come to Alu Keep to retrieve Sarah's belongings."

"I understand. I would still accompany you, though I will not board the Terran ship."

"Then you are certainly welcome." Jeryl looked at the sun. It was not yet mid-morning. "We will reach Alu just after dark. I can offer you the hospitality of the clan-hall tonight."

The youngling brought Jeryl's alep, and both he and Arien mounted. Viela had already climbed into the front seat of the cart, and a youngling was handing him the borra's reins. Jeryl turned his mount and led the way out of the stableyard and onto the road that led to Alu Keep.

In the early morning, the kitchen of Alu Keep's clan-hall was warm and inviting. Viela sat before the fire, sipping tea and listening to Jeryl and Arien make plans.

"I want to cremate Sarah today, this morning," said Jeryl. "We will place her urn in the mourning wall, next to Mrann's."

"Her people made no objection?" asked Viela.

"None. Captain Swenson told me they do not ship bodies back to Terra."

"I will help you with the cremation," said Arien.

"You will not!" Viela set his tea aside. "Neither of you is ready to channel that much energy."

"I am fine," protested Jeryl. "Arien should rest a few more days, but I can do this alone."

"I will not rest! I wish to honor the person who died in my place. I will not sit by while you perform the rites."

"Neither of you will do this. It is too soon!" Viela rose and walked between them, letting all his power shine in his aura.

They were not impressed. Their auras billowed out, bright flashes of topaz and ruby erupting where they touched his. He had no power to stand against two trained FreeMasters. If they chose to cremate the Terran, he could do nothing to stop them. He stepped back, and looked from one to the other.

"I will allow you to do this, but only if I am present.

I want to monitor both of you, to make certain you do not overstrain yourselves.''

A quick glance passed between Arien and Jeryl, and they shrugged capitulation. Just then, a youngling burst into the kitchen.

''Healer! Healer, you must come now! Torma says come.''

It was the summons he had been waiting for, to attend Torma and Eenar for Septi's emergence from the cocoon. Viela spared one last glare for Jeryl. ''Wait until I return,'' he said as he followed the youngling out.

Torma was waiting for him at House Kirlei. They passed through the outer rooms and into the Mother's chamber. Viela sealed the door behind them.

Septi was already emerging from his cocoon. Torma helped him tear away the soft white fibers, revealing his body. His newly-grown arms ended in perfect, six-fingered hands, and he stood on long, slender legs and broad feet. His tentacles were dormant, housed in nodules on his chest. He coughed, and Torma cleared the sticky gel from his face. Septi opened his eyes.

Eenar was waiting for them. Viela monitored her bloated, wrinkled body. She was not strong, and he would not let her leave the platform. Her six breasts, that had nursed the younglings she and Torma had conceived, were dessicated, wrinkled folds of flesh. She watched her mates with soft gray eyes, clouded with the weariness of time. Her aura was faded topaz, warm and loving. At the foot of her sleeping platform, her burial urn was waiting.

Her mates knelt beside her, paying homage to House Kirlei and the unbroken line of Mothers who had nurtured it. Eenar welcomed them with serenity, touching each of them with gentle hands, accepting the new Master into her House and her life. They came together on the platform, the Masters gently depositing their seed in Eenar's womb. The younglings would grow there, drawing nourishment from Eenar's body while her empathy sustained and enveloped them. She knew that the younglings would kill her, and she was not afraid.

The fear that permeated the room came from Torma. When the mating was complete, his body began the metamorphic processes that would make him a Mother. He lay on the platform beside Eenar, unable to move. Viela touched Torma, dropping into rapport to monitor the changes in his body, and was overwhelmed by Torma's fear. The paralysis terrified him. Torma tried to move his hands, but the muscles would not respond. He wanted to leap up and run from the chamber, but he could not move his legs. His fear blossomed and grew, filling his chest with tension. There was no escape.

Then Eenar's aura enveloped them all. Torma found peace and acceptance in that loving topaz glow. This was the natural order of things; he was fulfilling the destiny of his race. When Septi lifted him from the platform, his fear was gone.

The rapport ended, and Viela was an outsider again. He watched Septi carry Torma to the grotto and prop him against the stone. Septi spun white thread from his fingers, anchored it in the stone on either side of Torma, and began to weave a soft fabric to cover his body. As the delicate silk crept upward toward Torma's face, Viela could see that he was no longer afraid.

The great stone bier dwarfed Sarah's body and the funeral urn that rested by her head. Beside her lay the small rectangular case that she had said was a journal. Viela had seen her writing in it more than once. He touched it.

"Will you burn this with her?"

Jeryl picked it up. His fingers brushed the locking mechanism and it emitted a tiny beep. "No. I will give it to Captain Swenson before the *Blackhawk* leaves tomorrow. He will also take a copy of the trade agreement, and the metal box that is in her room."

"It is a radio transceiver," said Arien. "Terrans use it for talking over long distances. What of the rest of her belongings?"

"We must dispose of them. Swenson will not take them." Jeryl fingered the sash she had given him, which he wore tied at his waist.

"We can still rescind the trade agreement," said Viela hopefully. "Send the Terrans away and tell them not to return."

"No!" Jeryl turned on him. "Would you have all these deaths be for naught? Alu will trade with the Terrans!"

Arien stepped forward. "The FreeMasters Guild will help the Terrans build their spaceport, and will provide caravans to transport goods. No one else except Jeryl will be allowed to contact the Terrans. Captain Swenson has guaranteed that they will not try to contact any other Ardellans."

Viela shrugged. "You believe him?"

"Sarah Anders taught me that there are honorable Terrans. I will believe Swenson until I have proof that he lies."

"Enough," said Jeryl. He slipped the journal into his cloak and took up the runestaff. "We are here to honor Sarah, not debate the integrity of her people."

Viela watched the cremation from the clanhall's steps. He had witnessed the beginning of life; now he would witness its ending.

Flames burst from the somber green urn as Jeryl's runestaff touched it. They ignited the white cloth that bound Sarah's body. The bright conflagration engulfed the surface of the bier and the urn, and reached up to lick at Jeryl's hands. He held the runestaff firmly, even when Arien stepped back.

The flames died away, leaving the surface of the bier clean and cool. The funeral urn glowed with a light of its own. Soft sapphire clouds drifted across its surface, interspersed with streaks of emerald. Jeryl's scarred hands stroked it gently before he settled its lid in place.

He carried the urn to the mourning wall, to the niche that had been prepared beside Mrann and Elver. Viela followed with Arien, and watched as Jeryl copied the strange glyphs of Sarah's name into the stone. His finger traced the alien forms slowly, carefully, setting them forever into the rock of Alu.

Arien carved the final rune, his finger wavering slightly as he set it into the stone: HONOR.

DAW

NEW DIMENSIONS IN MILITARY SF

C.S. Friedman
☐ **IN CONQUEST BORN** (UE2198—$3.95)
Braxi and Azea—two super-races fighting an endless war. The Braxana—created to become the ultimate warriors. The Azeans, raised to master the powers of the mind, using telepathy to penetrate where mere weapons cannot. Now the final phase of their war is approaching, spearheaded by two opposing generals, lifetime enemies—and whole worlds will be set ablaze by the force of their hatred!

Kris Jensen
☐ **FREEMASTER** (UE2404—$3.95)
The Terran Union had sent Sarah Anders to Ardel to establish a trade agreement for materials vital to offworlders, but of little value to the low-tech Ardellans. But other, far more ruthless humans, were also after these materials—and were about to stake their claim with the aid of forbidden technology, double-dealing, and threats of destruction to the clans of Ardel. Yet the Ardellans had defenses of their own, based on powers of the mind, and only a human such as Sarah could begin to understand them. For she, too, had mind talents locked within her—and the Free-Masters of Ardel just might provide the key to releasing them.

John Steakley
☐ **ARMOR** (UE2368—$4.50)
Impervious body armor had been devised for the commando forces who were to be dropped onto the poisonous surface of A-9, the home world of mankind's most implacable enemy. But what of the man inside the armor? This tale of cosmic combat will stand against the best of Gordon Dickson or Poul Anderson.

DAW

Cosmic Battles To Come!

Charles Ingrid

☐ **THE MARKED MAN** (UE2395—$3.95)

A recurring plague was decimating mankind, linking to the DNA structure to create truly terrifying mutations. Desperately, a small group searched for a way to breed the shifting bloodlines back to a "pure" human form. And while they experimented, Thomas Blade and his fellow Lord Protectors, gifted with powerful psychic abilities, stood guard as the last defense against the forces of the mutant Denethan, who had sworn to complete the destruction of the "true" human race.

THE SAND WARS

☐ **SOLAR KILL: Book 1** (UE2391—$3.95)

He was the last Dominion Knight and he would challenge a star empire to gain his revenge!

☐ **LASERTOWN BLUES: Book 2** (UE2393—$3.95)

He'd won a place in the Emperor's Guard but could he hunt down the traitor who'd betrayed his Knights to an alien foe?

☐ **CELESTIAL HIT LIST: Book 3** (UE2394—$3.95)

Death stalked the Dominion Knight from the Emperor's Palace to a world on the brink of its prophesied age of destruction. . . .

☐ **ALIEN SALUTE: Book 4** (UE2329—$3.95)

As the Dominion and the Thrakian empires mobilize for all-out war, can Jack Storm find the means to defeat the ancient enemies of man?

☐ **RETURN FIRE: Book 5** (UE2363—$3.95)

Was someone again betraying the human worlds to the enemy—and would Jack Storm become pawn or player in these games of death?

☐ **CHALLENGE MET: Book 6** (UE2436—$3.95)

In this concluding volume of *The Sand Wars,* Jack Storm embarks on a dangerous mission which will lead to a final confrontation with the Ash-farel. *Coming in 1990*

DAW

BESTSELLERS BY MARION ZIMMER BRADLEY
THE DARKOVER NOVELS

The Founding

☐ DARKOVER LANDFALL   UE2234—$3.95

The Ages of Chaos

☐ HAWKMISTRESS!   UE2239—$3.95
☐ STORMQUEEN!   UE2310—$4.50

The Hundred Kingdoms

☐ TWO TO CONQUER   UE2174—$3.50
☐ THE HEIRS OF HAMMERFELL (hardcover)   UE2395—$18.95

The Renunciates (Free Amazons)

☐ THE SHATTERED CHAIN   UE2308—$3.95
☐ THENDARA HOUSE   UE2240—$3.95
☐ CITY OF SORCERY   UE2332—$3.95

Against the Terrans: The First Age

☐ THE SPELL SWORD   UE2237—$3.95
☐ THE FORBIDDEN TOWER   UE2373—$4.95

Against the Terrans: The Second Age

☐ THE HERITAGE OF HASTUR   UE2413—$4.50
☐ SHARRA'S EXILE   UE2309—$3.95

THE DARKOVER ANTHOLOGIES
with The Friends of Darkover

☐ DOMAINS OF DARKOVER   UE2407—$3.95
☐ FOUR MOONS OF DARKOVER   UE2305—$3.95
☐ FREE AMAZONS OF DARKOVER   UE2430—$3.95
☐ THE KEEPER'S PRICE   UE2236—$3.95
☐ THE OTHER SIDE OF THE MIRROR   UE2185—$3.50
☐ RED SUN OF DARKOVER   UE2230—$3.95
☐ SWORD OF CHAOS   UE2172—$3.50